THE DOGS IN THE STREETS

Also by Murray Davies

THE DRUMBEAT OF JIMMY SANDS

THE SAMSON OPTION

THE DEVIL'S HANDSHAKE

COLLABORATOR

THE DOGS IN THE STREETS

MURRAY DAVIES

MACMILLAN

First published 2005 by Macmillan
an imprint of Pan Macmillan Ltd
20 New Wharf Road, London N1 9RR
Basingstoke and Oxford
Associated companies throughout the world
www.panmacmillan.com

ISBN 1 4050 5168 X (hb)
ISBN 1 4050 4919 7 (tpb)

This book is a work of fiction. Names, characters, places,
organizations, and incidents are either products of the author's
imagination or used fictitiously. Any resemblance to actual events,
places, organizations, or persons, living or dead, is entirely coincidental.

1 3 5 7 9 8 6 4 2

A CIP catalogue record for this book is available from
the British Library.

Typeset by SetSystems Ltd, SaffronWalden, Essex
Printed and bound in Great Britain by
Mackays of Chatham plc, Chatham, Kent

For a different Maddy, far away.

Acknowledgements

I would like to warmly thank Goronwy Hughes, Peter MacAleese, Ted Oliver, Jeff Edwards, Charles Collier-Wright, Paul Crosbie, Ian Duff, Alison Crossley, Mark Hotson, Howard Feltham and Danny O'Connell for their help, expertise and advice.

Once again, I owe a special debt of gratitute – and another lunch – to Stef Bierwerth for her unflagging help and encouragement.

1

On the last day of his life Alfred was up early. Christmas was still two days away but Alfred had fallen in love with the tree that stood twice his height and gave off an elusive scent. He dragged himself from his bedroom to lie on the floor gazing happily up at the fairy lights that pulsed round and round in different patterns. The little boy had never seen such a tree before, never smelled pine resin, had never had the chance to marvel at the shining glass balls and glittering tinsel.

Just in front of his nose, there was a stack of presents wrapped in paper decorated with strange images of villages under snow, prickly green leaves and small birds with red breasts. And some of those presents, he knew because he was learning to spell, had 'Alfred' written on them.

'All right there?' Rob Sage bent to make sure that the metal cages encasing the boy's shattered legs were not chafing his skin. 'Shall I put the TV on for you?'

'I like the tree.' Alfred looked up, a huge grin splitting his face.

'You're the boss.'

Rob carried on into the kitchen, returning with a glass of orange juice for Alfred.

'What these?' asked the boy, pointing at shapes on a piece of wrapping paper.

Rob glanced down. 'Christmas crackers,' he announced. 'You pull them and they go bang.'

'Like a bomb?'

'No, not like a bomb. Crackers go *crack*, and then they split open and a present falls out. You'll see on Christmas Day. Okay, boss?'

'Okay, boss.'

Rob made two mugs of coffee and carried them back to the bedroom where Mekaela was peeping over the top of the thick duvet.

'Come back to bed. I'm cold.'

'The central heating's on.'

'I don't care. I'm freezing.'

Rob let his dressing gown fall to the floor and slid back into bed to wrap his arms around Mekaela. Outside, the day was beginning to break. This Christmas was going to be special. Really special. He was home on extended leave from Ethiopia with his beautiful girlfriend and little Alfred – the child at Christmas. Rob was going to make this a time that Alfred would remember for ever.

And then, straight after the holidays, the boy was going to have the first operation to start to rebuild his shattered legs.

The three of them had arrived back in Rob's Wiltshire village yesterday afternoon. Alfred, who had been chattering all through the flight from Addis Ababa, had fallen quickly asleep. So, too had Mekaela. While they slept, Rob had gone to shop for food and had come across a Christmas tree for sale.

He smiled as he recalled the wonder on Alfred's and Mekaela's faces when they'd woken to find the tree decorated with fairy lights and tinsel, and presents around the base.

Tonight they were going to the carol service in the village church, but first Rob and Mekaela were taking Alfred to visit Father Christmas at a store in Salisbury. Rob suspected that he had made a hash of explaining Santa Claus because the boy was now looking forward to meeting a fat, bearded old man, wearing a red jump suit, who would give him a present. Alfred thought this was wonderful. That sort of thing simply didn't happen in his country.

Mekaela's hand brushing downwards over Rob's chest brought him out of his reverie. Yes, it was going to be a very good Christmas.

At a farmhouse, less than fifteen miles from where Alfred was gazing up at the fairy lights, two men pulled on blue boiler suits and gloves and set about securing their Christmas tree onto the roof of the silver Ford Mondeo which had been stolen five days before. The tree, which overhung the windscreen, was not only a nice seasonal touch: it also helped to conceal the faces of the driver and his passenger.

The car sat low under the weight of the 300 pounds of explosives hidden in its boot. If the operation had been in Ireland, they would have welded on metal spars to reinforce the chassis. Here in the English shires the tell-tale sagging would pass unnoticed.

The bomb-maker had already departed – being driven to catch a plane home by one of the two 'lilywhite' helpers.

The block car had been parked last night at the same time as they had disabled the vital CCTV camera. This morning, the other lilywhite had regularly fed the car's parking meter in the shopping street. He was back now, carrying cans of petrol into the farmhouse.

At 11.28, the only woman in the bombing team picked up the smaller come-on device, hidden in a used red and white KFC box, and put it gingerly into a plastic bag.

The thickset man led the way in a belligerent swagger to a red Ford Sierra parked outside the farmhouse. He climbed in behind the wheel; the woman slid in alongside him, the plastic bag on her lap. Her fiancé sat in the back as they set off.

Five minutes later, the silver Mondeo with the Christmas tree on top set off after them. In addition to the boiler suits and gloves, the driver and his passenger now wore surgical masks hidden by long white beards and red Father Christmas hats.

Left by himself, the remaining lilywhite put down the can of petrol and walked away to light a cigarette.

On the last morning of his life, Tom Lipzinger sat opposite his wife Maddy and their daughter Mitch in the breakfast room of the Red Lion Hotel – and complained about the size of English hotel beds.

'I don't know how people over here sleep in them. They're so . . . small.' He made a play of stretching his large frame.

'Hey, come on, you were snoring loudly enough,' protested Maddy.

'Yeh, Pop, I heard you,' said Mitch.

Maddy brushed a strand of dark chestnut hair behind her ear and wondered what else her daughter had heard. The Red Lion might claim to be seven hundred and fifty years old but the wall separating their interconnecting family rooms was worryingly thin.

'Can I leave the table now, mommy?' asked Mitch.

Maddy sighed. It was rare for her family to share a meal together. She should be grateful that her nine-year-old daughter had stayed even this long. Mitch's younger brother Tom Junior had fidgeted himself back to the room five minutes ago.

'What's the hurry, honey?'

'I want to get back before TJ finds something really cruddy on TV.'

Back at home in upstate New York, the kids each had a TV in their bedroom. Sharing one here was proving a source of friction.

'We didn't come all this way for you guys to become couch potatoes,' warned Maddy. 'Come on, we'll go plan what we're going to do today.'

Her elder child could be a complete mystery, thought her mother. Yesterday Mitch had fallen in love with a beautifully illustrated book of English nursery rhymes that she'd found in a second-hand bookshop. She'd bought it with her own holiday money and had spent most of last evening reciting the rhymes aloud. That was yesterday.

Today she was back to being a snub-nosed brat determined to pick a fight with her brother.

By the time Maddy reached their room, Mitch was tussling for the TV remote control with TJ.

'That will do,' barked Maddy. 'Either you guys agree what you're going to watch or I'll switch off the set.'

Maddy was annoyed not just by the kids' squabbling but also by the way that her husband was able to ignore it. Instead of supporting her, Tom had just wandered off into their bedroom as if nothing was happening.

'Now, I've got some postcards to write,' continued Maddy. 'And I must send a couple of emails to confirm our arrangements in Ireland next week; then we can all go and visit Stonehenge.'

'They're just old stones.' TJ pretended to be sick. 'Yeuk.'

'Don't say "yeuk" like that,' snapped Maddy. 'You're lucky to be here.'

'I didn't want to come,' shouted TJ. 'I'm missing my friends' parties.'

Mitch took advantage of the moment to snatch the remote control out of TJ's hand. The cartoon on the TV was replaced by teenagers dancing.

'I was watching that,' wailed TJ.

Mitch backed behind a sofa and dangled the control teasingly out of reach. TJ launched himself at her, running over the seat to leap on his sister. They fell grappling to the floor.

Maddy flipped. 'That is *enough*!'

Tom emerged from the bedroom in a thick sweater.

'Take these two out before I kill them,' shouted Maddy.

'Where?'

'What do you mean, where? *Anywhere.* The cathedral . . .'

'Went there yesterday,' said Mitch quickly.

'There's that military museum.'

'That's for boys,' griped Mitch.

'All right. Go feed the swans, then. I don't care. Just get out of here and give me some peace.'

Tom shuffled his feet awkwardly. 'Actually, honey, I was planning some last-minute shopping. Just to see if—'

'Take them with you.'

'Um . . .'

'Get your anoraks, you guys. Chop-chop.'

'Aw, mom. It's cold,' whined TJ.

'Not as cold as home. Come on. Put this scarf on. You too, Mitch.' Maddy began dressing her protesting children.

'Not going.'

'Tom, speak to your daughter.'

'Come on, guys, you heard your mother.'

'Out. Out.' Maddy ignored Mitch's efforts to bat her away as she fastened zips and poppers on the children's matching orange anoraks.

'I hate you, mommy.' Mitch stamped her foot. 'I hate you, I hate you.'

Tom ushered the kids into the corridor. Maddy shut the door behind them and heaved a sigh of relief.

The bomb-maker climbed out of the old car and slung a holdall over his shoulder. He left behind a strong smell of soap and deodorant. Before leaving the farmhouse he had showered, methodically scrubbing himself clean of any traces of the Semtex explosive. He didn't think they had sniffer dogs at Bristol Airport – but that was when they got you, when you were least expecting it.

He had taken just two steps towards the distant passenger terminal when he spun around. Motioning to the driver to wind down his window, he leaned into the car.

'Don't get any ideas about keeping this banger. You take it to the scrappy to be destroyed as you've been told. D'you hear?'

The young driver nodded sullenly. The car, which had been used as a runabout to service the bombing team, had been bought for cash and was still registered to its previous owner.

'Right, then. Do it.' The bomb-maker strode off, not seeing the two-fingered gesture the driver made behind his back.

Sod him. After the way the big-time operators from Ireland had treated him and his brother the past week, he was keeping the car. They owed him that.

'Are you sure you've got the shopping list?' Rob asked Mekaela as they crawled into Salisbury in the growing stream of traffic.

'It's here.' Mekaela began to read. 'What is . . . Stilton?'

'It's a blue cheese.'

'You have *blue* cheeses. Why can't we have a white one?'

'We'll get one of those as well.' Rob grinned.

'Now you are laughing at me.' She tried to scowl at him. '*Aygidi-senin'yul.* I don't care.'

Alfred sat in the back of the old estate car, singing happily to himself. Mekaela went back to inspecting the shopping list – only to look up just as a car cut across them at a roundabout. 'Yiiyii!' She flung out a hand to protect herself. 'Is it always this busy?'

'The traffic will be worse in an hour or so. That's why I wanted to get here early.'

'If I'd known, I wouldn't have let you come back to bed.'

'And whose fault was it that we didn't get up for another hour?'

They swooped under the railway bridge and into Fisherton Street, now festooned with strings of Christmas lights.

'The city is very old, isn't it?' observed Mekaela.

'The cathedral was built in the thirteenth century, I think. We'll go round it sometime.'

'If you want.'

Rob picked up the note of boredom in Mekaela's voice. 'If *you* want.'

'You know what I want to do. *I* want to see the shops. Remember your promise.'

Mekaela was wrapped up in two of Rob's sweaters, a thick scarf and his duffel coat. She was used to dry, cold nights in the mountains of Tigray but her thin clothes had proved to be no protection against the damp English winter air. In bed that morning, she had complained that she had not felt warm since they'd arrived in England.

There's no such thing as bad weather, only bad clothing, Rob had said, quoting a Russian proverb. Mekaela had tilted her head to the side and flashed him a brilliant smile. Finding he had fallen into his own trap, Rob had burst out laughing and promised to buy her a warm winter coat.

'Okay, you help me buy the food and then you can shop until you drop while I take Alfred to see Father Christmas,' said Rob. 'Deal?'

'Deal,' she agreed.

They drove slowly past the Market Square with its orderly rows of covered stalls – before finding one of the last available places in the car park behind the Red Lion Hotel.

'Come on, boss.'

Alfred clapped his hands in glee as Rob swung him up on his shoulders. People stared curiously at the laughing crippled black boy and the tall sunburned man but, most of all, they were fascinated by Mekaela – as tall as Rob, with the unique elegant posture and blue-black skin of highland Ethiopians. But then, Mekaela was striking even in her own land.

Frequently in Tigray, Rob's arrival in a village would bring out the whole population to stare at him. He found it amusing that the English gawped at Mekaela in exactly the same way as her people looked at him.

'Where first?' Mekaela frowned at Rob's long shopping list.

'There's a good butcher's and cheesemonger's in the next street so we'll stock up there, dump that load back in the car and then go on to Marks & Spencer.' Rob smiled into Mekaela's eyes. 'You've been wanting to see England and you can't get more English than this.' He turned to Alfred. 'What do you think, boss?'

'Yeh, boss.' The boy punched the air in excitement. 'Yeh.'

'That's settled, then. Come on, gang. Christmas begins here.'

The scout car dropped down the hill into the Wylye Valley and set off between bare winter hedgerows towards Salisbury. On the other side of the valley, a slow-moving line of lorries marked where the main A36, with its traffic-monitoring cameras, ran parallel to the lane.

'It's really pretty around here,' murmured the woman, looking at sheep grazing in the water meadows. No one answered her.

At a red traffic light in the centre of the town of Wilton, the driver called the bomb-car team on his mobile phone to say that the way was clear so far.

But at the roundabout joining the main road, the Sierra was forced to wait for an unbroken stream of traffic from their right. As the seconds ticked by, everyone's thoughts came to focus on the device in the woman's lap. In theory, it was safe until the timer was set – but they had all known comrades who had died when their 'safe' bombs had exploded in their faces.

At last there was a gap and the scout car accelerated away. In Lower Road, on the outskirts of Salisbury – where the Mondeo would wait for the final go signal – the driver pulled in to announce that the route was still clear. He made two more calls before continuing into the city centre, where the woman and her fiancé left the car.

'Where are we going?' demanded Mitch grumpily as they stood around a display of leaflets in the hotel foyer.

'Well . . .' Tom Lipzinger seemed at a loss. 'Where do you guys want to go?'

'Nowhere.'

'You must be able to find something you want to see there.'

'Huh!' Mitch and TJ pretended to examine the leaflets until Tom grew impatient.

'Listen, I have to do some special shopping . . .'

'For Mommy?'

'Could be.'

'Mommy's horrid. I hate her,' exclaimed Mitch.

'No, you don't. And you mustn't say things like that.'

'Don't care.'

Tom gave up. 'All right, we'll go look at the shops.'

'Great,' sneered Mitch as her father went to ask the hotel receptionist for directions before leading his children out through the courtyard of the inn. TJ slouched behind, playing his Game Boy until they turned into a pedestrian shopping mall. Sixty or so yards on, they halted at a small square with stone benches where three branches of the mall met.

'You guys'll be okay here while I do my shopping?' asked Tom. 'Tell you what. I'll get you some doughnuts, huh? How about that?'

He hurried into the nearby baker's and returned with a bagful. Maddy would go ballistic if she discovered he'd given the kids treats straight after breakfast. But that wasn't the only secret Tom hoped to keep this morning.

At the farmhouse, the remaining lilywhite was splashing petrol around the main bedroom when he glanced out of the window to see a woman on a moped heading up the long track towards him.

He had no idea who she was or why she was here but he knew she mustn't be allowed inside the house in case she smelled the petrol. At the same time, he couldn't let her see his face. He didn't know what do. Maybe one of the Irish hard men would have murdered the woman in cold blood – but he couldn't do that. Helping to make a three-hundred-pound car bomb was different.

The lilywhite ran down the stairs and out of the back door to the old stables where they'd ground the fertilizer. He was watching the woman approach when his mobile phone rang.

'Yes?' He could not help whispering.

'Are ye done?'

'No. There's a woman coming up the track.'

'Who is she?'

'I don't know.'

'Just do your job and call me when she's gone.'

The line went dead.

Fuck it! That was how the Irish had ordered him and his brother around all week. *Do this. Get that.* He was sick of it.

He watched as the woman climbed off her moped and went up to the front door. She knocked and waited before stepping back and scanning the house. She knocked again – more loudly this time. For a moment he feared that she was about to try the door. Then she thought better of it. With one last backward glance, she mounted her moped and set off back down the track.

The lilywhite walked a safe distance away and lit another cigarette, his hands shaking.

In the last hour of her life, Leanne Burroughs was excited by seeing a celebrity in the flesh. That striking black woman at the Marks & Spencer's food checkout had to be a film star, or a supermodel at least. But try as she might, Leanne could not place her. And she knew her celebs. After a frustrating few minutes, Leanne gave up, cross that she couldn't name the woman, and went back to wondering why her bloke Wayne had been so keen for her to go shopping. Normally he complained that she spent too much money, but this morning he couldn't wait to get her out of the house.

Walking down the mall, she saw ahead a boy and a girl, in matching orange anoraks, devouring jam doughnuts. The children seemed to be alone. Leanne was about to ask if they were all right when she glanced in the cafe opposite.

Two men were sitting at a window table. One had a cup raised to his lips. He had short hair, turning prematurely grey, and wore steel-rimmed glasses. Now he *was* definitely a celebrity. He was someone on TV. Leanne furrowed her brow in concentration.

Oh, come on, come on. Who was he?

Of course. Doctor Samson in the hospital soap; he was the one who was having the affair with Sister Pidgeon. And she'd seen his name on the posters advertising the pantomime in Bath. Denny Fox. That was it. Denny Fox. He was also in the hysterical loo-paper commercial with the chimpanzee.

Leanne thought the actor looked older in real life – and smaller, somehow. She recognized the other man, too. He owned the posh coffee shop in the High Street. As she watched, he put his hand over Denny's, squeezed it and rose to his feet. He left the cafe to hurry away past the children in their matching anoraks.

The silver Mondeo with the Christmas tree on top was falling behind schedule. First, it had been forced to crawl behind a tractor the last mile into Wilton and then the driver had missed the back lane into the city through the village of Quidhampton.

'For fuck's sake, you drove this yesterday,' complained his passenger.

'That was yesterday,' replied the driver, fingering the brown paper bag containing a half-bottle of Scotch in the pocket of the boiler suit. He came to a junction and turned right.

'Jesus Christ! This is the main road. It's crawling with police cameras,' exploded the large raw-boned man. 'You're an idiot, you are. A fucking idiot.'

Beads of sweat erupted on the driver's scant hairline. He began unscrewing the cap of the whisky.

'Don't you dare.' The passenger peered round, trying to identify the passing side streets from the town map on his knee. If they continued along this road they'd pass the police station. Not a good idea.

'There. On the right. Cherry Tree Lane. Go down there.'

Obediently, the driver pulled across. At the bottom of the hill, he turned left into Lower Road and parked. The bomb was now less than a mile from the city centre.

Denny Fox sipped his tea and looked fondly after Clive's retreating figure. Last night, Denny had been short with the pantomime's principal boy because she'd ruined his big entrance. He hadn't said anything to Clive when he'd got home but now he'd casually mentioned that he needed to make amends. And Clive, being kindness itself, had gone straight off to fetch him a box of handmade chocolates to give to her.

He and Clive had been together almost two years now. Good years, too. Clive had brought him luck. Denny had always made a living from his talent for mimicry by doing voice-overs for TV commercials but the day after they'd met Denny had landed the part in the TV hospital soap. The breakthrough had led to steady work, including currently topping the bill in the panto at Bath.

'Excuse me.'

Denny looked up, startled out of his reverie. A girl in her mid-twenties stood at his shoulder, smiling uncertainly.

'I hope you don't mind me bothering you, but can I have your autograph?'

'I'd be honoured.'

The girl scrabbled in her handbag for a piece of paper.

'Who shall I say it's for?'

The girl cleared her throat. 'Leanne. Leanne Burroughs.' She carefully spelled out both names. 'Can I ask you a question?'

'Of course.' Denny braced himself for a query about the TV soap. Was the lead actress as saintly in real life as her character Nurse

Chapel was in the series? No, she was a bloody-minded coke-head whose mood depended on how recently she'd had her last line. Or if the bullying chief surgeon was really an ogre? No, again. He was an absolute pussy cat, and like Denny himself, in a long-term gay relationship. Denny despaired that viewers seemed unable to tell the difference between TV and real life.

'How do they make that chimp do . . . um, you know, what he does with the loo paper?'

'Kindness, my dear,' replied Denny, surprised at the unusual question. 'The director lets Gerald, that's the chimp's name, watch whenever he goes to the loo. Chimps are natural mimics.'

'Well, fancy that. Thank you so much. You're so sweet.'

'Thank *you*.'

The girl scurried away and Denny looked out of the window towards the mall entrance. There was no sign of Clive. Instead, two children in garish orange anoraks were tucking into a bag of doughnuts. Had to be American, Denny decided, and returned to his coffee.

The woman, plastic bag held tightly to her chest, did her best to stroll naturally along the High Street, her fiancé walking slightly ahead through the crowds to prevent anyone jogging her elbow. The man had the collar of his reefer jacket turned up and a woollen hat pulled low over his forehead. The woman wore glasses that she did not need and a dark auburn wig under a Paddington Bear hat.

A youth club's silver band was playing a carol on the corner. The man and the woman walked around the collecting bucket, avoiding eye contact with each other.

The red Sierra cruised past – just another car looking for a parking space.

The woman was close to her target.

Time to summon the bomb car.

*

Once her family had left, Maddy had looked around the kids' room, enjoying the silence before beginning to pick up discarded items of clothing and folding them away in the chest of drawers. Most belonged to Mitch. TJ was the tidy one.

A wave of depression swept over her, leaving her feeling hollow and sick. Hotel rooms were all the same – even in this lovely old inn. Impersonal, unloved, anybody's. They could have stayed with friends in England or, next week, with distant relations in Ireland but Maddy had wanted the four of them to be by themselves, together as one loving family.

She had told the kids that this holiday was a very special treat. They were going back to explore their roots, she had said, making a big play of how both her and Tom's families had originally come from Ireland; and how they had met at a St Patrick's Day dance. She had made the trip sound exciting and fun.

In reality, it was the last desperate effort to save her marriage. By flying to England, Maddy was keeping Tom away from *her*. Whoever she was.

Maddy returned to her room and began writing postcards to friends and relatives back home. She kept referring to the kids – and that made her feel guilty about the way she had packed them off. There was no getting away from the fact that she was turning into a tetchy old broad. It was the kids' holiday, too.

There was a tap on the door and a chambermaid appeared.

'Oh, sorry. I thought you'd all . . . I'll come back later.'

'No.' Maddy came to a decision. 'I've got to go out. Please come in.'

Maddy flung on her coat, slipped the postcards in her pocket and went off to make peace with her children.

'Kwer ida!' Rob lifted the bag containing the turkey and smoked ham into the back of his old estate car. 'That didn't take long, did it?'

'I've never seen so much food,' said Mekaela.

In the highlands of Tigray, farmers ploughed their fields with oxen, sowed seeds and harvested by hand. The harvest was threshed by the feet of animals. Little had changed since the days of the Queen of Sheba and King Solomon. Rob had thought Mekaela would be impressed by the shops but instead she'd been outraged. Not even rare visits to large stores in the Ethiopian capital had prepared her for the sight of a Western supermarket stocked for Christmas.

'Why do people buy so much? Are the shops closed for two weeks? A month?'

'I think they're open the day after Boxing Day,' admitted Rob.

'Crazy. No one can eat that much food.'

Rob pulled a face at Alfred, busily chewing on a liquorice stick. '*You* don't mind, do you, boss?'

Alfred shook his head solemnly. He loved the bright displays in the shop windows and the happy music coming from inside every store.

'When can I get to look at *my* shops?' demanded Mekaela. 'You promised. Before I get too tired.'

'Tired!' This was a woman who regularly walked ten miles a day over rough terrain at home. Rob knew that she meant bored. 'Okay.'

He hoisted the last bag into the estate car and waved apologetically to a driver looking hopefully towards their parking space.

'There were fashion shops back in that mall.' He remembered that there was also a toy shop for Alfred on the corner. 'If you find something you *really* like, I'll buy it for you on plastic.'

'*Rihus Lidet.*' Mekaela, all smiles, kissed him. 'Happy Christmas.'

No one spoke. In the bomb car, every second seemed a minute, every minute an hour. The big man in the passenger seat clenched and unclenched his fists, his eyes glazed with the tension of the moment. The driver, his throat constricting with fear, fought a private battle not to open his whisky bottle.

The mobile phone rang to summon them into the city.

Near the railway station, they were forced to halt behind a pantechnicon which blocked their view so they couldn't see the cause of the delay. The passenger swore before phoning the coordinator to warn him that they were falling behind schedule. Just as he ended the call, the big van in front pulled away. Not much longer now.

At Bristol Airport, the bomb-maker strolled through passport control with the confidence of knowing that his passport was genuine – even if it was in someone else's name.

Fergus O'Hanlon was a mentally retarded thirty-year-old who had never been abroad, nor was ever likely to. With his family's agreement, the bomb-maker had applied for a passport in Fergus's name, accompanied by photographs of himself wearing a beard and spectacles. Finding a priest to vouch for the authenticity of the application had not been a problem.

As the aircraft began its take-off roll, the bomb-maker could not resist checking his watch. The car should be in place now.

The explosive power of the bomb should normally shatter shop windows more than two hundred yards away but, if he had calculated correctly, the force of the blast from this device would be funnelled along the narrow street, vastly extending the killing zone.

He was looking forward to reading tomorrow's newspapers to learn by how much.

Now Leanne Burroughs knew why Wayne had been so keen for her to go shopping. He was cheating on her.

She had been idly looking in a shop window, thinking what a nice man Denny Fox was, when she'd spotted their next-door neighbour Scott walking past carrying a sports bag.

Strange! He worked nights so he was normally home asleep at this time of day.

Wayne had become very pally with Scott's wife Shaynee since

they'd moved in a couple of months ago. He was always finding excuses to pop round there. An unpleasant suspicion grew in Leanne's mind. What if Wayne had known Scott was going to be out this morning?

The devious little shit!

Leanne pulled out her mobile phone and called home. There was no reply. She tried Wayne's mobile. It was turned off. With an effort she made herself stay calm. There could be a totally innocent explanation why Wayne wasn't at home, slobbed out in front of the television set as normal.

Of course, there could be an innocent explanation – except she couldn't think of one.

He and Shaynee were probably on the job, this very moment. Sick in her stomach, Leanne slumped onto a stone bench in the small square and wondered what she was going to do.

Back at the farmhouse, the lilywhite's mobile rang.

'Have you torched it yet?'

'The woman's just gone.'

'For fuck's sake, you know we want the fire brigade out there when the big one goes up. Get a move on.'

'I'm just about to—'

The line went dead.

Muttering angrily to himself, the lilywhite poured petrol over the empty fertilizer bags and the grinders, splashed a trail out into the yard and tossed a match onto the petrol. The match went out. He tried again and again until finally he was rewarded by a blue flame that flickered, caught and raced along the trail. With a satisfying *whoosh,* deep red flames and oily smoke leaped from the outbuilding. He laid a similar petrol trail into the farmhouse kitchen and lit it before leaping onto his motorbike.

At the main road, he looked back at the column of dense smoke rising skywards.

'It's well torched,' he announced into his mobile phone. There was a deep explosion as the upstairs farmhouse windows blew out. 'Wow! You should see it.'

'Get your arse into town. You're running late.'

The line went dead. The lilywhite swore again. Then he opened the motorbike's throttle and sped off towards Salisbury.

'Ready.'

The woman was in position to plant the come-on bomb.

The thickset man coordinating the bombing noted with satisfaction how the stores and pavements were crammed with shoppers.

Many would not live through this day. Many, many more were about to have a Christmas they would never forget.

This would teach those cowards who had bargained and sold. Peace process! *Peace process, my arse.* There would never be peace while a single English soldier was left in Ireland. There could never be peace until the thirty-two counties were reunited.

His former comrades condemned him, and those who believed like him, as dissidents.

Fuck them.

The dissidents were about to make people around the world take notice.

He relayed the message to the bomb car.

In the last minutes of his life, Alfred saw a train set for the first time. He had been sitting on Rob's shoulders humming happily to himself when he called out and banged Rob on the head to stop in front of a shop window. At first, Rob failed to see what had attracted the boy's attention. Then a model train appeared from the back of the window display and Alfred began wriggling in excitement.

He couldn't take his eyes off the train, chuckling in unalloyed happiness each time the little wooden engine and its two trucks rattled towards him under the model bridge. After a while, the train stopped at the station, reversed into a siding and then set off in the opposite direction.

Alfred was beside himself.

Rob looked at Mekaela and shrugged.

'You spoil him,' she smiled.

'It's Christmas.'

'I'll hold him. Don't let him see you buying it. It'll be a surprise Christmas morning.'

'What about your shopping?'

'I can wait.'

Mitch found it impossible to play her Game Boy and eat a doughnut at the same time without dropping jam on the floor. She decided to concentrate on the doughnut. Leaving her brother occupied with his own computer battles, Mitch began a game of her own which involved smiling at passers-by and seeing how many acknowledged her.

Mitch was attracting smiles and nods from a succession of shoppers when she spotted a bespectacled woman with a Paddington Bear hat looking in the window of a menswear shop. Unlike most of the other women, who were laden with shopping, this one was clutching just an old plastic bag. There was something about her that wasn't right but Mitch couldn't put her finger on it.

Mitch was about to grin at her when the woman brought a mobile phone up to her ear. The woman listened, replied briefly then nodded to someone ahead. Mitch saw that she was signalling to a man who had been looking at holiday offers in a travel agent's. The man turned and hurried away towards the street. After a moment, the woman strolled over to where Mitch and TJ were sitting. She partly brought out a battered KFC box from the plastic bag, put her hand inside the box, scowled and then took off her glove before continuing to do something inside the box. Finally satisfied, she pushed the box through the slot in the black and gold trash can beside Mitch and dropped the bag in after it.

Mitch thought it odd that the woman should take so much care with a box of chicken bones. The woman looked straight through her before muttering into her mobile phone and striding off towards the street. As Mitch watched, she climbed into a parked car – only to reappear seconds later and start to walk back in her direction.

The little girl's imagination was stirred. Mitch told herself that the woman had abandoned her newborn baby in the garbage but now her conscience had got the better of her and she was coming back to reclaim her child.

But then the woman halted just a few yards into the mall. She was looking back to the road and was again talking into her mobile phone.

Intrigued, Mitch was about to rummage in the bin to see what the box really contained when her father came up, carrying a neatly wrapped package.

'A lady's just put a baby in the garbage,' she told him.

'No, she hasn't,' contradicted TJ. 'Mitch is just being stupid.'

'I'm not. Anyway, you didn't see. You were playing your stupid game.'

Tom held out his arms in a placatory gesture. 'Now then, you guys. No fighting.'

'There's mommy,' announced TJ, pointing towards the street.

Maddy saw them and waved. Only TJ waved back.

Waiting to pay in the toyshop, Rob watched as several men glanced covetously at Mekaela. He understood. Her beauty was enough to turn anyone's head. She had certainly turned his.

Rob saw too how Mekaela kept looking at her reflection in the shop window. She knew she was beautiful. Last night he'd been waiting in bed for her when she'd caught sight of herself in the full-length mirror. She had turned this way and that, admiring her naked perfection. He'd accused her of being vain and she had answered in an old Tigrinyan proverb.

'If I can't say that I admire myself, then who shall admire me?'

That sort of summed up Mekaela. She had come a long way, both geographically and figuratively, from the primitive schoolroom with its corrugated-iron roof and earthen floor where he had first seen her, teaching a class of traumatized war orphans.

But what did their future hold now?

Mekaela had begun to murmur 'I love you' each night as they were falling asleep. She spoke the words shyly, hesitantly, as if afraid of rejection. Rob had yet to reciprocate.

Was he in love with her? He certainly felt as much for Mekaela as he had ever felt for anyone. She was funny, giving, sexy and good with Alfred – but Rob was cautious. He told himself that he didn't *really* know what love was. He was too practical, too phlegmatic to ever fall head over heels in love – but he was as happy as he had ever been and aware that he wanted to make Mekaela happy. Was that love?

Perhaps he'd propose to Mekaela this Christmas. He knew she'd accept. Anyone in her position would. That was the problem. What if she wanted him just for a British passport?

But if they did marry, they could adopt Alfred . . .

The silver Mondeo turned the corner just as the woman emerged from the mall. Her fiancé, already behind the wheel of the block car, pushed open the passenger door for her to get in.

'Okay?'

'Yeh. Let's go.'

'Shit!'

'What is it?'

'Some fucking moron's trying to get into this parking space.'

The woman twisted round to see a small green car on their wing, its indicator light flashing.

'Get out. Pretend you've forgotten something.'

'You're fucking joking. You know the timer on that thing.'

'What else can we do?'

'Fuck it.'

The woman climbed out of the car. She held up ten fingers to tell the waiting driver that she would be ten minutes and retraced her steps back into the mall. As soon as she was out of sight, she stopped near a tall black girl holding a crippled boy and scowled at the green car through the corner windows of the toyshop, willing it to drive on.

It didn't. Instead, it sat obstinately behind the block car. She hit a button on her phone.

'Get out of the fucking car,' she hissed. 'They're not going to move with you sitting in there.'

Her fiancé did as he was told, and finally, reluctantly, the green car pulled away.

As soon as it did so, the Mondeo, with two men in white beards and red hats inside, drew up in its place. This time there could be no mistake.

The clock had been running for some time.

Maddy spotted her kids' anoraks as soon as she reached the entrance to the mall. There they were, sitting side by side on a bench. But where was Tom?

Out of the corner of her eye, she noticed a car with a Christmas tree tied on its roof making a hash of parking. It was good to know that she wasn't the only one who had problems with parallel parking.

Tom appeared, carrying a parcel. Maddy set off towards her family, stepping around a beautiful black girl holding a little boy with his legs in braces. His arms were going round like pistons and Maddy saw that he was imitating the toy train in the shop window.

Tom looked guilty, thought Maddy; probably expecting to be told off for leaving the kids by themselves. It crossed her mind that it was unusual for Tom to go shopping. He even got his secretary to buy Maddy's birthday presents.

Mitch burst out laughing and pointed at something behind her. Turning, Maddy saw that the driver getting out of the Christmas tree car was wearing a blue boiler suit, a white Santa Claus beard and a red hat. At the same time, she noticed a postbox on the far side of the road. It reminded her that she'd forgotten to hand in the postcards at the hotel. Pulling the cards out of her pocket, she waved them at her family to show what she was doing and hurried back towards the street.

The driver's first attempt to park the Mondeo left it sticking out at an angle to the kerb. He pulled back out into the stream of traffic and reversed again. This time the Mondeo ended up three feet from the kerb.

'You're too far out,' muttered his passenger.

'I know,' hissed the driver, wiping away the sweat running down his forehead.

The third time he parked successfully. No sooner had he switched off the engine than he flung open the door and leaped out into the street where he hopped from leg to leg in his impatience to get away. He unscrewed the cap of the whisky bottle and took a quick drink before scurrying off. Twenty yards away, he looked back over his shoulder once, took another stiff drink and hurried on.

Life had to go on, Leanne told herself. Anyway, maybe she was being fanciful. It was no good just sitting here. She'd know when she got home and confronted Wayne. She always knew when he was lying.

Come on. Stop feeling sorry for yourself.

Leanne rose to her feet. On the next bench, the two kids had been joined by a large man.

Denny Fox's friend came hurrying up, holding a large box of chocolates. Leanne thought he looked both kind and handsome. Why did she have to pick the wrong ones? *Bloody Wayne.*

Then the black girl was running towards her. She was holding a little boy and she was shouting something. She looked terrified. The girl stumbled and Leanne stepped forward to take the boy out of her arms.

Rob did not know why he first became suspicious.

Except that living and working near the Eritrean border, where booby traps, landmines and terrorist attacks were commonplace, meant that you had to keep your wits about you – or you ended up dead.

So when Rob saw the small man with his white beard and red cap leave the car and behave strangely, he watched him casually. At first, Rob thought that the man was desperate to get to a lavatory but then a second man, wearing identical clothing, emerged from the car to walk purposefully after the driver, talking into a mobile phone.

Rob wondered first if he was about to get caught up in a bank robbery. Then he noticed how the car sat low on its suspension. It looked as though it was heavily loaded, yet it appeared to be empty.

With a sinking heart, Rob remembered such cars on the streets of Northern Ireland waiting for a bomb-disposal team.

Suddenly, he realized that the Mondeo had pulled up to park in that spot *before* the other car had indicated that it was about to leave.

So that had been the block car.

And this was . . .

The bomb car.

God! Only yesterday he'd read a newspaper story that the police were braced for a terrorist bomb planted in Britain. You never thought that it would happen near you. And now it was.

Rob dashed out of the shop.

'Get away from here.' He snatched up Alfred, thrust him into Mekaela's arms and pushed her into the mall.

'What?'

'There's a bomb in that car. Get away from here. *Now.*'

Mekaela hesitated.

'Boss.' Alfred held out his arms to Rob, alarmed by his friend's intensity.

'Go.'

Mekaela clasped the boy to her and stumbled away down the mall.

Rob ran to the car and looked inside. A child's turquoise sandwich box sat on the back seat, partly covered by a newspaper. Rob tried the car door. It was locked. He smashed the side window with his elbow and pulled up the door catch. The piercing whistle of the car alarm made him wince. Inside the car, he gingerly lifted the newspaper to find red and blue wires running from the plastic box into the boot.

'What the hell do you think you're doing?' he heard a woman demand in an American accent.

'Get everyone away from here. Call the police.'

The box must contain the power timer unit. Rob went to pull off the lid – and stopped. What if it was booby-trapped?

'Say that again.'

The American woman was still on the pavement behind him.

'There's a bomb in this car,' said Rob without taking his eyes off the sandwich box. 'Move well away and get everyone else to do the same. And call the police.'

'Right.'

Rob heard her shout a warning.

He looked again at the wires disappearing into the boot. If his guess was right, the box concealed an electrical timer. The surge of power from its battery would send an electrical impulse to a detonator. But there had to be some form of booster explosive hidden in the boot, otherwise the detonator wave would be too weak to set off the whole bomb. You'd end up with just a low-order explosion.

And the bomb-maker would not want that.

Rob felt in his pocket for the Leatherman he always carried.

In the distance he heard a siren, followed by another. It struck him that no one could have sounded the alarm that quickly. It didn't matter.

He chewed his lip. He didn't dare try to open the lid of the sandwich box nor the car boot.

He took a deep breath and cut the blue wire.

For a moment there was an utter stillness that expanded to fill the universe before contracting so that it became bile in Rob's stomach.

Then came the explosion.

2

It was only four o'clock in the afternoon but already it was growing dark. Arc lamps, running off a throaty generator, cast a harsh light over scene-of-crime officers, in their white paper suits, picking their way methodically through the debris. Detective Superintendent Cyril Tanner stepped over a pool of blood which had dried as dark as varnish and crunched his way back to the street, finding it impossible not to walk on the shards of glass that covered the mall like an obscene carpet. Outside the toyshop, the contents of a mound of shopping bags leaked onto the pavement: runnels of milk and green washing-up liquid clinging to a thicker patch of golden syrup.

This part of Salisbury, which only hours ago had been busy with Christmas shoppers, was now a sealed-off ghost town. A police car's blue light cast its haunting reflection in a cracked window while in the distance the chimes of a church clock carried far on the chill silence.

'The Met's Anti-Terrorist team are here, sir,' announced Tanner's sergeant, Graham Pottidge, indicating where an immaculately groomed man in an open topcoat was leading a procession in Tanner's direction.

Detective Chief Superintendent David Hayward of the Metropolitan Police had been appointed to head the investigation within an hour of the bombing – much to the disgust of the Wiltshire force. No copper liked outsiders on their patch, especially city slickers from London.

'What have you found out about him?' asked Tanner.

'University graduate. He's just finished a year's sabbatical doing a Master's degree in criminology in America,' replied Pottidge. 'Still doesn't explain why's he muscling in on our patch.'

'Come on, Graham. You know SO13 head all investigations into acts of terrorism,' explained Tanner. 'In the jargon, the Anti-Terrorist squad have the ability to interface with other security organizations at home and abroad.'

Pottidge grunted.

Hayward halted to talk to his team when they were still twenty yards away. As they made no effort to approach, Tanner thought he had better go and pay his respects.

'Mr Hayward? I'm Cyril Tanner.'

'Good to meet you. I gather from your chief constable that you're the acting SIO on the inquiry. You're one of the older hands, he said.'

Tanner noticed that he had been described as the 'acting' senior investigating officer. As his immediate superior, the head of Wiltshire CID, had been rushed to hospital with a heart attack two days ago and was never likely to return to work, Tanner thought the chief constable could have dropped the adjective. There was no one else in the county capable of running the inquiry – whether the chief liked it or not.

But now, looking at Hayward, Tanner felt like a country bumpkin. Hayward was in his late thirties with neatly coiffured hair, silk tie and blue-striped shirt. Altogether too healthy-looking, thought Tanner, conscious of his own thinning sandy hair and podgy waistline.

God, it came to something when one's senior officers began looking young.

'No warning given, was there, Cyril?'

'No.'

'And no one's claimed responsibility?'

'Not yet. Any information from the intelligence side?'

Hayward shrugged. 'Early days. Might be Islamic terrorists. There's been a marked increase in chatter between extremist Islamic cells across Europe in the last week. But at the same time we've been picking up rumours that IRA splinter groups *might* try something on the mainland.'

'But why here in Salisbury? Why now?'

'The IRA always reckons that one bomb on the mainland is worth ten in Ireland. You're a soft target. And of course, there's the British Army HQ Land Command and Porton Down both on your doorstep,' replied Hayward. 'Anything from closed-circuit cameras?'

'The main CCTV camera in the shopping mall was sprayed over last night,' reported Tanner. 'But there are many other cameras in the vicinity. We'll ask store managers with their own systems to hand over their tapes as soon as the area's secure.'

'What about the bomb car itself?'

'Stolen five days ago from the Lewisham area of London and fitted with false plates matching make and model,' replied Tanner.

'If the bomb *is* down to dissident Irish republicans, then that marks a departure in their modus operandi,' observed Hayward. 'In the past, they've always bought cars for bomb operations at auctions.'

'Maybe they reckoned this time that it was safer to nick a car rather than risk being identified at an auction,' said Tanner. 'Stolen cars are hardly the Met's highest priority. The local CID only got around to interviewing the owner yesterday. Unfortunately the car's been used as a minicab, which'll mean that forensic will find a mass of fibres, DNA, et cetera.'

'Shows unusual foresight,' muttered Hayward.

'Or luck,' said Tanner.

'The terrorists must have stayed somewhere. They needed vehicles to move around. We need a witness appeal.'

'Our press office is working on one,' said Tanner. 'By the way, a farmhouse in the Wylye Valley was torched deliberately this morning just before the bomb went off. Could be where the gang laid up.'

'I'll get forensic back-up down from the Yard.'

'We'll be popular,' said Tanner.

'No one's going having a good Christmas, but at least we're alive.'

Breda Bridges waited inside the phone box on the coast road from Dundalk to Riverstown, watching a young boy and girl race each other along the pebble beach. Behind them the wind was whipping up white caps on the restless grey Irish Sea.

The phone rang once. She snatched it up.

'Yes.'

'I'm in Paris.'

'What the fuck happened?'

'What do you mean, what happened?'

'Don't you know?'

'Know what? The last I heard on the radio, it was all right.'

'Only the small one went off.'

'Are you saying the car didn't—'

'That's a lovely present for the police, so it is.'

'But I got the thumbs-up from Jimmy. He wouldn't have done that if he hadn't—'

'What a waste of a fucking operation.'

'We got some.'

'A fart in a bottle.' Breda put down the receiver.

The children were running to and fro along the breakwater, daring each other to defy the incoming waves until the last moment.

'You two. Stop that before you get wet.'

The little girl darted to the very end of breakwater so that the next wave broke over her shoes.

'Come here. Come here, I tell you. *Now.*'

When the little girl stood before her, Breda Bridges grabbed her, spun her around and smacked her bottom.

'You carry on like this, and *you* won't be seeing Father Christmas. Understand?'

'Yes, mam.'

'I'll put my money on the Irish,' decided Hayward after he had spent an hour inspecting the scene. 'Similar MO to the Ealing Broadway car bomb and the two incidents in 2001.'

'You got those, didn't you?' asked Tanner.

'They thought they were being clever by hiding their terrorist activities behind a diesel-washing scam. Ironically, it was the Customs investigation which got them.' Hayward waved a hand at the destruction. 'While I think of it, make sure you've got enough dustbins.'

'Dustbins?'

'After the Brighton bombing, the Sussex force ran out of dustbins to remove the debris for examination. If I were you, I'd write an action now and arrange with the army or RAF to use a hangar on one of their bases. The Met's search team will go through the debris.'

'I've never had to deal with a bomb before,' confessed Tanner.

'You've handled enough murders, though. Got a good clear-up rate, too, your chief said.'

'Eight out of nine. And I know who did the ninth but I'm buggered if I can prove it.'

'That's often the hardest part. Mark my words, we'll have the names of the bombers inside a week but getting them in the dock will be more difficult.'

The bomb-disposal captain and his warrant officer, both in full body armour, appeared from the tent set up around the silver Mondeo. They lifted the visors of their helmets. The captain pulled out two cigarettes, lit them and for a minute, both men inhaled deeply, not saying a word. Then the captain spotted the detectives and clumped towards them.

'The device is safe now,' he announced.

'I, er, I thought it was safe before,' said Tanner.

'Had to make sure there weren't any booby traps, that sort of thing. These bomb-makers can be devilishly cunning when they want to be.'

'But not in this case.'

'He never expected his work to be on display, did he?' The captain drew heavily on his cigarette and slowly exhaled.

'I don't suppose there's any indication which terrorist organization is responsible, is there?' asked Hayward.

The captain gave a barking laugh. He turned to his warrant officer. 'Here, Johnno, the detective wants to know if you've any idea which terrorist organization is behind this.'

'I can do better than that,' replied Johnno. 'I can tell you the bomb-maker's bloody name.'

Tanner slipped unnoticed past the media scrum around a police spokesman giving casualty figures outside the main entrance to Salisbury District Hospital. Tanner hated hospitals and their distinctive smell. He always had. This modern giant – the size of a village – sprawling across a windswept hill outside the city was no exception.

Inside the foyer, he found Graham Pottidge seething with fury.

'What's wrong?' demanded Tanner.

'I just phoned the missus to tell her I'd be working late, and you know what? She and our nipper were just one hundred yards away when that bomb went off. Helen's in a terrible state.'

'Easy now, Graham.' Tanner's deep gravelly voice carried a warning. 'Don't let yourself get too involved.'

'Helen always buys cakes for herself and Jack in that square. They sit and eat them on those benches. God, if she hadn't decided to go to Marks & Spencer first . . .'

'I understand your feeling but you can't do your job if you hate the people who did this.'

'Hate them?' echoed Pottidge. 'I'd pay money to throttle each and every one of them with my bare hands.'

Tanner halted at the foot of the staircase leading up to the intensive care unit and turned to scowl at his sergeant.

'Sorry, sir, but you must have hated some of the villains you've put away. What about that child-killer, Michael Rowe?'

'I didn't hate him. I just wanted to catch him so he couldn't kill again. The point is, Graham, that you mustn't get angry. Get even. That's what we do. Get even on behalf of society.'

'Justice, not revenge, eh?'

'Something like that. Hello, what's this?'

At the top of the stairs they saw two uniformed officers escorting a pale-faced man in his mid-twenties with greased spiky hair. One officer peeled off to talk to the detectives.

'Leanne Burroughs's partner Wayne Wallis, sir. He's come to formally ID her.'

'You've only just found him!'

The officer pulled a face. 'We spent an hour on the Bemerton Heath estate looking for him before he finally emerged from his next-door neighbour's house.'

'Didn't you try there?'

'Of course we did, sir, but we couldn't get an answer. Then out pops Wallis, bold as brass, claiming he hadn't heard us knock.'

'His face is familiar,' said Pottidge.

'Petty theft and fraud. Nothing major. Too thick and too lazy. Leanne Burroughs was all right, though. Kept him on the straight and narrow, said the neighbours.'

'It's always the good ones who go,' growled Pottidge.

Jimmy Burke discovered that the car bomb had failed to explode when he arrived at Dublin Airport off his flight from Amsterdam.

Five Feared Dead in English Bomb Blast, said the headlines in the *Evening Herald.*

Only five! Burke reckoned the bomb should have killed many more than that. He bought a paper.

It took a second for the implications to sink in, and when they did Burke was almost physically sick. He made himself think. Had he armed the device properly? In his mind's eye, he saw himself reaching into the lunch box and setting the timer. He had allowed just ten minutes, calculating that this would be the optimum time when shoppers, fleeing from the come-on bomb in the mall, would be milling around the car in the street.

Perhaps the Pizzaman had slipped up for once. But that wasn't very likely.

Then again, if Mikey Drumm's bottle hadn't gone, Burke would have had time to double-check the connection.

Everyone in the bombing team had taken strict precautions but if police DNA recovery techniques were as good as they had been told they were, then a little insurance was in order. Burke bought a phonecard and dialled a mobile number from memory. The number rang and rang.

Burke was about to put down the phone when a crisp English voice said, 'Hello.'

'It's me.'

'Yes.' The man's voice was cold, unwelcoming.

'You know about the bomb.'

There was a pause. 'What bomb?'

'Jesus, what do you mean, what bomb? The fucking bomb that's gone off in Salisbury.'

'Don't use that word again. Wait. I'll look on teletext . . .'

'You mean you're—'

'I'm on leave. Right. Yes, Salisbury blast. Five dead. You're a bit late in telling me, aren't you?'

Burke bit his lip. 'You don't understand. There were two . . . The car didn't go off.'

'So?'

'For fuck's sake . . .'

'Are you saying—?'

'I've just got back to Dublin.'

'I see.' There was a long silence. 'I'll call you later.'

The line went dead.

In the living room of his Chiswick flat, Damien Kilfoyle swore long and hard, then went into the kitchen and poured himself a large whisky.

Every intelligence officer's nightmare. An agent informer out of control. And not just out of control, but actually taking part in a bombing – and on the mainland. Happy fucking Christmas.

If Burke was ever arrested . . . Kilfoyle took a large gulp of Scotch. It was not a question of *if* but *when*. Burke would have left DNA in that car, which would link him to the bombing as surely as his fingerprints.

God, if it got out that an MI5 agent had actually planted a terrorist bomb, the consequences were unthinkable. The Security Service would be mauled, exposed, humiliated. Kilfoyle could kiss his career goodbye. Never mind promotion in the New Year. He'd be out on his arse.

All because of Jimmy fucking Burke.

Kilfoyle took another drink, breathed deeply to steady his voice, then picked up the phone and dialled the direct line to the Northern Ireland desk at Thames House.

As Tanner and Pottidge turned into the intensive care unit, a policeman cradling a Heckler & Koch MP5 sub-machine gun stepped forward to confront them. He recognized the detectives and relaxed. Tanner wondered why he was there. Did someone really expect the terrorists to return to finish off the wounded?

A rumpled-looking man with a large plaster on his forehead was shifting restlessly on a seat against the wall. The firearms officer leaned forward to say softly, 'Denny Fox, sir. His partner Clive Austin caught a piece of glass in his liver.'

'How is Austin?' asked Tanner.

'He's still in surgery. Doesn't look good, according to the nurses.'

A harassed-looking doctor in a white coat emerged from the room where Michelle Lipzinger lay unconscious.

Tanner introduced himself. 'How's the little girl?'

'Her father shielded her from the worst of the blast but she was thrown off her feet and struck her head against a brick wall.' Dr Amrit sighed as if the effort of speaking was too much. 'She has a fractured skull and suffered major bleeding in the basal artery.'

'The basal artery's one of the major ones in the skull,' ventured Pottidge, whose wife was a nurse.

'It could hardly be in a worse place. If you compare arteries to motorways, it's rather like the junction of the M1 and the M25,' agreed Dr Amrit. 'We have to stabilize her before we can do anything.'

'And then you'll operate?'

'Invasive surgery near the brain is never a good idea. We'll probably insert small platinum coils to stem the bleeding.'

'How is Mrs Lipzinger?'

'How would you be if you'd lost your husband and son, and your daughter had only a fifty-fifty chance of surviving?'

'Sorry. Stupid question.'

'No, I'm sorry.' The doctor pinched the top of his nose as if his sinuses were hurting. 'She appears to be holding together remarkably well. God only knows how she's feeling inside.'

'Can we see her?'

'As long as you don't stay too long.'

The little girl was all but surrounded by an array of monitors, drips and tubes. She lay with an oxygen mask over her waxy face; her eyes were closed and her fingers were curled over the edge of the bed sheet. A blue rubber tip on one finger recorded her carbon dioxide levels. One drip went into a giving set on her right wrist, another into her left ankle. Tanner's eyes followed the traces on the monitor above the bed as they described jagged peaks and heart-stopping troughs.

A woman with dark chestnut hair was bending over the bed, stroking the girl's cheek.

'Mrs Lipzinger, I'm Detective Superintendent Tanner. This is my colleague Detective Sergeant Pottidge.'

'Maddy. Call me Maddy,' said the woman softly, without turning round.

'Maddy.'

Maddy reluctantly rose to face the men and Tanner found himself looking at a slender, pretty woman with a strong face now abraded by grief. She held his eyes in hers and, for that second, Tanner felt he was the centre of her world.

Then she went back to smoothing her daughter's hair and did not look at the men again all the time they were there.

'The doctors say Michelle has a good chance,' murmured Pottidge.

'They say Mitch has a fifty-fifty chance,' corrected Maddy. She wondered what these two policemen wanted at her daughter's bedside. She told herself they were only doing their duty and that she must be pleasant to them.

The older one was speaking. Maddy made herself concentrate.

'Is there anything we can do?'

Bring my husband and my son back.

'No. Thank you. Some nice police lady helped me get through to Tom's dad.'

'No other relatives in the United States? Anyone over here?'

'I lost both my parents last year.' Maddy made a small noise deep in the back of her throat. 'My sister and I aren't close and she'll have her own family to look after. Tom's dad is trying to get on a flight to London. It won't be easy this time of year.' Her voice tailed off.

'We'll see if we can talk to the airlines. Get him some kind of priority.'

'Tom's dad is a former Congressman. If anyone can get a flight, he will.'

'I gather you're going to stay in the hospital with your daughter,' said Tanner, thinking that Maddy did not particularly like her father-in-law.

'Yes, until Mitch comes round.' Maddy gently enfolded her daughter's hand in her own. 'You *are* going to catch the people who did this, aren't you? You *will* get them?'

'We'll do our very best. I give you my word.'

'Do you have *any* idea who they are?'

'There's a suggestion that this was the work of dissident Irish republicans.'

'Irish.' Maddy gave a strangled laugh. 'But I'm Irish. American-Irish. My grandparents were from County Mayo. My maiden name is Donovan. Tom was half-Irish on his mother's side.'

'We'll get those who did it,' repeated Pottidge.

'This trip was my idea,' said Maddy in a dreamy voice. 'We were going to come here for Christmas and then go on to Ireland for New Year to explore our families' roots. Once we'd decided to come to England, Tom got all excited. His business had just sponsored a student production of T. S. Eliot's *Murder in the Cathedral* at our local college. Do you know the play?'

'Vaguely,' replied Tanner, wondering where Maddy was heading.

'Tom wanted to see the spot where Archbishop Becket was murdered so he could impress his pals at the country club.'

'But Thomas à Becket was slain in Canterbury.'

Maddy gave a small laugh. 'Funny, isn't it? Tom wasn't very good at English cathedrals. We should have spent Christmas in Canterbury, not in Salisbury.'

Then she laughed again.

*

'Damien, it's not like you to get your hands dirty at a crime scene.'

'Just wanted to see how the other half live.' Damien Kilfoyle and David Hayward shook hands.

'So what are you doing here?' inquired Hayward, lightly but insistently.

There was a mutual wariness, tempered with respect, between the two men. Both had done well for their age, and both were expected to go further. Each also knew the importance of personal contacts. More information was exchanged between friends over drinks than through formal channels.

'The DDG thought it would be a "good thing" for me to pitch in. We are the lead agency in intelligence-gathering in Irish counter-terrorism, remember.'

'Of course.' The two men began walking down the deserted street towards the site of the explosion. 'Well, what do you think?'

'It's eerie. What's in that tent?'

'Our star exhibit, the intact bomb car. The forensic lads are just about to ship it out.'

'Can I see?' Kilfoyle started to walk into the tent.

'Sorry, chum.' Hayward grasped his arm. 'Not even I am allowed in there. Strictly forensic only. What's the word from the Province about this caper?'

'Rather too soon to say.' Kilfoyle was clearly fascinated by the bomb car. He kept craning his neck to try to see through the gaps in the tent. 'Where's the car going?'

'The labs in Lambeth. Priority is to forensicate the Mondeo as soon as possible.'

'Forensicate! What sort of English is that?'

'Metropolitan Police-speak,' replied Hayward, totally unfazed. 'I'm meeting the local skipper and his team in ten minutes. Coming?'

'May as well.'

'And there's a major conference at the Yard at oh nine hundred hours tomorrow. Your mob, Six, SB, Northern Ireland SB, Garda, even our American cousins.'

'I'm supposed to be taking Felicity Christmas shopping tomorrow morning – but I've an idea I'll be in Belfast by then,' groaned Kilfoyle.

'Isn't it time you and the beautiful Miss Fakenham tied the knot?'

'We're both quite happy as we are, thank you.'

The crowded incident room – converted from the old snooker room – smelled of warm dust, paper and deodorant. There was a hum and bustle of activity with phone lights flashing and the muted clack of computer keyboards. One wall was filled by a large-scale street plan of Salisbury indicating the positions of the litter-bin bomb and the bomb car.

Tanner looked up as Hayward and Kilfoyle entered the room. He was struck by how they were two of a type. Confident, able young men who looked as if they spent more on their clothes than their salaries allowed.

Hayward introduced the MI5 man and asked for the latest casualty figures.

'Five dead and thirty-eight injured,' announced Tanner. 'Of the injured, two are in intensive care, twelve more are in a serious but stable condition. About half the remainder, suffering from minor cuts and shock, have already been discharged.'

'We got away lightly,' observed Hayward. 'The device was intended to panic the public towards the larger bomb.'

'Initial findings suggest that the device contained between one and two pounds of commercial explosive, probably Semtex,' continued Tanner. 'The Ethiopian boy Alfred, Leanne Burroughs and the American Tom Lipzinger bore the brunt of the explosion. Leanne, who was holding Alfred in her arms, had turned to shield the boy from the street, the direction from where she thought the blast would come – when the bomb went off in the litter bin. Consequently, the lad took most of the impact. Leanne died in A&E. Tom Junior and Mekaela Telassi were killed instantly.'

Tanner cleared his throat. Someone else in the room blew their nose.

'The device in the car appears to be the standard IRA mixture of finely ground fertilizer and sugar, weighing an estimated three hundred pounds, together with a small booster charge of commercial explosive, again believed to be Semtex, and a detonator,' said Hayward. 'The explosion was to be triggered by a commercial mechanical timer inside a child's Addis lunch box. The device has been recognized as bearing the hallmarks of a top IRA bomb-maker known as the Pizzaman. His defection to the dissidents has come as a surprise. The Garda are checking his whereabouts.'

'What's the score at the farmhouse?' asked Kilfoyle.

'It's pretty well gutted, the outbuildings too. A neighbouring farmer says he's seen a number of cars there over the past few days, including a silver one which may have been the Mondeo.'

'That would fit in,' said Kilfoyle. 'It takes two to three days to grind that much industrial fertilizer fine enough to become an effective explosive and then it has to be used within seven days or it loses its potency.'

'The farmhouse was rented for a fortnight,' reported Pottidge. 'The cleaning lady called there this morning to see if the tenants wanted her to go in over the Christmas holidays. She thought there was no one at home. The fire was reported ten minutes later so the arsonist must have been there then.'

'Anything on who actually rented the farmhouse?'

'The owners are in Spain. The local police are tracing them.'

'We're assuming that the core bombing team was around six strong.' Hayward began counting on his fingers. 'The scout-car driver, the litter-bin bomber, the two men in the bomb car, the block-car driver. Plus whoever torched the farmhouse. They'll have kept in touch by mobile phone. Of course, villains are too canny nowadays to use their own mobiles. They buy pay-as-you-go phones instead and then junk them. But we can still try to track them through their phones. Sergeant Pottidge, I'm told you know about this sort of thing.'

'Thank you, sir.' Pottidge stood up. 'Once a phone's switched on, it transmits a recognition signal to the nearest beacon, even if the phone's not in use. Assuming that the bombers turned on their phones before they travelled from the farmhouse to Salisbury, analysis of calls from cell sites along the route will reveal patterns of use. If we assume the scout car to be the coordinator then we'd expect calls to radiate out from him. Find *that* phone and see who he calls. It would make life easier if we could track down the pay-as-you-go phones and work from their numbers.'

'I'm told the Americans are keen to help,' interrupted Hayward.

'That's great, sir. Their National Security Agency routinely monitors calls from mobiles, emails, faxes, telexes, basically any electronic signals transmitted within Europe and picked up by a listening base at Menwith Hill near Harrogate. From there, recordings are sent to NSA headquarters at Fort Meade, Maryland, where they're run through some of the largest super-computers in the world.'

'Thank you. Now, any reports of Irish people staying in the area, Cyril?'

'Afraid not, sir. An initial trawl of shops, pubs and garages in a ten-mile radius around the farmhouse has drawn a blank.'

'Someone must have serviced the bombing team,' objected Hayward. 'Are we looking at English fellow travellers?'

'Could be. First witness accounts are also disappointing. Enough people saw the occupants of the bomb car in their Father Christmas beards but few agree even on their heights. We're hoping closed-circuit TV will give us something on them. We urgently need to find the driver and passenger of the green car who tried to park in the bomb car's place.'

'All CCTV tapes along routes from Lewisham – where the Mondeo was stolen – to Salisbury are being examined,' announced Hayward. 'It's a colossal task. Please pass on the word that I and my team, in fact, all senior officers, have cancelled Christmas leave.' There was a general murmur of understanding around the room. 'We owe it to the families of the dead and injured to catch the perpetrators of this crime. Let's just hope the bombers are still on the mainland.'

3

'Aoife, Bobby. It's time you were getting ready for bed.' Breda Bridges stubbed out a cigarette and rose from the armchair in front of the fake coal fire to go and see what her children were doing. She found Aoife up in her bedroom, playing with her doll's house.

'You said I could stay up to see daddy,' complained Aoife.

'That was when I expected him earlier than this. Put that away now.'

Bobby's room was empty. Breda found that the boy had sneaked down into the living room where he was pressing buttons on the TV remote control.

'What do you think you're doing?' demanded his mother.

'It's time for the news. I want to see the bomb that killed the frigging English.'

Breda made a half-hearted attempt to clip her seven-year-old son around the head. 'I do not want to hear you using that sort of language in this house.'

'You and dad do.'

'We're older, and be careful you don't knock over the Christmas tree.'

'Why did someone plant that bomb, mummy?' asked Aoife, coming into the room as images of the devastation in Salisbury began to fill the TV screen.

'I expect they were angry about an injustice,' replied Breda, lighting another cigarette. She saw that she had only three left and hoped there was another packet in her coat.

'Were they angry with the people they killed, then?'

'No, not necessarily.'

'Then why kill them?'

'To make a point that they had a wrong which should be righted.'

'So were those children who were killed bad?'

Breda was becoming angry at her daughter's logic. 'You're too young to understand.'

'No, I'm not. I'm nine,' objected Aoife. 'Anyway, I don't think I could *ever* kill anyone.'

'I could,' boasted Bobby. 'Easily.'

'I've got a question to ask you, mummy.' Aoife had forgotten the bombing on TV. 'Are you and daddy really married?'

'Of course we are. Why?'

'Because Marian said you and daddy have different surnames.'

Breda picked a piece of tobacco off her lower lip. 'Not every woman takes her husband's surname. I decided to keep my maiden name. Some women do.'

'Oh.' The little girl thought about it for a moment. 'So what's my name, then?'

'What are you known as in school?'

'Aoife Nolan.'

'Right, then.'

The kids exchanged glances and Breda saw that they were deliberately stringing her along so that they could stay up.

'Mu-um,' began Bobby.

'Bed or you'll feel the flat on my hand.' Breda knew they wouldn't go to sleep until Conn arrived home but she needed five minutes' peace to check the proofs of their political movement's next newsletter.

The newsletter was named after their movement *The True Guardians* – the umbrella group for all hardline Republicans.

Breda had written the editorial setting out their position:

Irish national sovereignty is the fundamental right of every Irishman. It is not negotiable; it cannot be haggled over like some trinket in a market place. It is beyond price.

What we are seeing now is not a peace process; it is a sell-out to the British. There can never be an end to the struggle while a single blade of Irish grass is under foreign rule.

The revolution will not end until our country is whole and British imperialism consigned to the dustbin of history where it belongs.

For too long, we have heard of the so-called benefits of the peace process. Men and women who were once proud to stand up for Irish nationalism now bend their knee to lap from the saucer of cream that the British government places before them.

That would get Adams and McGuinness spitting feathers – and bloody right too.

It is time for all who believe that the peace process has failed to rally together; to stand as one not only against the imperialists but also against the traitors who have betrayed Irish republicanism.

Tiocfaidh Ar La. Our Day will Come.

Breda paused, looked up and froze. There was the sound of a key turning in the front door. She had not heard a car pull up. The memory of that phone call from Belfast not half an hour ago returned. Surely they couldn't act this quickly.

There was a rattle and a thud as the door opened only as far as the length of the security chain.

'Breda, it's me.'

She heaved a sigh of relief at the sound of Conn's voice, stubbed out her cigarette in the already full ashtray and hurried to the front door.

'Sorry. I put the chain on . . .' She wasn't going to tell him about the phone call yet.

'Ay. Can't be too careful.'

She pulled back the door. They looked at each other without touching.

'Daddy, daddy.' Aoife and Bobby erupted out of their bedrooms. Conn Nolan just had time to put down his bag before they threw themselves on him. As he picked one up in each arm, Breda stepped around him to peer quickly out into the dark tree-lined street before shutting the door again. This time she locked and bolted it.

'What did you bring us, daddy?'

'Bring you?' Conn looked blank. 'Nothing.'

'It's against Santa's rules to give presents this close to Christmas,' said Breda quickly.

'Did you eat snails?' demanded Bobby.

'Snails?'

'In Paris,' reminded Breda.

'Oh, snails. Yeh, buckets full.'

'That's it, back to bed, now,' cried Breda. 'You can talk to daddy in the morning. He's had a long day.'

Reluctantly the children went back upstairs.

'What's this?' Breda spotted a carrier bag besides Conn's case. 'A takeaway? You could have asked *me* if I wanted something.'

'I picked up a curry. I thought you'd have eaten by now.'

'It's just as well I have, isn't it?' Her mouth compressed into an angry line. 'I'll get the kids settled.'

Breda returned to find Conn dishing out chicken vindaloo, rice and chips onto his plate on the coffee table in the living room. Normally she made him eat curries in the kitchen, otherwise it smelled terrible in here next morning. As a concession to his safe return, she let him continue. Breda fetched a bottle of Lambrusco and two glasses, picked up the ashtray from the floor and placed it on the coffee table next to Conn's plate. She poured the wine and lit another cigarette.

'So, what happened?'

'God knows. I thought it was all right.'

'Did you wear your masks, gloves and things like I told you?'

'Ay. The others didn't see the point but I told them to shut the fuck up and do as they were ordered. They're thanking you in their prayers now, I'm thinking.'

'The Pizzaman's as good as signed his name, now they've got that device intact. I've sent him a message telling him to make sure his alibi's watertight.'

'He'll be all right.' Conn dipped three chips in the curry and stuffed them in his mouth.

'What was the farmhouse like?'

'Grand. The fertilizer and the grinders were there waiting for us. But those two English brothers were stuck-up little gits.'

'They did what they were told?'

'They were too shit-scared not to.'

Breda took a large swig of wine. 'I've had someone from the Provos in Belfast swearing and hollering down the phone.'

Conn stopped chewing. 'We knew they wouldn't like it. Who was it?'

'I didn't recognize his voice. I told him to fuck off.'

'What time was this?'

'About half an hour before you arrived.'

'Stuff them.' Conn resumed eating. 'They had no qualms about planting bombs when it suited them.'

'You're sure that they won't try anything on?' Breda frowned. 'I'm thinking of the kids.'

'The days when the boys from West Belfast could come down here slapping us around are over. If they try it, they'll go home with bloody noses – and the next day there'll be one or two up there without a roof over their heads. We're not the ones who've gone soft – they have.'

'Ultimate violence will always succeed.'

'If you say so. You're the boss.'

'No,' she corrected. 'I'm just the vice-president of the *political* organization; you're in charge of the *military* side.'

The phone rang. Breda stiffened.

'Shall I answer it?' she whispered.

'Suppose so.' Conn put down his spoon and braced himself as if expecting a punch.

Breda crossed to the phone and picked it up. 'Who is it?' A pause. Then she let out a long breath. 'Oh, it's you, Teresa. Thank the fuck . . . No. No problems . . . You're back safe. That's grand . . . All right, now. See you both Christmas Day.'

'Well?'

'Teresa and Dessie are staying near Rosslare tonight and driving up in the morning.'

'Fine.' Conn picked up the spoon and continued eating.

'I taped the TV news for you, if you want to see it.'

'That'll be good.'

'They're whingeing on about the kids who got killed,' said Breda.

'They should think themselves lucky the big fucker didn't go off.'

'We'll blame the bomb on the inefficiency of the English police and express regret for the innocent victims of British imperialism. The old doublespeak: black is white, white is black and it's always the other side's fault. PIRA's been getting away with it for years.'

'Shame a couple of Yanks got zapped.'

'Yeh, we don't want to risk our fund-raising over there.'

The tape wound back to the start of the TV news. Conn Nolan poured the rest of the vindaloo curry into the carton of rice and leaned forward to drink in the scene that filled his living room.

'You're sure you want to go home? It's not too late to put you up in a hotel, you know.'

'I'd like to be at home,' replied Rob Sage as the police car pulled up outside his cottage.

Not twelve hours before, he had left here in high spirits with Mekaela and Alfred. Now they were dead, and this morning seemed to belong to another lifetime.

Rob unlocked the cottage door and stepped inside. As he turned on the wall switch, the Christmas-tree lights came on. The memory of Alfred's fascination with the tree combined with the sight of the presents around its base made him stop dead.

'Are you all right?' Tanner asked softly.

'Yes. Sorry about that.'

For Christ's sake. Pull yourself together.

But it got worse as a policewoman walked past him, carrying that morning's shopping into the kitchen.

'Do you know anyone who could use a turkey?' Rob asked Tanner. 'An orphanage, old people's home, anywhere.'

'But what will you . . .?'

'I'm not going to cook for myself, am I? There's a ham, a cake, cheese. It might help make someone's Christmas.'

'I'll find out for you.'

'Thanks. Would you like a drink? I'm going to have a large Scotch.'

'Just a small one, with water.' Tanner looked around the low room with its exposed oak beams and inglenook fireplace. It bore an unexpectedly female touch with its chintz-covered three-piece suite, watercolours and old plates on the walls. 'Nice room. It's got a warm feel to it.'

'The cottage belonged to my parents.' Rob found a bottle of Inchgower and two glasses. 'I use it when I'm in England.'

'It's bigger than it looks from the outside,' observed Tanner.

'We used to call it the Tardis, after Doctor Who's police phone box. There are three bedrooms and a self-contained granny wing around the corner.'

'Never thought of selling the place?'

'Not really. My parents bought it for their retirement.' Rob handed Tanner a glass and poured a larger measure for himself. 'Sadly, neither of them ever really got to use it.'

'Your parents were doctors, weren't they?'

'Dad was a surgeon at Cork Hospital for donkey's years. He had a very Irish view of life: live for today and to hell with tomorrow.

Both he and mum smoked like chimneys. Mercifully, he went very quickly.'

'And your mother?'

'She was a radiologist at the same hospital. She died less than a year later.' He did not tell Tanner that his mother had lost the will to live once her husband had died, nor that she had taken an overdose at the onset of the secondary cancer. The death certificate did not say that she had committed suicide. Doctors were good at protecting their own.

'You were brought up in Ireland?'

'I only spent the holidays there, really. I was sent to boarding school over here, university and then the army.'

'You never wanted to be a doctor?'

Rob grimaced. 'My parents inoculated me against *that* vocation. I never really knew what I wanted to do. A short-term commission in the Royal Engineers was my way of buying time.'

'And now you're in Ethiopia?'

Rob shrugged. 'I thought I'd try to put my training to good use.'

'What do you do out there?'

'Try to give people clean, accessible water. Most years more Ethiopians die from drinking contaminated water than from famine. Even then, many villagers have to spend hours a day trekking to get that water. The idea is that the time could be better spent on education or working.' Rob sipped his whisky.

The policewoman walked back through the living room with her face averted. Tanner guessed she had been crying. He finished his drink, thinking that he did not envy Rob the night ahead.

'You're sure you'll be all right?'

'The police doctor gave me some sleeping pills but I won't need them.'

On the threshold, they shook hands. Tanner spoke softly: 'I'm truly sorry. I really am. But we *will* get those responsible. Make no mistake. We'll get them, lock them up and throw away the key.'

'Until the next armistice,' said Rob.

He closed the door and listened as the police car pulled away. Then he poured himself another drink. For the first time, he heard the silence that surrounded him. Something drew him into Alfred's room. Rob had stuck up posters of footballers and men walking in space in an effort to turn the bare room into a little boy's den. Models of aeroplanes hung from the ceiling and a glove puppet lay on the brightly coloured duvet.

Rob paused. Where was the train set that he had gone to buy? Had he actually bought it? Had he left it in the shop or had he given it to Mekaela? He couldn't remember. It didn't matter now.

He wondered if he should sleep in the granny annex, but dismissed the idea as cowardice. Instead, he wandered into his own bedroom, glass in hand. There were indentations on both pillows. Mekaela's jeans and a T-shirt were draped over the back of a chair. He knew he would find her toiletries in the bathroom. Every room bore witness to the ghosts who this morning had laughed and loved.

Back in the living room, Rob slid down against the wall to stare sightlessly at the lights on the tree. Alfred's tree.

4

'He'll be here in a minute. He particularly wants to meet you, Mrs Lipzinger,' announced the hospital official.

'That's kind of him,' replied Maddy. 'But I'm not in a fit state to meet anyone, especially the Prime Minister.'

Her daughter had remained stable during the night but Maddy was gripped by the fear that Mitch would deteriorate as soon as she left her bedside. When, at four a.m., a nurse had found Maddy asleep in a chair she had been persuaded to lie down next door. But each time she'd drifted off she'd come to with a start, guilty that she was not watching over her daughter. By six a.m., she was back at Mitch's side. Consequently, Maddy was too tired to argue and gave in to entreaties that the Prime Minister *really* wanted to meet her. The nurse promised to stay with her daughter.

Maddy inspected herself in a mirror and was shocked at the haggard creature who stared back. Dark-rimmed, bloodshot eyes, puffy with fatigue and grief. She looked a complete mess – which was just how she felt.

There was a man already waiting in the ante-room. At first sight he was attractive, tall and tanned with fair hair bleached almost white by the sun. But then Maddy noticed that his face, too, was scoured with grief. There were bags under his eyes and an artificial tautness about his mouth. She realized she had seen him before.

'You're the guy who disarmed the bomb,' she said. 'Remember me? You told me to raise the alarm.'

Rob recalled an American woman asking what he was doing. He had not bothered to look up and then everything had become a kaleidoscope of confusion and panic.

'I gather your husband and son died in the bombing. I'm sorry.'

'Who did you . . .?' Maddy felt she should know. She was sure she had been told.

'My girlfriend and a little boy I owed my life to . . .'

Maddy reached out and took Rob's hand in both her own. 'Hurts, doesn't it?'

'Like hell. Someone forgot to stop the clocks. The pain goes on.'

'Yes.'

Rob found himself gazing into the woman's deep brown eyes, which held his as if in a traction beam, pulling him towards her. It frightened him that she seemed to see into his soul. He was the first to drop his eyes.

'How's your daughter?'

'Holding on. Will you say a prayer for her when you have a moment?'

'Of course.' Rob could not remember when he had last prayed. Curses were more in his line. 'I'll say a prayer for the dead as well.'

'I think the living need them more.'

The hospital official bustled in.

'This way, Mr Wallis. The Prime Minister will arrive shortly. I don't know if you know one another?'

'No.' Rob held out his hand to the stranger. 'Rob Sage.'

'I'm Maddy Lipzinger.' She, too, held out her hand.

'Hi, I'm Wayne Wallis. Leanne Burroughs's other half.'

Maddy found herself taking an instant dislike to Wayne Wallis. He was cocky when he should have been respectful. His eyes were too close together and she didn't like the way his hair was greased.

Stop. Stop. Stop. Maddy chided herself that she was wrong to be so judgemental about someone she did not know. She blamed her tiredness and apologized mentally to Wayne Wallis.

'I'm sorry about your girlfriend, Mr Wallis.'

'Yeh, you too. My Leanne was a saint. Would you like to see a photo?' Wayne was already pulling out a postcard-sized picture from an inside pocket. 'It was taken in Lanzarote this summer.'

Leanne grinned out of focus from over a thicket of wine bottles. The camera had turned her eyes red and washed her teeth a dazzling white but nothing could conceal the girl's love of life and sense of fun.

Maddy feared that her eyes would begin leaking tears again and quickly handed the photo to Rob.

'A lovely-looking girl,' he murmured.

'Yeh, she was a smasher. You two got any pictures?'

Maddy shook her head.

'No. Neither have I,' replied Rob. 'At least, not on me.'

Rob was not the type of person to carry his girlfriend's picture. But Mekaela had had lots of photographs taken. She had been convinced that she was going to become a supermodel one day. For her last birthday, Rob had paid for the best professional photographer in Addis – which wasn't saying much – to take enough photos of her to make up a modelling portfolio. He wondered what had happened to the photos. He couldn't remember seeing them on the trip.

Rob's thoughts were interrupted as the Prime Minister and his entourage flowed into the room in a flurry of suits and dark silk ties. He had clearly been well briefed. He went up to Maddy and took her hand. 'I'm sorry about your husband and son, Mrs Lipzinger,' he said quietly. 'A most cruel and needless blow.'

'Thank you.'

'I gather someone from the American embassy has been to see you – but if there's anything further we can do, anything at all?'

Maddy was about to tell the Prime Minister that he was mistaken when she remembered. Yes, some woman had come to see her last night. She'd left a card. Maddy had totally forgotten. The Prime Minister was still talking to her.

'The police forces of this country will not rest until those responsible for this cowardly act have been brought to justice.'

'Good,' muttered Maddy.

'The sooner we bring a lasting peace to Northern Ireland, the sooner the people who planted this bomb will find they have nowhere to hide. They are a sick minority, shunned by all decent men and women.' The Prime Minister finally released Maddy's hands. 'I spoke to your President last night. He pledged his unconditional support and asked me to tell you that his prayers are with you.'

'Thank you.'

'I give you my solemn word, Mrs Lipzinger, that I will go to the ends of the Earth to find those who killed your husband and your son.'

'Thank you, again.' Maddy was too choked with emotion to say more.

'Mr Sage.' The Prime Minister shook hands. 'It's an honour to meet you. That was an incredible act of bravery. It's a shame it can't be publicly recognized at the moment.'

'That suits me, sir.'

'I'm sure a time *will* come when your courage and quick thinking will be properly recognized. In fact, I'm convinced of it.' The Prime Minister gave Rob a meaningful look. 'What made you suspect the car was carrying a bomb?'

'There was just something about those men in their Father Christmas beards.'

'It was doubly fortunate that you also knew how to disarm the bomb. Was that something you'd done in your time with the Royal Engineers in Northern Ireland?'

Rob wished that the Prime Minister had not mentioned his past in front of the others.

'Only in training, sir. Never in real life. I wasn't in bomb disposal, I was just a sapper.'

'You're being too modest, Mr Sage. I gather you were attached to the elite 51 Independent Commando Royal Marine.'

Rob looked uncomfortable.

'Do you have family you can turn to this Christmas?'

'I have friends,' lied Rob, desperately wanting the Prime Minister to move on.

'It's important to have people around you at a time like this.'

With a last meaningful eye contact, the Prime Minister switched his attention to Wayne. 'Mr Wallis, you're Leanne Burroughs's . . .'

Rob closed his eyes for a second. When he opened them, Wayne was showing the premier the photograph of Leanne. The Prime Minister was making sympathetic noises. Rob was not listening. The PM's words had made him realize just how alone he was. He had no real family. He had not seen his cousins in the Midlands since his mother's funeral. He could take or leave his aunt and uncle in Cornwall, and that was it. There were friends from the army, and some mates from university, but they were scattered far and wide. He'd lost touch with lots of people during the last four years he'd spent in one African country after another.

Maybe Maddy was reading his mind, for when he next looked at her she was regarding him with a soft look in her eyes.

'She was a saint, a verifiable saint,' he heard Wayne say.

'Indeed.' The PM looked around to signal that he was about to address them all. 'I just want to say again how much I'd like to extend my deepest sympathy to you all. I have told Mrs Lipzinger that I will go to the ends of the Earth to catch the evil monsters who did this. I repeat that pledge to you now. We will get them, I swear it.'

The embarrassed silence that followed the departure of the Prime Minister and his party was broken by Wayne Wallis.

'I know what I was going to ask him,' exclaimed Wayne, looking for a moment as if he was going to pursue the premier's party. 'Criminal compensation.'

'What?'

'Are we entitled to criminal compensation?'

'I've no idea,' snapped Maddy. 'It's not something that crossed my mind.'

'You have to think about it sometime.' Wayne was unabashed. 'I don't suppose I'm allowed a fag in here? I'll have to go outside, then. See you later.'

'What did he mean, he'll see me later?' demanded Maddy as soon as Wayne had left.

'It's just an expression over here,' explained Rob.

Maddy's relief was so obvious that Rob couldn't help smiling.

'I'm sorry,' she muttered. 'He's just so . . . awful.'

'Everyone handles grief differently.'

'Sorry.'

'You're saying sorry a lot at the moment.'

'You're right.' Maddy hesitated. 'Would you like to see my daughter?'

'If I may.'

Rob did his best not to flinch when he saw the little girl's pale and waxen looks. He could tell that she was close to death.

'Everyone talks about my loss,' said Maddy, gazing down on her child. 'They make it sound as though I've squandered money gambling on the horses.'

'They mean no harm.'

'I know, but everyone's too timid, too afraid to come right out and say, "I'm sorry your husband and son have been killed by some terrorist scum who can only pick on the innocent."' Maddy needlessly smoothed Mitch's sheet. 'What has a shopping mall in Salisbury to do with the struggle for a united Ireland?'

'Or a bomb in Ealing Broadway or in Canary Wharf in London.'

'Sorry?'

'Other places where Irish terrorists have set off bombs in the past few years,' explained Rob.

'I've not heard of those attacks. We don't get a lot of foreign news in the States.'

'You must have heard of the bomb in Omagh, Northern Ireland. It killed twenty-nine and injured hundreds more.'

'Isn't that the one where everyone knows who did it but can't prove it?'

'That's the one.'

'God.' Maddy looked up from her daughter to face Rob. 'It must be terrible to be in that situation.'

'What would you do?'

'I'd kill them myself,' she said simply.

'You wouldn't!'

'I promise you I would. I've already thought about it. If the police don't get these bastards, then I will.'

In the following weeks, Rob struggled to recall how Maddy had looked as she spoke those words. It would have been easy if she had been contorted by hatred – but instead her face had settled into a mask of resolute calm with a slight smile lifting the corners of her mouth. At the same time, her eyes had turned as dead and expressionless as a still black pool.

Then she went back to smoothing Mitch's hair.

'It's all there, Conn, you have my word.'

Conn Nolan continued his inspection of the till roll. 'I believe you, Stozza, I believe you, though there's maybe thousands who wouldn't.'

Stozza McKenna, manager of Nolan's Bar, shifted his weight uneasily from foot to foot.

'Come on now, Conn. You know there's no way I'd cheat you.'

Nolan looked up from under his heavy brows. Stozza would cheat his grandmother if he reckoned he could get away with it, but he wouldn't take the piss out of Conn. He valued his kneecaps too much. Nolan believed that the only good lieutenant was a shit-scared one. Checking the till was an exercise in keeping Stozza on his toes. Let him relax and he'd take liberties.

Nolan made out the strains of 'Four Green Fields' coming from the juke box in the bar. The boys were starting to hit the sauce early today but then, of course, it *was* Christmas Eve. He'd lost track of time over the past days.

'No one's been here looking for me while I've been away?'

'Only Davy Guzzle. He's blown his club money and his missus is demanding the new TV and DVD player she thinks he's been saving for.'

Nolan gave a bellow of laughter. 'And?'

'Five hundred at forty per cent. Payable inside six months.'

'Good.' Nolan stretched back, rolling his neck so that the muscle and gristle ground together. 'Breda was banging on this morning about some young tearaways pushing dope near the kids' school.'

'That'll be Dapper Smith's lads. They're trying to build a patch there.'

'They won't be doing that when the new term starts, you hear me?' Nolan paused. 'Where are they getting the dope from, anyway?'

'Belfast, I'm told.'

'Get the lads in and have a chat. If they want to sell dope in this town, they can buy it from me – but they're not to deal near the kiddies' school.'

There was a knock on the door. Stozza disappeared to return a moment later.

'There's gyppos knocking out holly and mistletoe near the market place,' he reported. 'The stallholders are pissed off because they've coughed up.'

'Take some of the boys down there to see off the gyppos. No violent stuff in the open, mind.'

'The boys were wondering if they could buy you a drink, like – after, you know.'

Conn gave Stozza a hard look. 'What?'

'Hell, Conn. It's your bar.' Stozza opened out his hands in a placatory gesture. 'You're among friends here. Staunch republicans each and every one.'

'So?'

'They want to drink your health. It was a grand thing that you did. A grand thing.'

Wayne Wallis lit his cigarette as he walked out through the doors of the hospital. The flurry of media activity following the Prime Minister's visit was over and TV crews were leaving. Wayne looked at them with a benevolent eye. He was beginning to enjoy being a celebrity. Last night, a reporter and photographer had knocked on his door asking if he had any pictures of Leanne. Wayne had muttered about the high cost of funerals nowadays. A photographer had offered him £100 for an exclusive picture. Wayne had agreed to let him copy the one of Leanne in Lanzarote.

When the second news team arrived, Wayne did the same again. He was pleased with his £200, not knowing that the second team was from a news agency which promptly sold the picture to all the national newspapers and TV networks, earning themselves £5,000.

He inspected the depleted press pack for someone he recognized. Because there were no papers on Christmas Day, most of the nationals had already pulled out, leaving the agencies to cover. The *Evening Standard*'s Phil Spicer, who had paid £50 to listen to Wayne's grief last night, had been ordered to stay on until the last edition. He winced as he spotted Wayne heading towards him.

'Lowlife approaching,' he muttered to his photographer Bill Humphries.

'What's the toe-rag doing now? Flogging invitations to the funeral?'

'Well, he wants to give her a good send-off, doesn't he?' mimicked

Spicer before turning to greet Wayne Wallis. 'Morning. How are you feeling today?'

'Gutted. Too bereft to work, but I'll tell you what. I've been talking to the Prime Minister.'

'So have we. Once in the town centre and once here. Same platitudes, different place.'

'Did he tell you about the bloke who stopped the bomb exploding?'

'What bomb exploding?' Spicer was careful not to appear too interested.

'The bomb in the car.'

'I thought that had failed to explode for some technical reason,' said Spicer.

'That's just what the Bill are saying. The real reason is that some bloke disconnected it.' Wayne smirked.

Spicer and Humphries exchanged glances.

'How do you know that?' demanded Spicer.

'I told you, I've been talking to the PM.'

'And he told you this, did he?'

'I wasn't the only one he was talking to. But we were all in one room. I couldn't help overhearing.'

I bet you couldn't, thought Spicer. 'And do you know the name of this hero?'

'Yeh. But you know I'm trying to get together money for Leanne's—'

'Let me give my news desk a quick call.'

Spicer walked a few paces away and muttered into his mobile. He knew he had a splash on his hands – but the timing could not have been worse. There was just one more edition before Christmas.

The editor happened to be standing near the news desk so Spicer found himself talking to God in person. Go for it, the editor told Spicer. He'd had an idea.

Spicer was always distrustful of editors' ideas, but knew better than to say so. Instead, he muttered his compliance and went into an act.

'*Oh, come on.* Wayne's information is worth more than that,' he said, raising his voice. 'He was decent enough to tell us about this hero.' Spicer swung to face Wayne and rolled his eyes theatrically. 'Okay, I know there's only one edition before Christmas but still . . . He needs the money to give his girlfriend a decent send-off . . . *Two* hundred, that's better. Hang on.' Spicer made a play of covering the phone with his hand. 'Bloody lot of Scrooges. Two hundred quid. There's no paper tomorrow or Boxing Day so they're not that fussed. But I've got them up to two hundred.'

'Cash?'

'No, it'll be a cheque.'

'That's no use to me. I ain't got a bank account.'

'Okay – cash, then. I'll get it out of a hole in the wall. Now, what's the hero's name?'

The editor's plan was to cut a deal with ITN News on the understanding that they would show the *Standard*'s headline and masthead each time they ran the story.

And that was when the operation hit the buffers. As the editor told Spicer later – the sodding police went absolutely fucking ballistic.

Through the Attorney-General, the Metropolitan Police were granted an immediate injunction preventing Rob Sage's identity becoming publicly known on the grounds that Rob's name had clearly come from a leak by a police officer even though Mr Sage had requested anonymity. The injunction was to prevent a further breach of confidence.

The *Standard*'s lawyers reckoned that the injunction was weak enough to challenge in the courts but time and the political climate were against them. The Attorney-General's department suggested a compromise. The *Standard* and ITN could run the story of the bomb hero as long as they did not publish anything that could lead to Rob's identity becoming known.

'I don't have much time,' complained Jimmy Burke. 'I've got to get to the shops.'

'*You* don't have time.' Kilfoyle narrowed his eyes. 'Listen, matey, I'm doing you a favour. Some poor countryman of yours is stuck at Heathrow trying to get home for Christmas because of you. So don't tell me you're fucking busy when I'm trying to save your skin.'

A wave of resentment swept over Kilfoyle as he recalled how his girlfriend Fliss had thrown a wobbly when he'd announced that he had to come to Belfast today. He was disappointed in Fliss. She too worked in Five. She should have understood.

He looked around the cavernous bar, heavy with the stale fumes of last night's beer and cigarette smoke, and made himself concentrate on the interview in hand. Burke wouldn't tell him everything about the bombing, he knew. The Irishman would withhold some facts, deliberately get some details wrong and contradict himself at some future debriefing. That was the nature of agent running.

But before Kilfoyle could ask a question, Burke got in first. 'What's happening with the car?' he demanded.

'Forensic are examining it,' snapped Kilfoyle. 'Tell me *exactly* what precautions you took.'

'We wore those all-in-one overalls with the hood done up tight, gloves and plastic bags over our shoes. And those masks that make you look like a surgeon.'

'And this applied to anyone who went near the car.'

'Any-fucking-where-near-any-fucking-thing.' Burke took a deep draught of stout, wiping away the resulting creamy moustache in a fierce movement.

'Why?'

'Conn Nolan had heard horror stories about how clever the police were getting with DNA. Listen to this, right. Detectives wanted to link this drugs baron to a computer where they'd found details of his deals. He swore he'd never seen it before but scientists found samples of his DNA *inside* the computer where the cooling fan had sucked in his breath. Fucking terrifying.'

'You shouldn't have got involved in the first place.'

Kilfoyle's smugness infuriated Burke. 'You haven't got a fucking clue, have you? You sit in your office and tell others "Do this", "Don't do that". Try living in the real world. If you want others to trust me, then I've got to get my hands dirty. I can't say, "No, I can't do this because it's breaking the fucking law" – and the next minute expect them to tell me where they're going to plant a bomb. For Christ's sake.'

'You could have found an excuse to back out and then called me. That's what I pay you for.'

'Bollocks I could.' Burke pulled out a tobacco pouch and angrily began to roll a cigarette. 'And then, when the bombing team are nicked, who do you think their mates would come looking for? Me, that's who.'

An old man in a cloth cap and suit jacket torn on one pocket went to sit down at the next table. Burke gave him the hard eye and the man slouched off to drink elsewhere.

But Kilfoyle too was angry. 'So instead you go and plant this bomb and the first I know is when I get a phone call that your arse has fallen out.'

Burke leaned forward, eyes blazing with anger. 'My arse did not fall out.'

Kilfoyle ignored him. 'And now you want me to keep you out of the shit.'

'If I'm in the shit, where the fuck are you? If I'm going down, I'll make fucking sure the world knows about you.'

Burke swayed back in his chair and lit the roll-up. The loosely packed tobacco flared. He made a play of inspecting the end of the cigarette. Kilfoyle eyed Burke steadily and said nothing. The silence grew.

'I could, you know,' muttered Burke.

'Of course you could. The courts wouldn't believe you and you'd end up doing twenty years under Rule 43. Not a pretty prospect, is it? Most on rule go mental after five years. It's their own company. It gets to them.'

Burke kept his eyes on the beer-stained table between the two men and drew on his cigarette.

'Stick with me, and I'll see you right,' continued Kilfoyle. 'Now, what about these two English brothers you mentioned?'

'Tony and Darren. Don't know their surname. They were just there to run errands for the rest of us. Neither Conn nor Dessie Fitzgerald could stand them.'

'One of them had a motorbike?'

'Yeh. Monster of a fucking thing. Scared the shit out of me when he ran me to Gatwick.'

'And the other one drove the Pizzaman to Bristol?'

'Yeh, in a white car – which he was then told to crush.'

'What make was the car?'

'Dunno. I never really looked.'

'Not good enough, Jimmy.'

'What else do you want?'

'Details, Jimmy. Details. In exchange for which I'll see that you're left alone to run your rackets and scams.'

Kilfoyle's phone vibrated inside his jacket. He pulled it out, inspected the caller's number and turned away from Burke.

'Yes?' Kilfoyle listened intently. 'When? No, never heard of them . . . Fine. Thank you.' He put the phone back in his pocket. 'A new mob calling themselves the Sovereign IRA have just admitted planting the bomb in Salisbury.'

'I didn't know that's what we were called,' confessed Burke.

Kilfoyle thought long and hard on the way back to the airport. He had to protect Burke at all costs – but at the same time he had to come up with the goods. That meant identifying others in the bomb gang. On balance, he reckoned it was safe to finger the hard men like Conn Nolan and Dessie Fitzgerald. He wasn't providing evidence that would stand up in court – merely intelligence. And neither Nolan nor Fitzgerald would ever talk. But if word ever got back implicating Jimmy Burke – Christ, it didn't bear thinking about!

There were other problems, too. Competing agencies, including MI6, Army Intelligence, Northern Ireland SB and the Garda, all had their own informers who might come up with Burke's name. And there was still the possibility that the bombers had been sloppy when wearing protective clothing. It needed just one microscopic slip-up.

All in all, Kilfoyle felt like he was tap-dancing on water.

Rob Sage's head was swimming from the hours he'd just spent at the police station looking through hundreds of mug shots of known Irish terrorists. No one had leaped out but it was hard to recognize someone when they had been wearing a long white beard. After a while, he'd thought one man had looked familiar. A flurry of phone calls returned the news that the man was serving time for a failed post office robbery. Never mind, Tanner had reassured Rob. We'd rather you picked ten wrong ones than miss one.

But the experience unsettled Rob and he failed to point out anyone else.

Back in his cottage, the phone's ring shattered the silence. Rob Sage scowled at it, resentful that he had been wrenched out of his daydream and back into the real world. He tried to ignore it but the phone rang insistently. Finally he answered it.

'Rob, it's Hannah. I've just seen the news on TV. Why didn't you call me?'

He recognized the breathless voice of Hannah Beckford, the recently appointed London director of his employers, the charity Waterworks.

'I was meaning to but . . .' he lied.

'Is there anything I, we, can do?'

'No, I'm . . .'

'The news said two people from Ethiopia were killed in the bomb. They must have been with you. Was it anyone I know?' Hannah dropped her voice half an octave to sound sincere.

'Mekaela and Alfred, the little boy who stepped on that landmine.'

'Alfred! Why didn't you tell me? I'd have met you at the airport.'

Hannah would have seen Alfred's arrival as an opportunity for publicity. Which was exactly why Rob had not told her. Hannah, for all that she made it sound as though they were intimate friends, had never met either Mekaela or Alfred.

'I brought him over to have his legs rebuilt.'

'I've not seen any pictures of Mekaela and Alfred in the papers.' A beautiful woman and a crippled child would have been powerful images with which to sell the charity – and to please their headquarters in Chicago. 'I'm sure we've photos from the time that German journalist came out. He was quite taken with Mekaela. It was just after Alfred had come out of the local hospital. Perhaps I should go and look. You wouldn't mind, would you?' Hannah took Rob's silence for acquiescence and ploughed on. 'We could put out a press release. After all, you are a hero.'

'Apparently you'd be done for contempt and sent to jail if you tried,' warned Rob, repeating what Tanner had told him.

'But Mekaela and Alfred were innocent victims . . .' From the fractured silences at the other end, Rob guessed that Hannah's partner Lenny was talking to her; probably telling her to calm down. That seemed to be his role in life, scraping Hannah off the ceiling where her spirals of hyperactivity left her. 'Mekaela was very beautiful, wasn't she? But only a girl.'

'She was twenty-two.'

'Was she that old? And Alfred was . . .?'

'We thought he was six or maybe seven.'

'I know. Why don't you come and spend Christmas with Lenny

and me and the kids?' continued Hannah. 'You're more than welcome.'

'Neighbours have invited me around,' Rob lied again.

'Oh, good,' replied Hannah, a little too quickly. 'If you're sure.'

'I'm sure.'

Tanner pulled open the door to the King's Arms and groaned at the numbers of late-night drinkers crammed into the public bar determined to enjoy Christmas Eve. Squaring his shoulders, he led Pottidge towards the end of the bar where a florid-faced man in a bright red waistcoat was sitting on a stool.

'Evening, Cyril,' greeted the man. 'What'll you have?'

'Two pints of best. You don't know my sergeant, Graham Pottidge, do you? This is the guv'nor, Barry Hives.'

Barry signalled to a barmaid. 'Hope you're going to get the swine who planted that bomb.'

'It won't be through lacking of trying, I promise you,' said Pottidge, with venom in his tone.

'Graham's missus and son were near the bomb when it went off,' murmured Tanner.

'Helen always treats Jack to a cake when she takes him shopping,' explained Pottidge. 'They stop and he eats it in that little square in the mall. They put the paper in the very bin where the bomb was. If she hadn't decided to go to Marks & Spencer first . . .'

'Christ!' exclaimed Barry Hives.

Their drinks arrived and Tanner took a long pull from his glass.

'I've heard that some tossers calling themselves the Sovereign IRA planted the bomb,' said Barry.

'They've claimed responsibility,' agreed Tanner.

'There's only a couple of hundred active IRA members in the whole of Ireland, or so I've read,' continued Barry. 'Why don't you just lock them up and have done with it?'

'They tried. It was called internment. It didn't work.'

'Oh.' The landlord waved for a refill for himself, saw that his bar staff were too busy to take his order and lumbered behind the bar to get his own drink.

'What's it like up at the farmhouse?' Tanner asked Pottidge as soon as they were alone.

'The SOCOs have found the remains of a coffee grinder in an outbuilding.'

'That's good. John and Andrea Petherton, the retired couple who own the farm, have finally surfaced in Spain. They advertised the farmhouse in the *Salisbury Journal* in mid-October. It was snapped up the day the advert came out by a well-spoken woman calling herself Pearse who paid cash up front.'

'That suggests someone local,' said Pottidge. 'Any description?'

'In her late thirties, average height, probably brown hair. Andrea admits that she probably couldn't recognize the woman if she passed her in the street today.'

'Shame.'

'Anyway, the fire's really spoiled the Pethertons' Christmas. It seems they weren't insured for holiday lets.'

'You call an IRA bombing team a holiday let?'

'No, but their insurance company will.'

'What are you two doing for Christmas?' asked Barry, returning with his pint.

'Working,' replied Tanner shortly.

'I was really looking forward to spending Christmas Day with my lad,' said Pottidge. 'But he'll be in bed by the time I get home tomorrow.'

Outside the pub, Tanner paused to listen to bells pealing from a nearby church, calling worshippers to midnight Mass.

'This is the one time of the year I go to church,' he told Pottidge. 'I'm going to miss it tonight. Anyway, good night, Graham. See you in the morning.'

'Good night, sir, and Merry Christmas.'

'Merry Christmas.'

'Come on, Breda. Get a move on or we'll end up standing at the back.'

'You don't have to see God to be in his presence,' Breda Bridges chided her younger sister.

'Bog off. If *you* want to stand for an hour with a lot of drunken blokes farting and belching around you, you can. *I* want to sit in God's House.' Teresa Bridges topped up her glass of red wine and scooped up a handful of peanuts from the breakfast bar, envying her sister's luxurious fitted kitchen where tomorrow's feast lay in various stages of preparation. 'Are the kids coming?'

'They're still too young. Bobby would be bored shitless.' Breda emerged into the kitchen in her best blue coat, tying a headscarf under her chin. 'You all right in there, Marie?' she called to the babysitter, a neighbour's fifteen-year-old daughter who was watching TV with her boyfriend and counting the seconds until they were left alone.

'Ay, grand, thank you, Breda.'

'The kids are fast asleep. Conn and Dessie are in Conn's bar. You've got the number.'

'Ay, ay. Don't worry.'

'Now, where's my purse? Right. Come on, then.'

Teresa swallowed the wine in one gulp and followed her sister out of the door.

In Salisbury, Teresa had worn glasses, an auburn wig and cheek pads. Now, back in Dundalk, she had reverted to her true self. In the real world, she possessed a hollowed face, wasted in fanaticism, cropped dark hair and a piercing stare that crackled with a coruscating intensity.

Teresa linked her arm through Breda's as they set off. 'I didn't tell you about the dog, did I?'

'What dog?'

'Dessie reckoned we'd look more like an established married couple if we had a dog with us. We saw this fat old thing in a back street in Fishguard and borrowed it, like.'

'How did you get it into the back of the car?'

'Cheese. All dogs love cheese. Then we spread out a couple of towels to look like a dog bed and this thing sat happily in the back, scoffing this half-pound of Cheddar as we sailed through Customs.'

'So where's the dog now?'

'Somewhere in Rosslare. Dessie wanted to run over it, but I made him set it loose. It can live off its fat.'

Breda laughed. The night air was soft and damp. Along the road, almost every house had a Christmas tree with fairy lights in its window.

'I always love this time of year, Breda. Everyone's happy.'

'That they are not,' contradicted Breda. 'There are more suicides at Christmas than at any other time of year.'

'Och, there'll always be sad bastards – but generally, you know.'

'Conn said there was almost a cock-up with the block car,' said Breda, returning to the subject of the bombing.

'Jesus, yes. Some gits in a poxy green thing appeared from nowhere. I had to go back into the mall to pretend I'd forgotten something and all the time the clock was ticking.'

'That must have been something.'

'It got me wee heart a-fluttering, I can tell you.'

In the distance, they made out the spire of the church against the night sky.

'I didn't tell you I had a call from the boyos in West Belfast,' announced Breda.

'Ah.' A sharp intake of breath. 'What did they say?'

'That the bomb wasn't a clever thing to have done right now. I told the sod to bog off and put the phone down.'

'Oh, Breda.'

'I'm not putting up with any shit from that load of self-serving two-faced cowards.'

Near the church, Teresa slowed down. 'Breda, I've a wee favour to ask.'

'Ay?'

'You remember that night Dessie and me fell out about three weeks back?'

'You got drunk at that party.'

'He was being a prat. Anyway, I told him I stayed with you that night . . .'

'Thanks for letting me know,' said Breda drily.

'He wouldn't have asked you, but I'm late.'

'What do you mean, late?'

'Late. As in my period's late. I've been too busy to keep track what with one thing and another this last week but now I've looked at my diary . . .'

'What's this got to do with saying you stayed with me?'

'Because I stayed elsewhere. Jesus, Breda, keep up, girl.' Teresa halted and swung to face her sister. 'Dessie and I have been trying, well, not trying, but not minding if it happened, you know, but nothing did. Then I stray one night, just one frigging night . . .'

'So what are you going to do?'

'I've got a pregnancy test. I'm going to take it when I get back. Christmas morning. Symbolic, like.'

'And if it's positive?'

'We'll get married, I suppose.'

'What! You and the father?'

'Me and Dessie, stupid.'

'You'll tell him the child is his, then?'

'What else do you expect me to do?'

'You wouldn't think of an abortion?' Breda asked quietly as they began to ascend the steps to the church.

'Hell, no. I'm a good Catholic girl, me.'

Side by side the two sisters climbed the steps and passed into the church.

5

Christmas morning and Rob had never felt so alone in his entire life. Before Alfred had adopted him, he'd been used to his own company in Tigray but there was a hollowness inside him now he could neither ignore nor repair. He should keep himself busy, but how? He had showered and shaved and made toast for breakfast. That might have been the first food he'd eaten since the bomb went off. He honestly couldn't remember.

Rob turned on the radio, only to switch it off at the sound of a choir singing carols. For something to do, he collected Alfred's few scattered toys before tidying up his own bedroom, picking up Mekaela's clothes and putting them away neatly folded in a chest of drawers.

He found himself wondering what to do about the presents he had bought for Mekaela and Alfred, now piled under the tree. He thought he'd wait until after the funeral before giving them away. What was going to happen about the funeral? Mekaela was an Orthodox Coptic, like most Tigrinya, so cremation was in order. Alfred was an orphan boy who did not even know his own given name. It would be wrong to attach a religious tag to him like some luggage label.

Anyway, whoever Alfred's God was He had failed the boy. He had given up his right to Alfred the instant that bomb had gone off.

Rob found himself thinking about those who had planted the bomb and wondered what they were doing this Christmas Day.

Were they laughing, drinking and enjoying being with their families? A flash of hatred seared through the inertia that was his mind's way of dealing with the pain – then the dull ache returned.

He needed to talk to someone. He thought of Maddy Lipzinger. He could go to see if her daughter was better, and take along photos of Mekaela and Alfred.

In the bedroom, Rob looked in Mekaela's case for photos of herself. The only ones he found were the snapshots from when the three of them had visited the ancient city of Axum. Idly, he wondered where the rest were.

'Hello, I hope you don't mind me calling in on Christmas morning.'

'Not at all, Rob. Come in.' Maddy looked up, the pale skin around her glazed eyes creasing in welcome.

'How is she?'

'Hanging on in there.'

'I like the spotted dog.' Rob nodded at the black and white stuffed dog lying on the pillow alongside Mitch.

'That's Pooch. Mitch's favourite. I got the hotel to send it round.' Maddy turned back to watch over her daughter, still surrounded by the same monitors showing the same uneven patterns.

There was a pause before Rob said, 'I don't know if I can really wish you Happy Christmas.'

'It's not, is it? It's not a happy Christmas.' Maddy's voice came close to cracking. 'It's the worst Christmas of my life.'

'But I can *wish* you one,' said Rob after a moment.

'Yes, you can. Thank you.' She saw him glance at the photograph of her family she had put up on the bedside cabinet. 'My husband Tom and Tom Junior, TJ. It was taken this autumn up in the mountains. TJ had just caught his first wild trout. He was ever so proud but he insisted that we put it back. He said he didn't see the sense in killing the fish just for the sake of it. I liked that.' Maddy drifted into silence, lost in her memories.

'Where do you live?'

'A small town outside Buffalo, New York State.' Maddy shuffled through a batch of pictures and handed him one. 'This is our home.'

'What a lovely house,' remarked Rob, looking at a large white timber house in English Colonial style.

'We bought it a few years back when Tom's business really started to take off. He and his partner have the local franchise for Nissan cars and trucks.'

'Had you known each other long?'

'We met at a St Patrick's Day dance at college. I was in my sophomore year. Tom was the football jock every girl wanted to date.'

'And you did?'

'Somehow we clicked. We used to have a lot of fun together, do all sorts of mad things. God, if we'd ever been caught!'

Rob was curious what sort of mad things Maddy was talking about. He suspected he was catching a glimpse of the woman she really was. Someone who would be fun, and could be dangerous.

'We got married straight after I'd finished college,' she continued. 'I was going on to qualify as a veterinarian but Mitch came along and I became a mother instead. Tom and I would have been married ten years in June. Happy years . . . in the main.'

'In the main?'

'Every marriage has its ups and downs. Tom liked to work hard and play hard.'

Rob thought there was a hint of bitterness in Maddy's voice. 'But he did well to build up the business.'

'Tom's father was a local congressman so his son had a leg up to start with – but he did work hard,' she added, feeling she was betraying her husband's memory. 'His father is flying over tomorrow. No doubt he'll want to get involved in some way.'

Maddy moved aside as a nurse arrived to examine Mitch.

'Clive Austin has died,' announced the nurse as she lifted one of

Mitch's eyelids to shine a torch into the pupil. 'Poor man never really had a chance.'

'So that's six dead now,' said Rob.

'And that's all there's going to be,' declared the nurse stoutly. 'This young maid is a fighter, bless her.'

'I hope so,' breathed Maddy. 'She's certainly stubborn enough.'

The nurse brushed a strand of hair off Mitch's damp forehead. 'Sometimes God makes them that way for a purpose. Maybe He made her stubborn and determined because He knew she'd have this battle to fight, and win.'

'Maybe,' said Maddy.

She returned to her daughter's side, immediately the nurse had left. 'Now, that's enough about me,' she said, briskly. 'Tell me about yourself . . . and Mekaela and Alfred.'

'I've a photo of Mekaela, if you'd like . . .'

'Yes, please. Wow!' Maddy regarded Rob with something like new respect. 'She's very beautiful.'

'Yes.' Everyone said that. 'The Tigrinya people are noted for their beauty.'

'Pardon me?'

'Mekaela was from Tigray province in the north of Ethiopia.'

'How did you two come to know each other?'

'She was a primary-school teacher in a small town near the Eritrean border when I first met her. She spoke some English and we sort of got on well. After a while she came to work with me.'

'You build wells and things, I gather.'

'Sort of. I try to provide villagers with clean water. Less than a quarter of the population in Ethiopia have access to safe water supplies, and only fifteen per cent have adequate sanitation. Water-related diseases are rife.'

'It sounds very worthwhile.'

Rob shrugged, embarrassed as always at the hint of praise. 'Putting in a water supply is the easy part. The hard part is to make sure that it's still working a month later.'

'What did Mekaela do?'

'She'd teach people about hygiene. She was trying to help to eradicate trachoma.'

'Trachoma?'

'The single most common cause of preventable blindness – triggered by dirty water and poor hygiene,' explained Rob. 'It's prevalent all over Ethiopia.'

To stop himself lecturing, Rob handed Maddy a photo of Alfred grinning broadly into the camera, a picture of impish glee.

'Aaawww. He's a cutie.'

Rob felt a lump grow in his throat. 'Alfred and I sort of adopted each other. One morning up country I found him asleep under my truck. I shooed him off but he was there again next morning. No one in the village had ever seen him before. The locals thought he might have come from a valley twenty-odd miles away where the people had been massacred by Islamic extremists. He was so traumatized that he couldn't talk. When his speech did return, he seemed to have blanked out what had happened. Maybe it was his mind's way of handling what he'd gone through.'

'I didn't know there's a war going on there.'

'There's *always* a war going on there. More than seventy thousand died in the last dust-up between Eritrea and Ethiopia. Even today there're four thousand UN peacekeepers along the border and still countless landmines.'

'Gee!'

'But just when the region was settling down, a bunch of Islamic extremists calling themselves the Eritrean Islamic Jihad Movement have begun massacring villagers on both sides of the border. They're probably the ones who killed Alfred's parents.'

'How did he get his name?'

Rob chuckled. 'After a few weeks he began to talk, but he didn't know his own name. I tried every one I could think of in Tigrinya and Amharic, even in English. I'd almost given up when I said "Alfred". He jumped up and pointed at himself. I can't believe

Alfred *is* his real name but that's the one he chose, so that's what he was called.'

'And he came to travel with you?'

'The villagers didn't want him. I tried to put him in an orphanage in the regional capital but a week later he stumbled into my camp, hungry, exhausted and footsore. He'd walked fifty miles across some of the roughest terrain in the country to find me.' Rob shrugged. 'After that, what could I do?'

'You had a shadow.'

'He was a smashing kid, bright as a button, and could never do enough to help. Mekaela was teaching him to read and write in Tigrinya and he was picking up English at an amazing rate.'

'What happened to his legs?'

Maddy, who was studying Rob closely, shivered at the way his eyes, one minute smiling and soft with memory, hardened to a cold brilliance.

'He stepped on a landmine meant for me,' said Rob in a clipped, neutral voice.

'What!'

'The extremists don't want the villagers to have anything that might improve their lot,' Rob explained. 'One night, two guerillas placed landmines along the path leading to the well that I was digging. Next morning, Alfred, running ahead, stepped on one. He was due to have the first operation to rebuild his legs next week. That's why we came here.'

A thought struck Maddy. 'How do you know that there were *two* guerillas?'

There was a pause before Rob said simply. 'I tracked them down.'

Tracked them down and killed them.

Maddy sensed that she should change the subject. 'What were you doing in Salisbury that last morning?'

'We'd gone to get our Christmas shopping, buy Alfred a few presents and take him to see Santa Claus.'

'Do you remember me asking you what was going on?'

'And me telling you to get away and call the police.'

Maddy glimpsed the terrible truth. The bomb car had been parked outside the toyshop where Alfred had been looking at the train set. Rob had told Mekaela and Alfred to move away. He'd thought he was sending them to safety. Instead, he had sent them to their deaths.

'Oh, Rob, I'm so sorry.' Maddy reached out and held his hand.

'I thought it for the best. I didn't know.'

'Of course not. How could you?' Maddy felt that she had to offer something in return. 'Listen, that morning . . . my family were getting on my nerves. The kids just wanted to watch TV. I *made* them go shopping with Tom. If I hadn't lost my temper with them, Tom and TJ would be alive now. Do you know the last thing Mitch said to me? "I hate you, mommy. I hate you." '

'She didn't mean it.'

'She did at the time.'

'A further victim has died as a result of the Salisbury bombing, bringing the total number of deaths up to six. Police have confirmed that Clive Austin, a 38-year-old local businessman, died of wounds sustained in the blast, which took place in a crowded shopping mall two days before Christmas. A new terrorist organization calling itself the Sovereign IRA has claimed responsibility. The bombing has brought international condemnation . . .'

'Ya, bollocks.' Teresa Bridges jerked the middle finger of her right hand towards the TV screen.

A reporter in Washington began describing how the President had offered assistance in tracking down the killers. *'The fact that two of the victims were American citizens has struck home here. Their deaths could be very much an own goal for the bombers. If the President proscribes this new organization then the dissident republicans will be cut off from a traditional source of fund-raising for the Irish republican movement.'*

'Stuff it. We don't need your fucking charity.'

'Open the oven door, Ter,' commanded Breda. 'I want to test the roast spuds.'

Teresa did as she was asked before topping up her glass and continuing to glower at the television set.

'Look, Breda, there's the bloke who's trying to catch us.'

David Hayward was on the TV, standing in front of New Scotland Yard.

'We believe the device in the stolen Ford Mondeo car was assembled in an isolated farmhouse, called Sundial Farm, between the villages of Wylye and Dinton, some twelve miles from Salisbury. The bombers would have spent around five days there, so we are asking anyone who might have passed the farm in the last week to contact us. We also want to contact the occupants of a green car, possibly a Citroen Xsara, who tried to park in the space intended for the bomb car . . .'

'Bog off, nancy boy,' jeered Teresa.

Hayward was replaced by the newscaster. *'There will be a special edition of* Crimewatch *after the six o'clock news tomorrow evening. This will replace the scheduled programme. Now the rest of the news . . .'*

'Ter, switch off that telly and give me a hand. Start draining off that water for the gravy.'

Breda was becoming exasperated with her younger sister. Anyone else would have been bursting to tell her the news, but Teresa had to be different. In the fifteen minutes that she'd been in Breda's home, all she'd done was drink wine, scoff handfuls of crisps and try to pick a fight with the TV. Breda could contain herself no longer.

'Well?'

'Well what?'

'Are you?' Breda put her hand over her stomach.

'Oh, ay. I'm in the club all right.'

'What did Dessie say? You haven't had a row about it, have you?

'No. Anyway, you can't have a *row* with Dessie. He doesn't say a word, then he thumps you and walks out.'

'You have told him?'

'Ay, when he finally rolled in last night, or rather this morning.'

'What did he say?'

'His exact words were "Holy fuck", and then he passed out. I didn't know if he'd remembered so I told him again when he woke up. This time he said, "Fuck me." I declined.'

'He doesn't suspect?'

'No. I made sure we did it a few times during the past few weeks, just in case.'

Breda burst out laughing, as usual finding it impossible to stay cross with her sister for long.

'You're a canny one.'

'Hark who's talking. Anyway, seeing as it was confirmed at Christmas I thought we'd call it Jesus if it's a boy and Mary if it's a girl,' continued Teresa.

Breda stooped to take the turkey out of the oven. 'How's Dessie's business going?'

'It's always quiet this time of year but it's ticking along. It's good that he's got the only double-glazing company in the area.'

'Yeh, that fire at his rival's really helped,' said Breda drily.

'That it did.'

'It's just that Conn has just acquired an interest in an executive housing estate being built this side of Dublin. Dessie can supply the windows if he wants.'

'He'll do it, especially now there's going to be an extra mouth to feed. Maybe this'll be the start of a large family. I've always said I wanted three or more, and now I know where to find a high sperm count.'

'You're incorrigible.'

The women were still laughing when Dessie and Conn arrived back from Conn's bar. They looked as if they had been drinking heavily. Dessie was clutching a bottle of champagne.

'Me and Teresa are getting married,' he blurted out.

'Congratulations.' Breda smiled. 'When's the wedding?'

'It'll have to be soon. She's up the duff,' said Dessie.

'We thought around St Valentine's Day,' said Teresa serenely.

'Did we?' exclaimed her husband-to-be.

'Yes, *we* did.'

'Ay, all right, then. But I don't know where you're going to find room to put an engagement ring, never mind the wedding band, with all those bloody rings on your fingers.'

Teresa inspected her left hand. All four fingers already bore wide silver rings. 'I could put this one on my thumb, like. Or again, I might not bother with a wedding band at all.'

Breda called the children to join them for the meal.

'Aoife, my precious, would you like to be a bridesmaid?' asked Teresa.

'Oh, yes, please.' Aoife jumped up and down in excitement; then her brow furrowed. 'But aren't you already married?'

'No, darling, we're not.'

'But you live together.'

'That's sort of having a trial marriage to see if you get on,' explained Teresa.

'That's what I'm going to do,' exclaimed Aoife. 'I'm going to have lots of trial marriages before I choose the one I like.'

'Good girl,' laughed Teresa. 'You do that.'

When everyone was seated, Breda raised a glass. 'Absent friends.'

'Absent friends,' chorused the adults.

'What are you doing?' Bobby asked.

'Remembering loved ones who can't be with us on this special day,' explained Breda.

'Why not?'

'Because they're doing important work which keeps them away.'

'Like firemen or people on TV,' volunteered Bobby.

'A bit like that,' conceded Breda. 'While I remember.' She rose and went into the living room to return holding a large Christmas card showing the three wise men as women. 'It arrived yesterday.'

'Who's it from?' inquired Aoife.

'Never you mind,' said Teresa quickly.

'Another toast,' cried Breda. 'The True Guardians.'

'The True Guardians,' chorused the others.

'*Tiocfaidh Ar La.* Our day will come.'

Teresa drained her wine glass and reached for the bottle.

'Shouldn't you ease up on the drink in your condition?' ventured Dessie.

'Away with you, a drop of wine never harmed anyone.' Teresa glared at him, as if daring him to contradict her.

Finally the meal was finished and the children left to resume playing with their presents. The women cleared the table, piling the plates next to the dishwasher before sitting down again.

'That was lovely, Breda,' her sister complimented her, lighting a cigarette. 'It really was.'

'You shouldn't be smoking,' complained Dessie.

'Oh, don't fucking start,' snapped Teresa. 'I'm not going to have to put up with this for the next nine months, am I? Don't do this, don't do that. You'll be having me sitting at home with my feet up next.'

'I'm only thinking of the—'

'Fucking don't.'

'Another toast' cried Conn to dispel the atmosphere building up between Teresa and Dessie. 'To a mission accomplished.'

'I've been thinking about what we should do next,' announced Breda.

'Jesus Christ, Breda, we've only just got back,' complained her sister.

'These things take time to plan.'

The phone rang. 'Who'd that be, now of all times,' murmured Breda as Teresa saw the flicker of fear in her eyes.

'Yes . . . hello . . . oh, hello, Mrs McGuire.' There was a perceptible lessening of tension around the table. 'And Happy Christmas to you . . . Hang on, I'll ask him.' Breda put down the phone and went to the bottom of the stairs. 'Bobby, it's Kieron's mam, asking if you want to go around there and play with Kieron's new Scalextric racing set. Yes? He'd love to,' Breda said, returning to the phone. 'He'll cycle over now if that's all right.'

Bobby came flying down the stairs.

'You go straight there, mind, and phone when you arrive,' commanded Breda. 'And make sure you call me when you're leaving.'

'Yes, mam.' Bobby hurried out of the door.

'You can't be too careful nowadays,' Breda told her sister. 'You'll understand when you have a child of your own.'

6

Cyril Tanner sipped his coffee and looked around the windowless conference room in New Scotland Yard for faces he recognized. There was only David Hayward and the Security Service man Kilfoyle, deep in conversation together. The others, from MI6, NCIS, SB, Army Intelligence Northern Ireland, the Police Service of Northern Ireland and God knew who else, were of all of a type – lean, well dressed and well scrubbed. Tanner could tell the CIA man from the cut of his pale grey suit.

'Good morning, there.'

Tanner turned at the sound of an Irish accent to see a large man in a sports jacket and cords who had come in behind him.

'Morning. Cyril Tanner, Wiltshire police.'

'Pat Rodgers, Garda Siochana.' Rodgers held out a large hand.

Like Tanner, Rodgers was on the wrong side of fifty, with too much flesh around his face and the shambling bulk of a man whose physical activity was limited to the occasional round of golf or propping up the bar. Tanner recognized a kindred spirit.

'You've come over specially for this conference?'

'Ay. First flight this morning.'

'I gather there are names in the frame already,' said Tanner. 'That's fast work.'

'Names in the frame is the easy part. It's getting the proof that's harder.'

'As always.'

'Especially so dealing with terrorism. It can get you down sometimes,' confessed Rodgers, playing with an empty pipe. 'We know who they are. They know we know. Sometimes even the dogs in the bloody streets know – but we can't prove it.'

'It must be very frustrating.'

'It can destroy a man, Cyril. You remember the Droppin' Well bomb in 1982 – killed seventeen people, eleven of them squaddies. A good friend of mine – a fine detective – investigated that. He knew who was responsible; knew every last detail of the operation – but couldn't prove a single thing. It became an obsession with him. He felt he'd let down the families of the dead. When the bomber finally blew himself up some ten years later, my friend felt cheated.'

'I can understand that,' said Tanner slowly.

There was the sound of a spoon rapping on a cup. Hayward cleared his voice. 'Gentlemen, if you're ready . . .'

Tanner and Rodgers sat down next to each other, their combined bulk sending ripples of movement around the polished oval table as others inched sideways to make room. A blue folder lay in front of each man.

'MI5 have come up with the names of a number of suspects.' Hayward nodded towards Kilfoyle. 'In addition, the Garda are holding the bomb-maker in Dublin on the strength of his trademark on the unexploded device. I must stress that what we have at the moment is uncorroborated intelligence. We have no evidence against any of these players, but we are in a strong starting position.' He held up a folder. 'Biographical details of the suspects, together with an Intelligence overview and appreciation of the organization that has claimed responsibility, together with the bombing's likely impact on the peace process. Please study this in detail later. Now, let's look at the players.'

He nodded to the projectionist and a slab of a man with a thick neck and broad shoulders filled the screen. He was glowering directly at the camera with hard, don't-fuck-with-me eyes.

'Connor Adrian Nolan. Leader of the bomb gang. Date of birth

1–11–59. Long-term IRA activist, former quartermaster of the West Armagh brigade. When he broke with PIRA, he took their arms with him. Legally, Nolan owns a bar in Dundalk, together with a successful building company. Illegally, he's involved in drug trafficking on both sides of the border, extortion, racketeering and loan sharking. Altogether an unpleasant piece of work, the type who would be involved in criminal activity even without a political pretext.'

Hayward took a sip of water and continued. 'Apart from serving four years from 1984 to 1988 for illegal possession of explosives, Nolan is suspected by the Northern Irish police of being implicated in the murder of two Special Branch officers in Belfast docks in 1989. In the early 1990s, he became operations officer of the West Armagh brigade before becoming its quartermaster. It's surprising that he's still alive after stealing PIRA's weapons. And the next picture, please.'

Photographs of a man and a woman came up together.

'Lovely couple, aren't they?' said Hayward, stepping back to look at the screen. 'Teresa Sheila Bridges and Desmond Michael Fitzgerald. Take Fitzgerald first. He is believed to have planted the come-on bomb in the litter bin. Date of birth 12–4–68. Served six years for the attempted murder of an RUC man in the late 1980s. Also a former member of the West Armagh brigade. Owns a double-glazing firm in Dundalk where he lives with . . . Teresa. She is believed to have driven the getaway car. Date of birth 26–8–71. Owns a hairdressing salon in the town. Impeccable republican credentials. Her father Seamus was shot dead in 1982 as he went to visit an arms dump under SAS surveillance. His death sparked a week of rioting in West Belfast. As Seamus had been involved in at least three previous bombings there were few tears on the security side. Teresa's elder brother Bobby blew himself up eight years later in Monaghan, preparing a car bomb. Teresa herself was suspected of planting the bomb that blew up the Conglarie Arms, but again there was no proof. As far as the republican movement in Ireland is concerned, her family are royalty, if you'll forgive the paradox.'

Hayward nodded to the projectionist, who flashed up the next photograph.

'All three are connected to this woman. Breda Anne Nolan. Elder sister of Teresa, wife of Conn Nolan. The Godmother of dissident republicans. Breda Bridges, as she likes to be known, is the political brains of the organization; Nolan's the military brawn. She is *not* one of the suspects thrown up by Five, although it's inconceivable that the bombing could have taken place without her knowledge. At the very least, she would have had to give her approval; probably, she was responsible for the detailed planning behind the operation.'

Tanner found himself squinting to see more clearly. Superficially, Breda Bridges was a disappointment: the sort of person who would pass unnoticed in a crowd. No flame of fanaticism crackled in her eyes as it did in her sister's. Teresa's stark, almost gaunt face screamed zealotry. Breda's features were softer: an entirely ordinary face framed by hair that fell to her shoulders. Tanner thought that her mouth was a little thin and her eyes were hooded – but then he realized that he was trying to make her into a villain.

'The epitome of the banality of evil,' announced Hayward. 'Don't be fooled. Under that placid exterior she is as cold, as ruthless and as exploitative as anyone on the Provos' Supreme Army Council. She is a brilliant orator. I've heard her speak and I promise you she really is remarkable – she almost had me believing in the justice of her cause . . .' He waited for the ripple of laughter. 'And a formidable political organizer and publicist. Ally those talents with her family's place in the pantheon of Irish republicanism and you can see why her status with the hardliners is colossal. When she accused the peace process of being a betrayal of everything that her father and her brother had died for, a succession of very senior Provos made the pilgrimage to Dundalk to try to get her to change her mind. They were unsuccessful.'

'Her movement, called The True Guardians, has become *the* umbrella organization for hardline republicans who believe the peace process is a sell-out,' added Kilfoyle. 'Bridges has been canvassing hard on both sides of the border so that now she can probably muster more support there than the Provos could. The Salisbury bombing could be Bridges's way of proclaiming that she now feels strong enough to take centre stage.'

'But aren't these players too senior to be foot soldiers?' objected Tanner. 'These are all chiefs, not Indians.'

'It could be a measure of their confidence that they'll get away with it,' suggested Rodgers. 'Or, again, maybe they were worried about security and so kept the operation within the inner circle.'

'Is there any forensic yet on the bomb car?'

'There's a wealth of fingerprints, fibres, DNA. The car was used as a minicab, after all – but nothing specific yet,' said Hayward. 'Now, Pat, your turn. For those who don't know him, this is Detective Chief Superintendent Pat Rodgers of the Garda Siochana's Special Branch. Pat has been interviewing the bomb-maker Kevin O'Gara.'

Rodgers gave a throaty chuckle. 'And I'd just as well have saved my breath.'

'Tell us about him.'

'Kevin O'Gara, a.k.a. the Pizzaman, aged thirty-three. Lives in Dublin with girlfriend and twelve-month-old baby son Dean. Has always delivered pizzas ever since he left school, hence his nickname. O'Gara was PIRA's top bomb-maker. We hadn't known he'd left them. The Addis lunch box and the Coupatan timer found in the bomb car are his trademarks.'

'Sounds promising,' exclaimed Tanner.

'I'm afraid not,' said Rodgers. 'O'Gara's never been convicted of any offence other than speeding. *We* might know that O'Gara is the bomb-maker but it's going to take more than our word to convince a jury. I brought a sample of his DNA over with me so we'll keep our fingers crossed that we can find a match on the bomb components.'

'I take it the Pizzaman has an alibi?' said Hayward.

'Ay, he's got an alibi,' said Rodgers. 'He says he was in West Cork, near Skibbereen, with his girlfriend and baby, staying at a bungalow on his brother's farm. O'Gara was seen with his brother in a number of pubs in Skib on Wednesday and Thursday last week. From the way they made a point of talking to the bar staff wherever they went, I'd say they wanted to be noticed. O'Gara's girlfriend was remembered in Fields, the local supermarket, on Friday because her bag of groceries conveniently split open and spilled all her shopping everywhere.'

'No sightings of the Pizzaman over the weekend?'

'No. It's my belief that he left as soon as he'd established an alibi. We've been checking all flights to Britain and other parts of Europe.'

'What about the girlfriend?'

'Lorraine? A foul-mouthed cow who backs O'Gora's story when she's not spitting in policemen's faces,' replied Rodgers. 'O'Gara was certainly back at home in Dublin by nine o'clock on the evening of the bombing. In fact, one neighbour says she saw him early that afternoon.'

'But how could he have got home so quickly?'

'Once he'd assembled the device and tested it that morning, then there was nothing to keep him.' Rodgers sucked his empty pipe, ruing the fact that all police stations in England had become no-smoking zones. 'I can hold O'Gara for a total of seventy-two hours but I don't expect him to get any friendlier. Let's just hope we get a forensic match.'

'Did I tell you that Mitch played the cello in the school orchestra? Why a little girl would choose the cello! We used to say, honey, why don't you learn to play the violin? That's so much easier to carry. But she said . . .' Maddy paused and corrected herself. 'She *says* it makes her feel sad and happy at the same time. Then she loves the ballet, and acting. She's a born extrovert.' Maddy sighed. 'TJ was the quieter one. He always lived in the shadow of his sister.'

The woman with the sensible tweed skirt and large glasses gave Maddy an encouraging smile.

'Little girls can be bossy,' agreed Rose Allen.

Maddy smiled down at her daughter. 'Mitch is a right little tomboy. Never happier than when she's climbing a tree or building a dam in a stream. We were going to get her a pony this spring.'

'And TJ was more bookish?

'More into computers,' said Maddy, feeling at ease with her visitor. 'I don't think kids read any more. At least, mine didn't . . . don't.' Maddy swallowed. 'I'm sorry. I'm gabbling on here.'

'That's all right. I should have called in sooner but I didn't know how you were placed, and what with Christmas . . .'

'Please drop by any time.'

'That's very kind of you.' Rose Allen, from the local Victims Support Group, was in her early forties and had the sort of homely face that was made for sympathetic listening. 'I've just come from visiting an eighteen-year-old girl who was attacked in the street on Christmas Eve.'

'No!'

'She'd just left a pub with friends when this man who she'd never seen before came up and stabbed her. An inch to the left and she'd have been dead.'

'Have they got the man?'

'Her friends caught him. Physically the girl will heal but she'll be mentally scarred for ever.'

'Why did he attack her?'

'No one knows. Do you mind if I knit?' Rose pulled out a pair of knitting needles and a ball of wool from the large shopping bag at her feet. 'How are the police getting on in their hunt for the bombers?'

'They seem hopeful. They've got lots of leads and the Prime Minister was positive about bringing the murderers to justice.'

'Everyone will try very hard,' Rose reassured Maddy.

'Our National Security Agency are tracking the bombers' phone calls to each other.'

'Can they do that?'

'Apparently. I don't understand these things.' Maddy felt drained and empty again. She had been talking furiously in an effort to keep the real world at arm's length. Now it closed around her again, enveloping her with sadness that touched on despair.

'Are you all right?'

Maddy clenched her fists. 'I couldn't stand it if those scum were to get away with it, laughing all over their faces. I mean, what sort of goddam people are they? How can they *live* with themselves?'

Rose Allen looked into Maddy's staring, over-bright eyes and decided it was time to leave. She stood up but Maddy seemed not to notice.

'I'm ashamed of the Irish blood inside me,' confessed Maddy. 'Ashamed.'

'There are good Irish as well as the bad,' said Rose. 'You mustn't tar them all with the same brush.'

'I suppose so.' With an effort, Maddy regained control of herself. 'Have you ever been to Ireland?'

'Not for many a year now.'

There was a tap on the door and Rob appeared. 'Sorry, I didn't know you had company.'

Maddy introduced him to Rose Allen.

'You'll excuse me,' said Rose. 'I really must get on.'

'Please call in again.'

'I'll be saying prayers for Mitch's recovery.'

'What a nice woman,' remarked Maddy once Rose had left.

'How did you find her?'

'She found me. She wandered in half an hour ago and we've been chatting ever since.'

'How is Mitch?'

'The doctors are talking about a brain scan or something.'

'How are *you* feeling?'

'Hanging on in here. Thanks for staying so long yesterday.'

The door flew open and a steel-grey-haired man in a white Burberry raincoat and with a mahogany suntan burst into the ward.

'Alvin!'

'Maddy, honey.' The two embraced. 'And there's my Mitch. Hell! She sure does look pale. Maddy, are you getting the best treatment here? I mean, it's a long way from London. Maybe she'd be better off in a private clinic in Harley Street. Cost doesn't come into it.'

'We-ll.' Maddy glanced towards Rob.

'They couldn't handle a case like Mitch's,' he said. 'Private hospitals are fine for varicose veins but they pass the buck to the National Health Service in an emergency.'

The man glowered at Rob. 'You're a doctor, huh?'

'I know how health care works in Britain,' replied Rob evenly.

'Alvin, this is Rob Sage. He lost his girlfriend and a little boy in the bombing. Rob, this is Tom's father, Alvin Lipzinger.'

The two shook hands briefly before Alvin again bent to inspect the unconscious little girl.

'I must go,' said Rob.

'You've only just arrived.' Maddy pleaded with her eyes for him to stay.

'Everyone back home wants you to know that you're in their thoughts, Maddy,' announced Alvin. 'On Christmas morning Father McVay said special prayers for you and Mitch, and for Tom and TJ.'

'The whole world seems to be praying for me,' murmured Maddy.

'This is a time for prayer – a time to examine one's soul.'

Rob remembered Maddy had said that Alvin was a former congressman. Maybe that explained his way of speaking in vacuous soundbites.

'I reckon we should get Mitch back to the States as soon as possible,' said Alvin abruptly, coming to a decision. 'At least I'll know she'll be well looked after there.'

'She's being well looked after *here*,' said Maddy in a small voice.

'We'll see. I'll get the embassy doctor down to examine her.' Alvin swung around to face Maddy. 'And how are *you* holding up?'

'Fine.'

'We don't want you going off the rails again, do we?'

'I said I'm fine.'

'Good.' Alvin switched his attention to Rob. 'This is a terrible thing to have happened. After 9/1l, nowhere is safe.'

'The IRA's been planting bombs in Britain for decades,' pointed out Rob.

'Yeh, but you've never had anything like the Twin Towers. Come on, three thousand died there.' Alvin clearly did not like being contradicted.

'Seven thousand Muslim Croats were massacred in Srebrenica by Serbs in July 1995,' said Rob. 'At least one million – *one million* – Tutsis and Hutus died in genocide in Rwanda. Most Americans haven't even heard of Rwanda, and certainly couldn't point to it on a map.'

'What are you saying, young man?'

'That Americans notice only that which affects them.'

'Yeh, well, this bomb of yours affects me because I've lost my son and grandson. Is that all right for you?'

'I don't want *anyone* to die. One death is one too many.'

'Rob disarmed the car bomb,' said Maddy, her stare flicking from one man to the other. 'Hundreds would have been killed if that had gone off.'

Alvin gave a curt nod and turned back to address Maddy. 'I spoke with our deputy ambassador here. The Brits reckon it's down to some dissident Irish republicans. I find that hard to believe.'

'A new organization calling itself the Sovereign IRA has claimed responsibility,' said Rob.

Alvin continued to address Maddy. 'The Brits blame everything on the IRA. When I met with Gerry Adams in Washington, he talked a lot of sense. I'd say he was a man of peace.'

'He may be now,' retorted Rob. 'But there's plenty of others queuing up to take his former place as a man of violence.'

Alvin look at Rob. 'I was one of those who lobbied the White House to allow Adams into the country. Hell, he owes me.' He thought for a moment. 'Do you reckon the IRA will know who's behind the bomb that killed my son?'

'The world of Irish republicanism is a small one.'

'Then why don't they come forward and help the police?'

'Because they regard informing on their own kind as a worse crime than murder.'

'That's crazy. I'll ask Adams and the others for help.'

'They won't talk to you,' said Rob quietly.

Alvin bristled. 'They owe me,' he repeated. 'You'll see.'

'Good afternoon.' Dr Amrit took in the sight of the two men and pretended to scowl. 'Normally only two visitors at a time are allowed in ICU but Maddy is classed as a resident.'

'Thank you.' Maddy gave a weak smile.

Dr Amrit scanned the monitors, comparing their readings against those on the chart that he'd picked up from the foot of Mitch's bed. 'Brain-stem activity is still strong. That's good.'

'Is there any chance of flying her home?' demanded Alvin abruptly as Maddy introduced her father-in-law.

'None at all,' replied the doctor.

'How about a second opinion on that?'

'My dear fellow, you can have as many opinions as you want,' replied Dr Amrit equably. 'How many would you like?'

Alvin Lipzinger frowned, not sure if he was being laughed at. He decided to change the subject.

'When can we take Tom and TJ home?'

'The coroner has to formally open and adjourn the inquest before the bodies can be released,' explained Dr Amrit. 'Hopefully in the next week or so.'

'I'll speak to the embassy. See if we can apply some leverage here to speed things up.' Alvin Lipzinger tightened the belt around his raincoat. 'And now I'd like to see my son's body.'

'Of course. If you'll come with me.'

Once they had left, Maddy let out a long breath of air. Her whole body seemed to sag.

'I feel as if I've been run over by an express train.'

'Sure you're not going to go off the rails?' asked Rob, repeating Alvin's words.

'Not yet. I'll let you know when I do.' Maddy gave a bitter laugh. 'Actually, you'll notice it for yourself.'

He's behind you. Oh no, he's not. Oh yes, he is. Oh no, he's not. Oh yes, he is.

They had not expected him to show up tonight. The director and the cast had thought he would still be at home, grieving. His understudy as Doctor Coldfinger had been taking his part since the explosion. Denny was sorry to disappoint the lad tonight but his chance would come again.

The hospital doctors had been unable to save Clive but now Denny was turning to Dr Theatre to aid his own recovery. Dr Theatre could heal sore throats, colds, stomach upsets. *Let's see if he can cure a broken heart.* God, he felt wretched – but Dr Theatre did not allow you to show it.

Where is he? Behind you.

A little boy was trying to climb on his seat to point more clearly; his embarrassed mother struggling to pull him back down.

Denny made a big play of archly tiptoeing to his right, his evil shadow one pace behind. This was a difficult moment needing concentration and split-second timing.

Denny put up one hand to shield his eyes and the other hand, the one away from the auditorium, behind his back in the classic silent movie pose. He pretended to scan the faces of the audience.

'I can't see him. Where is he?'

'Behind you,' came the shrill chorus.

'Are you sure?'

'Yes.'

The director had a penchant for the quirky. This was difficult, but the looking-glass sketch – stolen straight from the Marx Brothers –

where Denny and his evil shadow had to perform an increasingly bizarre series of synchronized movements across the face of a gigantic mirror frame took even more exquisite timing. The scene ended when Denny produced an enormous cigar and his image struck a match to light it for him.

'You're having me on, aren't you?'

His shadow should now be leaping up and down behind him, pulling faces and sticking out his tongue.

'What's he doing?'

The children in the audience, and some of their parents, competed to show exactly what sort of faces his shadow was pulling.

Denny knew that he had been right to come. What else would he have been doing this Boxing Night? Sitting at home, feeling sorry for himself; ignoring the ringing phone, trying to avoid the well-meant platitudes of friends. He was not short of people offering their shoulders to cry on – but the one person he really wanted was dead.

The girl who had asked for his autograph was dead, too. And those kids in the orange anoraks. No, he'd heard on the news that the girl was still fighting for her life in intensive care – where Clive had been. Perhaps he should get in touch with her mother. That was the sort of thing Clive would have done, but then Clive had always been the sociable one. Clive was the party animal, and Denny had gone along.

Two years, two fulfilling, faithful years.

He had always said that Clive had brought him luck. That had remained true until the very end.

Denny fingered the silver four-leaf clover tucked inside his costume. Clive's good-luck charm had saved his life. Clive used to carry it on his keyring which he'd left on the coffee shop table when he'd hurried off for the chocolates.

If Denny had not brushed the keyring onto the floor as he waved to greet Clive's return; if he had not been reaching down to pick it up at the instant the bomb had gone off, shattering the glass window where he sat . . .

The woman at the next table had lost her voice box. She had needed eighty stitches in her face. Not a good thing to happen to an actor.

Denny had escaped with a cut to his forehead where he'd struck the underneath of the table as he'd straightened up.

But Clive, who had come to meet him for coffee in the middle of his Chistmas shopping expedition, was dead.

For a second, the delighted screams of the children in the audience threatened to become the screams of the dying and the injured. Denny couldn't, wouldn't, allow himself to see again the scene of devastation – not now. He concentrated on two little girls in the front row, holding hands, sitting right on the very edges of their seats, mouths open in wonder. He winked at them and their eyes popped.

And now for the song-and-dance finale. Energy levels high, wide smile in place; that frisson that came with forcing the rest of the cast to keep up; kick higher, swirl faster, faster.

And when he came to take his bow, as one, the whole cast burst into applause. Those nearest hugged him. When he looked out, the audience were on their feet, cheering. A standing ovation. In the wings, the stagehands were clapping above their heads. That was a new one; he'd never seen them do that before.

Denny struggled to hold back the tears.

'Last orders.'

'What do you mean, last orders? I'm just getting meself a thirst.'

Seamus, the club steward, wagged his finger at the leprechaun of a man who sat at the end of the bar with a pint of Murphy's and a glass of Paddy's whiskey in front of him.

Mikey Drumm had been the first through the door when the Irish Club had opened at noon. Eleven hours later he was still there – sitting on the same stool. He hadn't moved – apart from going to the bog at regular intervals. And Seamus was sure that Mikey had not eaten – not so much as a packet of pork scratchings.

Mikey used the club as his local whenever he stayed with his spinster sister in Camden. He was known to like a drop of the hard stuff, but Seamus had never seen him knock it back like this.

'Last orders. Thank you very much.'

Mikey's sister Deirdre said goodnight to her table of friends and weaved her way towards the bar.

'Time for home, Michael.'

'Wisht, woman. Can't a man enjoy a few drinks without being nagged?'

'You'll sober up and come with me if you want a bed for the night.'

A young man in a leather bomber jacket hurried up to the bar. He ordered drinks, then nodded familiarly to Mikey.

'Hey, Mikey, will you tell us what it was like, then?' The lad winked at Seamus who scowled back.

'What was what like?' asked Mikey.

'You know. When the bomb went off.'

'Holy Mary,' breathed Deirdre.

'I don't want to talk about it,' began Mikey. He grasped the whiskey and brought it to his lips with exaggerated care.

'I was told it was terrible,' coaxed the boy.

'That it was. If you'd seen those limbs lying in the gutter, torn-off chunks of bloody flesh like you see in the meat market. And the eyeballs . . . And the blood . . . You've never seen so much blood . . .'

'Were there screams?' The boy seemed to be enjoying himself.

'Screams! You should have heard them. They would rend a heart of stone, so they would, and the groaning and the moaning. I can hear them now.' Mikey Drumm sucked through his teeth. 'I'll just have a small Paddy's to keep you company.'

'That you will not.' Deirdre grasped her brother by his arms and glared into his rheumy blue eyes. 'For the love of Mary, you can stop talking like this or you'll pack your bags and be gone back to the Republic, so you can.'

'He's telling the same tale to anyone who'll buy him a drink,' warned Seamus, coming round to their side of the bar to indicate that he had stopped serving.

'But I saw it, I tell you.'

'You did not see anything,' hissed his sister.

'I'm just worried someone might take him seriously,' said Seamus.

In fact, two men in the club were taking a close interest in Mikey Drumm. One was giving him the hard eye while, three tables away, the other affected not to notice the drunken ramblings while striving to remember every word. Both had spoken separately to Drumm earlier and both were working out what to do with the information.

Deirdre, white-haired and as skinny as her brother, shook her fist in Mikey's face. 'You saw nothing. It's all in your imagination.'

'I did see it, I tell you. In Sal-is-bury.'

'Come with me now, or you'll find the door locked and your bag on the step.'

'I've never left a drink in me life . . .' Mikey Drumm saw the look in his sister's eye and quickly swallowed his whiskey. He swayed to his feet and took the first uncertain steps towards the exit.

As he did so the band struck up the Irish National Anthem, *Anhrán na bhFiann*, 'The Soldier's Song'. Everyone rose to their feet.

Soldiers are we whose lives are pledged to Ireland . . .

Mikey Drumm stood rock-steady, shoulders back, head high.

. . . Tonight we man the gap of danger.
In Erin's cause, come woe or weal,
'Mid cannons' roar and rifles' peal,
We'll chant a soldier's song.

Tears streamed down Mikey Drumm's stubbled cheeks.

7

Kilfoyle had provided the names of the suspects who had featured in the Scotland Yard conference. Now he had to put a little flesh on the bones.

He concocted a story that an agent needed to see him urgently about the bombing. His girlfriend Fliss was furious. This was his second trip to Ireland in three days while he was supposed to be on leave. What was the point of her taking time off and then him working? It wasn't good enough. Kilfoyle was just grateful that Fliss didn't have a clue why he was really going back to Belfast. If she had, she'd have dumped him like a sack of bricks. Fliss was not the sort of person who would jeopardize her career by associating with someone who risked bringing the Service into disrepute – especially as daddy had recently retired as a deputy director-general of the Service.

The knowledge that he stood to lose his girlfriend as well as his career depressed Kilfoyle throughout the long evening in Belfast as he built his alibi. He was taking a gamble. But, as he told himself, when you're tap-dancing on water – there was no other way.

Thanks to Jimmy Burke, Kilfoyle knew more than he wanted to about the bombing – but if he passed on that information it would inevitably lead back to Burke.

Yet if he came up with nothing, then other intelligence agencies would try to fill the information gap to rub Five's nose in it, his superiors would hold his failure against Kilfoyle when considering him for promotion and he would lose any control he had over the investigation. If the inquiry was heading anywhere near Jimmy Burke, he needed to know.

There was only one thing to do – play all ends against the middle.

Kilfoyle phoned Hayward at home just after six the next morning as he was about to board the first flight back to London. Stressing that his information was delicate, he arranged to meet Hayward in the coffee shop of the Intercontinental Hotel on Hyde Park corner.

The detective was picking at a Danish pastry when Kilfoyle arrived.

'Don't tell me. You've cast your bread on the water and a bakery's come in on the tide,' said Hayward.

'Not quite.' Kilfoyle allowed himself a hint of a triumphant smirk. 'A few stale crusts, maybe, but I don't want to put it on the intelligence net, not at this stage.'

Hayward lifted an interrogative eyebrow. 'We've failed to stand up any of your earlier steers so far.'

'Then maybe I can help.' Kilfoyle smiled. 'I have a source. Call the source Silvermouth. Well placed and suitably greedy but untested, if you get my drift.'

Hayward was not sure if he did, but he nodded anyway.

'Recently, I've wondered about Silvermouth's veracity. There wasn't anything inherently wrong with some of his offerings, simply that they couldn't be corroborated.' Kilfoyle waited until a waitress poured him coffee. 'But now he's come up with the same names that featured at yesterday's conference. The first whisper was right. Nolan was the coordinator.'

'That was predictable.'

'But . . . the come-on bomb was planted by Teresa Bridges. Dessie Fitzgerald drove the block car.'

'A woman planted the bomb!' Hayward leaned forward, eyes shining. 'That'll change how we look at the CCTV coverage.'

'Apparently she wore some kind of disguise.'

'And her sister, Breda Bridges?'

'Nothing so far. But the boys in West Belfast have already been on the phone to her to voice their displeasure.'

'Have they indeed!'

'One further thing. Conn Nolan and Dessie have been bought drinks in Nolan's bar to celebrate their safe return. Their part in the bombing appears to be common knowledge among the hardliners in Dundalk.'

'Any leads to other members of the bomb gang?'

'Not yet, but this is not a bad start, eh?'

As he sat in the taxi on the way to Thames House, Kilfoyle knew that he'd have to continue feeding small morsels of information into the investigation if he was to survive. Still, today he had reason to be pleased with himself. He had validated Hayward's knowledge while adding only a little collateral, he had placed his source firmly among the drinkers in Conn's bar – and he had said nothing that would lead to Jimmy fucking Burke.

'A woman! A woman planted that bomb! How could she? How could any woman of flesh and blood hurt a child?' Maddy Lipzinger gaped in disbelief.

'It's only a rumour,' said Tanner. 'We have no proof.'

'But a *woman*!' Maddy began to tremble with anger. God! If she could get hold of her, Maddy would break every bone in her body.

'Did you notice a woman behaving strangely in the mall?' inquired Tanner.

'No. I didn't. I only noticed the bomb car because it was having problems parking.'

'Try to picture it in your mind,' coaxed Tanner. 'You started to walk into the mall . . .'

'I saw the kids in the distance, then I remembered that I had to post the cards. Tom appeared holding a package.' *Tom had looked guilty. It had been the last time she had seen her husband alive – and he had looked guilty. Sort of summed up the last few years, really.* 'I wonder what happened to the package?'

'It should be at the police station with other items recovered from the scene,' said Tanner. 'It'll be returned to you soon. Tom appeared . . .'

'Right. I went back to post the cards. I'd just recrossed the road when I saw Rob trying to smash his way into a car. Actually, the first person I saw acting oddly *was* Rob.'

'What was the last you saw of the men in the Father Christmas beards?'

'Heading off up the street. Don't *you* know where they went?'

'A number of witnesses saw the men in their boiler suits but no one saw them take them off,' admitted Tanner. It was a source of some bewilderment that in a city centre blanketed with CCTV cameras the two men had just simply been able to vanish. 'They must have changed immediately after they left the scene.'

'If they had a van nearby, they could have changed in that,' suggested Maddy.

'We've thought of that. We're in the process of eliminating a number of vans from our inquiries.'

'What about a public lavatory?'

'There isn't one.'

'A private dwelling? Maybe a maisonette above one of the shops?'

'You two should be detectives. Sorry, but we've thought of that, too.'

'Only trying to help.'

'I gather your father-in-law is going to offer a large reward for information leading to the arrest and conviction of the bombers,' said Tanner.

'Is he?' shrieked Maddy.

'Didn't he tell you?' Tanner failed to hide his surprise.

'I haven't seen that much of Alvin. He only arrived yesterday and this afternoon he's flying to Belfast to try to talk to IRA leaders. How much is he offering?'

'One hundred thousand dollars,' replied Tanner as a nurse hurried in to tell him he was wanted on the phone.

'That should get them coming out of the woodwork,' exclaimed Rob.

'He likes to make waves,' said Maddy shortly.

Tanner returned to report that there might have been a breakthrough in the search for a witness and that he had to leave.

Maddy gravitated back to Mitch's bedside. Rob followed.

'What are you going to do today?' she asked, glancing up at the clock which announced it was just 11.30 a.m.

'Don't know,' he confessed. 'I seem to be in limbo land. Time's standing still.'

'Tell me about it,' said Maddy. 'I don't even know what day it is.'

'I *think* it's Friday.' Rob was not sure himself.

'Friday. God, we left New York a week ago today,' exclaimed Maddy.

'We were in Addis Ababa,' said Rob.

They both fell silent.

'I can't believe a woman did this,' repeated Maddy. She looked up to stare hard into Rob's eyes. 'I'll tell you what. I want that woman to suffer before she dies.'

'But she won't die,' Rob reminded her. 'This isn't the United States with its electric chairs and lethal injections. She could be out of prison in ten years.'

'But I'll still be weeping then,' cried Maddy.

'Do you know how many prepaid phones we sold in the run-up to Christmas?' demanded the young man with the shaven head. The badge on his company shirt proclaimed him as Mark the Manager. 'Get real.'

The manager turned to walk away. It had taken Graham Pottidge twenty minutes to get to see Mark who had allegedly been stocktaking in the back of the giant store. With difficulty, the detective controlled the anger surging inside him.

'Your company's very PR-conscious, aren't they?'

'Suppose so.'

'So when they read the national press that one of their pissy-arsed managers refused to cooperate in the hunt for the Salisbury bombers, they're not going to be too happy. Think you'll have a job this time tomorrow?'

'Nah, nah. Don't get me wrong. It's just that we were incredibly busy before Christmas.'

'Ask your staff. Hopefully they'll remember someone, before you start going through your records.'

'You what? Do you know what you're asking?' Mark accepted defeat. 'Hey, Lee. You don't remember selling anyone a bulk order of prepaid mobiles before Christmas, do you?'

'Not a bulk order,' corrected Pottidge. 'Maybe between three and six phones, certainly for cash.' He detected a flicker of interest in Lee's eyes. 'We believe the Salisbury bombers used those phones.'

'But you can't trace anyone from prepaid mobiles,' objected Lee.

'That's our problem.'

'I sold six Nokia 3410s to a guy who paid cash,' admitted Lee. 'Almost £500 in notes, it was.'

'And which day was this?'

'Don't know. But we'll have records – and the numbers of the phones.'

At the same time as Graham Pottidge was writing down the numbers of the mobile telephones, Tanner was walking around a green Citroen Xsara car parked outside a terrace of narrow houses near the centre of Wilton.

The front door opened while his hand was still on the brass knocker to reveal a sparrow of a woman, her white hair tied in a severe bun.

'Mrs Bella Fryer?' Tanner handed her his warrant card. 'I'm Detective Superintendent Tanner.'

'How do you do. This is my husband Frank.' A tall, stooped man, wearing glasses and dressed in a grey pullover, woollen tie and sports jacket, appeared from the gloom of the hall to give Tanner a watery smile. 'Do come in.'

The heat hit Tanner like a furnace as soon as he stepped inside the doorway. He was shown into a small, tidy front room as Frank shuffled off to make tea. Despite the heat, there was a coal fire in the grate. Christmas cards hung on ribbons over the mantelpiece and bottles of gin and sherry sat on the sideboard.

Two books lay face down on either side of the fire, a pair of reading glasses resting on one of them. Tanner guessed that this room was kept for high days and holidays – and for visitors. For the rest of the year, Frank and Bella would live out their lives in the back kitchen.

'You saw *Crimewatch* last night?' began Tanner.

'No. We don't have a TV set. Our son saw it and phoned us this morning,' Bella corrected him. 'He said we should call you.'

'We don't take newspapers, either,' added Frank, coming in with a tea tray. 'They're always full of such terrible things.'

'I heard people in the baker's shop talking about a bomb but I didn't know six had died,' admitted Bella. 'Poor things. So close to Christmas, too.'

Bella must be in her early seventies, thought Tanner. Alert, vital, wearing better than her husband. The couple's lack of curiosity about the outside world was odd but . . .

'Perhaps you can help us now,' said Tanner. 'We believe the terrorists tried to keep a parking space for the car containing the bomb, and you tried to park in that space.'

'That'd explain that woman coming and going,' said Frank. 'No sooner had she got in the car than she climbed out again – and then the driver got out, too. I was all for waiting but Bella's impatient. She made me drive on.'

'Can you describe the car? Was it a saloon car like yours or an estate car?'

'Like ours.'

'Colour?'

'Blue,' said Bella.

'Grey,' said Frank a microsecond later. He corrected himself. 'Blueish-grey.'

'It wasn't at all.' Bella swung towards her husband. 'It was a deep blue. Almost royal blue.'

Frank did not argue. Tanner suspected that he was used to being corrected.

'Can you remember anything about the number plate?' It was a long shot, Tanner knew, but he had to ask. 'No, all right. A detective will go through photographs of lots of different types of car with you, so hopefully you'll recognize the model.'

Inspection of CCTV tapes had suggested that the block car had been a blue Toyota saloon. Frank and Bella had validated the colour. Maybe, with a little work, they'd stand up the make.

'Now, what about the woman? You saw her come back to the car and then leave again. How old was she?'

'Early thirties,' said Bella decisively. 'She was about five foot five, five foot six. And she had a green coat and glasses.'

'Could you recognize her from a photo?'

Tanner handed over six colour photographs. One was of Teresa Bridges, taken without her knowledge at a republican rally that summer. The others, all of women in their thirties and similarly taken outdoors, had been carefully chosen from police files. After the Law Lords ruling on North Wales Police versus Brown, laying down strict rules on identity, Tanner was taking no chances.

Frank exchanged the pair of glasses resting on the book for the ones he was wearing. 'I don't know,' he said hesitantly.

Bella spent time inspecting the photos, turning them over in her hands before pointing at the one of Teresa. 'That's her. That's the woman.'

'But there was something different about her,' objected Frank. 'I thought she had a hat on?'

'I don't care. That's her.'

'You're sure?'

'Yes.'

'What about the man?'

'I can't remember him at all,' admitted Frank.

'He was stocky and he had a woollen hat and a coat with the collar turned up,' declared Bella.

Tanner handed over a second batch of six photographs. The one of Dessie Fitzgerald had been taken at the same rally.

Bella took her time, holding the pictures in a fan and again turning them over in her hands. She glanced back at Teresa's picture before picking out Dessie.

'You're sure?'

'No doubt.'

Tanner said a silent prayer. At last someone who could identify the bombing couple. He liked Bella Fryer as a witness. She'd stand up well under cross-examination and the jury would take to her.

His phone rang. It was Pottidge to tell him of his success with the mobile phones.

Between them, they had made a good beginning to cracking the investigation. There was a long way to go, but it was a start.

The knock on the door came at midday.

Conn had driven off to his bar only minutes earlier. Breda wondered if they had been watching the house, waiting until he left. She recognized them at once. Milo O'Connell and Nutter Hains. The velvet glove and the iron fist. Hains had got his nickname as the former head of the IRA's internal security unit, killing alleged traitors with a single round to the back of the head. He was just a thug – and Breda had her own thugs to match him.

No, it was the sight of O'Connell that unsettled Breda. Sixty years old if he was a day; a republican born and bred. While he had moved away from troubled Belfast to live in Dublin, placing himself above the strife, O'Connell remained the quiet, ruthless voice of experience who expected to be heeded and obeyed. Breda made herself stay calm.

No one moved.

'Yes?' she said, cracking first.

Hains made to step into the house but Breda folded her arms, barring him. His hard eyes darkened with anger.

'Will you not be inviting us in, Breda?' asked O'Connell softly.

'Why should I?'

'Because we have much to talk about and it wouldn't be seemly to conduct a long conversation on the doorstep, now, would it?'

Hains was sliding his hand inside his jacket. Breda wondered if he was stupid enough to be carrying a gun.

'Come in, then. Go into the front room.' She indicated the room on the right. 'I'll be right with you.'

She hurried into the kitchen where Teresa was smoking a cigarette over a cup of coffee.

'Who was that at the door?'

'It's them,' muttered Breda.

'Christ, what are you going to do?'

Breda thought quickly. 'Bobby's in the garden. Take him down to the bar, tell Conn what's happening and get him to bring back a few of the lads.'

'I'm not leaving you.'

'Just go.' The last thing Breda wanted was Teresa to lose her temper. She and Nutter Hains would end up killing each other. She pushed her sister towards the kitchen door. 'And make sure you take Bobby. I want him away from here.'

Breda watched as her sister slipped out. Then she picked up her cigarettes and walked into the living room with its mock Christmas tree and coloured lights around the window. Hains was just putting down the phone.

'Feel free,' she mocked, knowing that he had been listening to see if she made a call.

'Who were you talking to?' Hains demanded.

'Whoever I chose to in my own house,' replied Breda.

'Ah, Breda, Breda.' O'Connell's soft voice drifted over the jagged silence that filled the room. 'I would have thought more of you. What were you thinking of in Salisbury? If the big one had gone up . . .' He shook his head. 'The days of the bombs are over.'

'So *you* say.'

'Yes, so *we* say – and you'd be well advised to listen.'

'And if I don't, what then? A bullet in the back of the head like you did to Joe O'Connor in West Belfast?'

'O'Connor was a hard man who was a menace to all around him.'

'You were happy to use him when he did what he was told, but as soon as he went his own way you killed him.'

O'Connell ignored her sally. 'You hoped your bomb would shatter the peace. It won't. You are living in the past; the long past when Ireland preferred the drama of war to the routine of peace.'

'Your peace is not a routine. Your peace is a surrender. My father and brother fought and died for the freedom of our country. To suggest that they would have accepted less shows that you did not know them.'

'On the contrary, I knew both your father and your brother well,' said O'Connell in little more than a whisper.

'Really! Yet you betray their memory and the memory of all those who died for Ireland.'

'We are realists . . .'

'You are cowards. Remember the 1919 Declaration of Independence.' Breda began quoting: '"We declare foreign government in Ireland to be an invasion of our national right which we will *never* tolerate and we demand the evacuation of our country by the English Garrison."'

'The vast majority of republicans are with us,' insisted O'Connell.

'Shame. Didn't de Valera himself say that the majority has no right to be wrong. That's an irony, now.'

'Breda . . .'

'*Tiocfaidh Ar La*. Our day will come.

'It won't. You have no coherent political beliefs beyond the chant of "Brits Out". Face it, Breda, you are in a tiny minority.'

'We grow by the day – and that is what worries you. The lame, the dispirited, the tired – they'll stick with you, but the vigorous, the passionate and the young are with us.'

The door was flung open. Breda gasped. Aoife stood there. Breda had thought she was safely playing at a friend's house.

'Hello,' said Hains, making as if to move towards the child.

'Don't you dare go near her.' Breda flew across the room to throw her arms around her daughter.

'Mam!'

'We're busy in here, sweetheart. Why don't you go and make yourself a glass of squash?'

'Can I have a mince pie?'

'If you want.' Breda fixed Hains with a hard eye, demanding that he meet her gaze and not look at her daughter as she left.

But the interruption had changed the mood in the room. O'Connell was no longer content to exchange political slogans.

'I've a message for you and Conn.' O'Connell spoke louder now. 'No more bombs. That was the last. Is that understood?'

'Would you like to tell Conn that?'

'He's fortunate to be alive after the trick he pulled,' growled Hains.

O'Connell held up a hand to signal Hains to be quiet. 'Indeed, we do not take kindly to one of our own running off with the very munitions he was supposed to be guarding. Prudent counsels have so far held the day. Things can change.'

Breda said nothing.

'We'd prefer to see you and Conn back in the fold,' continued O'Connell. 'We are not opposed to his . . . outside interests. The drugs supply locally is his to control as he sees fit . . .'

O'Connell was holding out an olive branch of peace, Breda recognized. The stick, and now the carrot. 'Why don't you talk to Conn direct?' she said.

'We will. But the message is for both of you. No more unauthorized direct action or the pair of you will face the consequences.'

But Breda was thinking. O'Connell had not demanded that she should disband The True Guardians. And she knew why. Her hardliners were useful bogeymen with which PIRA could threaten the Brits. *We can't make too many concessions*, their leaders would argue, *or we'll drive our supporters into the arms of the dissidents*.

Something snapped inside her. 'Get out,' she yelled. 'You make me sick. What can you do to me and mine? Nothing at all. Your threats are as empty as your peace process. Get out of here, now.'

Breda marched to the front door and flung it open, sending the holly wreath flying to the ground. Two cars were pulling up outside. Conn leaped out of the first and strode up the path in his belligerent rolling swagger, Dessie close behind him. Four other men got out of the second car and stood looking up at the door.

'Are you all right, Breda?' Conn spoke to his wife but he was looking hard at Hains.

'Ay. These men are just leaving – or did you want to tell Conn himself your message?' Breda directed the question at O'Connell.

'You can pass it on,' said O'Connell evenly.

'Fuck off, the pair of you,' growled Conn.

He and Hains glared at each other.

'Remember, a nation cannot be free in which even a small section of its people have not freedom,' quoted Breda, jutting out her jaw.

'Then nothing remains to be said,' replied O'Connell. 'A volley is the only speech proper to make over the grave of a dead Fenian.'

Breda put her hand to her throat, but then she rallied. 'Typical of your lot to misquote that traitor Michael Collins.'

Tanner had received the new MI5 intelligence less than an hour ago. According to the tip-off, Conn Nolan had coordinated the bombing from a red Ford Sierra which he had then driven on to Southampton

Airport. While Nolan had flown to Dublin via Paris, an unknown helper had taken the car to this breaker's yard, hidden away deep in the Hampshire countryside.

Tanner wondered about this latest piece of intelligence to come out of Ireland as he followed his guide through the maze of back lanes. He thought it strange that while it named the breaker's yard there was no mention of who had brought the car there. Any informer who could come up with this sort of information must know more, he reckoned – but maybe they did things differently over the water. Tanner had to concede that *his* grasses seldom had to fear for their kneecaps – or their lives.

The breaker's yard was full of rusting automobile carcasses stacked in rows three or four high, divided by oil-blackened tracks and surrounded by a high wall of corrugated iron sheeting. In a clearing near the gate a beefy man wearing a blue fisherman's sweater full of holes sat outside a Portakabin office and watched Tanner's arrival with surly indifference.

'The owner, Billy Tugman,' muttered Detective Sergeant Waverley of the local police.

'You ought to have a search warrant,' called out Tugman as Tanner climbed out of the car.

'I've explained to Mr Tugman that we can apply to a magistrate for a warrant but that officers will remain here while we do,' said Waverley.

'You're wasting your time,' grunted Tugman. 'And mine, too.'

'Mr Tugman, you understand that we're looking for a red Sierra saloon which was brought here on December the twenty-third,' began Tanner in a reasonable tone.

'Don't know what you're talking about,' muttered Tugman sulkily.

'You must keep records of what comes in here,' said Tanner.

'Not really. Who'd want to know?'

'DVLA Swansea?'

'Nah. The wrecks have already been written off by the time they get here.'

'Do you remember a red Sierra being brought in?' repeated Tanner.

'I don't see everything. There's a couple of blokes who help me out. Why don't you talk to them?'

'Because they're both away on holiday and it's your yard,' said Waverley evenly.

Tanner decided it was time for another approach. 'In hock to an Irish mate, are you?'

'You what! I'm in hock to no one.'

'In that case, why did you agree to do a favour which'll see you banged up for seven years?'

Tugman blinked in shock. For a second, Tanner thought he had him. Then a supercilious leer spread over Tugman's face. 'You find a red Sierra in this yard and you're welcome to it.'

'Sir, sir.' A uniformed officer was waving from deep in the scrap yard.

Tanner glanced at Tugman. The man was puzzled – *but he was definitely not worried*. Whatever they had found did not alarm him. He ambled along behind the two policemen as they went to investigate.

There *was* a red Sierra in the breaker's yard but it was a flattened wreck at the bottom of a pile of cars. From the state of the ground with its nettles and dock, it was clear that no one had been near it for some time.

Tanner set off to explore by himself, followed at a distance by Tugman. He came to a clearing where the jib of a large crane towered over a high-sided machine with powerful hydraulic ramps. By the deep impressions in the blackened earth, small heavy objects had been stored here recently. He could see Tugman watching him as he hand-rolled a cigarette. Tanner looked up at the jib of a giant magnet on caterpillar tracks. A cube of crushed metal hung suspended in the air from the magnet. Looking closely, Tanner could make out streaks of red paint.

*

'For the record, this is a telephone conference between myself, David Hayward SO13 at Scotland Yard, Cyril Tanner, Wiltshire police in Salisbury and Pat Rodgers, Garda Special Branch in Dublin to report on progress in the inquiry into the Salisbury bombing. It is now . . . 1805 on Friday, 27 December. Pat, would you like to begin?'

'The bad news first. We had to release O'Gara.'

'And the good news?'

Rodgers chuckled. 'We calculated that the only way O'Gara could have made it back from Salisbury that morning to Dublin by three o'clock was on a Ryanair flight from Bristol. It didn't take long to find Fergus O'Hanlon on the passenger list.'

'Who's Fergus O'Hanlon?'

'A retarded thirty-year-old who lives in a secure home in Cavan. He goes no further than to the seaside twice a year as a treat.'

'So O'Gara got himself a passport in O'Hanlon's name?'

'O'Hanlon's correct date of birth, address – except the photograph bears a striking resemblance to O'Gara. Or rather, O'Gara with long hair, glasses, fat face and a beard.'

'A breakthrough?'

'If you were to knock on O'Gara's door today you'd find a clean-shaven man with a number one haircut, thin face and no glasses. No jury would make him from that passport picture.'

'What about fellow passengers on O'Gara's flight?' asked Tanner.

'The person who sat next to him is somewhere in Thailand. The cabin crew don't remember him. We're going through CCTV coverage at Dublin Airport now.'

'What did he look like when he arrived in Dublin?' asked Tanner.

'The old biddy thought he was clean-shaven. But one of Dublin's largest cab firms is solidly republican. O'Gara could have shaved somewhere on the way home.'

'What about O'Hanlon's family? Or the passport referee?'

'The family say this is news to them. The parish priest who countersigned the application claims his signature has been forged. They are all known republican sympathizers.'

'Any intelligence on the ground?' asked Hayward.

'No. There's better stuff coming out of the north than we're getting down here,' admitted Rodgers. 'The big-league players kept it in the family, so to speak.'

'Anything further on where Nolan, Teresa Bridges and Dessie Fitzgerald claim to have been in the days before the twenty-third?' asked Hayward.

'Nolan's put it around that he was in Paris on a business trip. Bridges and Fitzgerald are telling people they went to the Gower Peninsula in South Wales for a short break.'

'We've got nowhere so far on the source of the fertilizer,' admitted Tanner, going on to bring the other two up to date with Bella Fryer, the crushed Sierra and the discovery of the mobile phone numbers.

'We'll pass the mobile phone numbers on to the NSA to see what they come up with,' said Hayward. 'At the same time, we'll ask the phone service providers to conduct a cell site analysis.'

'The last time we asked for a phone company's help they tried to charge us £43,000,' recalled Tanner sourly.

'I think they'll be more sensitive to public opinion this time,' said Hayward.

'Tell me one thing,' said Tanner. 'Would this intelligence coming out of Ireland be admissible in court?'

'That'll depend on whether you'll be allowed to use a supergrass and grant that supergrass indemnity from prosecution,' replied Rodgers.

'That's a decision for our political masters,' added Hayward.

'The Prime Minister did say that he would go to the ends of the Earth to catch these bombers,' reminded Tanner.

'A prosecution based on supergrass evidence comes unstuck more times than not,' warned Rodgers.

'Then you wouldn't vote for one?' asked Tanner.

'I didn't say that,' chuckled Rodgers. 'They do get the villains in the dock – which is why the IRA hate them so much.'

8

Rob Sage's mind was in a whirl, racing with images, snatches of songs and conversations all spinning round in a frightening blur. At the same time, his stomach was churning with the strange restlessness he'd experienced since he'd woken.

Rob forced himself to stop pacing around the cottage, closed his eyes and wondered if he was going mad.

Since the explosion, he had been surrounded by a cloud of numbing fog – pierced only by an occasional flash of anger. Perhaps it had been his mind's way of coping, of stopping himself feeling, but he was feeling now – and, Christ, it hurt. He found he hated Mekaela's and Alfred's killers with a passion which surprised him. Rob had been trained to think, not feel. His chosen subject – engineering – was symbolic of his pragmatic, practical approach to life. Even when he had hunted down the guerrillas who had crippled Alfred he had done so methodically and coldly, knowing that if he did not do so they would come back and kill him.

This was something new.

He had to get out of the cottage; he had to do something. Rob picked up a half-bottle of brandy from the sideboard and slipped it into a pocket of his Barbour before going out to the car.

He set off to drive to the foot of Cotley Hill and from there climb up the vast Iron Age earthwork overlooking the Wylye Valley. He'd been planning to take Alfred up there to fly the kite he'd bought him for Christmas. Alfred would have enjoyed the ride on Rob's shoulders while Mekaela would grumble about the ascent. It was funny how she'd walk for miles in Tigray but in England she objected to putting one foot in front of another.

What was he thinking? Mekaela was dead.

Alfred was dead, too.

Don't forget it.

But how could they be dead when he could hear Alfred's chatter, Mekaela's slow laugh; see their faces and feel their presence, their very breath, in the car with him?

Rob blinked to see a white van hurtling towards him on the wrong side of the road. It was trying to overtake a lorry – and it was not going to make it.

Rob made no effort to slow down.

The van was about to smash head first into him.

Rob blinked again.

Jesus! This was not a dream. This was for real.

Catapulted out of his trance, Rob braked sharply and wrenched over the wheel. The van sped past, missing the car by inches.

That had been close. He must stay more alert. Rob glanced around to find he was driving along a winding road bordered by high hedges. Ahead, the road descended into a dip with woods on either side.

Rob didn't recognize this stretch. He peered down at the clock.

Midday.

A wave of panic and confusion swept over him. He had left home at around 10.30 a.m. That meant he had been driving for an hour and a half. Where the hell was he? What had he been doing?

A road sign loomed up ahead. *Dorchester 3 miles.*

Rob pulled in at the first lay-by and turned off the engine, the enormity of his memory loss making him feel physically sick.

He forced himself to calm down. Slowly, the glimmerings of memory returned. He'd been going to drive to Cotley Hill. But somehow, somewhere, an autopilot had cut in. It had taken that lunatic in the white van to wake him up.

But there was another puzzle. He had left home an hour and a half ago – but Dorchester was only thirty miles or so away. What had he been doing? Had he really been driving all this time? The petrol gauge showed that he had a quarter of a tank left. He wished he knew how full it had been when he had set off.

Rob opened the glove compartment to search for a tube of mints – and discovered the brandy. Who in their right mind left home in the morning with a half-bottle of brandy? Perhaps he was cracking up. Rob decided he'd go for that walk after all.

He drove back at a steady speed, trying to absorb what had happened. No doubt a psychiatrist would have a field day analysing what had happened – Rob was just bloody scared.

And now he was sitting on the earth ramparts of Scratchbury hill fort. It was almost dusk. Away to the right were the lights of Warminster; directly ahead, the dun-coloured ridge of Mere Down and the distant mass of Cley Hill. Below in the valley, church steeples showed where villages hid among the patchwork of fields. The river was a cold silver snake in the last of the late-afternoon sun. There was something achingly forlorn about the solemn stillness.

The first stars were appearing in the indigo sky. Rob pulled out the brandy bottle and took a swig. As he did so, he heard a train. Peering down into the cutting beneath he saw the lights of the two coaches as it rattled down the line towards Salisbury.

'Look, Alfred, a real train,' Rob said aloud.

'It's a big train,' he heard the little boy answer.

'You haven't been on a train, have you?'

'I've been on a donkey.'

'I know you've been on a donkey, numpty-head.'

'I'm not a numpty-head. You are.'

'How fast can you run?'

'As fast as the wind.'

'How high can you jump?'

'To the moon.'

'Good boy.' Rob took another large gulp of brandy. The temperature was falling. He wanted to be cold. He closed his eyes.

'What are you grinning at, Mekaela?'

'You. You love that boy more than you love me.'

'He saved my life.'

'I save your life every time I stop you going off with those bad village girls.'

'I don't have any energy left to go after anyone once you've finished rogering me.'

Rob laughed aloud at the turn the imaginary conversation had taken. Then he remembered what lay behind it – and laughed again.

One day, he had made the mistake of trying to tell Mekaela about the urban legend that peopled the *Captain Pugwash* TV cartoon with characters like Master Bates, Seaman Staines and Roger the Cabin Boy. The puns – and the concept of an urban legend – had been beyond Mekaela. Rob took another large drink as the memory flooded back. The more he had tried to explain, the deeper the hole he had dug for himself.

'The captain of a merchant ship is called the Master. And this captain's name is Bates but that sounds like masturbates . . .'

Mekaela had stared at him, a picture of utter incomprehension. 'They do that on your television?'

'No. No. Masturbates is a pun. Like Seaman Staines.' Rob found he was laughing.

'I know. He is a seaman called Staines.'

'No. Not seaman. Semen. S – e – m – e – n. Look it up in the dictionary I gave you.'

Mekaela had read aloud. 'Generative fluid of male animals, containing spermatozoa in suspension.'

Rob had hooted before trying to find an easier definition of semen. Mekaela had followed closely until she'd finally shaken her head in disagreement.

'But it doesn't.'

'Doesn't what?'

'Stain. It washes out.'

More brandy.

Then he'd tried to explain Roger the cabin boy. 'Roger is both a boy's name and a more polite way of saying fuck.'

'So they could not say Fuck the Cabin Boy on television.'

'Well, they could,' he'd said, gasping for air. 'But fuck's not a name.'

Mekaela was getting tired of being laughed at.

'Why are you mocking me?' She had folded her arms and glared at him.

Rob caught her eye and collapsed. She had launched into him, buffeting him with her fists, until he wrapped his arms around her and they had slid down onto the warm earth.

Rob drank again. The stars were out, twinkling icily in the sky. He was cold, very cold. That was good. But . . . but he'd thought he'd been on the scrubby grass and red earth of Tigray.

Never mind.

Then there was that time he'd tried to tell Mekaela the wide-mouth-frog joke. *Oh God!* Rob laughed aloud, a brittle crazy laugh which unsettled Cyril Tanner and the two police constables climbing the hill towards him.

'Simple,' said Tanner in reply to Rob's question. 'A traffic officer saw your car parked here at half-past two. It was still here at four o'clock. I told you we'd be keeping an eye on you.'

'I wasn't going to top myself or anything like that,' muttered Rob as he sat beside Tanner in the police car. Despite drinking most of the brandy, he still felt disappointingly sober. One of the police officers was driving Rob's car home.

'Never crossed my mind,' said Tanner heartily. 'I'd been trying to find you to tell you that the inquests will be formally opened and adjourned next Thursday so the bodies can be released. Do you know what you plan to do yet?'

'Cremation,' replied Rob, firmly. 'Then I'll take the ashes to Tigray. I'm not a great believer in life after death, and I don't think Mekaela was either, but it's right to take their ashes home.'

'What will you do with them there?' inquired Tanner gently.

'There is a green hill . . .' Rob gave a sour laugh. 'And it's without a city wall, or at least a town wall. We used to have picnics up there. Light a fire, cook luncheon meat and eggs in a frying pan. There'd be Mekaela teaching Alfred to write and me to speak Tigrinya, and me teaching both of them English. I used to worry that we'd overload Alfred by making him learn the different scripts – but he loved it.'

'Are they very different?' asked Tanner.

'Have you ever *seen* written Tigrinya? It's like a load of worms squiggling over a page.'

'When will you go back?'

'As soon as possible,' replied Rob. 'At least I'll feel useful there.'

He'd already left a message on Hannah's answerphone telling her that he was cutting short his leave. He was worried she'd descend out of the blue on him. He couldn't cope with her relentlessly cheerful energy at the moment. But as they neared his home, Rob began dreading being left by himself. The idea of spending the long evening ahead reading without taking anything in or skimming through TV channels was depressing. Tentatively he suggested that Tanner might like to stop for a pint in one of the pubs they were passing.

'Normally I'd say yes but I've got things to do in the incident room. I'll get to see my missus some time this Christmas.'

'Sorry.'

Tanner was instantly contrite. 'No, *I*'m sorry. I didn't mean it like that. After thirty-two years married to a copper, she's used to it.'

'You've been married thirty-two years?'

'We were wed just after I finished my probationary stint. I've been a copper for thirty-four years.'

'Don't you have to retire after thirty years?'

'That's when the pension kicks in. You don't gain a lot by doing more than thirty.'

'So why have you?'

'I wanted to see my son through medical school. Now he's qualified, I'm leaving the force in April. We bought a place in Portugal last year.'

'Will you miss the police force?'

'Ay, inevitably. But times have changed. The days when you could give some young tearaway a clip round the ear are long gone. Nowadays I think villains frequently have more rights than their victims.' The lights of an inn loomed up out of the darkness. 'Ah, now, the beer used to be excellent here.'

'Are you sure? I don't want . . .'

'Absolutely.' Tanner pulled in and led the way into the pub. He ordered a pint of Wadsworth bitter for himself and a pint of lager for Rob.

'I don't know if it's any help,' began Rob. 'But I've remembered something about the taller man in the bomb car.'

'Yes?'

'It was the way he moved. The smaller man was like a headless chicken bursting for a crap but the second guy had power inside him. I knew guys like that in the army. He'll work outside in some manual job, and not a builder either. Maybe a farmer. Does this sound too fanciful to you?'

'Not at all. We've nothing on those two yet so every little helps.'

Rob was about to ask a question when he noticed that Tanner was staring behind him at the doorway to the bar.

'Well, well.' Tanner waited a moment, then said loudly, 'Good evening, Mr Wallis.'

Rob swung round to find Wayne Wallis standing at the bar with a young woman with dyed blonde hair and wearing a T-shirt too thin for December. If ever a man looked guilty, Wayne Wallis did then. It was clear that he was not going to introduce them to the girl but Rob had had enough to drink to feel mischievous.

'I'm Rob Sage,' he said. 'This is Detective Superintendent Tanner.'

'Shaynee Fields,' smiled the girl.

'Shaynee's consoling me,' muttered Wayne. He escorted her to a table as far away as possible before returning to the bar.

'How come Rob's name was never in the papers?' he asked Tanner. 'He's a hero.'

'Security,' replied Tanner briefly before giving Wayne an old-fashioned look. 'And how do *you* know the newspapers have his name?'

Wayne didn't miss a beat. 'A reporter told me.'

Of course – Wayne Wallis must have overheard the Premier praise Rob's bravery, Tanner realized. Good. That would take the heat off the local bobbies who were being put through the wringer, suspected of leaking Rob's name to the press.

Wayne slapped Rob on the back. 'Well, you're a hero in my book.'

Rob wished that he'd been a coward. Then Mekaela and Alfred would still have been here.

9

'Mr Fox?'

'Yes.' Denny swung round to find a doctor in a white coat emerging from a side corridor.

'I'm glad I caught you. I'm Dr Mortenson.'

'I'm trying to find my way to Intensive Care,' admitted Denny. 'This hospital's a maze.'

'You're in the wrong building but it's fortunate we bumped into each other. You got my letter?'

'What letter?'

'I wrote to you two days ago. Hatch Cottage . . .?'

'Yes.'

'And you haven't received it.'

'No.'

'Perhaps you'd better come to my office.' Dr Mortenson led the way into a cluttered space barely larger than a broom cupboard. He moved a pile of folders off a chair, indicated for Denny to sit down and delved into a stack of buff files.

'What's this about?'

Dr Mortenson looked up. 'I'm afraid that blood tests on Clive Austin indicate that he was HIV positive. From the antibodies, it's clear that he only contracted the virus recently.'

'What!'

Mortenson pulled a regretful face. 'I'm sorry. I take it you didn't know?'

'But we both had tests two months ago. We were clear. Since then I'd thought . . .'

He'd thought that Clive had been as monogamous as he had been. A void of sadness opened inside Denny. Clive had betrayed him – and he had been caught out. So much for fulfilling, faithful years. Clive, the party animal, had not been able to help himself after all.

The doctor was talking to him ... something about needing further tests.

Denny nodded mutely. Good old Clive. Unfaithful unto death.

'So the police think a woman planted the bomb in the litter bin?' repeated Rose Allen, who had called in to visit Mitch.

'Yeh, but they've no proof,' said Maddy. 'God! How can that woman live with herself, knowing that she's killed two innocent children?'

Rose shrugged. 'I don't know.'

'People like her can't be *normal*, can they?'

'I suppose not.'

'She must have a screw loose.' Unable to sit still, Maddy rearranged the stuffed black and white dog at her daughter's side. 'Planting a small bomb to deliberately drive your victims towards a bigger bomb so that even more will be killed and mutilated. *Is that sick!*'

Tanner's revelation that a woman had planted the bomb in the litter bin still shocked Maddy to the core. She found it impossible to comprehend that a woman could do something like that.

'Drat!' Rose Allen peered down at her knitting. 'I've dropped a stitch. I don't know *why* I chose this pattern.'

'Sorry, Rose. It just gets to me when I think . . .' Maddy paused, grateful for her visitor's calming influence. 'That's so pretty. What is it going to be?'

'A bedjacket for an old lady who was robbed by bogus gasmen.' Rose began to count the stitches.

'That's really sweet of you.'

'But you were telling me about your family holiday,' encouraged Rose.

Maddy made herself concentrate. 'Well, it wasn't really a *family* holiday. For a start, Tom had to stay behind to work during the week so it was just me and the kids. Then at the weekend he came up with his partner Cy, and Cy's wife Miss Purple.'

'Miss Purple?'

'That's what we call her. Her real name's Trixie. She's obsessed by the colour purple. That's all she ever wears. She even got married in it.'

'And it suits her?'

'Yeh, actually it does.' Trixie was a southern belle with a large personality and an even larger bosom. It was hard not to be overwhelmed by her laughter, even if Maddy suspected that Trixie frequently didn't have a clue why she was laughing. God, she could be so stupid. Or was Maddy just being bitchy because Tom fancied Trixie?

Maddy had often wondered whether Trixie was her secret rival but she'd rejected the idea as being too obvious. *All* men fancied Trixie and she encouraged them evenly. A harmless flirt, decided Maddy. Anyway, Tom liked his women to be bright, not vacuous.

'I'm not kidding. She wears purple bikinis, purple ski outfits. Hell, she even has purple bras.'

The two women were still laughing when there was a knock on the door and Rob appeared. Rose Allen stood up sharply as if flustered by Rob's arrival.

'Oh dear. Is that the time already? You've got to go to your meeting.' Rose bundled up her knitting. 'I'll just get myself a cup of tea and then I'll be back to watch over Mitch.'

'Perhaps you could teach me to knit sometime,' said Maddy.

'I'd be happy to. Something rather easier than this, though.' Rose pushed up her glasses, which seemed to be permanently sliding down her nose, picked up her bag in both hands and scuttled out.

'She's sweet,' said Maddy. 'She's going to sit with Mitch while I'm at the police briefing.'

'Is she becoming a regular visitor?'

'She's taken to popping in. It's nice to have company.'

'I'm sorry.' Rob took it as a reprimand that he had not been to see her yesterday.

'Don't be silly. I didn't mean *you*. I'm happy to see you whenever, you know that.'

'You see, yesterday . . .' Rob hesitated, in two minds whether to tell Maddy about his lost hours. In the end he did, simply because he had no one else to confide in.

'Hey, that's scary.' Maddy put her head on one side and regarded Rob seriously. 'Perhaps you should get this checked out. It could mean that you're—'

There was another knock on the door.

'I hope you don't mind me intruding, Mrs Lipzinger,' began Denny Fox. 'I was Clive Austin's partner. I thought I'd come to wish your little girl well, if I may.'

'That's really nice. Thank you.'

'A Sleeping Princess,' he murmured, looking at Mitch. 'Is she . . .?'

'The doctors say it's a question of waiting. I don't know whether she can hear us or not. I talk to her about her friends, her favourite things, you know.' Maddy thought that she ought to be offering Denny her condolences. 'I'm really sorry about Clive.'

'So am I,' said Rob. Maddy introduced them.

'We're all in the same boat,' she said.

'I hope Hayward's going tell us they're about to catch these bastards,' exclaimed Denny. 'Sorry for my language.'

'Hey, listen. That's nothing to what I call the scum who did this. *Nothing*,' hissed Maddy. 'I've read about people who lose loved ones and turn the other cheek. I can't be like that. I want an eye for an eye, a tooth for a tooth. I don't just want those motherfuckers dead – I want them screaming in pain and fear and *then* I want them to die.'

'Maddy, are you all right?' Rob put his hand on her shoulder, shocked by her sudden vehemence.

Maddy gave a rancorous laugh. 'And I was just telling *you* to seek help. This thing is driving us all crazy.'

'It's not surprising,' said Denny.

'I gather you're an actor, Mr Fox,' said Rob to change the subject.

'Denny, please.'

'Aren't you in the funny loo-roll commercial with the chimp?' asked Rob.

'Mitch used to love that one,' exclaimed Maddy. 'Me, too.'

Denny gave a mock bow. 'Such is fame.'

Rob was struck by the very ordinariness of Denny Fox. He was around five feet nine tall, wirily built with steel-rimmed glasses and short hair with the grey showing through. Rob had never met an actor before but somehow he'd expected something more.

'It's not your voice on the razor-blade commercial, is it?' he asked. 'You know, the one with the eagle's talons.'

'You have a good ear,' Denny complimented him. 'To be honest, I largely make my living doing voice-overs for TV commercials.'

'Which others have you done?'

In the past week Rob had stared at a TV screen more than he had in his entire life. Maddy, too, had watched British television in their hotel room with the children.

'Um, well, currently, there's one for jeans, Irish butter . . .'

'The one with the cows stirring the cream?' demanded Maddy. 'But the narrator's got an Irish accent.'

'To be sure, that he does,' replied Denny in the rich Dublin brogue he used on the commercial.

'That must be wonderful to be able to do that,' said Maddy. 'Can you do American accents, too?'

'Let me see, I reckon you must be from upstate New York . . . But I can go to the Deep South . . . or the Midwest . . . or even be from the Lone Star State of Texas,' he said, changing the accent to match the region.

'That's really clever.'

Rose Allen swept back into the room. 'Now, away with you or you'll be late for your meeting. I'll call you if there's any change. You can tell me about the investigation when you get back.'

Hayward and Tanner were waiting to greet them in the incident room. Graham Pottidge poured cups of coffee and passed on his wife's condolences, before retelling Maddy how his wife and his son had narrowly escaped the attack.

'She has hardly slept a wink since,' Pottidge was saying when Wayne Wallis came in accompanied by a police officer.

Tanner frowned. He had deliberately excluded Wallis from this briefing because he feared that any confidential information divulged here would quickly find its way into the newspapers.

'Leanne's parents wanted me to come to see what's happening,' announced Wayne.

Tanner and Hayward exchanged helpless glances. Maddy and the others were already looking curiously around the incident room where a dozen or so tired-looking detectives sat at computer terminals. Long printouts were pinned up on the walls next to maps and large white boards covered in lists. A box of sandwiches, crisps and fruit sat in the middle of the room, surrounded by paper cups.

'This used to be the snooker room,' said Pottidge. 'Now it's kept aside for major incidents.'

'Who's that in there?' Rob pointed to a man in a small glass-fronted room, the only person without a computer screen.

'He's the statement reader,' explained Pottidge. 'Large investigations become paper jungles. Not only are there literally thousands of witness statements to go through, but we also conduct house-to-house inquiries with printed questionnaires which have to be filed.'

'It's the statement reader's job to look for the lie in the paper,' added Tanner. 'He's there to spot any inconsistencies or discrepancies. That's why he's left alone to concentrate.' He indicated other men in the large room. 'There's the officer manager, the action allocator who makes sure that the various tasks which are assigned are actually carried out, the receiver.'

'I didn't know so much is done on computer,' observed Rob.

'Every scrap of information goes into the computer. Mr Hayward at Scotland Yard can access it, and so, in this case, can Pat Rodgers in Dublin. Everyone involved in the inquiry is given a nominal, starting with the victims. For example, Tom Lipzinger is N 1.'

'What do you mean, everyone?'

'Relatives, witnesses, every household we visit. We also liaise with the Police National Computer at Hendon . . .'

Hayward gave a diplomatic cough and indicated that they should take their places around the table.

'I must emphasize that anything said in this room is strictly between ourselves.' Hayward glared at Wayne who stared innocently back. 'You'll understand that we can't go into operational details but, on the whole, we are pleased with the progress we've made in the six days since the bombing. Intelligence has provided a number of suspects. Our task now is to find the evidence to bring those suspects to justice while uncovering the identities of the rest of the bombing gang.' Hayward paused to take a sip of coffee. 'Sixty detectives are working full time on this case in mainland Britain. The Police Service of Northern Ireland and the Garda south of the border are liaising closely. We are in touch with the intelligence services not just of this country but also the United States.'

'What can you tell us about the woman who put the bomb in the trash can?' demanded Maddy.

'We don't know for certain that a woman *did* plant the bomb,' objected Hayward weakly. 'We have untried intelligence, that is all.'

'But your intelligence is normally correct, isn't it?' demanded Maddy.

'Not always, and, anyway, it's not admissible in a court of law.'

'I'd like to know something about this bitch from hell,' insisted Maddy.

'Mrs Lipzinger, please.'

'Why not?'

'Say the intelligence proves to be faulty and this woman's name entered the public domain through anything Mr Hayward or I said, then we'd be facing a large defamation case,' pointed out Tanner.

'According to the newspapers, this Sovereign IRA group is the paramilitary wing of an organization called The True Guardians,' said Rob. 'They're led by a Breda Bridges. Is she one of your suspects?'

Hayward hesitated. 'The answer is no.'

'What about her husband Conn Nolan? He was big in the IRA until he left because he didn't agree with the peace process, according to the newspapers. Is he involved?'

'I cannot answer that,' replied Hayward.

There was a silence before Wayne said, 'What about DNA from the bomb car?'

'Exhaustive tests are still continuing on the car,' said Hayward, clearly happy with the change of subject. 'DNA tests can take weeks or even months – but once we *have* firm DNA evidence, then it's impossible for a trial defence to stand against it. That's why it's so vital. And we must make sure we get it right.'

'I've read somewhere that every bomber makes a device slightly differently,' said Denny.

'It's called his signature,' agreed Hayward.

'So in this case you know who made the car bomb.'

'It's a matter of public record that a man was detained in Dublin in connection with the bombing,' replied Hayward. 'He was released because of lack of evidence.'

'Have you any idea why no warning was given?' asked Maddy.

'We can only surmise that the terrorists wanted to cause the highest number of casualties possible.'

'Holy Christ,' breathed Maddy.

'We *will* catch those responsible,' proclaimed Hayward.

Maddy thought Tanner looked more dubious but Pottidge was

nodding enthusiastically. 'You didn't get those responsible for the bombing in Omagh,' Denny reminded them.

'If that inquiry were to be conducted today, it would be done very differently,' said Hayward firmly. 'We've learnt a lot since then, and Omagh is still an ongoing investigation. It's my belief that those behind that outrage will be brought to justice one day.'

'One day,' repeated Maddy. 'A day in the future.'

'Remember that the Prime Minister himself is on record as saying that he's willing to go to the ends of the Earth to hunt down those who killed your loved ones. With that sort of backing, we *will* get them.'

'What was that all about?' asked Maddy as the four stood outside the police station. 'They didn't really tell us anything.'

'If they know who did it, they should send in the SAS and kill them,' exclaimed Wayne.

'You do that and you become as bad as the terrorists,' said Rob. 'Those who fight the monsters in our society must ensure they don't become monsters themselves.'

Wayne snorted impatiently.

'What do you think?' Maddy asked Denny.

'I don't know,' he replied, taking off his glasses to rub his eyes. 'The police don't have a great track record of solving bombings like this. And if they do, the bombers have a habit of walking free a few years later with bundles of dosh for wrongful arrest and imprisonment.'

'The police are always fitting people up,' agreed Wayne.

'If they know who planted the bomb but can't prove it, then I hope they *do* fit someone up,' said Maddy.

'Even if by breaking the law you become, in a small way, like the killers?' Rob asked her gently.

'I wouldn't care.'

Wayne sidled closer to Denny. 'I know what I really wanted to ask you,' he murmured 'Are you having it off with Sister Sex-on-Legs?'

'Who?'

'Sister Pidgeon,' reminded Wayne. 'At the end of the last series, you two were going up to the roof together and she seemed to be taking her uniform off.'

'Oh! On television. I don't know. I haven't seen the scripts for the new series. Do you think I should?'

Maddy moved to Rob's side. 'The police *will* get the killers, won't they?'

'I hope so,' he said.

'So do I.' It was time to return to Mitch's bedside.

10

'Ah, Teresa, Teresa, you're a lovely girl, so you are – but you're lying through your teeth.'

'Am I now? You prove it. Wasting my time, dragging me down here to your big police station in Dublin.'

'You were brought here from Dundalk to save my time, not yours. I don't care a damn about your time,' said Pat Rodgers, thinking that Teresa Bridges resembled a crack addict with her sunken features and over-bright eyes. Maybe she was just high on fanaticism.

'Nice.'

'And who knows, you might get to see some sense.'

'Me! You've never had anything on me before, so why try now?'

'This time it's different.'

'Sod off.' Teresa slouched back on her chair, a picture of insolence in her faded denim jeans and jacket.

'We'll see,' said Rodgers, wishing he felt as confident as he sounded. The chances of getting Teresa Bridges to cooperate in any police investigation were as remote as Ireland winning the Rugby World Cup.

Rodgers had tried to rattle Teresa and Dessie Fitzgerald by picking them up at their home at dawn and rushing them separately down to Dublin in Black Marias with sirens wailing. But it needed more than a piece of theatre to unsettle Teresa. A colleague was interviewing Fitzgerald while a third detective was going through the motions with Conn Nolan in Dundalk. Rodgers had chosen Teresa. The two men would hardly say a word, he knew. Teresa was different. She enjoyed a verbal joust – confident that she would come out on top. Rodgers had decided to play on that arrogance in the hope that she'd talk herself into prison. But now he was beginning to fear that her arrogance came from the sure knowledge that there was nothing to tie her to the Salisbury bombing.

'Do you have any idea how many cameras there are on the streets of Salisbury?'

'Nah. How many?'

'Probably a hundred. But only two matter.' Rodgers took his time lighting his pipe and continued to bluff. 'The ones that clocked you doing your dance with the block car.'

'What the fuck are you on about?'

Rodgers pulled out the chair on his side of the table and sat down heavily, thinking how he disliked these old interview rooms with their green and white walls and small high windows, now showing a patch of grey sky.

'All right. Let's start at the beginning? Where were you on December twenty-second?'

'How the fuck do I know?'

'It should be easy enough to remember. A few days before Christmas. You weren't at home.'

'Wasn't I?'

'No. You weren't even in Ireland.'

'Is that true? God almighty, now you're telling me something.'

'You were in an old farmhouse on the mainland with Dessie.'

'Was I?'

'Sundial Farm. Just outside Salisbury.'

Gotcha! Teresa could not help her eyes widening just that fraction. She blinked rapidly to cover up. Rodgers had won a small skirmish. By naming the day before the bombing, he'd led Teresa to believe he was referring to the alibi she and Dessie had laid down at a farmhouse on the Gower Peninsula in Wales. Rodgers's last-minute switch to the farm where the car bomb had been made had thrown Teresa off balance.

'You were staying at Sundial Farm with Dessie, Conn Nolan and the Pizzaman, making the bomb.'

'That wasn't me.'

'We know that *you* weren't actively making the bomb. Too much like hard work, grinding all that fertilizer. But the next day you were driven into Salisbury where you planted the come-on bomb in the mall.'

'Get real.'

'Oh, I am,' said Rodgers softly. He knitted together his sausage-like fingers and leaned onto the table to stare into Teresa's eyes before dropping his gaze to her hands, resting on the table. 'You personally planted that bomb, girl. You, with those very hands, put that device into the litter bin. It was a week ago today, about this very time. You managed to kill two children. Another might die. How does it feel?'

Teresa compressed her lips in hate.

Rodgers continued talking in the same soft way. 'One was a little boy who'd had his legs shredded when he stepped on a landmine in Ethiopia. His pal had brought him over for an operation to try to rebuild his legs. Well?'

'Born unlucky, wasn't he?'

Rodgers kept his face – and his hands – still.

He kept his face still because he knew the moment had passed when Teresa might have cracked.

He kept his hands still because he had seldom wanted to hit someone as much as he wanted to smack Teresa then.

'And after you planted that bomb, you walked through the mall to where Dessie was waiting in the block car.'

Teresa made a play of yawning, her mouth wide open.

'Close your mouth. I don't want to see your cheap fillings.'

'There's nothing fucking cheap about my fillings, I can tell you.'

Rodgers returned to the attack. 'But there was that cock-up. Instead of the bomb car, you found that another car was waiting to take your place. Old people can be stubborn buggers, can't they? You had to leave the car and then summon Dessie out as well before the old couple finally got the message.'

'Is there much more?'

'Oh, I'd say about thirty years.' Rodgers waited for the effect of his words to sink in. 'Teresa girl, I don't think you understand just how much of England is covered by these CCTV cameras. Not just in city centres like Salisbury but all along the motorways. That's how we can track you out of Salisbury and over the Severn Bridge into Wales.'

A shadow of doubt was growing behind Teresa's eyes.

'Then, of course, you're on the evening Fishguard to Rosslare ferry. Back home safely for Christmas. Teresa and Dessie's murderous little trip to England – and all captured on camera for the world – and the jury – to see.'

There was a silence. 'Of course you could cooperate . . .'

Hell's bells and damnation! Rodgers had become carried away by his own eloquence. Teresa's eyes were flashing with hate. To suggest that a member of the Bridges family might turn informer was like asking the Grand Master of the Orange Order to celebrate Mass at the Vatican.

'Fuck off, the fucking lot of you. Fuck off.' Teresa jerked forward. The policewoman by the door tensed as Teresa began rocking to and fro in her chair, lips curled tight in contempt.

Rodgers pulled out a stack of photographs.

'Here. Look.' He handed them to her.

'Yeh, so?' She glanced at the top photograph.

'It's one of the little boys you killed. The one with the shattered legs.'

'You're sick.' Teresa tossed the photographs onto the table.

Rodgers left them there. He had not expected her to look through them. If she had not been so agitated she probably would not even have touched them. He was glad she had. They already had Teresa's fingerprints on file. Now they had her DNA.

Rodgers felt a wave of tiredness sweep over him.

'We'll leave it there.' He rose, deliberately making no mention of the alibi he knew Teresa had been so keen to lay.

'I'm not denying going to England, you know.'

'Really.' Rodgers paused with one hand on the doorknob.

'Dessie and I were in Wales for a few days, staying in a bed-and-breakfast.'

'Queer time to go away, just before Christmas.'

'I had a special reason.' Teresa was glaring at him with a triumphant gleam in her eye. 'I was advised to take a few days of rest. Didn't you know? I'm having a baby.'

'You expect me to understand all this, do you, Graham?' Tanner scowled at the new wall maps covered in different-coloured pins, tapes and stickers showing different times.

'Piece of cake, sir,' replied Pottidge. 'The techies are making a computer graphic so it'll be easy to see where everyone is at a given moment. But until then, if you'll follow me through this?'

'I'll try.'

'The cell-site analysis was conducted by the phone-service providers. We're still waiting on the NSA.' Pottidge turned to the maps. 'First, the six pay-as-you-go mobile phones were used on *one* day only – 23 December. No signal has been heard from any one of them since. Five of the six come alive at the same time – 11.25 a.m. – and in the same place, the cell site covering the farmhouse where the bomb was assembled.' Pottidge indicated on a map. 'The other phone is switched on ten minutes later not far from Bristol Airport.'

'That'll be the Pizzaman on his way home.'

'Yes, sir. Now, the recognition signals of three of the five mobiles move away from the farmhouse, down the valley and on to the next beacon site. They travel together from site to site *all* the way into Salisbury. We reckon these phones belong to Conn Nolan, Dessie Fitzgerald and Teresa Bridges.'

'And they are in the same car, the red Sierra?'

'There's been no trace of another car so it's a fair assumption that the Sierra was used as a scout car before Nolan dropped off Dessie and Teresa. The Sierra takes the back lane towards Wilton. You can see that because if they'd been on the main road, their phones would have shown on this beacon here.' Pottidge pointed to a small blue triangle stuck on the map.

'What does the red ribbon represent?'

'That's the bomb car itself following the scout car's route towards Salisbury,' replied Pottidge. 'Nolan makes three calls to the bomb car, we assume to say that the way is clear.'

'Okay.'

'The Pizzaman calls Nolan at 12.05, probably to confirm his flight's on time. The sixth phone, belonging to an unknown helper, stays behind at the farmhouse. Nolan calls him twice. The helper calls back shortly after the second call.'

'He's reporting that he's set fire to the place.'

'Looks like it. Then the helper sets off towards Salisbury along the same route, and he's really motoring. The traffic guys say he's travelling too fast for a car so he must be on a motorbike. I'll come back to him later because . . .' Pottidge tapped at a street map of Salisbury. 'The bomb car has stopped near the station and Nolan has reached the centre of town. Nolan now splits up from Dessie and Teresa. Because cell sites cover much smaller areas in the city centre, we can plot their movements in more detail. You can see that Nolan's cruising, making calls to coordinate the come-on bomb and the arrival of the bomb car.'

'What about Teresa and Dessie?'

'They move to the site covering the mall where the bomb exploded. At 12.21, the bomb car arrives in their cell site. There is one phone call from Teresa to Dessie. Shortly afterwards, the two leave Salisbury and head towards Warminster, presumably in the block car. Nolan heads the opposite way, towards Southampton. At 12.31 the bomb-car phone calls the helper from the farmhouse who's just entered the city centre. They then set off together.'

'But you've said the helper is on a motorbike. He couldn't take away both car bombers,' objected Tanner.

'Then one car bomber had to leave another way,' said Pottidge. 'Because this one goes like a bat out of hell to Gatwick where both phones are switched off. Nolan, at Southampton Airport, gets one call from Dessie, west of Warminster, and then *all* the phones go dead.'

'Shame we can't hear what they said,' complained Tanner.

'The Americans can.'

'I don't like it. How come they've interviewed the four of us so quickly?'

Breda Bridges looked up from ironing her daughter's best party frock. 'Obvious suspects.'

'Then why haven't they picked up Jimmy Burke?' demanded her husband.

'Perhaps the Garda don't know he was out of the country. Anyway, you can ask him yourself. He's due any minute.'

'That detective knew I was the coordinator,' persisted Conn Nolan.

'They'd expect you to be.' Breda folded the frock away and held up one of Bobby's T-shirts and tutted.

'But how did the man *know* it was Teresa who planted the come-on bomb?' persisted Nolan.

'The police are bluffing. They're just trying it on.' Breda began rubbing at the stain on the shirt. 'If you all followed your instructions, then there'll be not a shred of evidence against us.'

'We did, Breda, I promise you. Mind you, there were those who believed I was making a fuss over nothing.'

It had taken Nolan's strength of character to ensure that members of the bombing team had worn protective clothing at crucial times. Jimmy Burke had objected that once the car bomb had exploded there'd be nothing left.

'Don't you believe it. The Omagh bomb car was blown to smithereens but scientists could lift new DNA off the wreck today – if the police hadn't fucked up by leaving it out in the open for twelve months.'

Now the bombers were grateful that Breda had insisted on them taking care. But that was Breda. She was taking the same painstaking trouble to remove a stain from her son's T-shirt as she had to plan the bombing.

Through her efforts, Conn had been able to stand up his alibi by showing restaurant bills and credit-card receipts for every day of his stay in Paris. The receptionist at his hotel had seen him check in and check out. The hotel bill showed nightly phone calls home and the room's minibar had been regularly used. Conn's fingerprints were in the room and he had even sent a postcard to his kids.

The French police might point out that the receptionist was part-time and there was no one on duty for much of the day. The daily meal receipts came from tourist restaurants which served hundreds of covers every day and wouldn't remember if Santa Claus had dined there. That wasn't Conn's fault.

A fellow traveller – the same one who had rumpled his sheets, made the phone calls and posted the card – would swear that he had met Conn on the morning of the twenty-third to talk about opening an Irish theme pub in the French capital.

The same attention to detail had been taken over the fictitious alibis of the Pizzaman and Dessie and Teresa. Jimmy Burke and Mikey Drumm were different. Not only would Jimmy Burke's brothers cover for him on their farm in the heart of the badlands but also a dozen men were willing to swear they had been drinking with him every night in December, while Drumm was an itinerant building labourer who never stayed in the same town or same lodgings for long.

The English lilywhites who had serviced the farm had no criminal records and no public links to the cause.

Breda inspected the T-shirt. That was better. She found ironing restful, enjoying the repetition and the satisfying way the laundry basket emptied as the pile of pressed clothing grew.

The front doorbell sounded. 'That'll be Jimmy Burke,' said Conn, going to let him in.

'How are you doing there?' Burke came into the room, his flat cap almost hidden in his huge hands.

'Fine. I'm fine.' Breda folded the shirt and added it to the pile.

'That's a grand job you're doing,' said Burke, admiringly. 'I can never iron like that.'

'Takes practice,' replied Breda.

'What do you think of that Yank offering reward money, then? Just because his son got zapped.'

'He'll get nowhere.' Conn brought two cans of lager out of the fridge and handed one to Burke.

'So, to what do we owe the pleasure of this visit?' asked Breda.

'I thought it best not to talk on the phone but I've a cousin, Vince O'Lone, who uses the same Irish club in London as Mikey Drumm. He says that Mikey has taken to drinking there every night in a big way.'

'That's not unusual for Mikey,' said Conn.

'I mean, in a *big* way.' Burke thought it was wrong of Breda to carry on ironing while he was talking. 'Worse, once Mikey's had a few, he goes on about seeing bodies being blown apart by a bomb.'

'But he didn't, did he?' Breda's head snapped up to glare at him. 'He couldn't have.'

'Not unless he went back. But it doesn't stop him getting the DTs. My cousin says he's very . . . colourful in his descriptions. It's getting to be his party piece.'

Breda glanced at her husband. 'You chose him.'

'We all knew Mikey likes a drink but he's never gone over the edge before.'

'You'll have to have a word with him, Conn,' declared Breda. 'We can't have him blabbing like this.'

'You think it'll be safe for me to go to England now, what with all the police interest and such?' asked Nolan.

'What police interest?' demanded Burke.

Breda recounted how Conn and the others had been interviewed by Garda Special Branch.

'Shit! How did they get on to you so quickly?'

'They knew more about the operation than they should have done,' answered Conn.

'Are you saying we've a grass in our ranks?'

'There are always informers, Jimmy. But you know what to say if the police come to you?'

'Fucking right, I do.' He crushed the beer can in his fist. 'I was never off the farm before Christmas – and I've witnesses to prove it.'

'How did they find *her*?' Pottidge steered the police car past a flock of indifferent hens and out through the narrow gateway into the spider's web of lanes that covered the Gower Peninsula. 'Mrs Morfen bloody Price.'

'What did you make of her, Graham?' demanded Tanner.

'It's not what I make of her, sir. It's what a jury would think,' he replied. 'She could tell them the world was created in six days and they'd believe her. And she's clean?'

'As white as her hair, apparently.'

And that was the problem. Mrs Morfen Price was sixty-two years old and had become a respected member of the local community since she had bought her lonely whitewashed farmhouse cottage near Penrice ten years ago, where she made ends meet offering bed and breakfast.

She had poured the policemen endless cups of tea, plied them with her home-made Welsh cakes and chatted away freely about her recent guests.

Yes, Dessie and Teresa had stayed with her from the eighteenth to the twenty-third of December, said Mrs Price. It was so nice to have people around at that time of year. That's why she took guests, she intimated, for the company as much as for the money. Dessie and Teresa were a nice couple, if rather like chalk and cheese. She was a talker while you were lucky to get two words out of him. Did they know Teresa had almost lost a baby? Her first, the one they'd been trying for. That's why they'd come here. For peace and quiet. They had asked if she would cook for them and of course she'd agreed. The couple had eaten with her every night. Normally, they had retired early. Of course, there was a TV in their en suite bedroom.

No, Mrs Morfen Price didn't know why they had chosen her place. Seen it on the Internet and liked what they saw, she expected. No, they had stayed every single night from the eighteenth to the twenty-third. Yes, she was sure. She'd know, wouldn't she.

And yes, she had heard from them again. Teresa had phoned, Boxing Day, she thought it had been, to say thank you again and tell her that she felt so much better for the rest.

'If I didn't know better, *I'd* have believed her,' moaned Pottidge. 'She reminded me of my gran.'

'She's everybody's bloody gran,' agreed Tanner. 'That's why the jury will buy every word she says unless we can shake her. We'll rerun background checks on her. There must be something somewhere to tie our perfect granny to Irish republicanism.'

'What if she's giving them a copper-bottomed alibi just for the money?'

'Well, at least it'll be easy to check her bank account.'

11

Maddy Lipzinger went to bed early on New Year's Eve. She kissed Mitch's forehead and slipped into the next room, not wanting to be awake at midnight, the time when normally she'd look back over the past twelve months and look forward to the next. Both Rob and Denny had also gone to bed early. Only Wayne celebrated – at a neighbour's party, without Shaynee who was with her husband. As Wayne explained, he had been advised to get out and meet people. It was bad for him to stay in moping. So he made the effort, even though his heart was breaking.

Maddy's first thought in the New Year was that the coroner's inquest was to be opened the next day which meant that Tom and TJ's bodies could finally be released for burial. Her father-in-law, who was still in Belfast as far as she knew, had taken charge of the arrangements to transport their bodies back home. But the funeral presented Maddy with a terrible dilemma – as she explained to Rob when he called in.

'I can't leave Mitch. I just can't.'

'But you have to go to the funeral,' he insisted. 'You must say goodbye to your husband and your son. You owe it to them.'

'I owe it to Mitch to be with her, *and* I've got this feeling that she won't wake unless I'm here.'

'What if I promise to stay and watch over her? Will that do?'

There was a long silence before Maddy whispered, 'Would you?'

'I'd be honoured.'

'I'll only be gone for a day or so.' Maddy calculated quickly. 'We'll fly into Toronto . . .'

'Toronto?'

'We're just over the border from Canada, a place called Tonawanda.'

'Where?'

'You mean you've never heard of beautiful Tonawanda on the banks of the Niagara River?' Maddy smiled. A natural warm, teasing smile. Rob caught his breath at the glimpse of Maddy as she had been before she'd been scoured by grief.

But before Rob could speak, Alvin Lipzinger exploded into the room.

'No change?'

'No, but how are you doing?' asked Maddy with a hint of irony.

'Fine. I've spoken to the coroner's officer and the funeral director. My people back home are sorting out Air Canada.' The big American spoke loudly and rapidly. 'They've assured me the paperwork will be completed in time to catch tomorrow's 1500 flight to Toronto.'

'Wait a minute, wait a minute.' Maddy swayed back as if recoiling from the force Alvin was generating. 'First tell me what happened in Ireland.'

'That's not important. Let's get our boys home.'

'Hang on there, Alvin. You went to Ireland to speak to the IRA to find out who was behind the bomb,' she reminded him. 'Well?'

'They couldn't see me.' Alvin wouldn't meet her eyes. Instead he peered at the monitors above Mitch's head. 'They were on holiday. Busy schedules, delicate time for the peace process over there. You know.'

'No, I don't.'

Alvin took a deep breath. 'I got the run-around. The bum's rush. Call it what you will.'

'So you're no further forward?'

'I guess not,' admitted Alvin. 'Shit! I helped get these guys visas to put their case in the States, and this is how they thank me. God-dam assholes.'

'Don't be hard on yourself, Alvin.' Maddy laid a gentle hand on his arm. 'You don't *know* they know who the bombers are.'

'Yeh, I do,' he confessed. 'I spoke to a lot of people in Northern Ireland, believe me. They know all right. They know *exactly* who planted the bomb that killed Tom and TJ – but they're too cowardly to say so.' Alvin paced the room, winding himself up into a fury. 'But I tell you what, it's time for those guys in Sinn Fein or PIRA or whatever they're calling themselves at this moment in time to piss or get off the pot. They can't have it both ways. They either have to stand up for peace with all the responsibilities that that entails or be branded as much a terrorist as the bombers themselves.'

'Did you speak to the police?'

'They suggested I went back to the States. They reckoned they couldn't guarantee my personal safety. But I haven't finished with this yet. Hell, I haven't started. By the time I'm through, the American people will be aware of the true colours of hypocrites who protect murderers.'

'At least you're back safely,' said Maddy in a small voice.

Alvin Lipzinger took a deep breath. 'Anyway, let's get our boys home. Give them a heros' burial. I've spoken to Father McVay. The interment is fixed for Monday the fifth. We'll have a memorial service in a month or so.'

'Hold on there. If I'm going to return with Tom and TJ, I want the service performed the next day so I can return here as soon as possible.'

'But that'll be Saturday. People need to organize . . .'

'Excuse me, I'll leave,' said Rob, making for the door.

'You stay,' ordered Maddy without taking her eyes off her father-in-law. 'Alvin, I am Tom's next of kin and TJ's mother. *I* say when they get buried. You understand.'

'But it's such short notice. People would have to cancel things to attend . . .' Maddy said nothing. The silence grew until Rob could feel its very weight. Alvin cracked first. 'Hell, Maddy. I'm only trying to help you.'

'And I'm grateful. But I need to get back to Mitch. Remember, she's yours as well.'

'Of course. I'll get onto Father McVay now.'

'And get me a return flight Saturday evening.'

Rob took his vigil seriously. The hospital authorities refused to let him stay overnight, but he was back by Mitch's side at eight next morning. Denny Fox arrived two hours later.

'I bring gifts to the keeper of the flame,' he announced as he unpacked Danish pastries and beakers of cappuccino from a brown paper bag. 'Real coffee as a change from hospital slops.'

'Thank you.'

Denny rearranged Pooch the stuffed dog to lie in the crook of Mitch's arm. 'Our Sleeping Princess has been unconscious for . . . eleven days now,' he calculated.

'A nurse was telling me that people can stay in a coma for months, even years,' said Rob. 'Mitch is breathing by herself, there's normal brain activity . . .'

'It's good of you to sit with her.'

'At least I'm being useful here,' confessed Rob. 'I envy you the stage. You're doing something.'

'Ah, yes. Dr Theatre,' sighed Denny.

'I was going to take Alfred to see your panto, you know, although I'm not sure how much he'd have understood.'

'Children don't have to understand language to enjoy a good panto. Heros and villains are the same in any language.' Denny took off his glasses and rubbed his knuckles into his eye sockets. 'You know, the woman who planted the bomb must have walked past me while I was sitting in that cafe window. I must have seen her.'

'I must have seen her, too,' said Rob. 'Shame we couldn't spot her.'

'At least you saw *something* was amiss. If it wasn't for you, there'd have been hundreds dead. Do you know what I find amusing about this, and it is the *only* thing I find amusing,' said Denny. 'People want *my* autograph because I pretend to be a hero on TV. You're a real-life one – and no one knows.'

'I hope it stays that way,' said Rob fervently.

Once he left Rob, Denny went to look for Dr Mortenson to see if the results of his blood tests had come back. It took a while to find Mortenson's office in the genito-urinary department and, when he did stumble upon it, it was closed. A nurse told him in a loud clear voice that Dr Mortenson was off duty.

Denny thanked her with theatrical hauteur, told himself off for slinking around and strode out with head held high.

Clive's infidelity nagged away like a bad tooth. Denny kept trying to work out when, where and, especially, from whom Clive had caught the virus. Denny could count the nights when he and Clive had been apart on the fingers of one hand. There was that weekend he'd spent in Yorkshire shooting a TV commercial, the two or three times he had overnighted in London for an early start in the studio on voice-overs, the hospital soap's end-of-series party . . . No, Clive had come up to that. He wasn't one to miss a party. So all in all, Clive had not had that many opportunities to stray – but he'd managed it.

Stop it. Stop it, or you'll turn into a bitchy old queen.

Magnanimity in death, dear heart. Magnanimity in death.

That afternoon a nurse put her head around the door of Mitch's room to say that Hannah Beckford was outside.

'Your next-door neighbour said you'd be here,' gushed Hannah. 'I've been trying to track you down. Everybody in London and Chicago sends their love. How've you been?'

'Fine. And you?'

Hannah rolled her eyes. 'We went to stay with my family directly after Christmas and then we went to Lenny's for the New Year. I feel I've done nothing but pack and unpack the car, but at least it meant we and the kids had Christmas by ourselves. You really should have come up.'

'Oh, well, you know.'

'Is there anything I can do to help?'

'Can you find out from the Ethiopian embassy whether I need special permission to take Mekaela's and Alfred's ashes back, and if I do, can you arrange it?'

'Of course. What do you intend to do then?'

'Stay in Tigray and get back to work, I suppose. There's nothing to keep me in Britain.'

'I'm due to go out to Ethiopia in February,' mused Hannah. 'After all, I've never been there and I've visited our sites in Tanzania twice. I could bring my trip forward and fly out with you, if you'd like.'

'Are you saying you've *never* been to Ethiopia?'

'Never. Stupid, isn't it?' she confessed. 'Now, have you thought any more about publicity?'

Rob grimaced. 'I've told you, Hannah, I prefer to remain anonymous.'

'I appreciate that . . . but do you know *how* many charities there are out there, all scrapping for the public's cash? You could give us an edge for a while. Help us raise more funds, do more good in Tigray.'

'Hannah!'

'I'm sorry to be so brutal, Rob, but it's a hard world.'

'I'd like to remain anonymous,' he insisted, angry at the attempt at moral blackmail.

Hannah controlled her temper with difficulty.

*

Rob was preparing to watch the news on the small TV set in the ante-room when Rose Allen arrived. She seemed confused to find Rob instead of Maddy.

'Oh dear, oh dear,' she repeated as Rob explained. 'I really should have called in before.' She blinked helplessly behind her large glasses.

'Please stay.'

Rose smiled shyly before taking off her overcoat to reveal a long, shapeless fawn cardigan over a sensible tweed skirt. Rob wondered if she knitted all her cardigans herself. She murmured endearments to Mitch before inspecting the medical charts.

'Can you understand those things?' asked Rob, who was watching her.

'I used to be a nurse,' she replied before bringing out her knitting. 'Have you heard any more from the police?'

'Not since that talk a few days ago.'

'Oh, look.' Rose pointed at the TV set.

There was Maddy at the funeral of her husband and son. She looked serene and composed, thought Rob. The epitome of grieving elegance. Rob turned up the volume so they caught the end of Alvin's soundbite speech to camera, something about revenge. Then the camera cut to Maddy again.

'She looks very beautiful, doesn't she?' murmured Rose, articulating Rob's own thoughts.

'Very beautiful.'

Maddy had left London Heathrow Airport at three p.m. on Friday afternoon on board an Air Canada flight to Toronto. She returned to Heathrow early Sunday morning. The intervening hours were a blur.

Alvin had organized everything. On the flight Maddy pretended to sleep and hid behind dark glasses. When the aircraft began its descent over Lake Ontario the ache deep inside her became unbearable. She insisted on waiting until she saw the two coffins being lowered from the hold of the aircraft before allowing herself to be led to where her sister and Tom's family were waiting. That evening was spent amid hushed voices and sympathetic murmurs of condolence. Someone gave her a sedative and her sense of unreality increased.

Next morning, others were on hand to do her hair, lay out her widow's weeds and make sure she had something to eat for breakfast.

It occurred to Maddy later that she had not participated in the funeral at all; she had merely observed it through a tear-etched pane of glass. She had been capable of focusing only on those close to her like Tom's partner Cy and his wife Trixie, in a black suit edged with purple, shedding copious tears from behind her purple veil. Maddy had felt a flash of anger that Trixie had pursued her affectation even at Tom's funeral – before her apathy, induced by grief and more sedatives, overcame her.

Alvin could not resist the TV cameras and had made a speech about the loss of two brave American lives, the need to root out terrorism in all its forms and how he, personally, would not rest until these murderers had been brought to justice.

Almost immediately after the service, Maddy had been driven back to the airport. She had to return to the bedside of her only surviving child who still lay in a coma. She hoped everyone would understand.

On the flight back, she thought long and deeply, grateful to be by herself.

Rob spotted Maddy as she emerged into the arrivals hall at Heathrow's Terminal Three, smartly dressed in a charcoal-grey trouser suit and with her hair pulled back into a ponytail. She was wheeling a suitcase and had another bag slung over her shoulder.

The moment Maddy saw him, she turned deathly white and stumbled as if about to fall. He hurried to her.

'What are you doing here?' she breathed, eyes wide with fear. 'It's Mitch, isn't it?'

'No, no. She's okay. Well, she's the same.'

'Then why are you here?' Maddy's fear switched to anger. 'You said you'd stay and look after her.'

Rob went to take her suitcase but she snatched it away.

'Hang on,' he pleaded. 'Her fairy godparents are watching over her.'

'What?' She turned around.

'Denny and Rose Allen are both with her as we speak. The hospital wasn't happy about all of us being around Mitch so those two suggested I came to collect you.'

Maddy gave a strangled laugh, then another. People were staring curiously at them.

'Maddy. Maddy.' Rob grasped her shoulders.

'I'm sorry, Rob. I'm sorry.' With an effort, she regained her composure. 'I can cope with hardness. I can cope with indifference, but when people are nice, I just fall apart.'

She finally allowed him to take her case. Rob led the way towards the car park as Maddy stuttered her apologies for misjudging him.

In the car, he asked, 'How did it all go? I saw you on TV. You looked . . .'

'Gone out?' offered Maddy.

'I was going to say serene.'

'That's because I was drugged up to the eyeballs. I was like a zombie most of the time.'

'You must be exhausted.'

'I don't feel too bad. I thought through a lot of things on the flight back.' Maddy eyed him nervously. 'I've made one decision.'

'Yes?'

'Spending every minute by Mitch's bedside is crazy. I don't know how long she'll take to pull through.' Maddy was watching

Rob closely to see his reaction. 'I'll get a cellphone. The nurses can call me if there's any change. I'll never be far from the hospital but I mustn't spend all my time there. Do you think I'm being heartless?'

'Don't be silly. You're being sensible.'

Maddy sighed. 'You don't know how much it means to hear you say that.'

'Will you go back to the Red Lion Hotel?'

'No. I'll rent a cottage.'

'Stay in my place,' Rob heard himself saying. 'I'm going back to Tigray to start work again straight after the cremation. You're welcome to have the cottage for as long as you like.'

'I don't know.'

'There's no charge. Just use it.'

'Money's not a problem. It's just that I don't want to take advantage.'

'You're not taking advantage. Would you like to see it?'

'Yes, please.' Maddy squeezed Rob's hand. 'I'd like to go straight to the hospital now, but will you take me there later?'

'Of course,' said Rob.

They were silent for a while, then Maddy asked, 'Do you ever think about God?'

'Um, no. Not really.'

'The priest at the funeral kept going on about how we had to have faith in God at times like this. According to him, losing my husband and son is supposed to strengthen my belief. Can you understand that?'

'No, I can't.'

'Nor can I,' said Maddy.

'I reckon you need a very special faith to believe that God is testing you by taking away a loved one,' reasoned Rob. 'That sort of faith is beyond my comprehension.'

'Yeh, I just feel angry at God for letting them die.'

'And angry at those who killed them.'

'And *very* angry at those who killed them,' repeated Maddy.

'You told me about that Sierra knowing it'd be a block of metal by the time the police got there,' Kilfoyle accused Jimmy Burke.

Burke shrugged. 'So?'

'Who drove the Sierra to the breaker's yard?'

'I don't know. Breda did the planning but I think she had someone on the mainland helping to set up the job.'

'Why do you say that?' Kilfoyle rubbed the condensation off the car window to peer out at the afternoon mist settling over the rolling hills and, behind them, the bulk of Slieve Beagh rising in the distant north.

'Someone had to rent the farmhouse. The fertilizer and the grinders were there waiting for us. Someone recruited those English boys.'

Kilfoyle winced. More cracks in the thin ice he was skating on. He'd rather the police inquiry focused on the hardbitten likes of Conn Nolan, Breda, Dessie and Teresa and the Pizzaman. The mountains of Mourne would tumble down to the sea before any of them would talk.

'What's happening about the bomb car?' demanded Burke. 'Have they found anything?'

'Too many things. You just want to hope that none of them's yours.' Kilfoyle became aware of the strong smell of diesel and cow shit coming off the big raw-boned farmer. He let down the driver's window.

'That's all right, then.' Burke began to roll a cigarette.

Kilfoyle bit back his anger at the man's complacency. Burke was relying on Kilfoyle to cover up for him – not aware that he was more likely to pull Kilfoyle *into* the shit than Kilfoyle was to pull him out of it.

'What else do you have for me?' asked Kilfoyle.

'What do you mean, what do I have for you?'

'Christ, Jimmy, I've told you. Unless I keep producing intelligence about the bombing, other agencies will step into the breach . . .'

'They won't get anything.'

'Don't you be so sure,' snapped Kilfoyle. 'Who was in the bomb car with you, for instance?'

Burke jerked as if he had been stung. 'Leave him alone. He's been hitting the sauce. Tell you what, though – Nolan went from Paris to London and back on a false passport.'

'I think we've deduced that,' replied Kilfoyle sarcastically. 'Whose idea was it to torch the farmhouse?'

'Breda's. She's scared shitless about DNA.'

'What about the lilywhites?'

'Christ. Don't go and be finding those now. They'll blab within five minutes.'

'So why were they recruited?'

'They ran the errands so none of us had to leave the farm.' Burke put a match to his roll-up. 'I'll tell you one thing. Breda's already talking about the next big one.'

'What?'

'Conn was complaining that Breda was going on about it Christmas afternoon. He said she never gives it a rest.'

'What's the target?'

'No idea. But I know she wants to make a big impact, like.'

'Find out what she's planning – but keep your fucking distance this time.'

Burke grunted and let the ash from his cigarette fall on the floor. 'My neighbours the Kennedys were lifted by Irish Customs two days ago. Now there's no one moving the fags and baccy over the border. Me and my brothers thought we'd step in to fill the gap. It'd be a shame to see a business opportunity go begging, like.'

'Don't push it,' warned Kilfoyle.

'What have I got to worry about with you as my mate? You'll not want anything happening to me, will you?'

12

It was Tanner's third funeral within a week – and it had rained at every one of them. He thought this one for Mekaela and Alfred at the Salisbury crematorium was the saddest because it was the most sparsely attended.

Leanne Burroughs had been given a good send-off. So too, had Clive Austin – although the funerals had been very different.

Bemerton Heath had turned out in force for Leanne. The estate could be as rough as sin, but, by Christ, it had done Leanne proud. The hearse had been drawn by matching black horses with a mummer walking in front. You could hardly see the hearse for the floral tributes. Pride of place was divided between a huge yellow and white cushion saying *Our Daughter* and an equally large heart of red roses from Wayne, paid for by a national newspaper and proclaiming *Always Mine*.

Every curtain had been drawn along the route to the church and, for once, there were no kids out playing in the streets.

Tanner had been surprised to see Rob and Denny slip into the back of the modern church as the service, full of pop music and windcheaters, was about to begin. No one recognized Rob but afterwards Wayne had intercepted Denny and introduced him to Leanne's parents and most of the mourners.

Clive Austin's funeral had been more sedate. Well-enunciated readings from Auden and Joyce Grenfell, music by Scott Joplin, Piaf and Bach. The mourners, divided between Salisbury's chamber of commerce and the local gay community, had sipped sparkling wine and nibbled canapés in an upstairs room at the White Hart.

And now Tanner and Pottidge stood in the back row of Salisbury Crematorium's small chapel, damp raincoats folded by their sides, listening to the heavy percussion and thin horns of a Coptic hymn. The congregation had consisted of just nine – Rob, Hannah Beckford and three colleagues, Rob's next-door neighbours and the policemen – when, at the last minute, Denny had entered with Maddy.

Rob stood by himself in the front row, head bowed as the priest urged Rob not to dwell on the loss of his friends' lives but instead to remember the happy times they had shared together. As Pottidge pointed out later, there was nothing else he could have said.

After the service, Tanner was inspecting the few flowers when Denny Fox approached. 'I'm going to try to get Rob to come for a drink. Will you join us?'

'Sorry, we've got to get back to the station.'

'Developments?'

'Not really,' replied Tanner, shortly.

But there *were* hopes of the breakthrough they needed. Tanner had had a brainwave. He had remembered that most farmhouses and many villages outside Salisbury were not on mains drainage. Instead, they relied on septic tanks.

That morning, the contents of Sundial Farm's septic tank had been pumped into a brand new stainless-steel container. In theory, the DNA of everyone who had used the lavatories at the farm was now in that container.

The police certainly needed a break. Interrogations of the four suspects had got nowhere, searches of their homes had uncovered nothing. The Toyota block car had vanished somewhere in South Wales. Witnesses in Salisbury were few and shaky in their recall and although cell-site analysis had revealed the pattern of conversations among the bombers there was nothing to tie the suspects to the phones. The police were still waiting for NSA's voice analysis of the calls.

The Met were making life unpleasant for South London pond life in their search for the thief who had stolen the bomb car – but it was beginning to look as if he was a professional who had stolen to order.

Mrs Morfen Price on the Gower Peninsula was sticking to her story – though they couldn't understand her motives. There was nothing in her history, nor her bank balance, to explain why she was lying.

Hopes for the success of the investigation were currently pinned on NSA's space-age technology and the contents of a septic tank.

Rob gazed at the few flowers, oblivious to the grey bands of rain sweeping over the distant council estate and the facing hills. Hannah had already left for London with her team, explaining that she had a lot to do before she flew off with Rob the next day.

'Thank you for coming,' he murmured to Maddy, who had materialized by his side.

'I wanted to come,' she replied softly. 'Part of my new resolution.'

Denny appeared, holding a raised umbrella over Maddy's head. 'You need a drink, Rob. In fact, we all do.'

'Do you know, I've not had a drink since . . . before Christmas,' said Maddy.

'All the more reason, then,' replied Denny.

Maddy was not certain. 'Do you think I should?'

'Rose Allen is happy to sit with Mitch,' Denny reminded her. 'She told you to get a breath of air. Now, I know of a nice pub just outside the city where we can have lunch.'

The three set off in silence. For a while the only sound in the car was the hum of the heater and the swish of the wiper blades battling against the heavy rain. Maddy leaned forward from the back seat.

'How're you feeling, Rob?'

'Strange,' he replied after a moment.

'It's over now,' she said.

'But it's not, is it? It's not over for you – with Mitch still unconscious – and it's certainly not over for any of us as long as those bombers are still out there.'

'What do you reckon, Denny?' asked Maddy.

'"The tumult and the shouting dies; The Captains and the Kings depart: Still stands Thine ancient sacrifice, An humble and a contrite heart. Lord God of Hosts, be with us yet, Lest we forget – lest we forget."'

'Gee, Denny, sounds as though you're about to go into battle.'

'Kipling, dear heart. I did a one-man show of his work once. Actually I might launch it again.' Denny switched into a Mancunian accent. 'Now I'm on telly, like.'

'I love all those accents,' laughed Maddy.

'Why does it always rain at funerals?' asked Rob.

'It's called pathetic fallacy,' announced Denny. 'When the weather is in accord with one's mood.'

'It's going to bucket down, then,' said Rob morosely.

Denny was clearly known at the pub. After a few words, the three of them were led to a secluded alcove. Maddy agreed to have a glass of wine. Rob ordered a pint of lager and Denny drank mineral water. A waitress brought the menu and Maddy, who had told herself she was only there for Rob, was surprised to find she was looking forward to lunch.

'A toast,' said Denny, once the drinks had arrived. 'To our loved ones. In our thoughts. In our hearts.'

'That's beautiful.' Maddy turned to Rob. 'Here's to a safe flight. I promise I'll look after your cottage while you're away.'

'A safe flight,' echoed Denny, before adding, 'I know that this is going to sound like a platitude, Rob, but it will get better.'

'I was just thinking that Alfred would have been coming out of hospital around now after his first operation.' In his mind's eye, Rob saw the little boy lying on the floor playing with his new train set. 'He'd have been home with me.'

'Taking the ashes back to Tigray will be a closure for you,' said Maddy.

'Closure!'

'Sorry. Hey, listen. Can you believe that Tom, me and the kids were supposed to have gone to Ireland for New Year?' said Maddy. 'I'd totally forgotten. I suppose Alvin must have cancelled for me. I don't like to ask him now. It makes me look stupid.'

'You had other things to think about.'

'Yeh, but you've not forgotten to turn up at the theatre, have you, Denny?'

'No, although I am having difficulty coming to terms with some things,' Denny replied. 'The little things, mainly.'

'The little things add up,' said Maddy.

'You know the hardest part? Clive used to prepare a light meal for me when I got home after the panto. I'd arrive drained and he'd have supper waiting in front of the fire. Clive could only have been doing this for a fortnight but, looking back, it seems that he did it for ever.' Denny removed his spectacles and began to rub his eyes.

Denny was going through a different experience from her or Rob, thought Maddy. His everyday life had been torn apart while she was still living an unreal existence centred around Mitch's hospital bed and Rob had never lived with Mekaela and Alfred in England. Only Denny – and Wayne, she supposed – knew what it was like to go home and find part of that home missing.

'I don't know where you live, Denny,' said Maddy.

'We shared a small place on the edge of the city. We bought it together almost eighteen months ago. You must come and see it.'

'Thank you. I'd like that.'

'It's a shame that Clive's not here to cook for you. He loved entertaining. We used to give lunch to friends every Sunday. The house seems so empty now.' Denny gave a bitter laugh. 'This is turning into a group therapy session. More wine. Let the show go on.'

'Stuff it! You're right, Denny,' cried Rob. 'I'll get another bottle.'

Seized with the idea, Rob leaped to his feet and strode towards the bar.

Maddy grinned, seeing for the first time the raw energy and incisiveness that ran deep inside Rob. Denny, too had changed. He had become more theatrical with his flowery quotations. It occurred to her that all three of them were beginning to reveal their true natures as they got to know each other better.

The food arrived, and Maddy's mouth fell open.

'Wow, you guys! Is this what real food looks like?'

'Eat up. You've lost weight,' said Denny. 'You can't afford to lose any more.'

'No, doctor.' A thought struck Maddy. 'Tanner didn't look too cheerful, did he? He looked . . . troubled, somehow.'

'I wonder if the investigation's going as well as the police are pretending,' said Rob.

'It's only been just over a fortnight since the bomb,' said Denny.

'Almost three weeks,' corrected Maddy.

She took another sip of wine. It tasted good. No one would know how good. Sometimes she just *needed* a drink. She'd held off since the bombing. Others would have turned to alcohol to forget but she'd been strong. She wondered how she'd have managed if she had not been cooped up in a hospital.

'The intelligence services must know who's behind this Sovereign IRA,' said Denny.

'I'll probably be in a minority of one here, but I don't see why, if they know who did it, they don't just go off and shoot them,' said Maddy.

'It's funny how one's personal experiences affect one's political thinking,' declared Denny.

'Pardon me?'

'Three weeks ago, I was a *Guardian*-reading, dyed-in-the-wool, pinko liberal. Since then, my views have lurched strongly in the direction of the hanging, drawing and quartering tendency.'

'So you agree with me?'

'Totally. What about you, Rob?'

Rob paused. 'You'd have to *know* the identity of the bombers. The police say they have suspects but no proof. That's not the same thing.'

'But assume that the police really were one hundred per cent sure who did it but couldn't bring them to trial. Then would you take the law into your own hands?'

'Yes, I would.'

'Do you think you could kill someone?' asked Denny doubtfully.

'I know I can,' said Rob softly.

There was a silence as Maddy and Denny absorbed his words.

'But what about this woman who planted the bomb?' inquired Denny. 'Could you kill her?'

'Rob wouldn't need to,' exclaimed Maddy. 'I would.'

'Really!'

'Why not? She knew what she was doing. She should get what's coming.'

'What if she has children?' persisted Denny.

'*I* had children,' spat Maddy, her eyes burning with hate. 'I wouldn't care if she's got half a dozen brats. I'd kill her in front of them – and tell them why.'

'Is *every* woman sick in the mornings?' demanded Teresa, pouring herself a glass of red wine from the bottle she had found in Breda's kitchen cupboard. 'Christ, I can't go on like this. I'll have an abortion, so I will.'

'I was bad with Aoife but I don't think I was sick when I was expecting Bobby.'

'It's not fair. Noreen, in the salon, sailed through her three pregnancies. She didn't even know she was expecting.'

'I'm surprised she knew who the fathers were.'

Teresa chuckled. 'I haven't told you about the girl today who came in and demanded a Mohican cut in bright red?'

'Never.' Breda gave up trying to work on the draft of the next newsletter, knowing it was impossible to concentrate when Teresa was in this chatty mood.

'She was pissed, stoned, whatever. She was certainly out of her tree.'

'What did you do? Send her off to sober up?'

'Did we fuck! We made sure she had the money on her and then had some fun. We shaved her head apart from this one strip in the middle which we dyed a brilliant red and then gelled up. It looks more like a cock's comb than a Mohican.'

'What did she say?'

'She seemed happy enough. Like I said, she was out of it. Cost her forty quid, though.'

'Who is she?'

'No idea. But you can't miss her.' Teresa finished her glass and helped herself to another.

'Are you sure you wouldn't rather a cup of tea? This is the danger time for you, you know.'

'Christ, Breda, don't *you* start. The only reason I'm drinking this wine now is that Dessie won't let me have any at home. He smashed my glass against the kitchen wall last night.'

'Never!'

'Prat. I made him tidy it up. You should have seen him trying to get the red stain off the wall. If he carries on like this, I'm going to end up with a newly decorated kitchen.'

'Oh, Ter,' laughed Breda. 'What's happening with your wedding plans?'

'We've settled on that wee church in Knockbridge. You know the one on that hill with the woods behind it.'

'It's a beautiful setting,' agreed Breda. 'What about the reception?'

'Drummore House Hotel.'

'Swanky. You were lucky to get in there so late.'

'I wanted Valentine's Day. No chance, but they had a cancellation for the following week.'

'That must be costing a bit.'

'Dessie can afford it. Well, he can if he works his arse off.' Teresa pulled out a cigarette and lit it. 'What do you reckon to a white wedding?'

'White!'

She caught Breda's old-fashioned look. 'All right, cream? Off-white, that sort of thing?'

'There's only five weeks or so to go to the wedding. You're really rushing this, Ter.'

'I want to *walk* up the aisle, not waddle up it, six months gone.'

'Dessie still doesn't suspect anything?'

'Not a thing. And he's getting quite paternal. I told you, he's throwing things at the wall now instead of at me. I want you to come to Dublin this weekend to look at wedding dresses and a little bridesmaid's dress for Aoife.'

'She can't wait. She's so excited about it. Did I tell you she got a gold star for a story she wrote about the famine? I don't know where she gets the imagination.'

'How's Bobby getting on?'

'Bobby's Bobby. He's never going to set the academic world alight, but he's happy plodding along. He's just been picked for the school's under-eight soccer team so he's well pleased.'

'And no more trouble from the boyos in Belfast?'

'They wouldn't dare,' replied Breda, handing her sister an ashtray just before she dropped ash on the floor. 'I reckon we've more support in South Armagh than the Provos now. People know they've been duped by the sell-out . . .'

'Right enough, Breda.' Teresa quickly choked off her sister.

'We'd thought we'd test the water by holding a rally just this side of the border, maybe in Castleblayney.'

'Christ. That's Provo country, that is.'

'That *was* Provo country.'

'That's taking the piss.'

'I'm not taking the fucking piss. Why is it that only the fucking

Provos have the God-given right to speak for the Irish people?' Breda rose to begin rooting around in the freezer in barely concealed anger.

'You're right, Breda. Me and Dessie'll be there. You can count on us.'

'Yeh, I know.' Breda smiled at her sister as Aoife and Bobby burst in through the kitchen door. 'Thanks.'

'Hello, you two.'

'Hello, Auntie Ter,' chorused the kids.

'Go and wash your hands. Your food won't be long.' Breda placed chicken nuggets in the microwave and began opening a tin of baked beans.

'Aoife, your mam and I are going to look for my wedding dress this weekend, so we'll get your bridesmaid's outfit, all right?'

'Grand.' The little girl was clapping her hands in excitement when there was a heavy knock on the front door. As Breda turned, she glimpsed a man in the garden. The knocking at the front door came again.

Breda and Teresa looked at each other.

The figure of a man filled the glass panel of the kitchen door. Teresa sprung to her feet, her eyes darting this way and that.

'What the fuck!'

The knocking was repeated. A deep voice called out. 'Garda. Open up.'

'Jesus!'

'What do they want, mummy?' Aoife looked as if she was about to burst into tears.

'Mrs Nolan. We have a warrant to search this house and the garden,' called the same deep voice.

Breda took a deep breath and walked into the hall. She opened the door a crack. A group of uniformed officers led by an inspector stood on her step.

'Mrs Breda Nolan? Please stand aside.' Breda folded her arms but the inspector brushed past her. 'Who's in the house, Mrs Nolan?'

'My sister and my daughter are in the kitchen. You can see my son there on the stairs.'

'If you'd all return to the kitchen, then.'

Breda was seething in fury but she knew she had to stay calm and make sure that Teresa didn't lose her rag. The police would love it if she flew off the handle and attacked one of them.

'Mummy, why are the police going upstairs?' demanded Bobby.

'Hush, darling. It's all right. Nothing to worry about.' Breda gathered her children to her side as an avuncular bear of a man in plain clothes shambled through the door.

'Aw, fuck. You!' Teresa glared.

'Do you have to swear in front of the weans?' complained Pat Rodgers.

'You stalking me or something?' demanded Teresa.

'Ay, you could say that, Teresa, girl. Ay, I am stalking you. The lot of you.'

'Who's this, Ter?' asked Breda.

'He's the git who had me and Dessie taken down to Dublin.'

'I want to see this warrant of yours,' began Breda. 'I'm getting my lawyer down here now.'

'Mrs Nolan, you can summon the Lord High Executioner himself,' replied Rodgers equably. 'It'll make no difference.'

Breda bent down to address her children. 'All right, you two. Why don't you go out to play for a while.'

'I'm afraid no one's allowed to leave the house while the search is being conducted,' said Rodgers.

'But they're children.'

'Did you know that two children were killed in the very bombing I'm investigating? Just about the age of your two, they were as well.'

'You're sick,' spat Teresa.

Rodgers ignored her. Instead he called to the inspector. 'Make sure you take the laptop computer in here as well as the desktop one.'

'How am I supposed to get out my newsletter without the computer?' Breda regretted her words as soon as she had spoken.

'That's not my concern.'

Despite his show of confidence, Rodgers was not optimistic. He saw only anger in Breda Bridges's eyes. She knew her computer's hard drive contained no incriminating evidence. Hell, she'd had plenty of time to get one of her computer geeks to destroy the old hard drive and install a new one by now. This raid should have taken place immediately after the first word pointed at Bridges and Conn Nolan but the powers that be had decided there'd been no prima facie case. Too sensitive, they had said. Bloody political policemen!

So now they were carrying out a fruitless raid while giving Bridges and her lot the opportunity to boast of police harassment.

'Go ahead and get the weans their tea,' said Rodgers. 'They'll be hungry after school.'

'And what are you going to do?'

'My team are going to search every drawer, every cupboard.'

'Be sure to look in the dirty-laundry basket,' sneered Teresa, pouring herself the last of the wine.

13

There is a green hill far away without a city wall, Rob Sage had told Tanner.

And now he stood here, high on this ridge above the medieval Tigrinyan town of Himora, holding the urns containing Alfred's and Mekaela's ashes.

His foreman Tabur Abebe had been waiting for him at the airstrip, wearing a clean white shirt over his frayed trousers as if going to a funeral. Rob handed him a leather bag containing the urns and climbed behind the wheel of the battered pick-up truck.

Tabur, tall and dignified, nodded. 'You have brought them home.'

'Yes.'

'That is right.' He regarded Rob with unblinking dark eyes. 'Where to, boss?'

'Up Abiy K'embo hill. Where we used to go. Remember?'

'You want priest?'

'Just you and me.' A priest would involve religion – and Rob wasn't talking to God at the moment. 'Let's go.'

He and Hannah had been whisked though Addis Ababa's new airport terminal by an Ethiopian protocol official who had driven them directly to the Addis Hilton Hotel, a well-watered oasis of luxury set in immaculate lawns. A junior minister and the British Embassy councillor were waiting at the pool bar to offer their condolences. Rob was puzzled at their presence until it emerged that the Ethiopian government had used the deaths of Mekaela and

Alfred to pledge its support for the international war on terror. Rob saw through their game. We're with you, America – so how about a few more million dollars in aid?

Surrounded by the fragrance of jacaranda, bougainvillea and jasmine, Rob had lunched on griddled diced steak seasoned with rosemary, thinking that while he was in the same country as poverty-ridden Tigray – he was in a different world.

Hannah was in her element, managing to be flirtatious, efficient, enthusiastic and sincere – all at the same time.

Rob was eager to return up-country and when he discovered that there was a flight to Himora that same afternoon, he was determined to catch it. Hannah would stay in Addis to inspect a drainage project in the capital's southern slums and follow on in a few days.

Now Tabur held the urn with the gentleness with which he would cradle a child as the truck bounced over the rough track. A few years ago, the Tekeze River had broken its banks here. Famine and disease had followed in the wake of the flood. And yet not ten miles away, up in the hills towards the Sudan border, there were women and children who walked four hours a day to fetch water, and bad water at that.

The track climbed steeply between eucalyptus trees until they came to a spur covered in coarse grass. Rob turned off the engine. He heard the call of an oriole and, looking up, saw high overhead the shape of a huge lammergeyer vulture. The air was warm and still.

Down in the valley, wisps of smoke rising from dried-dung fires marked where Himora lay within its ancient mud walls. Ahead, the sun was posed to plunge down behind peaks shaped like dragon's teeth. Dusk did not exist here in the Tropic of Cancer.

Rob placed the two urns on the red earth.

It was here, on this wedge-shaped ridge, that Rob had tried to explain about the Captain Pugwash characters. There was the blackened site of the fires he had lit to keep them warm at night. The rope hanging from the branch, Alfred's swing. Back under that acacia bush, he and Mekaela had liked to make love when they were alone – which hadn't been often with Alfred around.

In Rob's bag was a tape of the Coptic hymns that had been so emotive at the crematorium chapel in Salisbury. Out here, the idea seemed artificial and superfluous. Rob felt the inertness of the timeless land and knew he needed nothing but the silence.

The sun was impaling itself on the far peaks, throwing the mountainside into a swirl of indigo and black.

'Let their spirits free in their world, Tabur. Let their spirits free.' A breeze rose from nowhere. Rob released a handful of ashes onto the wind as the sun's last crimson ray flared – and then all was darkness.

'What a lovely cottage,' exclaimed Rose Allen, standing in the middle of the low-beamed living room of Rob's home.

'I can't believe how cute it is,' agreed Maddy, carefully spooning tea into the pot. 'Wait until I tell folks at home that I'm staying in a *thatched* cottage.'

'You're doing Rob a favour. Old cottages need to be lived in, especially over winter.'

'That's exactly what Rob said.'

Maddy set out cups, saucers and biscuits on the small table in front of the fire that she had painstakingly lit. It was all very English – but the room encouraged that sort of behaviour. It had not taken much to persuade her to stay in the cottage instead of the annex. She marvelled at the thickness of the walls, forgave the tiny windows which made the place gloomy and remembered to duck when going into the kitchen.

'I've bought a cellphone, I've got Rob's old station wagon and I've even been shopping to fill the freezer.'

Maddy did not say that she had also steeled herself to clear their rooms in the Red Lion. She had packed Tom and TJ's clothing into one large suitcase and arranged for the nearest charity shop to collect it. Rob must have done the same here for there was no evidence of Mekaela or Alfred's possessions.

'So, you're all set up.'

'I'm starting to be.' Maddy smiled, pouring the tea. 'But listen, I know so little about you. Do you live in Salisbury?'

'No. Up on the edge of the Plain. Really tucked away.'

'In a thatched cottage?'

Rose laughed. 'Not everyone's as fortunate as Rob. No, I've a small modern bungalow. You must come and visit some time.'

'Thank you. I'd like that.'

Rose was a type – that much was clear. A do-gooder who was more interested in others than in talking about herself. Maddy didn't think Rose was married – she didn't wear a wedding ring, or any rings at all. She might have been divorced or widowed, but Maddy would be prepared to bet she was a spinster. Maddy did not want to pry – still, a few gentle questions couldn't do any harm. 'Have you been down here long?'

'Less than a year. I was in London before that.'

'Didn't you once say you used to be a nurse?'

'Oh, that was a long time ago. Don't you miss all the modern appliances you have in the States?'

And that was all Maddy could get out of her. Later that afternoon, after Rose had left, Maddy wandered around the cottage, thinking that it possessed a warm, friendly feeling, when she remembered the parcel the police had left for her at the Red Lion; the parcel that Tom had been holding when he'd been killed.

She picked it up, turning it in her hands with an odd sense of foreboding. There was no name on it. Apart from one tear in the wrapping paper, it was remarkably intact. It felt soft and had been wrapped by someone who knew what they were doing.

The wrapping paper was not the usual Christmas sort. In fact, it looked more like birthday paper. But it wasn't her birthday, nor the kids'. Maddy prodded the contents with her fingers. Definitely clothing, probably wool from its springiness, she decided.

It was no good. She was going to have to open it.

With difficulty, Maddy peeled back a strip of adhesive tape. A cashmere jumper in a rich purple slowly revealed itself.

Purple!

Of course. It had been Trixie's birthday on 30 December.

But why hadn't Tom said anything?

Maddy held up the sweater. It really was beautiful.

Something fell out. Something purple. Maddy bent down to pick it up and found herself staring at one of the briefest thongs she had ever seen.

Special Agent Jorge Brupp fingered the knot in his tie and regarded the four men sitting in the secure office inside the American Embassy in London's Grosvenor Square. Outside, evening rush-hour traffic had clogged Mayfair in a gridlock of blaring horns but the only sound in this windowless room was the hum of the air-conditioning.

'Detective Chief Superintendent Hayward, I am authorized by the Director-General of the National Security Agency of the United States to release this transcript to you as a token of our cooperation and in the sincere hope that it will aid you in your investigation.'

'Thank you.' Hayward took the transcript, found there was a copy for everyone and handed them around to Tanner, Kilfoyle and Pat Rodgers.

'We've taken the liberty of overlaying the voice data onto our own cell-site analysis,' continued Special Agent Brupp, with a patronizing smile. 'And where possible we've ascribed the names of suspects to the phone calls. So now you not only know *what* they said but *when* and *where* they said it.'

The room fell silent as the four men read the transcripts.

11.35 Wylye cell site. Male believed to be Conn Nolan to unknown male in bomb car:

'All clear.'

'Got yer.'

11.49 Wilton. Nolan to same unknown male in bomb car:

'All clear.'

'Okay.'

11.51 Wilton. Nolan to unknown male at farmhouse:

'Are ye done?'

'No. There's a woman coming up the track.'

'Who is she?'

'I don't know.'

'Just do your job and call me when she's gone.'

11.54 Salisbury outskirts. Nolan to suspect believed to be Kevin O'Gara near Bristol Airport:

'All okay?'

'No probs. Your end?'

'So far . . .'

12.03 Fisherton Street area of Salisbury. Nolan to unknown male in bomb car:

'Clear to Lower Road. Proceed to lying-up point.'

'Got yer.'

12.04 Fisherton Street. Nolan to unknown male at farmhouse:

'Have you torched it yet?'

'The woman's just gone.'

'For fuck's sake, you can tell the time, can't ye? We want the fucking brigade out there when the big one goes up. Get a move on.'

'I'm just about to . . .'

12.10 Salisbury city centre. Female believed to be Teresa Bridges to Nolan:

'We're here. Toyota's okay.'

'Good. Stand by.'

12.11 Salisbury city centre. Nolan to bomb car:

'Move up now.'

'Got yer.'

12.11 Bristol Airport. O'Gara to Nolan:

'I'm through. Flight's on time.'

'Speak tomorrow.'

'Yeh, best of luck. Slay the bastards.'

12.12 Unknown male at farmhouse to Nolan:

'It's well torched . . . Wow! You should see it.'

'Get your arse into town. You're running late.'

12.14 Near Salisbury railway station. Unknown male in bomb car to Nolan:

'We're stuck in fucking traffic.'

'Okay. Call me when you're moving.'

12.14 Salisbury city centre. Nolan to Teresa Bridges:

'Wait. Wait. Hang on. Don't do anything yet.'

'Fuck!'

12.15 Near Salisbury railway station. Unknown male in bomb car to Nolan:

'It's okay. We're moving. On our way.'

'Good.'

12.16 Salisbury city centre. Nolan to Teresa Bridges:

'Car's on its way.'

'Thank fuck.'

'Get ready.'

12.19 Salisbury city centre. Unknown male in bomb car to Teresa Bridges:

'We're turning into the street. We've got the Toyota.'

12.20 Salisbury city centre. Teresa Bridges to Nolan:

'I've left the baby. Clock's running.'

12.20 Salisbury city centre. Nolan to unknown male in bomb car:

'Clock's running.'

'Okay . . . Fuck. There's a fucking car up the Toyota's arse.'

'Stay cool.'

12.21 Salisbury city centre. Nolan to Dessie Fitzgerald:

'There's a car behind you, he's between you and Big Brother.'

'Fuck! I see it.'

12.24 Salisbury city centre. Teresa Bridges to Dessie Fitzgerald:

'Get out of the fucking car. They're not going to move with you in there.'

12.26 Salisbury city centre. Teresa Bridges to Nolan:

'At last. The green car's moving away. Tell big brother to move up real fucking tight this time.'

'Will do.'

12.28 Salisbury city centre. Unknown male in bomb car to Nolan:

'In position. This is going to be a tight one. We're shaving it. I'm out of here.'

12.29 Salisbury city centre. Same unknown male to the unknown male from farmhouse:

'Where the fuck are you? No, it's okay. Got you.'

Pat Rodgers was the first to break the silence. 'This is good stuff.'

'Thank you.' Brupp accepted the praise as the Agency's due.

'But when do we get to hear the actual tape?'

'Er . . . we'd rather not do that at this moment in time.'

'Is there a reason for that?' inquired Tanner.

'It's . . . not the Agency's practice.'

'But surely in this case, after your President pledged his unconditional assistance,' pressed Rodgers.

'I hear what you're saying, sir, but I must repeat that it is not the Agency's policy to allow non-Agency staff to hear audio evidence. Not even the CIA or FBI get to hear it.'

'But . . .'

'Sir. This is as good as it gets. Most times, when we cooperate with outside agencies, we offer them an edited digest of what has been said. I've never known us hand over anything like this before.'

'And we're grateful,' muttered Kilfoyle.

'Forgive me. Perhaps I was being naive,' continued Tanner. 'But I was under the impression that we would actually get to hear the tapes, in the hope of identifying the speakers.'

'Sir, you *were* being naive.'

*

'So what was that about?' demanded Pat Rodgers as the four lowered themselves around a quiet table in a pub in Mayfair's Brook Street. 'I expected to hear a tape recording, not be given a transcript.'

'I'd say we're the victims of a turf war between the NSA and its rivals,' judged Kilfoyle. 'Sometimes the CIA, FBI and NSA spend more time fighting each other than they do fighting terrorism.'

'Can we go over Brupp's head?' asked Rodgers.

'We can try,' conceded Kilfoyle, turning a gold cuff link. 'Though it won't be easy.'

'Don't the two dead Americans count for anything?'

Kilfoyle looked into his glass and did not reply.

It was the first time the four men had met up in some days and Tanner and Rodgers at least were determined to use the occasion to hold a case conference.

Rodgers reported that, as expected, the examination of both Breda Bridges's personal computer and her laptop had drawn blanks. There had been nothing incriminating in the rest of the house, either.

'What's happening with the shit-shovellers, Cyril?' he asked, referring to the team going through the contents of the farmhouse's septic tank.

'It's taking longer to separate the DNA than Forensic first thought,' said Tanner. 'But I still can't understand how Intelligence could throw up names of the big three so quickly and then fail to provide anything about the foot soldiers.'

'That's the way it goes sometimes,' replied Kilfoyle. 'Maybe Nolan, Bridges and Fitzgerald are the only ones who live in Dundalk.'

'So that's where your informer is?' demanded Rodgers.

'I didn't say that.'

'Indeed you didn't. Because if he was, you'd be trespassing.'

Hayward cleared his throat. 'Before we start another turf war, I may have something. On the afternoon of the bombing, Michael Drumm, a fifty-five-year-old building labourer with known links to the IRA, arrived to stay with his sister in Camden Town. He immediately started drinking at a local Irish club where he attracted attention to himself because every time he got drunk he'd graphically describe people being blown up in an explosion. At least once, he actually mentioned Salisbury by name.'

'How do you know this?'

'One of our undercover men is a regular at the club. According to him, Drumm got plastered every night between 23 December and New Year's Eve and then, all of a sudden, stopped drinking.'

'Perhaps he made a New Year's resolution.'

'Perhaps Conn Nolan put the frighteners on him.'

'I'm sorry, you've lost me.' Tanner had the unpleasant feeling that he had been excluded from something.

'Nolan made a flying visit to London on New Year's Day,' confessed Hayward.

'I didn't know that,' exclaimed Tanner.

'It wasn't SB's finest moment,' continued Hayward quickly. 'Nolan caught them on the hop at Stansted Airport. They tried to follow him and lost him. Nolan returned to Dublin that afternoon. We don't know why he was here.'

'Why didn't anyone tell me?' demanded Tanner.

'You should have been told, I agree,' said Hayward.

'These things happen, Cyril,' Rodgers reassured Tanner. 'Not worth getting cross over.'

'Let's go back a bit,' said Tanner, staring hard at Hayward who refused to meet his eye. 'You say Drumm arrived at his sister's on the afternoon of the twenty-third? How did he get there?'

'We don't know.'

'One of the men in the bomb car was taken to Gatwick. That couldn't have been Drumm if he was going to London. Drumm made no phone calls to link up with transport so it's probable that he travelled to London by train or coach. Let's check CCTV footage at bus and railway stations to see if we can spot him. Do the Garda have his mugshot?' he asked Rodgers.

'I'll have it emailed over within half an hour.'

'But we still don't know for sure that Nolan warned off Drumm,' objected Kilfoyle.

'Our man's made a point of bumping into Drumm to invite him for a drink,' said Hayward. 'He refused. It's a shame, because Drumm could be the weak link we've been looking for.'

'I wonder,' mused Rodgers. 'On 31 December, a small-time villain called Jimmy Burke visited Bridges and Nolan at their home. Burke dabbles in petrol washing and smuggling on his cross-border farm. He *was* a signed-up member of PIRA. We didn't know he'd broken with them.'

'How do you know he has?'

'He wouldn't be visiting PIRA's Antichrists if he was still a moderate.' Rodgers downed the last of his drink. 'And if you put timings together . . . Burke calls to see Nolan on New Year's Eve. Nolan, who normally gets roaring drunk at his own New Year's parties, stays sober and flies to London early New Year's Day. The day Drumm stops drinking.'

'You can read too much into things, surely?' objected Kilfoyle.

'Ay, you can. But I've a feeling that these things are connected.' Rodgers looked towards Hayward. 'Can you get me the membership list of that Irish club? I'll see if my lads can make a connection with Burke. Maybe it's time we gave him a spin.'

'We may have a lead on the man who drove O'Gara to Bristol Airport,' announced Hayward. 'A camera covering the cargo area picked up a white Vauxhall Astra round the time O'Gara arrived. A man with a shoulder bag is seen to get out, walks away out of shot, then returns briefly for a word with the driver before leaving again. Unfortunately, the car is right on the edge of the camera's field of vision. The passenger *could* be the Pizzaman, although the quality is so poor that it wouldn't stand up in court. We've enhanced the film and we can make out the beginning of the registration plate: N20. Those letters are being run through the computers now.'

'Could the man be an airport employee?'

'We've eliminated all of them. The fact that this man was dropped some way from the departure terminal suggests that he was deliberately trying to avoid being seen.' Hayward glanced at his watch. 'Now I'm afraid I must tell you that I will no longer be running this case on a full-time basis. A parliamentary report out next week will identify the Al Qaeda terrorist organization as *the* major threat facing Britain. Consequently, I have to begin sharing my time between this inquiry and operations against them. Of course, the Anti-Terrorist Squad will continue as the clearing house for all intelligence information about the Sovereign IRA and this bombing.'

A few minutes later Hayward and Kilfoyle hurried off into the night, leaving Tanner and Rodgers sitting over their drinks.

'Don't look so fed up, Cyril. It was inevitable that Hayward would have to divide his time sooner or later,' said Rodgers.

'I can see what's going to happen,' replied Tanner bitterly. 'In a couple of months, there'll be just me, Graham and a few others. Then comes the first serious murder on my patch, I'll be taken off to run it, so the bomb inquiry will be down to two men and a dog. And we'll still be telling the relatives that we're pulling out all the stops.' He drained his glass. 'Bugger it. Another pint?'

'Why not?'

'I've been thinking about Mikey Drumm,' said Rodgers when Tanner returned. 'Not only is there no hard evidence against him, but if the Met's undercover man makes a witness statement it'll be uncorroborated.'

'And I'd bet you a pound to a penny that the undercover man's been plying Drumm with drink. Think of what the defence will make of that.' Tanner's mobile phone rang. A smile spread across his face as he listened. 'The shit-shovellers have just found traces of O'Gara's and Teresa Bridges's DNA in the septic tank,' he announced, putting down the phone. 'That pins them to the farmhouse. Just as well you had their DNA on file.'

'They're not exactly on file.' Rodgers looked embarrassed. 'They're what we took when we interviewed them recently. You know, off their mugs of tea and such.'

There was a moment's silence.

'But those samples won't be admissible as evidence,' said Tanner heavily. 'The defence will argue that they weren't legally and properly obtained. We're still no further forward.'

'Oh, Jesus. I thought I'd find you in here.' Deirdre Drumm marched furiously up to her brother sitting at the bar of the Irish Club. 'Your first day at work and what do you do afterwards? Go and get drunk. Saints alive. What are you doing serving him, Seamus? You should be ashamed of yourself, so you should.'

'You can't stop a man drinking – just because his sister says so,' muttered Seamus. 'Mikey's no trouble. He just sits there and drinks.'

'And just how long has he been sitting there and drinking, as you put it?'

'How do I know? I've better things to do than look at the clock all day.'

Deirdre glared around the drinkers at the bar as if defying anyone to argue with her before turning back to her brother. She did not see the man who had been plying Mikey with whiskey pick up the butt end of a roll-up from an ashtray and slip away. Outside the club he placed it inside a plastic envelope to drop off at the nick.

Mikey was still in his work clothes, a pint of Murphy's and a glass of Paddy's in front of him, smiling benignly at his own reflection in the mirror behind the bar. Alongside him another man shifted uneasily.

'Deirdre. You know Vince O'Lone. He's a cousin of Jimmy Burke.'

'Of course I know Vince O'Lone,' snapped Deirdre, squaring up to O'Lone. 'I trust you haven't been feeding him drink.'

'Not me, missus.'

'Has he said anything, like?'

'About what, now?'

'About . . . dead bodies, explosions, that sort of thing.'

'You mean like he was doing before Christmas? No. Not a word.'

Deirdre uttered a small prayer that she had been in time. She knew her brother's drinking moods better than he knew them himself. Mikey was in his at-peace-with-the-world stage of drunkenness but soon the calm would be replaced by the jumble of memory and imagination that was his recurrent living nightmare.

It had been Mikey's idea to work in England for a while – but if he was back on the drink, then he could return to Ireland tomorrow. Deirdre grasped the collar of her brother's donkey jacket and pulled his head down towards her own.

'You're a fool, drinking again after what Conn Nolan told you,' she hissed. 'If he hears you're back on it, he'll do you. You know he will. He's a nasty piece of work, that one.'

'Conn's a mate of mine. We go back a long way. Done great deeds together, me and Conn.'

'Then you'll know him for the man he is.'

'Away with ye.'

'Mikey, the man came to London to warn you himself, so he did. You carry on like this and you're a dead man walking.'

Mikey Drumm gave her a beatific smile.

The report of Mikey Drumm's reappearance in the Irish Club was on Hayward's desk when he arrived at Scotland Yard at six-thirty the next morning.

Hayward was keen to start his new duties. But first he had to deal with Mikey Drumm.

Drumm was picked up at the kerbside while waiting for the van to take him to the building site. He was driven to Paddington Green police station where he was held under the Prevention of Terrorism Act and the half-bottle of whiskey that he'd planned to drink for his breakfast was confiscated.

By noon Drumm was a sweating, trembling wreck – but he had

not uttered a single word. He refused to confirm his identity. He refused even to ask to go to the lavatory.

Deirdre, hearing that her brother had been picked up, left a message for Conn at his bar as soon as it opened at eleven o'clock.

Her conversation was recorded by the Garda and played back to Pat Rodgers within half an hour.

Nolan picked up the message at the same time. He said publicly that he had no idea why the London police had seen fit to arrest an old comrade like Mikey Drumm but he was sure that Mikey would not give them so much as the time of day. Not so much as the dirt from under his fingernails – and knowing Mikey, there'd be a lot of that. Privately, he started making inquiries and learned that last night Drumm had been drinking heavily again in the Irish Club. Nolan's eyes hardened.

At Paddington Green police station, Drumm continued to refuse to speak. He accepted cups of tea when they were offered, but he never asked for one. He took every cigarette he was given and went without when none was. Even the sight of his whiskey bottle, even the smell of the drink, brought not a sound from the shaking man.

But Deirdre's phone call had established a connection between Nolan and her brother. Soon Pat Rodgers had established that before Christmas Drumm had been working on a housing estate near Dublin for Nolan's building company. Although records showed Drumm had been paid up to Christmas Eve, he had not been seen on site since 18 December.

Finally, embarrassed British Transport police called to report that someone had accidentally erased the CCTV footage from Salisbury railway station. They were re-examining footage from Waterloo station at the London end.

Hayward shook his head in despair – then turned his attention to a mosque in East Ham with unhealthy links to Algerian fundamentalists.

14

'Welcome to Tigray,' said Rob, meeting Hannah as she stepped down from the Twin Otter aircraft. 'How did you enjoy the flight?'

'Terrifying. Some of those ravines make the Grand Canyon look like Cheddar Gorge.'

Rob was pleased to see Hannah wearing a sensible old bush shirt, slacks and boots. Her only concession to fashion was a baseball hat, with a blonde ponytail swishing out of the back, and a pair of wraparound sunglasses. Rob favoured an old floppy hat and hated wearing sunglasses.

He introduced her to Tabur who collected her bag and led the way to the pick-up. Rob set off, explaining about the local area.

'Himora is the chief town of the *wedera* or district. Population's around 18,000. It's doubled in four years, swelled by refugees from the war with Eritrea. In one refugee camp, a charity put in a standpipe, then promptly left the locals to get on with it. Of course, when it broke down no one took responsibility so the people went back to their old dirty wells. A classic case of unsustained development.'

'What happened?'

'That was my first job – to get it up and running and make sure the locals took charge of it.'

'Well done.' Hannah pointed out of the window. 'What strange-looking huts!'

'They're called *tukels*. They're made from stone because there's so little timber. Up here, you only find trees around a church or in a village. Centuries of erosion, deforestation and overgrazing have left the whole region dry and treeless.' Rob slowed to allow a small girl in an electric-blue frock to drive a flock of scrawny sheep and goats across the road. The girl waved and called out.

'Faranji.'

'Habesha,' replied Rob. The girl dissolved in delighted giggles.

'What was that about?' asked Hannah.

'She called us strangers so I called her Ethiopian,' explained Rob.

A group of men squatting in the shade of an acacia tree watched them pass, their faces expressionless as an ancient bus, belching blue smoke, swayed and growled towards them. A thicket of thin arms protruded from the open side windows and the roof was packed with people clutching huge bundles and crates of fowls.

Rob drove through Himora's outskirts speckled with shanties and ramshackle dirty white bungalows roofed with corrugated tin. Few had glass in the windows. Once in the mud-walled town itself, he turned off into a potholed lane which lay half in brilliant sunshine, half in dark afternoon shadow. Hannah glimpsed a street market through a mud archway.

'I love markets. Can we go and see?'

'Of course,' said Rob. 'We'll walk the rest of the way.'

Tabur slid behind the wheel of the pick-up as Rob and Hannah set off up the narrow alley that reeked of the open sewer which ran down one side. Hannah was immediately surrounded by chattering street urchins who each grasped one of her fingers and trotted beside her.

In the market square, women sat cross-legged on the ground with tiny scales to measure out the spices and chilli peppers used in *wat* – the staple spicy stew. Sacks of grain, called *tef*, sat next to meagre offerings of misshapen lemons and custard apples. Alongside them, traders were selling everything from bolts of brightly coloured cloth to treadle sewing machines and plastic tea strainers.

Rob made a play at bargaining before handing a woman three *birr* for five shrivelled oranges.

'How much is that?' asked Hannah as Rob led her to a rusty gateway set in a stone and mud wall.

'About eighteen pence. The locals would have had them for less than half that.'

'At least you speak Tigrinya.'

'Not really.' He did not say that Alfred was the one who loved haggling or that Rob would not be learning Tigrinya any more, now that his teacher was dead.

They passed into a compound resembling a builder's yard. In the far corner was the climbing frame and a swing he had built for Alfred.

'Welcome to our home.'

'Please sit.' Rob indicated a low couch while he perched on a stool at one side. Hannah had changed into a thin black cotton dress which enabled Rob to see exactly how much or, rather, how little she had on underneath. 'Tabur's wife Marta has prepared a feast to welcome you.'

'Please tell Marta that I'm honoured,' replied Hannah, taking in the sparsely furnished room with its whitewashed walls. Above their heads, a ceiling fan whirred and groaned.

'Try this *myes*.' Rob held up a glass to the solitary flickering light bulb so that Hannah could see the amber colour. 'It's a sort of mead.'

Marta, clothed in gauzelike white fabric from head to foot, glided in carrying a copper ewer in her right hand. In her left she held a bowl. A white towel was draped over her left arm. She bowed before Hannah.

'Ritual hand-washing,' explained Rob. 'Hold out your right hand.'

Marta poured warm water over Hannah's fingers, catching the

drops in the basin. She handed Hannah the towel before repeating the ceremony with Rob. She left to return with an hourglass-shaped wicker table covered with what appeared to be a coarse grey cloth.

'It's sourdough bread called *injera*. Watch.'

Marta emptied the contents of a number of small bowls onto the bread. Rob ripped off a small piece of *injera*, spooned on a little of one of the dishes and rolled it into a pancake. He held it delicately up to Hannah's mouth.

'I can help myself, thank you.'

'It's the custom. You're my guest.'

'If you're sure.' Hannah allowed Rob to pop the parcel into her mouth, saw Marta watch in approval from the doorway, smiled back – and then her mouth caught fire.

'Ethiopian cuisine is the spiciest in Africa,' explained Rob, after he had refused her demand for water – like throwing kerosene on flames, he said – and made her eat a purée of ground peas instead.

'What the hell was it?' gasped Hannah, fanning her mouth.

'*Derho wat* – chicken stew with hard-boiled eggs. It shouldn't be *that* hot.'

'You try it, then.'

Rob did so. 'No, that's all right,' he declared judiciously.

'What's that one?' Hannah pointed suspiciously at a dark red dish.

'*Tibsi.* Beef in hot pepper paste. That *can* be a little hot,' he admitted. 'Keep drinking the mead.'

'What's that one?'

'*Kitfo.* Like beef tartar. You eat it last.'

'If I get that far.' Hannah leaned forward to try to make a pancake of the vegetable stew. As she did so her dress gaped, allowing Rob to glimpse her naked breasts.

Rob dropped his eyes and concentrated on making his own pancake.

'Did you know Ethiopia claims to be the only country in the

world to have thirteen months of sunshine?' he asked. 'It has a thirteen-month calendar. Twelve months of thirty days and one of five; six in a leap year. Ethiopia's also eight years behind our Gregorian calendar.'

'Really.'

The light bulb flickered, then went out. The fan creaked to a halt.

'Happens most nights,' explained Rob as Marta came in carrying two oil lamps. 'I'll get the generator going if you like.'

'No. This light is beautifully soft. Let's keep it.'

'It'll be warm without the fan.'

'I don't mind if you don't.' Hannah leaned forward again.

Rob had stopped averting his eyes by now. He reckoned she must know what she was doing and if she didn't mind him looking at her breasts – then he certainly didn't.

'You must try to get to Axum while you're in Tigray. The Ark of the Covenant is meant to be hidden somewhere there,' said Rob.

'I won't have time.' Hannah held up her food parcel for Rob's approval. 'I'm looking forward to travelling around with you. I hope I'll be some company.'

He noticed Hannah was regarding him from sleepy, half-closed eyes. It occurred to him that she was letting him make the first move. The air had become heavy, embracing him in its cloying warmth.

Marta brought in a tray of coffee in tiny metal cups.

'Good night,' she managed in English.

'Good night,' chorused Rob and Hannah.

There was a silence before Hannah said gently, 'It doesn't do any good to dwell on the past, Rob. Life must go on.'

'I know.'

He looked up from his coffee cup to find that Hannah had slipped her dress over her shoulders so that it fell around her waist.

Life for Wayne Wallis was going from bad to worse.

Three nights ago Shaynee's muscle-bound husband Scott had

accused his wife of having it off with Wayne, she had gleefully told him the next morning, relating how she had laughed in Scott's face. This morning Scott had arrived home unexpectedly early. While the increased risk of discovery was fuelling Shaynee's sexual excitement, it was having the opposite effect on Wayne who found it hard to concentrate with Scott liable to burst in at any moment.

And it was not just his sexual failures that were depressing Wayne. He had relied on Leanne's wages from the bakery to top up his dole money while he ducked and dived, scraping together a few quid from his scams. But yesterday he'd had a letter from the local social security office telling him that full benefit was about to end, pointing out that he had failed to attend any job interviews.

Wayne had hurried around to the office to explain that he was receiving grief counselling, and that he couldn't possibly be considered for full-time employment – only to be ordered to produce a medical certificate to that effect or his benefit would be cut.

The final blow had come an hour ago when his solicitor had told Wayne bluntly that he was not eligible for criminal compensation for the death of Leanne. Wayne was still feeling sorry for himself three pints of lager later.

He had just left the pub when he spotted a slim attractive woman walking towards him. There was something familiar about her.

'Hi. How're you doing?'

As soon as Wayne heard the American accent, he realized it was Maddy Lipzinger – but a different Maddy. And looking good in a long sheepskin coat, blue denims and ankle boots. Wayne knew nothing about women's clothing but he recognized class when he saw it.

'Yeh, all right. I didn't expect to see you here.'

'I needed to get out.'

Wayne remembered that Maddy's daughter was still unconscious in intensive care. 'How is Mitch?'

'The doctors say she could wake up tomorrow or next month. I've got a cellphone so they'll call me if anything happens.'

'Keep your pecker up.'

'Sorry?'

'Keep your pecker up. Don't lose hope, yeh?'

'Right. Keep your pecker up.' Maddy made herself overcome her reservations about Wayne, and smiled back. 'I'll remember that one.'

'How do you cope for money when you're over here?'

'It's not a problem,' replied Maddy, startled at the directness of the question.

'You're lucky.'

'Aren't you working?'

'I'm still not up to it, really.'

'What do you do?'

'Bit of this, bit of that. Decorating, painting, gardening. I'll turn my hand to anything. I've just been to the Job Centre – but there's nothing there.' Wayne brightened up. 'I might try becoming an actor like Denny. Can't be difficult, can it? I mean, just learn some lines and spout them out again.'

'I think there's a bit more to it than that,' replied Maddy. 'I know Denny went to RADA, but why don't you ask him? I'm sure he'd help you.'

'You think so.'

'Let me have your telephone number and when I see Denny, I'll ask him to call you.'

'I don't mind telling you, I miss my Leanne.'

'I understand.'

'Leanne was shopping for my Christmas present that morning. I didn't want her to come into town. I told her not to bother but she was determined to get me a surprise. She'd been saving, doing overtime. We didn't have much money but we were happy. We were going to get married, have kids.'

'She sounds a lovely girl.'

'She was.'

Maddy was overwhelmed by guilt. She had instinctively disliked

Wayne as an unfeeling Jack the Lad. Now here he was, talking movingly about the woman he had loved and lost.

Yes, it just went to show how wrong you could be about people, thought Maddy as she walked towards the car park.

She had put on a cheerful front to Wayne but, in fact, the three days since she had opened Tom's parcel had been dark days indeed.

As Maddy had held up the purple thong, a wave of nausea had washed over her. She did not know how long she had stood there. In a daze, she had opened a bottle of wine, poured herself a glass and subsided onto the floor in front of the fire.

It was only as she was finishing her second glass that Maddy became aware that she was drinking by herself – something she had vowed never to do again. Fuck it. She was angry with the world as a whole and with herself in particular. She poured herself another glass.

So Trixie had not been a harmless flirt, after all. Despite sneering at Trixie's affectations, Tom had fallen for her large bosom and her bubbly laugh – even though the woman was pig thick. Maddy had thought that her husband preferred intelligent women – but then, what had she known?

Those times when Tom had encouraged Maddy to take the kids up to the cabin for a few days, saying *he* was too busy working but that *she* should enjoy herself. Those nights when he was supposed to be at motor dealers' gatherings in Albany or New York city.

What a fool she had been. What a gullible fool.

After the fury had come the self-analysis. Why had he gone off with another woman? How had Maddy failed him?

It'd been inevitable that their sex life hadn't retained the white heat of the early days but she'd always been willing when he'd wanted her. Though now, thinking about it, when she'd suggested it just before they came away Tom had pleaded tiredness. Now she knew why.

Maddy was confused to find the wine bottle was only one-third empty. Surely she'd drunk more than that. Then she saw the other bottle empty in the hearth. She'd opened a second one without knowing.

Feeling the first pangs of fear, Maddy put a log on the fire and stared at the flames.

A dread knowledge seeped into her mind – and that scared her even more than her return to drinking alone. She had not loved Tom. She understood that now. The pain she was feeling was from the blow to her pride.

In fact, if she was brutally honest with herself, she hadn't loved Tom for some time. But then why had she demanded that they come to England for Christmas? Because she had refused to admit it to herself, and because she was desperate to keep her family together. Maddy had coped with Tom's one-night stands – with the help of a bottle – but this time she had sensed he was getting in deeper.

Miss fucking Purple. She could scratch the bitch's eyes out for what she had done to her family.

It was an odd feeling – grieving for a husband you knew you didn't love.

Maddy stared into the flames and wept.

A cold rain had been falling since breakfast but now the low clouds had finally moved off to the east to allow patches of blue sky in the last hour of daylight. Tanner and Pottidge had taken advantage of the dry spell to get out of the Wilton Road incident room, now just ticking over as the team ran out of leads to follow. The loss of the closed-circuit film from the railway station more or less summed up the inquiry team's luck with CCTV. Not only had the bombers taken out the main one in the mall but another, covering a busy junction, had been blocked by a delivery van while a nineteen-year-old assistant in the shop opposite the bomb car had forgotten to change the film on the morning of the attack because of her hangover.

Tanner was getting the feeling that this investigation was jinxed.

There was good circumstantial evidence linking Drumm to the bomb car. Not only did Drumm's build match that of the smaller bomber but Rob had described how the man had taken a swig from a bottle as soon as he'd left the car. That sounded like Drumm. But that was not enough. Tanner desperately needed solid evidence.

Searches of footage from the bus station had drawn a blank. So too had footage from his direct route to the station along busy Fisherton Street. That left the longer route along residential Crane Bridge Road and Mill Road. The route that Pottidge and Tanner set off to walk now.

To their left the pale wintry sun was beginning to set over the deserted water meadows. In the summer they were packed with tourists feeding the ducks. Now a solitary swan was holding station against the flow of the river Avon.

Tanner needed to walk. He needed to get out of the claustrophobic incident room and think in the fresh air. He was dismayed that, although DNA matches for Teresa and the Pizzaman had been found at the farmhouse, Crown Prosecution Service lawyers reckoned that not only were they inadmissible but their very possession might taint future sound evidence.

Pottidge was outraged – and failed to understand how they had arrived at their decision.

'The lawyers reckon that because the evidence was illegally acquired, then anything else that we get out of the line of inquiry arising from that evidence is also tainted,' explained Tanner.

'Don't you feel we're fighting with one arm tied behind our backs?'

'Very often, Graham,' replied Tanner gravely. '*Too* often, in fact.'

'And the bloody Yanks let us down.'

'The NSA now say that voice recordings of mobile-phone intercepts have never been accepted as evidence, even in the States, because you can't be one hundred per cent certain of identifying the voice.'

The detectives passed the roundabout where the bomb car had

been delayed. As they neared the station, Tanner pointed to a deserted shop. 'What was there?'

'A children's-wear shop which folded in October,' replied Pottidge. 'A couple of Asian traders moved in for a couple of weeks in December selling stocking-fillers, Christmas decorations, that sort of thing.'

'Did they have a camera?'

The two detectives peered through the whitewashed windows. 'Yes. There it is. Pointing at the door.'

'When would this place have finally closed?' asked Tanner.

'Probably Christmas Eve.'

'So the previous day's footage might still be in there?'

'It's worth a try,' agreed Pottidge.

'At this stage, Graham, anything's worth a try. Let's find the keyholder and get him down here.'

The two men had just turned back into Fisherton Street when Tanner spotted Bella Fryer and her husband Frank, peering in the window of a fabric shop, Bella's nose close to the glass. As he approached, the couple turned away and made to cross the road. At the kerb they halted and looked right and then left, straight at Tanner. He waved but they ignored him.

'Mrs Fryer,' Tanner called out, striding towards her.

'Yes?'

'It's Detective Superintendent Tanner. You remember.'

'Of course. How are you, Mr Tanner?'

'Fine. And you?'

'This weather doesn't agree with my old bones.' She had recognized him now, but Tanner was troubled.

'Mrs Fryer, can you read the name of that greengrocer's shop across the road?'

'Trumble's.'

Bella replied before even looking. Something made Tanner eye her husband. Frank gave a weak smile.

'We shop there,' he said mildly.

Bella shot her husband a filthy look.

'What about the number plate on that white van, then?'

Bella squinted, blinked and squinted again.

'I haven't time for these games,' she said impatiently.

'Mrs Fryer, the defence counsel will want to test your eyesight in the courtroom. It's best that I know now,' said Tanner.

'Our Bella's got wonderful near sight,' explained Frank. 'But she needs glasses for long distance and she won't wear them.'

'Can't stand glasses,' muttered Bella angrily.

'But how did . . .?' Tanner suddenly knew how Bella had managed to identify Teresa and Dessie. There had been tiny pencil marks on the backs of the photographs he had handed her, identifying their provenance. Tanner couldn't make them out without his glasses but Bella had managed to. He bet that he'd find the pictures of Dessie and Teresa were inscribed with *Garda* on the back while the others would say *Wilts Police*.

'I was only trying to help,' Bella mumbled sullenly.

Just when Tanner thought things could get no worse, he had just lost his one and only witness.

'Daddy thinks we should get married, Damien.'

'Sorry?' Damien Kilfoyle adjusted his black bow tie in the bedroom mirror and pretended not to have heard his girlfriend.

'Here, let me do that. We're going to be late at the embassy reception at this rate.' Fliss Fakenham tugged at the ends of the tie. 'Daddy thinks we should get married,' she repeated.

'With all respects to Daddy, darling, it's fuck all to do with him.'

'He can be a bit of an old fuddy-duddy, I know, but he's got your best interests at heart.'

Calling Fliss's father a bit of an old fuddy-duddy was like calling the emperor Caligula a bit of a madman, thought Kilfoyle, but held his peace. Even though Hector Fakenham CMG had retired a year ago, he was still a byword for moral rectitude inside the Service. It was fear of his disapproval that made Kilfoyle and Fliss maintain separate residences. Kilfoyle had his place here in Chiswick and she kept a small apartment in Wandsworth.

'What do you mean?'

'In our new positions it would be considered . . . inappropriate to live in sin.'

'What new positions?'

Fliss stretched her long neck to one side to judge if her diamond pendant earrings went with her cocktail dress before turning to look over her shoulder.

'Are my seams straight?'

'Yes, darling. They're perfect. Now, what new positions?'

Fliss winked at Kilfoyle. 'Daddy tells me you are about to be transferred to the vastly enlarged, new super-duper, all-singing, all-dancing International Counter-Terrorism department.'

'Really! And how does Daddy know this?' Kilfoyle lightly kissed the end of her nose.

'Watch my make-up.' Fliss examined her nose in the mirror. 'He had dinner with the director of personnel at his club yesterday.'

'Ah. Any clue of my role in the new department?'

'Oh, yes, darling. You're going to be deputy head boy.'

'What!' Such a high-ranking appointment at his age was virtually unprecedented in the Service. Normally he'd have to wait five years or more even to be considered.

'It seems you are dearly beloved by the powers that be.'

'What's *your* new job?'

Fliss smiled. 'I'm to be deputy head girl of Serious Crime.'

'Congratulations.'

'Thank you. But you see why Daddy feels we're rather too . . . senior to be shacking up together.' The doorbell sounded. 'That'll be the taxi. Don't stand there gawping. We'll make this *our* year, Damien, darling.'

'Yes. Yes, we will.'

They would, too. The Service's golden couple, blessed with both looks and brains. But even as he followed Fliss out of the door, Kilfoyle found himself wondering what Jimmy Burke was doing at that moment. And for the first time in his life, Kilfoyle wished another man dead.

15

Rob enjoyed the drive up into the hills. They set off just after dawn, the pick-up's rear packed with bags of cement and sand, pipes, sheets of corrugated iron, entrenching tools, pickaxes and spades.

And under the rear seat, within easy reach, was a blanket covering something that Rob hoped he would not need – and which he hoped Hannah need never know existed.

The metalled road ended within twenty minutes of leaving Himora, and the going became slower. Soon the conical hills gave way to a wild mountainous landscape full of hard angular shapes. They passed flocks of sheep and goats, tended by small children who waved excitedly at the sight of the white faces.

Hannah was unusually silent this morning. Rob had to stop himself from pointing out things as he had done with Alfred. He missed the boy's chatter and his endless questions which could fill up a whole journey.

He heard the pair of them talking in his head.

'See the sparrow weaver bird.'

'Why's it called a sparrow weaver?'

'Why do you think?'

Alfred put his finger to his lips. 'I don't know,' he said finally.

'Because it's a sparrow that weaves its nest, numpty head.'

'Not a numpty head. Why does it weave its own nest?'

'Because it can't afford to buy one.'

'Why?'

'Do you know how much sparrows earn?'

'Five *birr* a week?' hazarded Alfred seriously.

'Five *birr* a week! Not even big vultures earn that much.'

'How much, then?'

'Enough to feed their family, if they're lucky.'

'Who pays them?'

'Ah.' Now it was getting serious. Rob would not mislead Alfred. 'No one pays them.'

'That's why they can't afford to buy a house.'

'Exactly.'

Shit! He missed the little boy.

They climbed steadily through terraced valleys, passing a crocodile of women, each with an earthen pot strapped to her back. Rob pointed out a rock-hewn church and a huge cave which served as a monastery.

'There seem to be a lot of churches,' observed Hannah.

'There's one priest for every ninety-two members of the Coptic faith,' said Rob. 'And one doctor for every twenty-eight thousand patients.'

Finally the track emerged onto a dun-coloured plateau dotted with thorny scrub.

'We're now in the triangle of land between Eritrea and the Sudan. The badlands.'

'Is it dangerous?'

'The local bandits know me, so they're not a problem. The same can't be said for the Eritrea Islamic Jihad Movement.'

'They're the ones who planted the mine that crippled Alfred?'

'Yeh. They're trying to destabilize the region. They murdered two Dutch aid workers in southern Eritrea last year, and they've destroyed irrigation projects further east in Afar province.'

'If it's not safe, then you should pull out.'

Rob bristled. 'I'm not running away from terrorists.'

'It's not a question of running away. One of my tasks is to assess the security situation. We can't have our people working in a danger area.'

'So you'd abandon thousands of Tigrinya for the sake of one white man, would you?'

'No, but . . .'

'You'd be playing into the EIJM's hands. I am *not* leaving here until I've finished the projects I've started.' They pulled up alongside a well on the edge of a sprawling village of conical stone huts. 'Come and see what we're trying to do here.'

Rob's arrival was greeted by a crowd who seemed to appear magically from nowhere. Once the introductions had been made, Hannah peered at the stone-lined well capped by an ancient-looking pump.

'As you can see, it's very basic. That way, there are fewer things to go wrong. Before I dug this, the women had to walk three miles for water, often to find that it had been contaminated by cattle faeces. Now we must have coffee with the headman while Tabur starts taking water samples and checks the latrines.'

'The latrines?'

'The villagers will look after the water supply because it's in their interest to do so,' explained Rob. 'They aren't so good at using the latrines. Part of Mekaela's job was to get the locals to understand basic hygiene.'

Surrounded by excited villagers in grubby *shamas*, they made their way past browsing donkeys and a few thin-legged goats to enter a dark stone hut with an earthen floor. Hannah and Rob sat on a low wooden bench as women began roasting coffee beans. When the beans were smoking they were passed to their guests.

'The smoke is supposed to be a blessing,' explained Rob.

'So tell me about this well, then.'

'It's ten metres deep and lined, partly to prevent pollution and partly to make it more stable. Because we couldn't get pre-cast concrete rings up here, we built a drystone casing. At the level of the water table, the lining's porous to allow the water to seep into the well.'

The thick coffee was served to them in tiny ceramic cups without handles. Hannah drank, scalding her tongue.

'We had to decide between a pump or bucket and windlass. If you can get the spares, then hand pumps are better because they prevent contamination,' continued Rob. 'Did you know that just one gram of faeces can contain one hundred parasite eggs, a thousand parasite cysts, one million bacteria and ten million viruses?'

'Golly. You really know how to talk dirty to a girl.'

Rob spent the next hours working on the well and servicing the pump. Half an hour before sunset, Tabur came up, looking worried.

'*Gele koynka alokha?* What's wrong?'

'Stranger come. He say *shifta* in next valley.' Tabur pointed to the north. *Shifta* was the all-encompassing word for brigands. In this case Tabur meant EIJM terrorists.

'How far away?'

'Three hours, maybe four.'

'How many?'

Tabur held up two hands.

'It's okay. We're not going in that direction. We're taking Hannah to look at the well at Adi Ajari.' Rob calculated. 'If we set off now, we could end up breaking an axle in the dark, then we'd be sitting ducks. We'll leave at first light.'

Rob relayed the news to Hannah.

'We'll give them a wide berth. Don't worry.'

That night they camped alongside the pick-up – preferring the cold to the bedbugs that infested the huts – and ate omelettes with *injera* and a can of sliced peaches. Later, when everyone was asleep, Rob lay in his sleeping bag and marvelled at the stars.

He listened to the utter silence and felt a long way from anywhere. Under the bundle which served as his pillow was a 9mm Makarov automatic pistol.

*

Mikey Drumm had finally broken his silence. Not so much broken it but shattered it into a thousand babbling fragments. He had started talking in his sleep and continued to talk to himself when he had woken.

Hayward and Tanner stood outside Drumm's cell listening to his ramblings.

'Oh, mother of God, save me now. Look at that wee child. Where's her eyes? For pity's sake. Oh, Jesus, it's terrible, so it is. Don't step in that blood, girlie. Don't. Don't. Sweet Jesus.'

'I'd say he was going round the twist,' said Tanner. 'Has a police doctor seen him?'

'When he was first brought in,' replied Hayward. 'He said Drumm might exhibit symptoms of alcohol-dependency withdrawal in a day or two.'

'They were called DTs in my day.'

'The doctor said he'd give Drumm something to sedate him if they got too bad.'

Tanner shot Hayward a sharp glance. 'He looks all right to me.'

'Just what I was thinking,' said Hayward. 'Let's have him in the interview room.'

The man who shuffled in was a stooped, slack-jawed wreck. Drumm had difficulty controlling the saliva dribbling from the corner of his mouth while his eyes, moist and reddened, had sunk into the putty of his unshaven face. Even though he was wearing a paper boiler suit while his own clothes were being forensically examined, he reeked of urine and stale rancid sweat. Drumm sat down at the small table, one hand clenched tightly around the other. A police officer came in with a cup of sweet tea and a bacon sandwich.

Drumm retched. 'Och. I've no stomach for food.'

'Drink that tea. You need the fluid,' said Tanner, worried now that they might have to send Drumm to hospital after all.

'Can't drink it.' Drumm huddled into himself even further.

'If you don't drink that, we'll get a doctor to section you under the Mental Health Act,' warned Hayward sternly. 'You'll be committed to a psychiatric ward while they evaluate you.'

'And then you won't get to *see* a drink for months,' said Tanner, finding that he and Hayward had already fallen into the good cop, bad cop double act.

Drumm groaned. 'Oh, please God. Don't be a-doing that now.'

'Drink your tea, then. Here's a packet of fags.'

Drumm wrapped first one hand and then the other around the mug. His hands, then his whole forearms began to shake as he fought to lift it off the table. Tanner found he was willing the little man on but Drumm's hands were trembling too much. After one seismic effort, when his whole body convulsed, he gave up and lowered his head to sip from the mug on the table.

Tanner lit a cigarette and passed it to Drumm.

The little man drew on it greedily. Then he jerked upright. 'Jesus, I've never seen so much blood. Not even in my time in the slaughterhouse in Wexford. The gutters ran red, so they did.' Drumm was staring sightlessly straight ahead. 'That poor little girl. Her arm still holding those flowers. Severed it was. Severed like a piece of raw meat.'

'What's he seeing?' mouthed Hayward.

Tanner shrugged. 'Christ knows. Nothing from Salisbury, that's for sure. Maybe he took part in another bombing we don't know about.'

'The only bombing in recent years with the sort of injuries he's describing was at Omagh – but Drumm wasn't involved. I reckon he's making it up.'

'It's real enough for him,' whispered Tanner.

Drumm blinked and seemed to see the two detectives for the first time. 'Holy mother of God, I need a drink. I need a drink, I tell you.'

'There's a few things we want to talk about and then we'll see about that drink.'

'Fuck off.'

'Why did they leave you to take the train by yourself?' asked

Tanner. 'Everyone else left by car or motorbike. Why did *you* have to take public transport?'

'What?'

'It doesn't seem right. Why should you, the oldest, be the poor bugger who has to do it the hard way?'

'It's always the same,' muttered Drumm.

'Why's that?'

Drumm shrugged.

'Your mate had a motorbike to take him to Gatwick, yet you had to hoof it.'

'Was it because you fucked up and let that green car get between you and the block car?' demanded Hayward brutally.

'Bollocks I did. I could do with a drink.'

'Talk to us, then.'

'I'm not talking myself into a jail cell.'

'Look, Mikey, this is just between us.' Tanner came round to perch on the table. 'You've not been cautioned, have you?'

Drumm's eyes narrowed as though he suspected a trap. 'Haven't I?'

'No. This whole conversation is off the record. We're just having a chat. If you want, this hasn't taken place.'

'Well, then, if this isn't taking place, I'd as well go back to my cell, if it's all the same to you.'

'That'll be a shame, Mikey.' Tanner drew Drumm's bottle of whiskey out of his pocket.

The little man's eyes followed the bottle as if he was hypnotized.

'Just a wee dram,' he wheedled.

'We need to chat.'

'I've told you, I'm not talking myself into twenty years.'

'What if we gave you immunity from prosecution?' asked Hayward.

'And a new identity and a fat wad of cash to start a new life somewhere. Maybe in the States. You could spend the rest of your days at ease, drinking Jack Daniel's.'

'Don't like Jack Daniel's.'

'Whiskey, then. Just think of it, Mikey. A new name, never having to work again and whiskey. All the whiskey you want.'

'You mean I wouldn't have my sister nagging me all the time?'

'Ay.'

'I want a drink.'

'What if we grant you immunity from prosecution for what you did?

'What if you gave me that bottle?'

'What if we gave you this bottle and immunity?'

'And what would you want from me?'

'Just tell us what happened.'

'You'd want me to grass up me mates.'

'Mikey, your mates are already wondering what you're telling us. You're going to have a hard job convincing them that you managed to go without a drink for all this time. They'll think you came to a deal.'

'They know me better.'

'Not when we put the word out on the streets,' said Hayward.

'Fuck off.'

'Listen, Mikey, we know most of it, anyway,' said Tanner. 'We know Conn Nolan was the coordinator. We know the Pizzaman made the bombs, Teresa planted the come-on and Dessie drove away the block car. You'll be amazed how much we know.'

'So you don't need me, then.'

'And you don't need this bottle.' Tanner went to put it back in his pocket.

Drumm stretched out his arm towards the whiskey. Tanner could almost see the demons battling inside the little man.

Tanner placed the bottle on the table. Drumm looked at it for a long long time. Tanner thought he was about to refuse, but slowly Drumm's clawlike hand reached out and closed over the whiskey.

Tanner expected Drumm to twist open the cap and drink immediately, but it was enough that Drumm had the bottle safely in his possession.

'I'm not going to jail. I want a bit of paper that says that, all official-like. And I know bugger-all about the English brothers who ran the errands.'

'But you'd know them again if you saw them?'

'Oh, ay. But I'm not saying a dicky until I get a proper bit of paper.'

'Wayne said what!'

'He wants to become an actor. He reckons there's nothing to it but learning a few lines.' Maddy smiled at Denny Fox's indignation.

'He didn't say anything about avoiding knocking over the furniture as well, did he? By the way, I love that trench coat. Miu Miu, isn't it?'

'How did you know that?' Last night Denny had phoned to invite her for morning coffee. Now they had met up outside Salisbury's Guildhall, he was being secretive about where they were heading.

'No more news from the police?' he asked as he led the way across the city.

'None at all. I think they reckon they need a bit of luck.'

Denny began declaiming. 'Good Luck, she is never a lady, But the cursedest quean alive, Tricksy, wincing, and jady – Kittle to lead or to drive. Greet her – she's hailing a stranger! Meet her – she's busking to leave! Let her alone for a shrew to the bone And the hussy comes plucking your sleeve.'

'Denny, that's wonderful but I don't understand a word of it.'

Denny continued. 'Largesse! Largesse, O Fortune! Give or hold at your will. If I've no care for Fortune, Fortune must follow me still!'

'That's really good.'

'Kipling, dear heart. This way.'

They entered a quaint, old-fashioned room permeated with the aroma of coffee and chocolate. A grey-haired waitress removed a Reserved sign from a table in the mullioned window.

'Salisbury's premier coffee shop selling the finest handmade chocolates and pastries,' announced Denny, showing Maddy to the table.

'You obviously have influence here.' Maddy smiled, sitting down.

'This, dear heart, is my inheritance. Clive left it to me. I found out yesterday.'

'You mustn't change anything. It's perfect.'

'I agree. It attracts a steady business among ladies of a certain age and class, and the amount of chocolates people buy is astonishing.' The waitress approached. 'What will you have, Maddy? What about Blue Mountain? Yes? Good. A cafetière, please, Betty, and a selection of pastries, especially your wonderful chocolate eclairs.'

Betty simpered with pleasure and left.

'You've already won over the staff,' observed Maddy.

'As soon as the panto finishes I begin shooting the next thirteen episodes of the hospital horror so Betty is going to manage the place for me.'

'Don't you ever want to do something serious?'

'Join the ensemble at the National, a season with the RSC at Stratford?' Denny sighed. 'I have played Shakespeare. Tybalt in *Romeo and Juliet* in Regent's Park, Fluellen in *Henry V*.'

'But surely, you can . . .' Maddy paused, head cocked. 'I think that's my cellphone.'

They both listened to the faint ringing coming from under the table.

'Shit! It *is* my phone.' Maddy snatched up her handbag and scrabbled inside. She was all fingers and thumbs, frantically pressing this button and that.

'Oh . . . Come on . . . Come on . . . It's a text message . . . from the hospital. *Urgent you come ASAP Amrit.*' Her eyes widened in fear. 'Oh, God, Denny.'

Maddy was on her feet; Denny signalling to the waitresses to get their coats. Then they were out of the door.

'This way,' called Denny and set off at a fast jogtrot.

'You don't have to come.'

'You'll get lost.'

Clutching her coat around her, Maddy ran after him. The cold air rasped in her lungs as she dodged around knots of pedestrians and darted across roads. Near the car park, Denny demanded her keys and sprinted ahead so that by the time she arrived he had the old estate car already backed out. With Denny at the wheel, flashers going and headlights on, they roared through the narrow streets.

Mitch must have taken a turn for the worse – and Maddy had been out enjoying herself. Perhaps her daughter was already dead. Maddy would never forgive herself. She had let Mitch down.

'Don't die on me, Mitch. Don't die.' Maddy's lips were moving in a silent prayer. 'I'm coming.'

Denny swung off the final roundabout and up the hill towards Salisbury Hospital. He braked sharply outside the entrance, Maddy leaping out of the car while it was still moving. She dashed through the foyer and up the stairs, trench coat flying behind her. Wide-eyed, tears streaking her white face, Maddy ran as she had never run before. A security man called out to her but she ignored him. She dashed around wheelchairs along the broad corridor that she knew so well; past signs for various wards, past the operating theatres, past an unconscious patient on a trolley. All the time she was sobbing, 'Please God, please God.'

Maddy crashed through the doors into Intensive Care. Dr Amrit was standing in the doorway to Mitch's room. He was saying something. Maddy swallowed once and barged past him.

Mitch turned her head and smiled up at her.

The tears flowed. Tears of relief and gratitude mingling with tears of pain and anguish. Maddy fumbled sightlessly for her handkerchief.

'Mommy, are you all right?'

'Oh, yes, honey. I'm all right.' Maddy dried her eyes, mumbling apologies for making a fool of herself. 'How are *you*?'

'Kinda woozy, I guess. Where am I?'

'In a hospital, honey. But you're all right now.'

Mitch was struggling to keep her eyes open. Pooch lay in the crook of her arm. She was absent-mindedly sucking her right thumb – something Maddy hadn't seen her do for years.

'What happened?' Maddy whispered to Dr Amrit.

'Rose Allen popped in to see Mitch and noticed an increase in brain-stem activity on the monitor. She told the nurse, who told me and I called you.'

'Rose Allen!' Maddy looked around for her friend.

'She's gone to see another client,' said Dr Amrit. 'She'll be back.'

'And Mitch woke up, just like that?'

'We said it would happen one day. Today's the day.'

'Hmmmm.' Mitch yawned. 'Mom, what's happening?'

Maddy gazed fondly down at her daughter. The first blush of colour was emerging in Mitch's waxy cheeks.

'You've been asleep, sweetheart.'

'I've had funny dreams.'

'You've been asleep a long, long time.' Mitch was trying to sit up. 'Careful, honey.'

'We can take most of these monitors away now,' said Dr Amrit.

'Does this mean the worst is over?' asked Maddy quietly.

'We'd hope so. Let's see what happens in the next day or two but it should be plain sailing from here on in.'

'Mom?'

'Yes, honey?'

'I'm hungry.'

'That's my girl.' Maddy laughed and choked back her tears at the same time.

The Minister of State for Security, Policing and Prisons at the Northern Ireland Office initialled the bottom of a page of the report in front of her and turned over to the next page. Tanner shifted his weight from foot to foot, glowering with impatience. Alongside him, Hayward stood absolutely still.

Petula Anstey crossed out a line with her silver propelling pencil, and spoke without bothering to look at the two men.

'So, as I understand it, you want NIO approval to come to a deal with a confessed terrorist?'

'That's not quite accurate, Minister,' replied Hayward smoothly. 'We are making informal soundings, as the DAC made clear to your officials, before we approach the Home Office.'

Anstey peered up sharply at the implied rebuke. In her late thirties and in her first government post, she was a woman to watch, said the parliamentary gallery. One who would go far through perseverance and devotion to whoever was in power and whatever their policies.

'So what do you want, then?'

'We need to know whether the NIO would countenance granting immunity from prosecution to someone who would give evidence leading to the conviction of those responsible for the Salisbury bombing.'

'You have such a man, or woman?'

'We believe so.'

'And he, or she, is one of the bombers?'

'Yes.'

'A known criminal?'

'No record as such, Minister, although he is known to be a member of the IRA.'

Anstey tutted in disapproval.

'Minister, many of today's senior Sinn Fein politicians are known to be yesterday's IRA men.'

Anstey bristled. 'I take it that this request means that your investigation has stalled.'

'Nothing of the kind – as our reports to Number Ten indicate.'

Tanner noticed the way Hayward had slipped in a reminder of the Prime Minister's personal interest in the outrage. Hayward had moved fast since Drumm had signalled his willingness to do a deal. Tanner had assumed that the speed with which this meeting had been set up was an indication of the investigation's importance. Now he was disconcerted by the Minister's belligerence.

Petula Anstey blinked twice and returned to the attack. 'Basically, you want me to countenance a supergrass. That's what they're called, aren't they? Supergrasses?'

'It's not a word I would choose,' replied Hayward.

'But that's what you want, isn't it? To recruit someone inside the gang willing to turn Queen's evidence in return for cutting a deal. Then a new identity, a pot of gold and we pay for them to live abroad.'

'I take it that you personally, Minister, are against the concept?'

'It is not a question of my personal inclinations. There are many factors to be weighed here. Apart from consulting the Attorney General and the Home Office, we have to consider Sinn Fein's reaction to a supergrass.'

'What's it got to do with them?' demanded Tanner.

'One would have thought that Sinn Fein would welcome the removal of the dissident hardliners who are currently undermining their position,' said Hayward smoothly as Anstey looked disdainfully at Tanner's naivety.

'The Prime Minister has promised the relatives that he would do everything to help bring the bombers to justice,' Tanner reminded her. 'In fact, he said he'd go to the ends of the Earth to nail them.'

'I am aware of the Prime Minister's words.' Petula Anstey pressed a bell on her desk to signify that the interview was over. 'I will take soundings among my colleagues.'

'And when may we expect to hear back from you?' asked Hayward.

'When I have completed my soundings. Good day.'

For Maddy, the past few hours had passed in a wonderful blur. Her miracle had happened. There was a God after all – even if he was only a part-time god.

Denny, who'd been expecting to find Mitch dead, was now wooing her with his charm.

'I'm Denny. I've seen a lot of you, but you've never seen me, have you?'

'No.'

'Yes, you have,' coaxed Maddy. 'Denny's on TV – in that commercial you like.'

Mitch frowned in concentration. Then her face lifted. 'With the chimp. Yeh!'

'The chimp's called Gerald. Would you like to meet him?'

'Can I?'

'When you're better, he'll come and have tea with you, if that's all right with your mum.'

'Wow! Cool.'

Maddy and Denny were sent outside while a team of senior doctors and consultants descended to conduct a series of tests. They emerged to tell Maddy that first indications were good. Very good indeed. Physical and cognitive functions had returned intact. Mitch was still very weak, of course, and there were more tests to be conducted – but the general prognosis looked excellent. Denny left to go back to the coffee shop to spread the good news. Mitch drifted in and out of sleep.

When Rose Allen arrived, Maddy threw her arms around her.

'Rose, I can't thank you enough.'

'The lamb was waking up by herself.'

'Mitch, this is Rose. She's a good friend.'

The little girl sat up and sipped orange cordial. 'Mom, what happened?'

'What do you remember?' asked Maddy, softly.

'I don't know . . .'

'There was an explosion . . .' began Maddy.

'A bomb?'

Maddy hesitated. 'Yes, a bomb. You were blown backwards and you hit your head.'

'How's daddy?'

'Daddy's fine.'

'And TJ?'

'TJ's fine, too.' Maddy pressed her tongue hard against her front teeth to stop herself crying. Doctors had warned her that to tell Mitch the truth now could be disastrous for her recovery. Maddy hated herself for lying.

'Where are they? I want to see them.'

'Um . . .' Maddy swallowed hard.

'They're in another part of the hospital, my lovely,' said Rose.

Maddy said a silent thank-you. Her own brain was refusing to work when it came to answering – or not answering – Mitch's questions.

'Can I see them?'

'When you're better. What do you remember?'

'Me and TJ were waiting in the mall for daddy. TJ was playing on his stupid Game Boy. Daddy bought us doughnuts. He said not to tell you because you'd be cross.' Mitch looked up at her mother. 'But you're not cross, are you, mommy?'

'No, honey. I'm not cross.'

'I was playing smiling at people. I got lots of smiles . . . except from this one lady. She was weird.'

'How was she weird?' Maddy struggled to keep the edge out of her voice.

'She was carrying an old bag and pretending to look in shop windows, except she wasn't. I could tell.'

Maddy shot a glance at Rose who was listening intently.

'How could you tell?'

But Mitch ignored the question. 'Then she pulled out this old KFC box and put it in the trash can real careful. I said it was a baby.'

'A baby?'

'I only said it to wind up TJ.'

'What did this lady look like?'

'She had glasses. She wasn't . . . right.' Mitch was getting tired.

'I know, she was like the lady at Banbury Cross . . . on a white horse.'

'What's that, sweetheart?'

But Mitch was drifting off to sleep again.

'What was she saying?' asked Rose.

'I think it was something to do with a nursery rhyme,' whispered Maddy excitedly. 'The day before the bomb, Mitch bought this book of nursery rhymes. She kept reading them over and over. Is there one about a lady on a white horse?'

Rose shook her head. 'Don't you think Mitch was just dreaming about nursery rhymes?'

'Could be,' agreed Maddy. 'But it does sound as if Mitch saw the woman who planted the bomb.'

Rose Allen left soon afterwards. Maddy was sitting by the bedside, listening to her daughter's rhythmic breathing, when Graham Pottidge burst in, a huge grin on his face.

'Isn't it great?' He beamed. 'After all this time.'

'Twenty-five days. It's like the end of a long tunnel,' Maddy replied.

'Mr Tanner's in London. I've told him the news. He's going to call in tomorrow morning. My wife sends her best wishes. She's been saying a prayer every night for Mitch.'

'Thank you.' Tears welled in Maddy's eyes. It was always the same when someone was being genuinely nice.

'Is it possible to talk to her?'

'Not today,' said Dr Amrit, appearing at his elbow. 'Remember, Mitch doesn't know that her father and her brother are dead.'

'Of course, I'm sorry. Whatever you say.'

'Once a paediatric psychiatrist has visited her, we'll see then. We have to take these things gradually.'

Dr Amrit's bleeper sounded and he scurried off, muttering to himself.

'I think Mitch saw the bomber,' whispered Maddy. 'She's talked about a woman acting oddly.'

'Great.'

'What do you know about nursery rhymes?'

'Helen used to recite them to Jack . . .'

'Is there one about a lady at Banbury Cross and a white horse?'

'Ride a cock horse to Banbury Cross. See a fine lady on a white horse. With rings on her fingers and bells on her toes, she shall have music wherever she goes,' recited Pottidge.

'Mitch said the woman behaving oddly was like the lady on the white horse.'

'With rings on her fingers and bells on her toes, she shall have music wherever she goes,' repeated Pottidge slowly. 'She certainly wouldn't have bells on her toes. Rings on her fingers? I'd have thought the bomber would have worn gloves.'

'So what's Mitch talking about?' demanded Maddy.

'I wish I knew.'

16

Rob and Hannah were breakfasting on luncheon meat and cups of tea as the first rays of sunlight pierced the gloom over the distant hills. To dispel Hannah's fears about the terrorists, Rob pointed out that they were heading away from where the guerrillas had been sighted. He did not tell her they'd be travelling towards to the Sudanese border where EIJM had their secret training camps.

It was a bone-rattling drive to the next well. At first the track fell away from the plateau down to a steep fertile valley with extensive stone terracing. But soon the greenery ended and they found themselves travelling along hot dry valley floors where the earth was a dirty white and even the scrub looked unhealthy. They passed tiny naked boys, their *shamas* folded on their heads like pads, tending emaciated long-horned cattle. Once they met a donkey caravan loaded with salt coming the other way.

After six hours Rob's shoulders were aching from grappling with the steering wheel. But now they were close to their destination he started to relax. Not for long.

The first indication that something was wrong came as they approached a tiny compound, inhabited by a single poor family. On Rob's first visit here, he'd spotted that the wife and her three small children all had discharges from their eyes – the first symptom of the trachoma that would ultimately blind them.

Antibiotic ointment and a lecture on hygiene from Mekaela had cured them. Ever since, as soon as they heard the sound of the pick-up's engine, the family would be standing in the track to greet Rob.

This time the compound was deserted. Rob and Tabur exchanged glances.

From the top of the ridge they gazed down on a broad shallow valley where settlements of stone houses could be seen as white specks in the distance. To the right, giant terraces stepped down to a slumbering brown wattled plain. Here and there rose table mountains with vertical sides of blue-grey rock. Above each mountain floated its own white cloud.

'Look at that,' breathed Hannah.

They followed the winding track down into the valley. They were rounding a bend near the first village when Rob spotted a man cowering inside an acacia bush. As Rob pulled up, the man shrank back, his eyes rolling in fear.

'Ask him what's happening, Tabur.'

The answer came in a torrent. Four EIJM soldiers, armed with Kalashnikov assault rifles, had taken over the village and executed the headman. Now they were charging fifty cents for a can of water from the well – instead of the normal two and a half cents.

'We'll have to go and get the police,' said Hannah.

'The nearest police post is three hours away,' Rob pointed out. 'They're poorly armed and not equipped to take on terrorists like these. They wouldn't even try.'

'What are we going to do, then?'

The face in the bush vanished. In the rear-view mirror, Rob saw that a man had appeared on the track behind them. He wore a military-style shirt and carried a Kalashnikov.

'We don't have any choice,' said Rob. 'We have to go on into the village.'

The gunman began hurrying towards them. Rob accelerated around the bend. When he knew he could not be seen, he halted and jumped out. Tabur reached under the rear seat and slipped him the Makarov pistol without Hannah noticing.

'What are you doing?' she demanded.

'Checking the load's secure in case we've got to get out in a hurry,' called Rob.

He checked the Makarov's safety catch was up before putting the pistol down his waistband in the small of his back. It was not ideal and certainly did not make for a fast draw – but it was all Rob could think of.

They drove slowly passed the first stone huts. There was not a soul to be seen. A flock of brown and white goats bleated forlornly.

The well was in a clearing of red earth backed by low scrub. Three men, who had been squatting on their haunches, rose to confront them. Each carried a Kalashnikov. Rob halted some distance off.

'You stay in the cab,' he ordered Hannah. 'I'll go and talk to them.'

'I'm coming with you.'

'I don't know how those men will react to the sight of a white woman.' He hoped Hannah would take the hint. 'Let's not inflame the situation more than we can help.'

Rob and Tabur climbed out. Rob held up his hands, palms outwards, to show that he was unarmed, then made a show of stretching as if he had been on the road for hours. He was in no hurry to approach the gunmen. Instead he carried on stretching, putting his hands in the small of his back and arching backwards. As he did so, he weighed up the fighters.

One was much older and lighter-skinned than the others, with a quiet air of authority. The other two were in their late teens. The one on the right was stocky, bristling with anger, with restless eyes and coarse features. The one on the left was slighter and looked nervous.

Finally, when Rob was satisfied they were comfortable with his hands disappearing behind his back, he walked towards them. Tabur followed, clutching his *dula*, the hefty walking stick that all highlanders carried.

Rob and Tabur were committed now. It would be no use trying to flee. Rob ran his eyes over the assault rifles. You could tell the quality of troops from the way they looked after their weapons. These Kalashnikovs were soiled and dirty. Rob was marginally reassured.

'Why are you here?' asked Rob in faltering Tigrinya.

To his surprise the older man – Rob reckoned he must have Arab blood – answered in American-accented English. 'This is our land. You are an imperialist dog meddling in things that do not concern you. Get out of Africa. Go back to the Great Satan.'

'I came to see that the well is working.'

'It is working.'

'Why are you charging the people money for their own water?' Rob wished he could turn to see where the fourth man was. He did not like the idea of someone behind him, or near Hannah.

'It is of no concern to you.'

The stocky thug brought up his AK to point it at Rob.

Rob tensed. The older man and the thug began to speak very rapidly among themselves. Rob guessed that they were arguing about the implications of killing the *Faranji*. Tabur clearly thought so because he growled deep in his throat and moved imperceptibly closer to the men fingering his club.

'No,' commanded Rob beneath his breath. Tabur would be mown down before he'd gone three yards.

Rob slid his right hand towards the butt of the automatic. He decided he'd take out the angry young thug first because his reactions would be the fastest. Then the older man in the centre and finally the nervous young boy – if he got the chance.

The men stopped arguing. Instead, they were staring at something over Rob's shoulder.

Oh, shit.

Hannah appeared in the corner of his eye. She had taken off her baseball cap and her blonde hair hung down to her shoulders.

The mood changed. The gunmen gawped at Hannah as if she was a vision. The only sound was the bleating of the untended goats. The atmosphere had become electric.

The young thug stepped up towards Hannah, reached out and stroked her hair. Then, before Hannah could move, he grasped the top of her bush shirt and tore downwards. As Hannah went to cross her hands over her naked breasts, the thug pulled the shirt down over her shoulders, pinning her arms by her side.

The men gave an audible hiss. For a second they stood mesmerized by Hannah's bare white breasts. Rob stepped towards her. The older man thrust the muzzle of his AK hard into Rob's cheek as Hannah wriggled free. She clenched her shirt tightly around herself and whimpered.

'Stop,' cried Rob.

The man struck him in the face with the gun barrel, cutting his cheek with the front sight. Rob stumbled back. The thug raised his AK, pointing it straight at Rob. Tabur must have been about to make a move because the older man's rifle swung towards him.

'No.'

Hannah's breath was coming in rapid shallow bursts.

'Listen to me, Hannah,' muttered Rob, hardly moving his lips. 'I want you to move away from me to your right and slowly open your shirt.'

'What?' The word came out as a plaintive sob.

'Move away and open your shirt.' Rob looked the older man in the eye, shrugged as if to accept the situation and placed his hands on his hips. Then he took a step away from Hannah. 'I want them looking at your tits – not at me. And when I say *down*, hit the deck.'

The thug began closing on Hannah. In a second Rob would not have a clear shot.

'For fuck's sake. Open your shirt.'

There was no mistaking the desperate urgency in Rob's voice.

With a small mewing sound, Hannah pulled her shirt wide open. The thug licked his lips. The other two made hissing noises between their teeth.

Rob grasped the butt of the Makarov and eased it out of his waistband, flicking down the safety with his thumb.

Now! He dropped into a crouch, his right hand coming up fast, his left hand wrapping around his right.

'Down.'

Both eyes open, he fired twice at the stocky gunman.

Tap-tap.

Saw both rounds hit the upper torso.

Swung to his left. The older man was bringing up his Kalashnikov. Too late, sunshine.

Tap-tap.

One shot was high. Blood spurted from the man's neck.

Rob swung further to the left. The boy had not moved. He was just standing there, mouth open. But he still held his gun.

Rob had more time to aim.

Tap-tap. Both rounds entered the boy's chest.

Rob spun around, searching for the fourth gunman. There he was – just fifty yards away. He was making no effort to fire. Instead, he began backing away. Then he turned and ran.

Rob jammed the pistol back into his waistband, wincing at the heat of the barrel against his skin, and picked up the nearest AK. It was set on full automatic. He slammed back the operating handle, dropped on one knee and fired.

The first shots went wide. Then, as he mastered the gun, Rob brought the rounds on target. The gunman twitched like a demented marionette and crumpled to the ground.

All was silent apart from the bleating of the goats. The smell of cordite lay heavy in the still air. Hannah wrapped her torn shirt tightly around herself, swayed backwards and forwards and began wailing.

Ten minutes later, Rob held a cold compress to the wound on his cheek and watched as the villagers, who had reappeared as if by magic, carried the four bodies into the scrub. Three of the Kalashnikovs had already vanished. Rob held on to the fourth, and a spare magazine. The Makarov had only two rounds left, and he was taking no chances.

Reaction had set in as soon as Hannah had been taken away by the women to be comforted and have her shirt repaired. Rob had felt the wave of nausea coming from deep in his guts. He had stepped into the bush, dropped to his knees and vomited until he tasted the bitter juices. Back in the clearing he was given a mug of *tella* and a double shot of arak, which he drank gratefully.

He found Hannah sitting naked to the waist at the centre of a circle of women marvelling at her pale skin. She seemed not to notice that two or three had plucked up the courage to gently stroke her back.

He dropped down level with her. 'How are you feeling?'

'Why did you do that?' she demanded in little more than a whisper.

Rob opened out his hands helplessly.

'You killed four men.'

'Miss, they bad, bad men,' said Tabur in his slow deep voice. 'You be dead and . . . if not for boss.'

'But why did you kill the one who was running away?'

'If he'd escaped, he'd have brought back his comrades to massacre the whole village.'

'What happens when the police find out what you've done?'

'No one here will ever breathe a word.'

'So that's it, is it? You kill four men but there's no blame. No punishment. You just get on with your life.'

'Whoa. Slow down. You're becoming hysterical.'

'But you can't just *kill* people.'

'Hannah, get real.' Rob grasped her wrists and made her look him in the eye. 'They were going to kill us, and rape you. Remember!'

'Oh, Rob. I'm sorry. Rob . . . I'm going to be sick.'

Hannah rose and staggered away. She returned, hands still across her breasts, looking even paler. Rob begged a little of the arak for her. Once she had drunk it and put her shirt back on Hannah pulled herself together.

'I think we should leave now.'

'Hannah, we cannot drive over that track in the dark. We have to wait until dawn. And anyway, the villagers are having a feast in our honour.'

'Oh, yes. Rob the saviour. You're making quite a habit of being a hero, aren't you?' Hannah sipped more arak, coughing at the fiery spirit. 'I'm sorry, I know I should say thank you. But it's all too raw at the moment. I've never seen anyone killed before.'

'I know.'

'It's not what we're supposed to do. We're supposed to help people.' Hannah recognized the paradox. 'Yes, all right. You saved the well and stopped me being raped, and it would have been my fault, and we would all have been killed, but . . . but . . . I've never heard of a charity worker killing people before.'

'No. We're usually the ones who get killed.'

'You're God's warrior, aren't you, Rob?'

'No, Hannah. I'm just a bloke who digs wells.'

'Not here. Not any more. You can't stay in Ethiopia after this. Suppose it got out.'

'It won't.'

'It might,' she insisted. 'If you want to carry on working on water projects then I'll get you a transfer to somewhere else. Tanzania, or somewhere. But you *cannot* stay in Ethiopia. You must be able to see that.'

Rob was not sure that he could. 'What'll I do?'

'Go back to the UK while I work things out.'

'But I came here to get away from there.'

'Sorry, Rob.'

17

'I thought I told Conn to do something about those kids selling drugs near Aoife's school.' Breda Bridges braked sharply to a halt.

'The shortarse is Jake, Dapper Smith's eldest. I've never seen the other one, though,' said Teresa. 'Ignore them, Breda. Let Conn and Dessie sort it out.'

'I thought Conn *had* sorted it out,' hissed Breda. 'And where are the Garda to let this sort of thing go on in broad daylight?'

She leaped out onto the pavement in front of the startled teenage boys. 'You two. What the fuck do you think you're doing? Piss off out of it.'

'You talking to us, missus?' demanded the taller boy. Jake Smith whispered to him but his mate shrugged defiantly.

'Conn said we could sell here, Breda,' mumbled Jake.

'That he did not.'

'We don't need your fucking permission, anyway,' said the stranger.

Crack. Teresa charged past Breda and caught the boy an open-handed blow. He reeled back, blood spurting as Teresa's heavy rings broke his nose.

'Time you learned some manners, yer bit of shite.'

'Leave it, Ter,' ordered Breda as her sister raised her hand to strike again. She addressed the teenagers. 'You two are young to be doing without your kneecaps, so you are, but if you ever come within a mile of this school you can kiss the fuckers goodbye. Is that understood? Good – now fuck off.'

'You'll be getting a call,' Teresa shouted after them as they scuffed away. She glared at the taller boy, defying him to open his mouth, but he was too intent on trying to staunch the flow of blood dripping onto the pavement.

Breda pulled out her mobile phone. 'Conn . . . There's lowlife back near the kids' school. Dapper Smith's boy Jake and some older kid I didn't know . . . Someone's putting them up to it, then . . . From West Belfast? Taking the piss, like? You need to get it sorted.'

She closed the phone to report. 'Conn's sending Stozza and a couple of the lads around to Dapper's place. Sounds like someone's trying to stir it on our patch.'

'Conn won't like that,' said Teresa.

'Bloody right, he won't. Very territorial, is our Conn.' Breda swung out to overtake a milk float.

'Christ, Breda. Slow down. I feel sick enough in the mornings as it is.'

The sisters were on their way to Dublin in a second attempt to buy Teresa's wedding dress after their previous shopping expedition had floundered on Teresa's unusual indecisiveness. Should the dress be ivory or buttermilk, with a train or without, plain or elaborate? Breda did not think she had ever seen her sister dither so much.

'Sorry.' Breda remembered something that she had been meaning to raise. 'Ter, do you know what blood group the father is?'

Teresa snorted with derision. 'Blood group! I don't even know his surname. Why?'

'You're blood group O, the same as me, aren't you? If the child turns out to be blood group A and Dessie's group B, then the child can't be his.'

'Dessie'll never notice.'

'What blood group is Dessie?'

'How the fuck do I know? Anyway, don't worry. Dessie's not the sort to wonder about blood groups.'

'Just trying to think of everything.'

'As always.' Teresa glanced affectionately at her sister.

'If it's not one thing, it's another,' groaned Breda. 'I just hope Mikey Drumm's keeping his lip buttoned.'

'Mikey Drumm'll not say a word.'

'That's what Conn says but drink changes a man. Mikey's not the fighter he once was. You can't trust a man when he's in hock to the demon alcohol.'

'You sound like some old-time preacher.'

'I want Mikey back this side of the water as soon as he's freed. Assuming they do spring him.'

'Coppers here are just as bad as in London. Have the Garda handed back your computers yet?'

'No. I've had to borrow a laptop to get out the newsletter announcing the Castleblayney rally a week today. Recruiting's really picked up since the bomb.'

'Are the weans going?'

'No. There could be trouble.'

'That's grand, that is,' laughed Teresa. 'You don't mind your pregnant sister getting involved in a free-for-all.'

'Ter, I'd back you against six of those PIRA wankers any time – even when you were nine months pregnant.'

Teresa took that as a compliment. She flipped down the sun visor to examine herself in the vanity mirror.

'Do you think my face is getting fatter?'

'No. And anyway you could do with a little more flesh on your bones.'

'I'm already starting to swell up. Look at the way these rings are cutting into my hand. I reckon I'm going to be a size.'

'You'll be biggest in the summer months, too.'

'Aw, thanks, Breda. You know how to cheer a girl up.' Teresa swivelled towards her sister. 'I finally got Dessie to talk about the honeymoon last night. He wanted to go to Miami, but I told him he wouldn't get a visa with his track record so we're going to Gambia instead.'

'Sounds great.'

'And I've agreed the menu at the reception. Waiter service for the top table. And a buffet for the others. Five bottles of wine per table – works out at about half a bottle each. If they want more, the buggers can pay for it themselves. The meal's costing a fortune as it is.'

'Well, you couldn't have chosen a posher place.'

'I'm worth it.'

'So now we're waiting on our political masters to see whether we can use Mikey Drumm or not,' Tanner told Pat Rodgers on the phone. 'Drumm's not going to play ball unless he has immunity and the full protection package. I can't say I blame him. He'll be crossing a hard bunch of bastards.'

'I'd say you've got yourself a prize there, Cyril. Drumm's been around a long time. He knows where the bodies are buried. He probably helped to dig the graves. That was his sort of role. If he opens up, he could crucify not just the Salisbury bombers but also a lot of republicans who've now gone legit,' declared Rodgers. 'And we may have something else. You remember the hidden camera outside Nolan's house picking up a character called Jimmy Burke who we thought tipped off Nolan about Drumm's drinking?'

'Ay.'

'Our Customs boys searched his farm yesterday on an unconnected tip-off. Burke was furious. Kept dropping hints about friends in high places.'

'Interesting.'

'Customs didn't find the cigarettes they were looking for, but in Burke's bedroom they came across a plastic bag from Amsterdam's Schiphol Airport decorated with Christmas scenes. Burke claims he hasn't been abroad for two years. He could be the other man in the bomb car, the one who was taken to Gatwick. From there, he could have flown home via Amsterdam. We're getting the bag dated now.'

'It's another line of inquiry. God knows we need them,' admitted Tanner. 'Now, I've a question for you.'

'Fire away.'

'Why would Teresa Bridges remind someone of the nursery rhyme "Ride a Cock Horse to Banbury Cross"?'

'*See a fine lady on a white horse, with rings on her fingers and bells on her toes,*' completed Rodgers. 'That's easy. You've never seen anyone with so many rings as Teresa wears. Huge, heavy things like knuckledusters. Why?'

'Because it sounds as if the little girl actually saw Teresa put the bomb in the litter bin.'

Rodgers whistled.

'I'm going up to the hospital now to have a chat . . .'

Graham Pottidge burst in, looking wild and distraught.

'It's Mitch Lipzinger. She's dead.'

The first thing that struck Tanner was the empty bed. He had become used to seeing Mitch surrounded by drip stands and monitors. Now the bed looked naked, somehow. The drama played out over almost four weeks had ended. And without the participants, this became just one unoccupied room in intensive care – waiting for the next patient, the next crisis. Tanner shook his head sadly.

A nurse had discovered during a routine check at seven o'clock that morning that Mitch had stopped breathing. An hour earlier, the little girl had been sleeping soundly. Every attempt had been made to resuscitate her but Mitch had been pronounced dead at 8.05 a.m. – just as Maddy had arrived to have breakfast with her daughter.

Tanner examined Mitch's body in the mortuary. There were no obvious signs of a struggle, no defence injuries. No bruising. The post-mortem would reveal more. At this stage, no one knew whether her death was suspicious or not.

It could be something as simple and as tragic as sudden death syndrome, said Dr Amrit, who kept shaking his head as if he could not believe what had happened.

'What a terrible, terrible thing,' he kept repeating. 'To fight all this time and then just slip away. Terrible.'

Graham Pottidge too was taking Mitch's death personally – more personally than a police officer should. To give him something to do, Tanner sent him to interview the head of hospital security who volunteered that the closed-circuit cameras on the ICU floor had gone blank for twenty minutes from 6.35 a.m. Engineers were on their way to check the system.

'Suspicious?' asked Pottidge.

'Happens sometimes.' The security man shrugged.

Tanner, with his distrust of coincidences, demanded that everyone on duty in the hospital between six and seven o'clock that morning should be interviewed. Videotapes from the hospital's other closed-circuit cameras were to be checked immediately.

'This is a terrible tragedy,' murmured Rose Allen, who had already been with Maddy when the detectives arrived.

'You're here early,' observed Tanner.

'I was going to do Maddy's shopping so she could spend the day with Mitch,' Rose replied.

Finally Maddy came out of her trance to acknowledge Tanner's presence.

'I'm sorry, I'm not . . .'

'I understand.'

'Just when I thought . . . You know, last night I phoned friends back in the States. I told them Mitch was getting better. She'd be coming home soon. Now she'll never . . .' Maddy broke down in tears. Pottidge put his arm around her and she leaned into him, weeping helplessly on his shoulder, her body racked with sobs. 'I'd started planning our future. Me and Mitch. Together . . . Everyone . . . I've lost everyone.'

'Get this straight, my Pet. We are not going to upset mainstream republicans and jeopardize the whole Irish peace process for the sake of two Yanks, two Ethiopians, a gay cafe-owner and a factory girl. Is that understood?'

'Yes, Secretary of State.' Petula Anstey hesitated. 'But the Prime Minister did say . . .'

'I am not responsible for what His Holiness the Blabbermouth says in moments of high emotion. It was a mistake letting him visit that hospital.'

'But if it gets out that you've, we've, come out against the use of a supergrass . . .'

'But it won't come out, will it, young Anstey? You are going to make sure it doesn't. Anyway, it's all down to political expediency.'

'I wish you could tell the PM that, Secretary of State.'

'Rather difficult since I'm halfway up a Swiss Alp as we speak. You don't know how much I've been looking forward to this week's skiing. It's my first real break since God knows when.'

Since less than a month ago at Christmas, she could have told him. But you didn't say those sorts of things to your senior minister – not unless you wanted to rejoin the back benches at the next reshuffle.

'Yes, Secretary of State.'

'Come on, Petula. I've always told you that if you can cut the mustard at the Northern Ireland Office, then any other department will be a doddle.'

'Will you be on your mobile?'

'Not until this evening. Reception around here is notoriously bad. All the mountains and things, I suppose. Must go. Our party's leaving.' The line went dead.

Petula Anstey swore softly. The old bastard could have flown back to see the PM and still not have missed more than an afternoon's skiing. He had clearly decided he was not going to risk being implicated in any potential fallout. No wonder he was known as Old Teflon Hands.

Kilfoyle gazed again at the announcement of his engagement to Felicity Fakenham in that Monday morning's *Times* and folded the paper back into his overcoat pocket. He was glad that Jimmy Burke would not have seen it. The very idea of that man knowing anything about his personal life made Kilfoyle shudder.

As the investigation had inched remorselessly closer to Burke, Kilfoyle had begun to feel more and more sorry for himself. It wasn't *his* fault that Burke had done the dirty on him. All right, in retrospect, Kilfoyle knew he should have reported Burke's phone call the day of the bombing. Instead he'd panicked.

It was ironic that friends and colleagues thought that his life was going swimmingly. His new job was an open secret and tonight, back in London, he was hosting a black-tie dinner for his and Fliss's parents. Normally he would have looked forward to the occasion – but Burke was gnawing at him like some malignant worm in his guts.

Where was the bloody man?

There he was, coming across a field in his tractor, heading for the lonely corrugated-iron barn where they had arranged to meet. One night Burke had drunkenly boasted that part of the Provisionals' arsenal that Nolan had stolen was hidden under the barn's earthen floor. Kilfoyle had not known whether to believe him or not.

Kilfoyle left the car, wrapped his coat around himself and watched as Burke turned through a gateway into a narrow lane, the giant wheels of the tractor brushing the bare hedgerow. Last night had been the coldest of the year and the edges of the fields were still covered in a thick white frost. There was not another building to be seen, just rolling fields, broken here and there with outcrops of rock and bracken.

'You're late,' called Kilfoyle.

Burke, wearing blue overalls tucked into wellington boots, climbed down. 'I had things to do.'

The studied insolence of Burke's tone told Kilfoyle that it was not going to be a comfortable interview. Burke went on the attack immediately.

'What the fuck were Customs men doing on my farm? I told you to see them off.'

'And I've told you I've no control over Irish Customs and Excise. I warned you they were coming. What else do you want?'

If Kilfoyle was expecting thanks, he was mistaken.

'We had to turn back a load of fifty thousand fags because of that raid,' complained Burke. 'No one will do business with us if we do that too often.'

Kilfoyle controlled his temper with difficulty. 'You know the Customs men found a plastic bag from Schiphol Airport in your bedroom?'

'Yeh. So what?'

'It was a one-off design this Christmas.'

'Someone could have brought me a present in the bag.'

'So they could. But the police are checking passenger lists on all flights from Schiphol to Ireland on the day of the bombing.'

'They'll never find anything. They've still got nothing from the car.'

'It's still early days. Forensic will take that car apart nut by nut and bolt by bolt if they have to.'

'I didn't touch no nuts or bolts,' sneered Burke.

Kilfoyle knew then just how much he hated Burke. Hated his raw potato face, his huge red hands, his uncouthness which reeked of farmyard smells. But most of all Kilfoyle hated Burke's vacuous arrogance that was going to land them both in the shit.

He decided to rattle the man's cage. 'Did you know Mikey Drumm's being questioned in London?'

Burke started, then gave a supercilious leer. 'Who's this Mikey Drumm when he's at home?'

'Good question. Just hope he doesn't talk.'

'He won't talk. Not Mikey Drumm.'

'You just said you'd never heard of him.'

'Mikey Drumm's been around for ever. Just likes a drop too much. He'll never talk.'

Kilfoyle hoped that Burke was right. He was getting no feedback from Hayward about Drumm's interrogation. This was probably an indication that Hayward was getting nowhere – but it could be a sign that there had been a breakthrough and old interdepartmental rivalries were raising their heads.

'What do you know about Breda Bridges's next target?'

'Nothing.'

'But you said . . .'

'That was before the Customs put the squeeze on me. I'm telling you, the minute the heavy brigade turn up I'm off across the fields into the North. I'll put myself under your protection.'

'Don't be hasty. All the Garda have on you is that you visited Conn Nolan on New Year's Eve . . .'

'And how do they know that?'

'They reckon you tipped off Nolan about Drumm's drinking.'

'Holy fuck!' Burke rounded on Kilfoyle, eyes blazing. 'You told them.'

'How could I tell them? You've never told me the name of the man in the bomb car with you, have you? *Think.*'

'You could have worked it out.'

'*I* didn't work out anything. *They* put two and two together and found that your first cousin Vince O'Lone is a regular in Drumm's drinking club. You'd better lay off your scams for a while.'

'If me and my brothers don't stake our claim now, others will step in.'

'You're asking for trouble.'

'Don't fucking tell me what to do, right.' Burke began to climb back up into the cab of his tractor. He swung around to stab his finger at Kilfoyle. 'You keep the fuckers out of my hair, d'you hear? The first night I spend in a prison cell is the night you'll be getting a call from my solicitors to get me out.'

'Supergrass? Ugly word. Unpleasant connotations.'

'Yes, Prime Minister.' Petula Anstey had known that – which was why she had deliberately chosen the word.

'Let me get this right,' began the Prime Minister, slowly turning a pencil in his fingers. 'The police are holding one of the Salisbury bombers who says he will play ball if they grant him immunity from prosecution.'

'Yes, sir.'

'So why don't they just charge him normally and bring him to court?'

'I gather that they don't have sufficient evidence, sir.'

'Yes, the investigation does seem to have stalled somewhat.' The Prime Minister painstakingly aligned the box of briefing papers with the edge of the long Cabinet table. 'What does the Attorney-General say?'

'We haven't consulted him yet, sir. We – that is, the Secretary of State and I thought of the political repercussions foremost.'

'Spoken to the Secretary of State, then, have you?'

'Only briefly, sir. He's . . . away.'

'He's no one's fool. Never around when the hard decisions are taken.' The Prime Minister turned back to look at Anstey. 'So, let this man turn Queen's evidence and put him under the police witness-protection programme.'

'The mainstream republicans won't like it.'

'Why not? I thought they'd be glad to get rid of these dissident extremists.'

'No, sir. I've spoken to Sinn Fein ministers. They won't tolerate a prosecution based upon supergrass evidence. Such a prosecution would send shock waves through PIRA's grass roots. It could upset the whole equilibrium of the peace process.'

'Surely Sinn Fein has an interest in bringing those responsible for the atrocity to justice?'

'Between the lines, sir, they're worried that such a supergrass could dredge up evidence of past crimes involving the current leadership.'

'Scared of washing old dirty linen in public, eh?'

'There's rumblings that Sinn Fein might withdraw from Stormont if we went ahead with a supergrass.'

'But I promised the relatives that I'd do everything I could to help. I can't go back on that pledge now.'

'But surely the peace process is more important than any single bombing, sir. By persuading mainstream republicans to support that process, you would be preventing future atrocities.'

'I don't know.' The Prime Minister swung to look out of the window where the London sky had darkened in heavy cloud. 'Is this police witness reliable?'

'I'm told that he's an alcoholic.'

'That doesn't bode well. It'll take a strong man to stand up in a witness box and give evidence against his former comrades.'

'Even if we go ahead, there's no guarantee that the Republic of Ireland will extradite suspects on the word of this one man alone.'

'Thank you, Petula, I'm beginning to get the picture. You're saying that if we employ this supergrass we'll alienate our mainstream allies among the republicans, Dublin might refuse to play ball and then, if it finally reaches the Old Bailey, our star witness would crumble in court.'

'Something like that, sir.'

'Old Teflon Hands should be proud of his young apprentice.' The Prime Minister gave a wry smile. 'Possibly a little worried by her, too.'

'Thank you, Prime Minister.' Petula Anstey tried hard not to smirk.

'The relatives of those killed in Salisbury have asked to see me to review the investigation,' continued the Prime Minister. 'As you know, I'm flying to Washington this evening. You can see them in my absence.'

Not twenty miles away from where Kilfoyle and Burke were snarling at one another, another meeting was taking place.

The call from Milo O'Connell had been succinct but urgent. He needed to talk to Conn Nolan – not on the phone. Nolan suspected a PIRA ambush. O'Connell let Nolan choose the venue – the Five Ways public house outside Carrickmacross – and the time. Nolan still sent Stozza and two carloads of men on ahead. Only when Stozza reported that there was no sign of rival gunmen did Nolan and Breda Bridges drive up to the pub sitting alone on the main road to Monaghan.

Nolan shouldered his way into the deserted bar, Breda following. The solitary barman jerked his head towards a passageway leading to the back.

Milo O'Connell and Nutter Hains were sitting at a table, glasses of stout in front of them. Both men had their coats on. The room smelled of damp and neglect. As Nolan entered, Hains moved to stand behind O'Connell, his hands deep in his raincoat pockets.

'Well?' Nolan stood four square across the table from O'Connell.

'Good day to you both. Will you not be joining me in a glass?'

'What do you want, Milo? Say your piece.'

'I always think a little civility never does any harm,' sighed O'Connell. 'But all right, if that's the way you want it. It's not a piece I have to say, but a question I have to ask.'

'Ask your question, then.'

'Would you be knowing any reason why the British government is contemplating a criminal trial involving a supergrass?'

'What are you talking about?' demanded Nolan.

'The Northern Irish Office made, shall we say, discreet approaches to some of our senior people, asking how the republican movement would feel about the use of a supergrass in a trial involving terrorists.'

'Irish terrorists?'

'Well, they wouldn't be asking Sinn Fein about Islamic fundamentalists, now, would they?'

'What did your people say?'

'That we could never countenance a trial based solely on the evidence of an informer. If the British government insisted, then they would jeopardize the peace process.'

'Peace process,' spat Breda.

O'Connell ignored her. 'You know that Mikey Drumm is being questioned by the Anti-Terrorist Squad in London.'

'Mikey! He wouldn't talk.'

'Wouldn't he? He's been hitting the bottle, I hear.'

'I'd trust him with my life,' avowed Nolan.

'Maybe you're doing just that.' O'Connell opened out his hands in a gesture of reasonableness. 'If we've a grass who's willing to turn Queen's evidence then it affects us all.'

'I can see that,' said Breda. 'Mikey Drumm's been around a long time. What he knows could be very embarrassing for the comrades who are now helping the British rule in Northern Ireland. Maybe they'd have to give up their ministerial salaries. What a shame.'

'Ah, Breda, Breda. Won't you rise above our dispute for the moment to join against a common enemy? No republican likes an informer. Christ knows, there's been too many of them over the years.'

'But I don't know that we have a common enemy,' argued Breda. 'You've no proof that Mikey Drumm's about to become a traitor. For all I know, you're just saying this to get us to turn against our own.'

'Breda, you're an intelligent woman. Think it through. Mikey

Drumm's arrested. Two days later, the NIO starts making informal soundings. The Anti-Terrorist Squad are not holding any other republicans – as far as I know.'

Breda shook her head.

'Right, then. A bit of a coincidence, wouldn't you say?'

Rob Sage was astonished to find Maddy waiting for him as he pushed his trolley into the arrivals hall at Heathrow's Terminal Four. He would have missed her had she not called out his name. She appeared at his elbow, wearing denim jeans and a sleeveless waistcoat. She looked tired and worn, with dark shadows under her eyes, but the eyes themselves were vital. There was an alertness and a hardness about her that hadn't been there previously.

'What do you want me to do? Stay at home and weep?' she asked when he expressed his surprise at seeing her. 'I've done enough of that. It's better if I do something. At least then I'm not thinking about it *all* the time.'

'It's lovely to see you and I am so sorry about Mitch. Really, really sorry.' He had tried to phone her from Addis Ababa but she had been out. He'd called Denny to say he was on his way back home – and had heard the bad news.

'No one knows why she died,' replied Maddy in answer to his question. 'The autopsy was inconclusive. Tanner wants a Home Office pathologist from London to perform another one.'

'Does he think her death's suspicious?'

Maddy shrugged. 'I don't know. Dr Amrit mentioned something called sudden death syndrome. Apparently you can just stop breathing and no one knows why.'

At the car park, Maddy held out the keys for Rob to drive.

'It's been a long flight. You drive, if you want.'

'Sure you trust me?'

'Sure.'

'Now you're back, you can come up to the Northern Ireland Office with us,' she said.

'Sorry?'

'The Prime Minister's abroad on business so me, Denny and Wayne are meeting with the Minister of State the day after tomorrow to find out where the investigation's going.'

'Okay.'

'But now tell me – why are you back so soon?'

'I'm sorry. Don't worry about the cottage.' Rob tried to deflect the question. 'Denny's offered to put me up so I'll move in with him.'

'Don't be silly.'

'I'm not turfing you out. I offered you my place. You have it.'

'Rob, if you think that I'm going back to the States now that Mitch is dead, you're wrong. I'm not leaving this country until I've seen justice done.'

'I know, I'll move into the granny flat.'

'Why don't I move into the annexe and you have the cottage?'

'No, I'll move into the granny flat . . .'

'No. *I'll* move. Don't be so damned stubborn or I'll go and stay with Denny. Deal?'

'Deal.'

'Right. Now, why are you back so soon?'

'It's . . . um . . . difficult.' Hannah had sketched out a public explanation along the lines that returning to Tigray had proved too painful for Rob. He was under strict orders never to tell anyone what had really happened – but he couldn't lie to Maddy. They'd been through too much together. 'We had a run-in with Islamic terrorists.'

'God! What happened?'

'I had to kill them,' replied Rob simply.

'Them? How many?'

'Four.'

'Four! Shit. Tell me the whole story.'

So he did, slowly and hesitantly.

'But you saved Hannah's life,' exclaimed Maddy. 'She should be grateful. Stupid bitch.'

'No. You can't have aid workers going round killing people, even terrorists. I shouldn't have told you. Promise me you'll never say a word of this to anyone.'

'I promise.' She nodded thoughtfully. 'It's good to know I've got you on my side, but what'll happen to you now?'

'There's a colleague in Tanzania coming to the end of his contract. Hannah's going to see if I can exchange territories with him. I don't mind, in a way. Maybe it was a mistake going back to Tigray. Too many ghosts.'

'Ghosts!' Maddy gave a strange little laugh. 'There are ghosts everywhere.'

That evening Maddy moved into the annexe. She cooked pasta for both of them – and broke her news.

'I'm off to Ireland tomorrow.'

'I thought we were going to see this Northern Ireland Minister.'

'That's the day after tomorrow,' said Maddy. 'I'm going to try to see Breda Bridges. Maybe ask for her help.'

'Why?'

'I just feel I should talk to her. What do I have to lose?'

'Maddy, Bridges's husband is an IRA thug who was almost certainly involved in the bombing. She's not going to help you.'

'You don't know *she* was involved,' argued Maddy. 'Bridges might have children too. Maybe if I appeal to her, mother to mother. It can't do any harm.'

'Anyway, how do you know where this woman lives?'

'It wasn't hard to find her address in Dundalk.'

'You could be taking your life into your hands.'

'Who cares? And if Bridges won't help me, then at least I'll have seen her. If nothing else, I can rattle her cage. Share some grief.'

'You're getting to be a right bloodthirsty little madam, aren't you?'

'Rob, you just don't know how dark my thoughts are.'

18

Maddy had not expected Breda Bridges to live in a genteel suburb of detached houses sitting back from wide, tree-lined roads, BMWs and Audis filling the drives.

'I thought she'd be in some republican ghetto with kerbstones painted green and gold and murals of masked gunmen on the gable ends,' muttered Maddy, staring at the modern red-brick house. Flower beds ran up to the garage where a new blue people-carrier was parked. A children's slide and swing sat on one side of the pristine lawn. A little boy, about the same age as TJ, emerged from the front door to be followed, a second later, by an older girl. They were shorter than her children and the boy in particular appeared to be a right little bruiser but they were squabbling as they walked off down the road together – just as her children used to do.

'Are you sure you want to go through with this?' asked Rob.

'Yeh, I'm sure.' Maddy took a deep breath to calm the butterflies in her stomach, strode up the path and pressed the front doorbell. From inside the house she heard cheap electrical chimes. After a moment the door opened a fraction.

'Mrs Bridges?' In her nervousness, Maddy got the woman's name wrong. She cursed herself.

'I'm Breda Bridges,' replied the woman in a soft Irish lilt.

'I'm Maddy Lipzinger. My husband, my son and my daughter were killed when that bomb exploded in Salisbury.'

'Yes?' Breda Bridges's eyes flickered past Maddy and Rob to check the street. She kept her hand firmly on the door as if ready to close it at any second.

'I'd like to talk to you about their deaths.' Maddy looked closely at the woman. She was smallish, with mousy hair and a full face. Not someone who would stand out in a crowd.

'That bomb was nothing to do with me.'

'You're the vice-president of The True Guardians. Their paramilitary wing is the Sovereign IRA who have admitted they planted the bomb. How can you say that it's nothing to do with you?'

'I don't have anything to say to you.'

'But you're a mother, too. I've just seen your kids.'

A fire ignited behind the Irish woman's eyes. 'You forget you saw those kids. They're nothing to do with you.'

'But that's the point. You have children. I don't.'

Breda Bridges began to close the door.

'I take it you haven't the moral courage to ask me in?'

'Ask you in! You've a fucking neck, coming here.'

'Your people had some "fucking neck" coming to Salisbury. The difference is that I have the courage to face you whereas your scum could only kill children and then flee like the cowards they are. Was your husband involved in planting that bomb?'

'What do you want?'

'I was going to ask for your help but I can see now that I'd be wasting my breath. Instead, I want you to feel the pain I'm feeling. I want you to imagine something happening to your kids.'

'Are you threatening me?'

'I'm interested in what sort of woman can countenance the murder of innocent children and show no remorse.'

'How little you know.'

'No. It's how little *you* understand,' declared Maddy, holding Bridges's stare. 'I've read your newsletters. They're a travesty of the truth.'

'You're an American. What can you know of Ireland?'

'I'm second-generation American,' corrected Maddy. 'My mother's and my father's families came from County Mayo.'

A silver Ford Escort XR3 pulled up outside. A woman with cropped hair and a thin angry face got out of the car to stride belligerently up the path.

'Who's this?' Teresa cocked an eye at Maddy and Rob.

'People who are just leaving.'

Teresa jerked her thumb towards the road. 'You heard my sister. You're leaving.'

'I'm Maddy Lipzinger. My husband and children were killed in the Salisbury bomb. I wanted to meet your sister.'

'And now you have, you can fuck off.' Teresa glared at Maddy.

'It's all right,' said Breda Bridges, her hand still holding the edge of the door. 'I'll phone Conn to come and get rid of them.'

'You don't need Conn, for fuck's sake. They are leaving.' Teresa pointed her finger at the road. *'Now.'*

But Maddy was staring at the heavy silver rings on the woman's fingers. A sledgehammer struck her above her heart. Maddy gasped, her knees buckling.

'Are you all right?' Rob put out an arm to steady her. 'Come on. Back to the car.'

'Yeh, fuck off out of it.'

Rob met Teresa's challenge with eyes iced with such a chilling hatred that for a moment Teresa was cowed. Then he took Maddy's arm and led her back to the road. At the gate, Rob turned to look back. Bridges and her sister were standing on the doorstep, staring after them. Teresa jerked two fingers up. 'And don't be coming back.'

'I've never struck a woman in my life,' muttered Rob. 'But I could have happily laid her out.'

As they halted by the car for Maddy to collect herself, the boy and girl they had seen earlier rounded the corner towards them. The girl was carrying a loaf of sliced bread and they were still squabbling.

Rob climbed in behind the driver's wheel but Maddy remained in the path of the children.

'Hi,' she smiled. 'What're your names?'

There was an explosion of fury from the doorstep.

'Don't talk to her,' screamed Breda Bridges. 'Get away from that car.'

'Here, kids. Have one each.' Maddy thrust something in their hands, waved mockingly towards the women running down the path towards them and got into the car. She and Rob drove off to the sound of curses from Teresa.

'What did she give you?' demanded Breda Bridges. 'Show me.'

Aoife and Bobby each held out a £10 note.

Maddy was feeling curiously elated. She was incredibly tired, physically tired – but content, as if she had just completed some mammoth task.

'At least we know now that Breda Bridges has one weak spot,' mused Rob. 'She's very protective of her kids.'

'Strange world where a mother's love is her weak spot,' replied Maddy.

Petula Anstey arrived fifteen minutes late for her nine o'clock meeting. Maddy, Rob, Denny and Wayne, who had been waiting in an ante-room high in the tower block overlooking the river Thames, suddenly found the Minister in their midst, gushing her apologies and ushering them into her office. She dropped an armful of files onto a chair and turned to face the four. Rob, watching closely, saw the transformation come over her. It took just a deep breath, two blinks and she mutated from a busy career woman with a hectic schedule into a caring person who was about to shake hands with their hearts.

Rob did not like chameleons – nor did he trust them.

'First of all,' began the Minister. 'Mrs Lipzinger, the Prime Minister has asked me to express his condolences on the death of your daughter. Naturally, I wish to offer my sympathy also.'

'Thank you.'

Petula Anstey put her hands down to grasp the edge of the desk behind her in one of her favourite poses. The body language said, *Look at me. I've nothing to hide. I'm open and honest.*

'Now, you wanted to see me.'

'With respect, we asked to see the Prime Minster,' said Denny.

'I'm afraid he's in Washington to confer with the President about the war on terror. But as I'm in charge of security in Northern Ireland he's asked me to see you.'

'I don't understand,' said Denny. 'The bomb went off on English soil, the bombers live in Southern Ireland, so why you?'

'You don't *know* that the bombers live in Southern Ireland,' replied Petula Anstey.

'We gather the police have a good idea *who* they are and *where* they live,' interrupted Maddy. 'It's merely a question of proving it.'

'And that's what you must give the police time to do,' said Anstey. 'It's only four weeks since the bombing. These investigations can take months. The police *have* to get it right.'

'One hopes,' muttered Maddy.

The Minister gave a sympathetic smile. 'I gather you're concerned that the inquiry has seemingly made little progress.'

'Yes, in a nutshell,' replied Maddy. 'We've heard of suspects being arrested, questioned and then released. Not a single person has been charged.'

'Let me assure you that there is no hiding place for terrorists of whatever sort, whether dissident Irish republicans or Islamic extremists. The world is united behind the war on terror.'

'That's all very well,' argued Maddy. 'But you're talking in generalities. I'd prefer to speak specifically about our case.'

'Mrs Lipzinger, I share your concerns. Truly, I do. But there are many things going on behind the scenes that *I* do not know about. The Intelligence Services and police forces on both sides of the border in Ireland have made the hunt for the Salisbury bombers their number one priority. The resources of the British government, together with the those of our American allies, are being utilized to bring these murderers to justice. Of course, you appreciate that the individual intelligence agencies or police forces cannot say what they are doing on a day-to-day basis, but we will get there.'

'That's what everyone says,' declared Maddy.

'The Prime Minister told us he would go to the ends of the Earth to catch those responsible for the bombing,' said Denny.

Petula Anstey shifted uncomfortably. 'I'm aware of that.'

'He doesn't appear to have gone to the end of Downing Street yet,' muttered Rob, breaking his silence.

Anger flashed behind Petula Anstey's eyes. 'The Prime Minister is a man of his word,' she said shortly.

'He'd better be,' replied Rob, meeting her glare.

Behind them, the parliamentary private secretary coughed discreetly and rustled papers.

'Oh, God. Is it time for yet another meeting?' exclaimed Anstey theatrically. 'I'm glad we've spoken but now I'm due to meet my officials before my counterpart in Dublin arrives to discuss a joint crime-computer program – something, in fact, that would help in this case.'

'Thank you for meeting with us,' said Maddy.

Rob glanced at his watch. 'And you've caught up with your schedule now.'

'Sorry.' Petula Anstey was finding it hard to disguise her dislike of Rob.

Rob made no such effort. He merely shook his head, looking grim.

'We are doing everything we can to bring these murderers to justice. Everything,' insisted the Minister of State as they reached the door. 'Trust me.'

'Bugger and damnation.' Tanner strode out of his office with a face like thunder. 'Those bloody politicians have vetoed granting Mikey Drumm immunity.'

'Why?' demanded Pottidge.

'Some twaddle about being unable to guarantee a conviction, says Hayward.'

'That means Drumm won't do a deal?'

'No, and we haven't a single shred of evidence against him,' confirmed Tanner. 'Bloody meddling politicians.'

'At least we've found the keyholder of that shop near the station. He's been in India visiting relations but he's letting us in first thing tomorrow.'

'It's taken long enough,' complained Tanner.

'Also, nothing on flights from Amsterdam to Dublin on the afternoon of 23 December so far,' reported Pottidge.

'Yet another failure.' Tanner sighed. 'Get your coat. I've got to pick up some shoes from the cobbler's so we'll have a pint in the market place.'

'Why didn't you tell me that you planned to go to Ireland?' demanded Rose Allen as she and Maddy sat in Denny's coffee shop in the middle of Salisbury. 'And seeing the Minister! You're having a busy time.'

'I've told Tanner about seeing that bitch with all those rings,' said Maddy.

'What did he say?'

'He already knew. She's Bridges's younger sister Teresa. She was questioned by the Irish police but had to be released for lack of evidence.' Maddy grimaced. '*And* he knew we'd been to Breda Bridges's.'

'How did he know that?'

'There's a secret police camera trained on the house, but don't say anything.'

'Who am I going to tell?'

'Sorry. That was wrong of me.'

'What did the Minister have to say?'

'The police and intelligence services are working flat out. America's intelligence agencies are weighing in as never before. Blah blah blah. We just have to be patient. Denny and Wayne thought she was convincing.'

'And Rob?'

'A little too smarmy for his liking. Mine, too.'

'Why's Rob back from Ethiopia so soon?'

'I think he found the memories were too painful,' replied Maddy carefully. 'He's hoping to go back out to a different part of Africa.'

'And you'll be going back home.'

'We're still waiting for the second autopsy on Mitch.'

'A second autopsy?'

'Mr Tanner's not satisfied that Mitch did die of natural causes.'

'Surely, he doesn't suspect . . . I mean, who would want to do such a thing? Why?' Rose lifted her glasses and rubbed at the indentation on the side of her nose.

'I don't know,' replied Maddy. 'But I'm not quitting England until I've seen justice done.'

19

'Have you seen this newspaper story?'

'Sorry.' Tanner looked up from his pint of beer to find Maddy Lipzinger at his elbow. Her face was black with anger and she was waving a copy of the *Evening Standard* under his nose. On her way from the coffee shop to the car park, a newspaper billboard had caught her eye. She had bought a newspaper, read the front-page story there and then – and her blood had run cold. Just as Maddy had thought she would explode with anger, she had glimpsed Tanner and Pottidge heading into a pub. Maddy had chased after them.

'Read this.'

Salisbury Bombers To Escape Justice, screamed the headline. *Politicians Refuse Police Supergrass.*

Tanner began reading, thinking that the reporter had been well briefed, probably by someone in the Anti-Terrorist Squad who was as fed up as he was with bloody politicians.

The story led off with the impending release of an Irish labourer from Paddington Green police station where he had been held in connection with the Salisbury bombing. The labourer, a former member of the IRA, had refused to say a word.

Clever – whoever was tipping off the press was still protecting Drumm.

The release of the Irish labourer was yet another failure in the ill-fated Salisbury bombing investigation. There was a vital witness – willing to turn supergrass – who could blow the case wide open. But politicians were frightened of upsetting Sinn Fein and damaging the peace process.

From intercepts of calls between the terrorists' mobile phones, detectives knew that the bombers had moved into Salisbury in two teams, the story went on. The come-on bomb had been planted by a woman whose identity was known. So, too were the identities of the driver of the escape car, one of the men in the bomb car, which had failed to explode, together with the man who had coordinated the attack.

Police even had DNA linking four suspects to the crime but the Crown Prosecution Service had ruled that the samples were not admissible in court.

The explosive device in the car bore the hallmarks of a well-known bomb-maker from Dublin. His girlfriend and his brother had given him an alibi that could not be shaken.

Already the investigation was being run down. Detective Chief Superintendent Hayward was already working on another major case.

All in all, the story was bang to rights. Tanner passed the paper to Pottidge to read.

'Is this true?' demanded Maddy, peeling off her gloves as if preparing for a fight.

'More or less.' Tanner opened out his hands in a show of helplessness. 'English justice is based on proof, not truth. It's one thing to know who was responsible and another to prove it to a jury. We're only allowed to try the bombers once. These people are experts in wriggling through any legal loophole so we have to make sure we have a watertight case against them.'

'It says here that you know the names of at least four of the bombers, including the woman who planted the bomb in the trash can. It was that Teresa Bridges, wasn't it?'

'You know I can't confirm that. Anyway, how did you find us here?'

'I saw you walk in. You see, Mr Tanner, there's no hiding place. For you or the killers.'

'That goddam Anstey woman. I could throttle her,' declared Maddy. 'She lied to us.'

'Only by omission,' Rob pointed out. 'We didn't ask the right questions.'

'We didn't know enough to ask them.'

'That's what she was banking on.'

'Perhaps we should *demand* to see the Prime Minister. Ask him why one of his ministers misled us.'

'Politicians. Liars, cheats and hypocrites, the lot of them.'

'The world is forgetting about us,' sighed Denny. 'Our dead will be added to the long list of victims of violence. And no one will ever pay.'

'Oh, they'll pay,' said Maddy softly. 'They'll pay all right.'

'Bloody right. I'll kill the bastards myself, if I have to,' proclaimed Wayne, draining his glass and helping himself to another.

The newspaper story had prompted a flurry of phone calls between the four that had resulted in a council of war in the staff room above the now-closed coffee shop. Denny provided the wine.

'I wish I'd had a gun when I met with that Teresa,' muttered Maddy. 'I'd have shot the bitch there and then.'

'What about suing the bombers for compensation, like they did with OJ Simpson in the States?' suggested Wayne, reaching for the bottle again. Maddy frowned at the way Wayne was freely helping himself to Denny's wine.

'The burden of proof in a civil court is far less than in a criminal one,' agreed Denny.

'It would take money and time,' objected Rob.

'Money's not a problem,' said Maddy. 'But that sounds more like the last resort, when all else has failed.'

'I reckon we should take the law into our own hands,' announced Wayne. 'What's Scotland's motto? *Touch me with impunity.* That's what we should be like.'

'*No one touches me with impunity*,' corrected Rob. 'It's the motto of the Royal Scots Regiment. *Nemo me impune lacessit*.'

'Yeh, that's what I said. And it's in the Bible. An eye for an eye, a tooth for a tooth.'

'There's also something in the Bible about turning the other cheek,' Denny reminded him.

'Bollocks to that, mate. I'm not going to sit on my arse doing nothing while those murderers take the piss.'

'I could put it differently,' murmured Maddy. 'But I think I share those sentiments.'

Wayne pointed to the byline of the reporter who had written the story. 'That bloke was down here when the bomb went off,' he said. 'I've still got his card. These reporters always know more than they say. I'm going to give him a ring and see what he can tell me.'

'About what?'

'That building labourer in Paddington Green nick for starters.'

'The police have probably let him go by now.'

'All the better, then.'

'What do you think, Rob?' asked Maddy, becoming impatient with Wayne's show of bravado.

'If you prick us, do we not bleed?' Rob began quoting softly. 'If you tickle us, do we not laugh? If you poison us, do we not die? *And if you wrong us, shall we not revenge?*'

'Yeh, right.' Wayne punched the air in agreement.

'So you'll have your pound of flesh too, will you?' asked Denny.

'It's tempting,' Rob admitted. 'And I wouldn't mind spilling the blood either.'

'What are you two on about?' demanded Maddy.

'*Merchant of Venice*, dear heart.' It was Denny's turn to start quoting. 'The quality of mercy is not strain'd, It droppeth as the gentle rain from heaven Upon the place beneath: it is twice bless'd; It blesseth him that gives and him that takes.'

'Fuck that,' said Wayne.

'All those days and I didn't say a word. Not even to ask to go to the lavvy.'

'So how did you manage to have a piss, then, Mikey?' demanded Seamus the barman.

Mikey Drumm held up a gnarled finger. 'They asked me. They asked me if I wanted a piss and I nodded, so I did.'

'You're a great man, Mikey,' proclaimed Vincent O'Lone. The circle of drinkers around Drumm at the bar of the Irish Club grinned in agreement. 'But why did the police arrest you in the first place?'

'For the Salisbury bomb,' said Drumm. 'They thought I had something to do with that.' He closed his right eye in a slow exaggerated wink. 'The very notion.'

'But how did you manage without a drink? That's what I want to know,' asked Seamus.

Drumm paused, a pint of Murphy's held to his lips. 'If it's there, I'll take it. If it's not, then I can go without. They tried to bribe me with drink, you know, but I was having none of it.'

Mikey Drumm was enjoying his first hours of freedom. He had come straight to the Irish Club from the police station – and he hadn't had to put his hand in his pocket since walking in.

Drumm had decided that in the morning he'd return to Ireland and make his peace with Conn Nolan. He was glad it had worked out this way. He wasn't cut out to be a supergrass. The idea of standing up in a witness box and denouncing old comrades was a frightening one, he saw now. He'd go back to work on the building site outside Dublin and find lodgings nearby.

In his mind, Drumm was already remembering how he had withstood the days of interrogation, never speaking a word.

And in the meantime ... Ay, grand. Another glass of Paddy's would be fine.

Mikey Drumm left the club at 11.30 p.m., weaving gently along the deserted pavements, making his way back to his sister's.

He hoped that Deirdre wouldn't mind him waking her up. She could be terribly cross when she had a mind to be but, hopefully, she'd be so relieved to see him that she wouldn't give him a hard time. And tomorrow he'd be out of the reach of any British bobbies. He began humming tunelessly to himself.

In the shadows, a car pulled out from the kerbside and began to follow him.

'There. Look. Run it back. Yes. There.' Tanner pointed excitedly at the video images. 'As I live and breathe, that's Mikey Drumm walking past the open shop doorway, and he's heading towards the station.'

Pottidge peered at the time displayed at the top of the picture. '12.33. The time the bomb went off.'

'So there is a God after all.' Tanner sat back, a huge smile spreading across his face. 'Now we've placed Drumm in Salisbury, he'll have to do a deal – politicians or no bloody politicians.'

'How do you mean, sir?'

'Once Drumm knows he's going to get done, he'll turn Queen's evidence. That'll present the politicians with a fait accompli. They can't stop someone giving evidence in an English court – never mind what bloody Sinn Fein say.'

The phone rang. Pottidge picked it up and announced, 'Mr Hayward for you, sir.'

'David. I was just about to call you ... What! When? And no one made the connection until now. Shit.' Tanner slumped in his chair and rested his head in his hand. 'No, it doesn't matter now. It doesn't matter at all.'

Maddy was in the kitchen of her granny flat making herself a cup of coffee to take back to bed when she heard the knock on the front door. She glanced down at her T-shirt which came down to the middle of her thighs – and judged she was decent enough to peep around the door.

The first thing that struck her was the strange look on Rob's face. The second was the Arctic wind.

'Have you heard the news?'

'No. What news?' Maddy pressed her knees together as the wind lanced through her. 'Come in. A girl could die in this weather.'

'It's a cold wind,' conceded Rob.

'Especially around Nebraska.'

'What?'

'American girlie word. You wouldn't understand. Come in before I freeze to death.' She shut the door quickly behind him and hugged herself to warm up. Her action made her T-shirt ride up higher. She saw Rob's eyes drop towards her thighs – and found, surprisingly, that she did not mind. In fact she was rather flattered. 'So what's happened?'

'I've just had Tanner on the phone. Remember that Irish labourer the police were questioning in London in connection with the bombing?'

'Yes.'

'Well, his name's Mikey Drumm – and he's been killed.'

'No!' Maddy led the way into the kitchen, feeling Rob's eyes on her legs.

'He was released from police custody yesterday, celebrated by getting rolling drunk at an Irish club all evening before being knocked down by a hit-and-run driver on his way home.'

'Wayne?'

Rob shrugged. 'I thought he was all mouth and no trousers.'

'All mouth and no trousers,' she repeated. 'What a quaint phrase.'

'Like Nebraska?'

Maddy grinned at Rob before turning serious. 'You really think Wayne could have done that?'

'It's a bit of a coincidence. I'm going to drive down and see if he's at home.'

'I'll come with you. Help yourself to coffee while I get dressed.'

'Don't be long. You don't want Nebraska to get cold.'

Maddy put her tongue out at him and disappeared into the bedroom.

Bemerton Heath estate was a side of the historic city that Maddy had not known existed. The front gardens were barren, muddy plots littered with discarded toys and junk. Litter blew in the wind, and the occasional abandoned car sat on its wheel hubs, surrounded by shattered glass. This was the poor part.

A free newspaper jammed in the letter box of Wayne's home suggested that there was no one in. Rob and Maddy knocked twice and then gave up. They were walking back to the car when an elderly woman came out of the house opposite.

'You don't know where Wayne is, do you?' asked Rob.

'He's not at home. He didn't spend the night there, either.'

'When did you last see him?' inquired Maddy.

'Yesterday afternoon. He was ranting and raving about what he was going to do to the people who'd killed his girlfriend Leanne. She was blown up in the bomb, you know. He swore he was going to take revenge. He reckoned if the law couldn't get them, he would.'

20

Maddy shivered uncontrollably and eased the weight off her left leg, which had gone numb. The movement snapped the stem of a fern, brittle in the freezing cold of the January night. There was not a single light to be seen in the darkness as the countryside crackled with frost. At other times, Maddy would have enjoyed the myriad of silver stars twinkling brilliantly in the clear sky. Now she stared hard at the outline of the barn two hundred yards away, and wiped her running nose on her sleeve.

The reality of embarking upon revenge was far different from how she had imagined it would be as she had sat on the floor in front of the fire and drank herself into a blazing hatred. Her craving for revenge had made her turn the red wine into the blood of a bomber – and she had laughed in an ugly, locked-jaw fashion, allowing the wine to trickle out of her mouth before wiping it off her chin and licking her fingertips clean.

That night, Maddy had yearned for the deaths of those who had killed her children. It wasn't enough for them simply to die; they had to be tortured to death, mutilated, disfigured. Pleading for mercy; pleading for death as a release. *Die bad, you bastards. Die bad.*

But now it was for real she found that revenge was not taken in the blood heat – but in the dark, waiting for your opportunity.

Maddy had been hiding here on the border between Southern Ireland and the North since just before dusk. As the temperature plummeted, the icy stillness had penetrated to her very marrow. She had wrapped her arms around herself to stop her teeth chattering and tried to keep herself warm thinking of good times with her kids; remembering indulgently Mitch's stubborn glare, the way she would never accept help as she struggled to carry her cello. How TJ had looked in his first junior baseball uniform; his freckles, and how he had always slept with his hand under his chin so that it made him look as if he was thinking.

The sound of a vehicle crawling up the track made Maddy snap back to the present. She looked at her watch again. It was nine o'clock. Almost the time that the note had said Burke would arrive.

The man who armed the Salisbury bomb is a terrorist named Jimmy Burke. At 9.10 p.m. tomorrow he will arrive alone at an isolated barn on his land. I will help you to see that justice is done. Trust me and destroy this.

The message had gone on to give precise Ordnance Survey map coordinates as well as instructions on how to get to the barn.

Maddy had burned the message – but the words were locked in her memory.

The vehicle stopped. A minute later she made out a faint gleam coming through chinks in the barn's corrugated-iron sides. Maddy rose, finding the cold had turned her legs into blocks of wood. She began stumbling awkwardly over the hard uneven earth. Something rustled in the hedgerow alongside her and she started, her hand leaping to her throat.

She found she was wading into a bank of nettles and veered towards the hedgerow where an old gate hung off its hinges. She tried to move it, but it was embedded in the earth. Maddy climbed over slowly, flattening herself on the top bar before sliding down the other side. She bent her knees to absorb the impact of her landing and complimented herself on her stealth.

A dark figure in a black balaclava rose behind her, clamped a hand firmly over her mouth and kicked her legs away from under her.

*

'Quiet! Quiet! I could hear you coming a hundred yards away.'

'There was no need to be so violent,' hissed Maddy. 'You scared the life out of me. Anyway, I thought you were supposed to be in Cornwall.'

'And you said you were going to London,' replied Rob.

'Hmmph.' Maddy did not know whether to be angry with Rob – or just very relieved.

They were lying on a groundsheet in a lair that Rob had fashioned inside a thicket of brambles and blackthorn. Maddy found it snug and sheltered after her own exposed hiding place and when Rob passed her a thermos flask of lukewarm tomato soup she thought it was the finest thing she had ever tasted.

'How long have you been here?' she asked.

'Since before dawn. I saw you arrive. You chose a daft place to lie up.'

'I'm not an expert like you,' sniffed Maddy.

'I take it you also had a note about this Jimmy Burke character?'

'Delivered through my letter box a couple of nights ago.'

'What are you going to do when you see Burke?'

'You're not going to believe this.' Maddy pulled a heavy pistol from her pocket.

'Where did you get *that* from?' Rob examined the old RUC standard-issue Ruger in amazement.

'Behind the crucifix where the lane turns off the main road. A text message on my cellphone told me where to look. The sender blanked his identity.'

'Do you know how to use it?'

'All American women know how to use guns. I'm currently the Tonawanda ladies' pistol champion.'

'I don't like this,' decided Rob slowly. 'First, someone sends us anonymous letters telling us where to find one of the bombers and then gives you a gun to deal with him. How many people know your mobile phone number?'

'Not many,' admitted Maddy.

'Someone's making it too easy for us.'

'Never look a gift horse in the mouth.'

'What if we're about to walk into an ambush?'

'I'll risk it. Come on, Rob. If this guy Burke armed those bombs then he deserves to die.'

'*If* Burke is the guy. I'd never heard of him until I got that note. Tanner's never mentioned him. And how can anyone know where Burke will be at ten past nine this evening – unless he's been set up. This stinks.'

'Look, Wayne's done his bit. I reckon it's my turn. Now you're here, we can do it together.'

'And you're going to kill Burke in cold blood?'

'Yeh, I suppose so.' Maddy had not thought things through that far.

'Do you want me to have the gun?'

'I can use it,' said Maddy defiantly.

'Okay, but I want to hear Burke condemn himself from his own mouth before we do anything.' Rob began putting things in his small rucksack. 'Now, stay behind me – and try not to make so much noise.'

'Huh.'

They set off, Maddy walking in Rob's tracks. She tried to copy the way his light, easy crouch covered the ground soundlessly. She saw that he was using every inch of cover, every small dip and depression, to reach the hedge which led towards the barn itself.

Rob slipped off the rucksack and motioned Maddy to stay under cover as he crept up to the barn. Through a chink in the corrugated iron he made out two naked bulbs, hanging from rafters and casting pools of weak light onto an earth floor. Bales of hay were stacked at one end and a row of empty cattle pens lined the far wall. Near them was a large trough full of water.

At first Rob failed to spot Burke. Then he saw the top half of his body appear out of a hole in the ground next to the bales. He had a pump-action shotgun in his right hand.

There was the sound of a car engine in the distance. Burke must have heard it too for he climbed out of the hole and eased down a wooden flap over the opening, covering it with earth and hay bales. Headlights played over the barn, then the car picked up speed and headed off into the night.

Rob waved Maddy to come forward through the nettles to join him.

He heard the rustle of her clothing as she rose from the hedge. He swung round to raise his finger to his lips. Maddy looked up at him.

Clang. Her boot struck something metallic hidden in the nettles.

Shit.

Rob pressed his eye back to the chink but Burke had disappeared. A second later, the lights went off, leaving the interior of the barn in darkness. Rob started to retrace his steps. Too late.

A torch beam snapped on not twelve paces away. It began to swing in Rob's direction.

'Who's there?' Rob heard the slide of the pump-action shotgun being slammed back. 'Come out or I'll fucking do you.'

'Don't shoot.' Rob headed through the nettles towards the light.

Burke shone the torch into Rob's face. 'Who else is with you?'

'No one. I've come to talk to Jimmy Burke.'

'The fuck you have! Get into the barn.'

Burke gave Rob a hefty shove through the Judas gate in the barn's door. He switched on the light and pulled the door behind him. For the first time Rob saw that a broad ramp ran along one wall, leading up to a loft that was lost in the shadows.

'Right. Who the fuck are you?'

'My name's Rob Sage. As I said, I want to talk to you.' Rob backed away from the door to bring Burke after him so that Maddy would have a clear shot when she followed them in.

'You turned up on Breda's doorstep with that American bird,' rasped Burke. 'Where is she?'

'Back in England,' lied Rob.

'How did you know where to find me?' Burke answered his own

question. '*He* put you up to it, didn't he? The bastard. I'll kill the pair of you.'

Outside, Maddy pressed her eye to a hole in the barn wall. The Irishman was as tall as Rob, but much more powerful across the shoulders and neck, and a good thirty pounds heavier. He was pointing the shotgun straight at Rob's chest.

'No one's put me up to anything,' Rob was telling Burke coolly. 'I just wanted to see what sort of man can murder small children.'

'You've got a fucking nerve.'

'You armed the two bombs at Salisbury.'

'That shows how little *you* know,' sneered Burke.

Rob thought quickly. Of course, Burke could not have armed *both* bombs. How could he? The woman who planted the come-on bomb would have armed hers just before she put it in the bin.

'You armed the bomb in the car, then,' declared Rob. '*And I disarmed it.*'

'It was you, you interfering bastard!' Burke's eyes blazed. 'You've come to your own execution. I'm going to cut you in two.'

Burke slowly raised the shotgun until Rob was staring directly down the muzzle.

'Now, Maddy. Shoot,' called Rob.

Burke snorted in derision. 'You think I'm going to fall for that old trick.'

'Maddy. He killed your kids.' There was desperation in Rob's voice now. 'Shoot him.'

Maddy appeared in the doorway. Even in the dim light, Rob saw that she was as white as a sheet. She held the pistol limply by her side in her gloved hand.

'Shoot,' pleaded Rob.

Maddy made a helpless sound like a small kitten.

It was enough for Burke to jerk his head around. Rob leaped at him, kicking him hard on the shin and knocking away the shotgun. The gun sailed out of Burke's hands, through the air and straight into the water trough. For a second, both men stood motionless, watching the gun sink in a stream of bubbles.

Rob went to jab at Burke's throat but the farmer pivoted on his heel and snatched up a wicked-looking billhook. He lunged at Rob with a wild backhand slash. Rob jumped back, the tip of the billhook missing his face by an inch.

Rob knew his only hope was to keep his distance and wear Burke down. Rob turned and ran for the ramp leading to the loft. Burke followed, screaming obscenities. The ramp was treacherously slippery. After a few steps, Rob's feet slid from under him. He twisted to land on his back. As Burke reared over him, Rob drew his legs up into his chest and kicked out, catching Burke in the stomach. The farmer reeled back but Rob had only gained a moment's respite. With an angry grunt, Burke straightened up, raised the billhook and took a step forward.

'You're dead meat.'

Rob tried to scramble to his feet, the billhook poised above him.

Then Burke was staggering backwards, his mouth gaping in surprise. His head jerked as the second bullet slammed into his back. He turned, blood already running out of the corner of his mouth. Maddy fired for a third time and Burke slid down against a hay bale.

Maddy let the gun drop to her side and advanced across the dirt floor as if walking in her sleep.

'I'm sorry, Rob. I couldn't kill him in cold blood. It was only when he . . .' She coughed as if she was about to retch.

Rob put his arm around Maddy. 'Are you all right?'

'Yeh.' She exhaled deeply. 'What about someone hearing the shots?'

'No one around here's going to investigate gunshots in a hurry. This is bandit country, remember.'

Rob looked towards where Burke was sitting upright against a bale, head lolling onto his chest, the rivulet of blood drying on his chin. His eyes were wide open and he was dead.

'We should get out of here.' Maddy glanced around nervously.

'I want to see what he was doing in the pit first.'

Rob cleared away the earth and hay bales. Pulling open the flap, he found a steep ladder descending into the hole. There was a light switch next to the ladder. Rob leaned down to turn it on – and gasped. He was looking into a concrete-lined arms bunker, measuring about ten feet by eight. He climbed down to stand among a rack of rocket-propelled grenades with two launchers, a case of M1 carbines, assorted automatic rifles including a British Army SLR, a selection of pistols, four Israeli Uzi machine pistols and various boxes of ammunition. The presence of a holdall, plus several lengths of tarpaulin and oiled paper, suggested that the arms had been moved around the country.

'Christ! You could start a war with this lot,' he exclaimed.

'Perhaps that's the intention,' said Maddy.

Rob began inspecting blocks of Semtex plastic explosive, detonator pencils and cord with professional interest.

'We really should get away,' insisted Maddy.

But Rob swooped on a Coupatan timer, identical to the one in the bomb car in Salisbury. An idea entered his head. 'Maddy, how do you feel about blowing this lot sky-high?'

'Can you do that?'

'Easy.' He climbed up back into the barn to drag Burke to the edge of the pit. 'Wipe your pistol clean and put it on the floor,' he ordered Maddy before hurrying back down into the bunker, where he began filling the holdall with explosives and detonators.

Old army instincts kicked in. If it was there – nick it. Rob added two Walther PPKs and, as an afterthought, an Uzi and ammunition. He couldn't believe that he'd ever use them – but who knew? He wrapped the holdall in tarpaulin and handed it up to Maddy.

'What are you going to do with these?'

'Set up our own arms dump.'

Down in the hole, Rob inserted a detonator pencil into a block of Semtex and wired up the Coupatan timer. He set it on thirty minutes, allowing enough time for them to get well away but not too long so that someone might come looking for Burke. Finally he tumbled Burke's body into the pit and covered up the flap with the bales.

'Come on.' Rob snatched up a spade and switched off the light. 'The clock's running.'

Maddy led the way to her car. They drove to Rob's car, where they split up. If Maddy hurried she could make the last flight back to London.

Rob had to cache the arms. It could be difficult at night, he knew. What looked like a perfect place in the dark could stand out like a bulldog's balls in daylight. After a quick search, Rob chose an almost impenetrable tangle of bramble, stunted blackthorn and white beam. He wormed his way into the middle. The earth was soft beneath the leaf mould and soon he had a large enough hole to cover the holdall. He made a mental note of its location and hoped that he could find the arms again in daylight – and that Maddy was safely on her way back to England.

But Maddy hadn't tried to catch her last flight. She had driven to the nearest high point, just a mile away, turned off her car engine and waited.

When the white flash lit up the sky to the north, Maddy leaped out of the car and began jumping up and down, clapping her hands like an excited child. Seconds later, the air vibrated with an enormous deep rumble. Then the ammunition began exploding.

'Oh, yes, Oh, yes. That's for TJ. That's for Mitch.' Maddy laughed and wept and capered all at the same time. 'This is just the start. You're walking dead, you motherfuckers.'

21

Rob arrived back at his cottage mid-morning and peered down the side lane, looking for signs of life in the granny annex. Maddy must have been keeping an eye out for him because she opened the door straightaway.

'Beat you to it,' she called. 'Come in for coffee.'

Rob threw his bag into his cottage and went to join Maddy.

'No problems?'

'No. I missed the last flight so I came back this morning.' She did not tell him that she had stayed to watch the explosion. 'The Irish papers are over there if you want a look.'

'We seem to have made a bang.'

'You can say that again.'

Rob picked up the *Irish Times* off the pile sitting on the breakfast bar which separated the kitchen area from the living room. He had already read one account on the flight but he enjoyed reading the story again. The explosion had been heard twenty miles away in Dundalk itself. The farmer who owned the barn was missing. His two brothers had been arrested under anti-terrorism laws.

'So, how do you feel this morning?' asked Rob, putting down the paper. 'No regrets?'

'No,' replied Maddy. 'I slept like a baby and my first thought today was, "We did good!" And you?'

'I'm all right.'

'I'm sorry I froze last night.' Maddy dropped her eyes. 'I'd talked so big and then, when it came to it, I just couldn't do it.'

'But you did – in the end.'

'I had to. He would have killed you.'

'You saved my life. Thank you.'

'That's what friends do for each other.' She smiled. 'Hey, why don't I fix you a meal tonight to celebrate? I promise you something better than pasta this time.'

'I can't, I'm sorry. Hannah's back from Ethiopia. I'm due to see her at four o'clock in London. There's a tradition that whenever a field man calls in at headquarters, the office staff take him out for a drink and a meal. Why don't I cook you supper tomorrow night?'

'You cook?'

'You'd better believe it.'

'Okay.'

Rob changed the subject. 'Why didn't you tell me about that note?'

'It said not to tell anyone. Anyway, *you* didn't tell *me*,' said Maddy.

'We should have trusted each other.'

'Yes.' Maddy put her head on one side. 'Shall we agree to trust each other in future?'

'Only if you promise *not* to bump into things,' Rob replied gravely.

'Wise guy.'

'I wonder if Denny or Wayne received the same note?'

Maddy opened her mouth to speak when they heard a faint knocking.

'There's someone at my front door,' announced Rob. 'It might be Denny.'

Rob hurried around the corner to find Detective Superintendent Tanner.

'Oh, hello. I was just talking to Maddy,' stuttered Rob.

'Sorry to trouble you. I called yesterday but neither of you were in,' replied Tanner.

'No.' The two men looked at each other as Rob became conscious of the biting wind. Normally he would have invited Tanner in, but his overnight bag sat just inside the front door. Rob hoped he wasn't looking as guilty as he felt. Maddy solved his dilemma.

'Hi. What are you two doing standing out there in the cold?' she cried. 'Come on in.'

Rob winced. Tanner was the last person he wanted to see right now. His guilty conscience set his brain racing. Did Tanner already suspect their part in last night's explosion? If he bothered to check, he'd find out about their trip easily enough. Rob had bought his air ticket with his credit card. He assumed Maddy had done the same. Then there were the hire cars from Dublin, the hotel bills. Rob followed Tanner back into the granny annex, feeling a growing sense of foreboding.

'You'll have some coffee?' asked Maddy. 'Or would you rather have tea?'

'Coffee's fine, thank you,' replied Tanner. 'I see you've been to Ireland.'

Rob's stomach lurched. He followed Tanner's eye to where Maddy's overnight bag lay on the floor. Around the handle was wrapped a distinctive Aer Lingus cabin luggage label.

'What!' Maddy spun around. 'Oh, that's from when we went to see that Bridges woman. I must get round to taking that label off.'

'I thought you might have been away?'

'No,' said Maddy, evenly. 'Please sit down.'

Tanner lowered his bulk onto the sofa. 'I've called in to tell you that we've found pictures of Mikey Drumm on a closed-circuit TV near Salisbury station at the time of the bombing.'

'But it's too late now,' protested Maddy. 'He's dead.'

'I know. Sometimes I think that this inquiry's jinxed.'

'And you had such high hopes from forensic,' prompted Maddy, feeling that Tanner was about to share a confidence.

'When it works, it's brilliant, but coppers are only human.' Tanner sighed. 'We'll find a cigarette butt and get excited, but invariably it'll turn out that it belonged to a bobby. We discover a shoe print – and it'll be a bobby's size twelve. There's always someone who will step in the wrong place at the wrong time.'

'But it didn't happen in our case, did it?'

'We hope not. But an investigation is only as good as its weakest link. A copper'll be thinking about a row he's had with his girlfriend and he'll miss something. The technology is never all that's it's claimed to be. It's all very well having these facial recognition cameras at airports but I've never known one to work yet.'

'Cheer up,' said Maddy, handing Tanner a cup of coffee.

'Sorry. Sometimes it gets to you. All this effort and nothing to show for it.'

'Any idea who killed Drumm?' asked Rob, embarrassed by Tanner's confidences.

'Hit-and-run driver. Probably from his own side. Drumm's drinking was making him a liability.'

Maddy caught Rob's eye as Tanner stirred sugar into his cup with slow methodical movements.

'But Drumm's not the only bomber to have died,' continued Tanner.

'No?' exclaimed Rob.

'A suspect called Jimmy Burke was blown up on the border with Northern Ireland last night.'

'Really!'

Rob's heart stopped. The Irish newspapers were sitting just feet behind Tanner's head. Luckily, they were folded face down so that their titles were not visible, but . . .

Rob rose and moved towards the kitchen.

'Sugar's already on the table,' called Maddy.

Rob could have killed her.

'I'm just looking for . . . um . . .' He opened a cupboard door. 'Sorry, Mr Tanner. What happened to this Jimmy Burke?'

Maddy was looking at him oddly, wondering what he was doing poking around in her kitchen. Tanner was casually following his movements.

'He was in a barn used as a secret arms dump when the lot went up. There's nothing left of him,' he said. 'The Garda are in two minds whether it's a home goal or the result of a turf war between smuggling gangs.'

'Burke's not a name you've mentioned before,' said Maddy.

Tanner swung to look at her as she came to sit down opposite him. 'He was only just emerging as a suspect.'

Rob opened a drawer and quickly stuffed in the newspapers. As Tanner turned back to see what he was doing, Rob made a play of peering into a cupboard.

'No biscuits, Maddy?'

The fleeting look of horror on Maddy's face told him she had realized her mistake.

'In the other one, Rob.' She stared hard at Tanner, compelling him to meet her eye. 'What was Burke's part in the bombing?'

'He was possibly in the bomb car.'

Rob offered a packet of semi-coated chocolate biscuits to Tanner who declined regretfully.

'My missus tells me I must lose two stone before I retire or I'll never make it around the golf course.'

'You've a few months to go yet.'

'You don't know how much I like my food,' said Tanner, patting his paunch. 'Or my beer.'

There was a knock on the door. Maddy opened it to find Denny, huddling in a thick overcoat with a scarf around his face.

'Hi, good to see you. Come in. I'll get some more coffee going.'

'Thanks.' Denny looked as if he was about to say something else when he spotted Tanner.

'I must be going,' said the detective, rising.

'Thanks for coming around,' said Maddy. 'You have a good day, now.'

Tanner looked thoughtful as he climbed into his car. There'd been something of an atmosphere in the room. And that business of Rob rooting around in Maddy's kitchen. Denny too had looked guilty when he'd spotted him. Strange.

Rob felt a weight lift off his shoulders as he closed the door behind the policeman. He and Maddy exchanged relieved looks. She picked up the overnight bag and carried it into the bedroom as Rob and Denny exchanged comments about the appalling weather. Maddy returned as Rob was recounting what Tanner had told them about the death of a suspect Salisbury bomber in an explosion in Ireland.

'You don't think Wayne killed him, do you?' demanded Denny.

'What?'

'You remember how Wayne threatened revenge a few days ago. I thought it was just the drink talking but then that Mikey Drumm was knocked down in London and now this man Burke's been blown up.'

'It's possible, I suppose,' said Rob.

'There is another thing . . .' Denny took off his glasses and pinched the bridge of his nose. 'Forgive me for asking, but did either of you get a strange note through the door?'

'What sort of note?' asked Maddy in a guarded way.

'It . . . um . . . indicated where Jimmy Burke would be last night,' stuttered Denny.

'What are you saying, exactly?' breathed Maddy.

'I don't know. This note seemed to be offering an opportunity.' Denny shrugged in a helpless gesture. 'I'm not the bravest of men. Maybe Wayne has put us all to shame.'

Maddy looked across at Rob, a question in her eyes. Rob gave a slight nod.

'Sit down, Denny. We've something to tell you.'

*

Breda Bridges fixed the headmistress with an unblinking stare. 'Sister Martha, I don't care what the other girls say. I'm telling you, they are picking on my daughter – *and I'm not having it.*'

'But . . .'

'Aoife came home in tears on Friday and this morning she didn't want to come to school. Aoife loves school normally.'

'Mrs Nolan, you know young girls. One day, they're all best pals. The next, they've fallen out. Aoife's group of playmates seem to have taken against her. I'm sure it's only temporary.'

'Aoife's told me that a gang of girls pushed her over in the playground and one of them deliberately trod on her hand. That's not friends falling out. That's bullying.'

'I've heard a rather different story . . .'

'Bridget Morris and Kirstie Rance are behind this,' continued Breda Bridges. 'You get their mothers up here and sort it out or, by the love of Christ, I'll sort it out myself.'

'Mrs Nolan, Aoife has been known to rile her classmates by flaunting her academic prowess.'

'Aoife can't help it if she's bright,' snapped Breda.

'Maybe if she tried not to show off . . .'

Breda was having difficulty keeping her temper. She had been up half the night as Conn had received a stream of reports about the explosion in Jimmy Burke's barn. The loss of their weapons and the lack of sleep had put her in a foul mood even before this meeting with the headmistress.

'Sister Martha. I will not have my daughter being unhappy. I expect you to put an end to this bullying or I will stop it myself. Do you hear me?' Breda Bridges gave the headmistress one last hard stare and swept out.

She returned home to find her husband finishing a mobile phone conversation.

'The other dump's safe and secured,' he told her. 'Just as well I listened to you and divided the stuff up.'

'What do you reckon happened?'

'God knows! It's not the Provos, that's for sure. They'd have nicked the stuff and then rubbed our faces in it.'

'They won't be happy that our rally went so well – especially after all the newspaper coverage. Did you read that piece in the *Irish Independent*, reckoning we're about to become the alternative mainstream opposition?'

'We're putting the fear of God into Sinn Fein, so we are.'

'They don't like the way we're reinventing their philosophy of the bullet and the ballot box. I'm looking forward to the local elections.'

'I bet Sinn Fein aren't.'

It had been a hectic – and heady – weekend. First Aoife coming home in tears on Friday, then on Saturday the political rally in Castleblayney had turned out to be an outstanding success, far exceeding Breda's wildest hopes, and finally the explosion last night. Breda felt as though she had been through the wringer.

'While I think of it, we must organize a full military funeral for Mikey Drumm. Get someone to talk to his sister and arrange for a funeral director to bring his body back here when the police release it.'

'I'll speak to Deirdre myself.'

'Another thing. I can't get that American cow out of my mind. The fucking cheek, coming here and talking to my children.'

'You don't think . . .'

'She looked mad and bad to me. I want to know if she comes back.'

'I'll get Stozza to see that her photo goes up behind every bar in town. If she sets foot here again I'll know.'

'Stozza did a good job in London.'

'Yeh. Poor Mikey Drumm. Still, we'll make sure he has a decent send-off.'

Rob sensed that something was wrong as soon as he arrived at the charity's headquarters behind St Pancras station in a run-down area of London. A handful of project managers, chatting around the reception desk, gave him an embarrassed, over-effusive welcome and then vanished. He was steered directly into Hannah Beckford's office.

The meeting was strangely formal. Hannah, looking tired under her tan, positioned herself behind her desk while Rob sat in a chair opposite her. There was a small sofa and an occasional table in the office, but Hannah had set the agenda.

They shadow-boxed through the preliminary welcomes until Hannah leaned forward and dropped her voice significantly.

'Rob, there's good news and bad news.' When Rob did not reply, she continued, 'The good news is that no one in Ethiopia seems to have picked up on that . . . incident in the mountains. It's as though it never happened.'

As she sat there, looking every inch a successful career woman in her tailored business suit, Rob recalled her standing, trembling and bare-breasted, under the Tigrinyan sun as he'd been about to gamble with their lives. It seemed a long time ago. So long, in fact, that Hannah appeared to have forgotten all about it!

'Good.'

'But I'm afraid I have bad news as well.' Again Hannah dropped her voice. 'Alasdair Dowling doesn't want to come out of Tanzania. It seems he's involved with some local chief's daughter. I never understand why . . .' She stopped, remembering that Rob too had had a local liaison. 'But we are pledged to continue the work in Ethiopia. We've signed binding agreements with the Ethiopian government.'

'There's nothing stopping me going back.'

'I'm afraid we've hired someone else to take your place in Tigray.'

'Oh.'

'We couldn't afford to let things drift. You know what happens. Miss a month and it takes a year to catch up.'

'So where does that leave me?'

Hannah glanced down at a piece of paper before her on her desk. 'There's still twelve months of your contract left to run. Of course, you're entitled to your salary, but, as I say, we've had to take on this new engineer to replace you, and you know how tight money is. The public's going through a bad patch of charity fatigue. We're having to compete for funds in an ever harder market . . .'

Rob almost bought it. If Ali Dowling had ties in Tanzania, he understood that. And, of course, it wasn't fair that Rob should be paid for doing nothing when the charity needed every penny it could get. He'd resign. That would be the honourable thing to do. Yes, he'd resign – but then . . .

'Hang on, if there's no repercussions in Ethiopia, then there's nothing preventing *me* from going back.'

'Who knows what might leak out in the future? We couldn't risk it. Anyway, like I said, we've already hired someone to take your place.'

'All right, then. How about one of the other projects. Malawi, Somalia, Sudan.'

Hannah opened out her hands. 'If only it were that simple . . .'

Rob understood. She was expecting him to resign. She'd put herself in a spot and now she was relying on him to do the decent thing. Maybe his presence inside the organization reminded her of a memory she was trying to forget. She clearly did not want to talk about it.

A month or so ago, Rob would have helped her by quitting. But he'd changed. If Hannah had jumped the gun – that was her lookout.

'Find me something,' he said.

'I suppose we'll have to, seeing as we're paying you. God knows what. You know nothing about the office side of things.'

'You decided to take someone else on,' he'd reminded her.

Hannah had not liked that. Rob left the building directly after the interview. He had never seen the place so empty. People were keeping out of his way.

God, how things change. One minute he'd been the best thing since sliced bread. Today he was an unwanted stale crust.

Tough.

22

David Hayward spotted Damien Kilfoyle at the centre of a circle of acolytes and admirers as soon as he entered the ante-room where intelligence experts were waiting for the start of MI6's presentation on international terrorism and money laundering.

Hayward was flattered when Kilfoyle broke away and steered him to a corner by themselves.

'Congratulations on your new job, and your engagement.'

'Thanks. I've been meaning to call you. Now that we're going to be working more closely together, let's fix lunch,' suggested Kilfoyle.

'Fine by me,' replied Hayward. 'By the way, surveillance on that East Ham mosque has come up trumps. It turns out to be a staging post between Algerian fundamentalists and cells in the Midlands. Something for your people to run with.'

'Splendid.' Kilfoyle dropped his voice to a conspiratorial whisper. 'Between ourselves, I'm planning to give my department a higher public profile.'

'Really!' Hayward was intrigued.

'Now that the Commissioner has publicly admitted that a suicide bomber on British soil is inevitable, it made me realize that when it does happen we're going to get a lot of flak. Yet we've intercepted four attempted suicide bombers in the past year alone. It's time we received some credit.'

'Come out of the shadows to take a bow, you mean?' suggested Hayward.

Kilfoyle slapped him on the back in delight. 'I'll use that phrase in my submission to the DG. Yes, stepping out of the shadows to take a bow and then returning to the shadows to continue protecting the people. I like it.'

They joined the general movement towards the doors of the lecture theatre. 'What did you make of that explosion outside Monaghan on Sunday night?' inquired Hayward.

'I've not had time to assess it,' lied Kilfoyle.

'It rather looks as if Jimmy Burke blew himself up.' Hayward dropped his voice. 'Does your man "Silvermouth" have anything to say on the matter?'

'No. He's gone very quiet,' lied Kilfoyle smoothly. 'And he's not in a position where we can pressure him to come up with the goods.' Kilfoyle told himself he'd have to give Silvermouth the chop and slip the word to Hayward to stop the detective asking about him.

Kilfoyle had already closed Five's file on Burke. No one in any of the other agencies would ever know that he had been their informer. Few in Five would either, if Kilfoyle could manage to fillet the records.

'By the way, Tanner's getting close to the two English brothers,' announced Hayward. 'I gather he's had a bit of luck at last . . .'

'Ladies and gentlemen, if you are ready . . .'

Kilfoyle took his seat in the front row. But behind his mask of attentiveness he was running through his final meeting with Jimmy Burke last week. For no obvious reason, the farmer had begun ranting against the two lilywhites.

'I don't know why Breda chose those two wankers! That Tony Larkin not only writes his name in his books but his address as well. Bloody little schoolboy.'

It was the first time Burke had mentioned the brothers' surname. Previously he had denied he'd known it. But that was Burke's way. He enjoyed dropping small pearls of information when Kilfoyle was least expecting it.

'Really, and what book was he reading?'

'One about the big feller – Michael Collins.' The irony passed over Burke's head. 'I had a look at it. That's when I saw Larkin's address in London. I only remembered it because I lived in a Gordon Road in Dublin for a while.'

A pearl indeed. But not one that Kilfoyle wanted to pick up.

The English brothers were the only weak link now that Burke was dead. They'd squeal their heads off – and now Tanner was getting close to them. *Shit!*

Tanner liked to say that while every investigation had its moment of luck, the skill came in recognizing that moment. For him, it came when a white Vauxhall Astra, registration N209 PTM, was recorded on camera breaking the speed limit on the Uxbridge Road in West London.

The National Police Computer flagged it as a possible suspect vehicle wanted in connection with the Salisbury bombing.

The owner of the car was registered as Richard Kenneth Ashdown of Clifton, Bristol. Mr Ashdown swore that he had sold the car a couple of weeks before Christmas for £800 cash.

It wasn't his fault that the bloke hadn't registered the ownership of the car, was it? Yes, he knew he should have sent the strip from the registration document back to the DVLA, but the buyer had offered to do that for him. He'd had no reason to disbelieve him.

The buyer? Young, maybe twenty-three or so. Well-spoken. Posh. Tall, say six feet one. Long fair hair with blond highlights, parted in the middle. Looked a bit of a prat, really. He'd come on the back of a motorbike. Didn't get a look at the driver, who hadn't taken his helmet off. But it was a big powerful bike.

Mr Ashdown was taken to the Portishead headquarters of the Avon and Somerset police to help artists recreate a computer photofit of the buyer.

Tanner had no way of knowing if this was the suspect car or not. It could be a blind alley into which he would wastefully direct men before coming to a brick wall. God knows there'd been enough of those on this case. But this time he had a gut feeling. This was the car that had been used to drive the Pizzaman to the airport.

That day it had been last clocked by camera on the M4 as it approached West London. How it had managed to avoid being spotted in the capital was a mystery. But, Tanner started wondering, what if it had never gone further than West London? What if the mystery buyer lived there?

Tanner's theory received a boost when the same car was spotted on camera driving illegally in a bus lane in Acton, not far from the first offence.

Every police officer in West London was ordered to be on the lookout for the white Astra. It could only be a matter of time.

'God, it feels good, Rob. It really does.' Maddy finished her glass of wine with a flourish. She picked up a corkscrew and began to open the next bottle. Rob smiled. One bottle down and the meal not even begun. At this rate they were going to get plastered.

'Let's eat in front of the fire,' he suggested. 'It'll be cosier. There's a nest of small tables . . .'

'I'll put them out.' Maddy bustled off, keeping up an endless stream of chatter – but under the surface there was a feverish quality about her which Rob found unsettling.

He followed her into the living room. She was standing in front of the inglenook, head on one side.

'This is so quaint, Rob,' she sighed. 'It's just like I always dreamed a cottage should look.'

Rob knew what she meant. The log fire, the exposed beams in the low ceiling, the soft lighting from the standard lamps conspired to make the room homely and welcoming. The wind howling in the chimney and the rain lashing the windows were a reminder of the storm raging in the night outside. In here, though, all was warmth and safety.

Maddy burst out laughing.

'What is it?' asked Rob.

'The look on Denny's face yesterday when we told him.'

'Do you really think he's with us?'

'Yeh, I do,' declared Maddy, following Rob back into the kitchen, where he began mashing potatoes. 'So, what are we eating?'

'Beef braised in Guinness, celeriac mash and cabbage with caraway seeds – just right for a foul night like this.'

They settled in front of the fire. Maddy held up her glass, the wine a rich red against the flames. 'A toast. Vengeance.'

'Vengeance.' They drank. 'You know that the Sicilians have a saying that vengeance is a dish best served cold?' he asked.

'I can see what they mean,' said Maddy slowly. 'But no, that's not for me. Every day, it eats at me that those scum are alive and my family's dead. It's like a serpent boring into my innards. I won't be satisfied until everyone, and I mean everyone, involved in planting that bomb is dead. And sooner rather than later. Surely you must feel that?'

'I want retribution as much as you. I just don't have your anger.'

Maddy giggled. 'It's the bad blood of the Hallorans coming out.'

'What?'

'On my mother's side. She used to say there was bad blood in her family which came out in the women every other generation or so.'

'Go on!' Rob reached over to top up Maddy's glass.

'No, it's true. Back in Ireland in the 1840s, Kitty Halloran was transported for setting fire to an absentee landlord's mansion; in the 1880s, Liza Halloran was hanged for shooting the land agent who had just thrown her out of her house. Her daughter Fanny went to the Yukon where she ran a miners' brothel until they discovered she was killing her punters and stealing their gold.'

'What happened to her?'

'Hanged,' replied Maddy simply. 'Then there was Cousin Geraldine who poisoned three of her husbands, but they could never prove it. She became a nun in Cork about the time of the First World War.

In New York in the 1930s Great-aunt Josephine killed two Italians who tried to rape her.'

'Self-defence?'

'Next day, in their butchers' shop with one of their own meat cleavers? And in front of customers?'

'Ah.'

'She was lucky not to get the electric chair. But it's always the female side. Now I reckon it's coming out in me.'

'Is that what your father-in-law meant by saying he hoped that you didn't go off the rails?'

'You've got a good memory,' exclaimed Maddy. 'This food is really excellent, Rob. You must give me the recipe.'

'There isn't one. I made it up.'

'Still, it's very good.' Maddy brushed her hair back over one ear and drank again.

'Off the rails?' he repeated.

Maddy took a deep breath. 'When Tom first started . . . playing around, I handled it badly. I drank too much. I don't mean like this. This is in company and we're celebrating,' she added quickly. 'I used to drink by myself. I crashed the car one night. Another time the kitchen in the cabin caught fire. Cries for help, the psychiatrist said.'

'What happened?'

'Tom stopped playing around, or so I thought. Looking back, I reckon he just became more discreet.'

Rob put another log on the fire and they sat quietly watching the blue flames flicker delicately around its edges.

'A fire is rather like revenge,' declared Rob. 'It has to destroy to exist. I hope we don't get like that.'

'You're being fanciful,' murmured Maddy.

The window panes rattled under a squall. A log fell, sending up a display of sparks.

'You know, there's only one thing wrong with what we did to Burke,' said Maddy dreamily.

'What's that?'

'Burke didn't know he was going to die. He wasn't frightened.'

'I don't understand.'

'It's not enough just to kill someone. You put a gun to someone's head and pull a trigger. So what? Their lights go out. They don't know about it. Probably they don't even feel it. I want them to be crapping themselves when I kill them.' Maddy's brown eyes had gone black and as pitiless as a dungeon. 'They have to know that they're going to die.'

'Do you think we'll live to see the end of our quest?'

'The idea of revenge is all that's keeping me alive. I won't care what happens to me as long as I can avenge Mitch and TJ.' Maddy paused. 'And Tom.'

'Who do you think sent that note?'

'We've been through this with Denny. As I said, it doesn't matter as long as—'

The phone rang, making them both start. Ten o'clock. Who could be calling now? Reluctantly, Rob reached for the receiver.

'Hello?'

'Can I speak with Mekaela Telassi?' An American voice distorted by a bad line. The request threw Rob.

'Um, she's not here right now,' he stuttered.

'This is Wolfgang Mayer at the BPL Agency in Manhattan, New York.'

'Yes?'

'Tell Mekaela that her portfolio ain't the classiest we've ever seen, but she sure does have something special. She needs to get herself over here in person, though. She said in her letter that that wouldn't be a problem.'

'Um . . .'

'Tell her she needs to get rid of that Ethiopian passport. She'll never get an American visa with that. She mentioned she's planning to become a British citizen. That'll be fine. Just tell her to hurry up and marry this guy. One last thing, tell her accommodation won't be a problem. We've got lots of girls sharing apartments around New York. She'll find a room easy.'

Rob put down the phone, his stare glassy-eyed.

'Is everything all right?' asked Maddy.

Rob began recounting the telephone conversation. 'So that's why Mekaela wanted to get married. She needed a British passport.'

And then she would have flown off to New York to begin her modelling career, leaving him and Alfred behind. Rob had had his suspicions. He had put them out of his mind as being unworthy once Mekaela had been killed. But he had been right all along.

'Just shows you can't trust women,' he mumbled, largely to himself.

'You can – at least, some women.' Maddy slid onto the floor in front of the fire and held out an arm for Rob to join her. She thought how vulnerable and young he looked then. He wore his heart on his sleeve and he had just been deeply hurt. She felt an overwhelming urge to ease his pain.

Maddy reached out to wrap her hands around his neck. 'We're not all bad, you know.'

She leaned her head to one side and gave him a sleepy smile. Rob locked his hands around her neck and gazed into her eyes. Maddy's head swooned with the wine. *That's my excuse,* she told herself. *I'm drunk, and women do stupid things when they're drunk.*

But I'm not so drunk that I don't know what I'm doing. And what I want to do.

Maddy cupped Rob's face with her hands and brushed his lips with hers. At the back of her mind she was aware that her husband had been killed less than a month ago – but in many ways he had been dead for years.

Maddy undid the top button of Rob's shirt.

*

'Did you enjoy the panto?'

Five-year-old Jack Pottidge stared at his shoes and mumbled indistinctly.

'What do you say, Jack?' coaxed his father Graham.

'Thank you,' the little boy finally managed.

'He loved it.' His mother Helen beamed. 'You should have heard him cheering and booing. I had to stop him from standing on the seat at one point.'

'I saw him,' admitted Denny.

'You could see that!' Graham Pottidge was astonished. He found it unnerving to stand here on stage after the show, even in front of an empty auditorium.

'It's a knack,' explained Denny.

'Which bit did you like best, Jack?' prompted his mother.

'The mirror with the bad man,' replied Jack. 'When he lit the cigar.'

'Did you like the wicked witch, Jack?'

'She was frightening.'

'Carole.' Denny waved to a nondescript young girl in jeans and with short hair who had just appeared. 'Come and meet Jack. He thinks you're frightening.'

'You're not the wicked witch,' proclaimed Jack uncertainly as Carole approached. After all, in the panto she had worn a black cape, and had had protruding teeth and a spider's web painted on her face. And she'd kept snapping black chewing gum at the audience.

'Oh yes, I am, young man,' replied Carole in her stage voice. 'I'm in disguise.'

She gave a manic cackle, pulled out a length of black gum she was still chewing and let it snap back. Jack gulped and scuttled behind his mother's skirt.

'See you later.' Carole winked at Denny and strode off. Jack's eyes followed her, his mouth gaping open.

'We really can't thank you enough,' repeated Graham Pottidge for the fourth time.

'I'm glad you made it before we closed,' replied Denny. 'I remembered you saying you were about to come when the . . . before Christmas.'

'If there's anything I can do.'

'Come on, Jack. You should go to the toilet before we get in the car.' Ann led her son away.

'Catch the bombers,' replied Denny. *Or we'll kill them*, he could have added.

A look of pain crossed Pottidge's earnest face. 'We are trying, I promise you.'

'It must be very frustrating, knowing who did it but being unable to bring them to court.'

'Tell me about it,' said Pottidge.

They waved goodbye. Denny, who had stayed in character for the backstage visit, returned to his dressing room to change. He began wiping away the pancake make-up in front of the mirror, thinking that he had aged. After the events of the past days, it was not surprising.

He was still reeling at Rob and Maddy's revelations. Two sane, likeable people had confessed to killing a man – *and he had cheered.* The world was going mad.

Then, this morning, he had finally received the phone call from the genito-urinary department of Salisbury District Hospital confirming his worse fears. He was indeed HIV positive. Dr Mortenson was very reassuring. It wasn't immediately life-threatening – not like it used to be.

He did not know that Denny had always been susceptible to illness and infections. He had only to cut his finger and it went septic. He had even gone down with two bouts of pneumonia when he'd been otherwise healthy. What chance did he have now that his immune system was crumbling?

And yet he had given his word to Rob and Maddy that he would help them in their quest to be avenged on the bombers. What else could he do – when all the others had done their bit?

But did Clive deserve to be avenged? Denny felt disgusted with himself for even entertaining the thought. Of course Clive must be avenged. To err was human; to forgive was divine. He forgave Clive – but he'd never forgive those who had murdered him.

'Good morning, I've brought you a cup of tea.'

Maddy opened her eyes and blinked at the sight of the lime-washed ceiling. What? Where? She was confused. Then she turned to see Rob in a dressing gown, a mug in each hand. He appeared to be about to get into bed with her.

The memories of last night flooded back. Maddy closed her eyes again.

What could Rob think of her? Not just a bloodthirsty murderess but a trollop as well. She had thrown herself at him. He had been the calm one: the voice of reason, asking her if she was really sure she wanted to do this. Maddy had let her body and her hands reply. God, she'd been all over him, she'd almost eaten him alive. He hadn't had a chance. No wonder their lovemaking hadn't been all that successful – she'd terrified the poor man.

Tom used to tell her she was sexually demanding – but last night she'd been something else. She'd needed that release. But why had she let herself get that drunk?

But then the memory of what had happened in the middle of the night returned. She'd been facing away from Rob when she'd woken to feel his hand gliding over her thigh, shaping her body into a foetal position before he'd gently entered her from behind.

That had worked. Jesus, how it had worked! Fulfilled and complete, she had turned her head to kiss him, murmuring her pleasure. Then she'd wrapped her body around his and fallen asleep.

That memory made her feel better. She became aware that Rob was still hesitating by the side of the bed, unsure of whether or not to join her.

She held out a hand. 'Thank you for last night.'

'Thank *you*.'

Maddy sat up and watched as Rob's gaze dropped to her breasts. She liked her breasts, in fact she liked her whole body. She knew she was in good shape.

'Come back to bed, and talk to me.'

'Talk?'

'Well . . .' Maddy rolled over and stood up.

'I thought you wanted me to come to bed.'

'And I need to go to the little girls' room and clean my teeth.'

'Who said that romance was dead?'

'The longer you wait, the better it'll be.'

This wasn't supposed to happen, Maddy told herself. None of it was supposed to happen. She wasn't supposed to have slept with Rob, she wasn't supposed to have enjoyed it or to want to do it again. Most of all, she wasn't supposed to be getting this strange exhilarating feeling. She thought it was called falling in love.

Maddy returned to the bedroom to find Rob staring transfixed at an envelope he was holding in his hands.

'Look what I found on the doormat,' he whispered.

23

Darren Larkin was bored. His girlfriend Leila had insisted on going to work on a display stand at some poxy exhibition at the Birmingham NEC rather than staying home with him. They'd been rowing about it for days. Darren didn't know what the exhibition was about. It didn't matter. They were all the same. There'd be Leila in a microskirt and tight T-shirt, handing out brochures to sad old businessmen. She was nothing but a tramp. But Leila was going to get her come-uppance – and soon . . .

But, shit, he was bored. Seven o'clock and the night loomed emptily ahead of him. He'd stopped going to the Irish pub after the woman had warned him and his brother off doing anything that might identify themselves with the cause.

That woman had been brilliant. Just like a spymaster in the books he loved to read. She had known he'd read Gaelic studies at Dublin for two years before dropping out of university; she'd known of his sympathies, and had even been able to produce copies of his letters to the nationalist news-sheets arguing against the peace process. She hadn't had to try hard to persuade him to join the bombers. And his brother Tony would go along with anything he did.

But the adventure had not turned out as he'd envisaged. He hadn't liked the attitudes of the Irish contingent at all. He'd found them boorish, uncultured, patronizing and thuggish. And he'd never heard anyone so foul-mouthed as that Teresa woman.

It had been made clear from the start that he and Tony were mere skivvies. They had not minded doing the shopping – but not all the washing-up and clearing up as well.

Darren wished he had gone snowboarding in France with Tony now, but he hadn't fancied riding on the back of his brother's bike as he raced along the autoroutes. And he couldn't risk taking the Astra because he wasn't sure it would get to the Alps and back without breaking down. He hardly drove it anyway. Leila used it more than he did.

But soon it would be his twenty-third birthday. Then, at last, he'd get his hands on his share of the trust fund. No more living on mummy's little hand-outs. He'd be a major player in his own right. A cool £3 million to spend as he liked. He'd buy a Porsche, or were they becoming passé? Maybe a BMW sports job or a convertible for summer. But a month in the West Indies first. He'd have a surprise for Leila. He'd tell her about his legacy, show her his airline ticket to paradise and then give her the boot. That would serve her right for going off with fat old businessmen and leaving him alone in Ealing.

He who laughs last laughs longest.

Feeling smug, Darren Larkin wandered into the kitchen to fetch a lager from the fridge. He was opening the can when he glanced out of the window. A police car was slowly turning into the cul-de-sac behind the house where he'd parked the Astra. Strange. He'd never seen a police car there before.

The doorbell rang. Darren put down his beer to answer it. He opened the door to find two policemen in blue sweaters and flat caps standing there. The world swam in front of his eyes.

He faintly heard one of the policemen demand if he was Darren or Tony Larkin.

'Darren,' he replied weakly.

'Do you mind if we come in?' Without waiting for a reply, the policemen pushed past, closing the door behind them. In a daze, Darren wandered back into the kitchen. Looking out of the window he saw that the police car had stopped beside the Astra.

'Are you all right, Darren?' asked the shorter, bespectacled policeman.

'Yeh, yeh, I'm fine.' Darren made himself concentrate.

The policeman followed Darren's gaze out of the window. 'Does that white car belong to you?'

'No. Nothing to do with me.'

The policeman regarded him steadily through metal-framed glasses. Darren thought for a moment that he looked vaguely familiar but then he dismissed the idea.

'Anyway, what do you want?' he blustered. 'You can't just barge in here like this.'

'You're going to be glad we're here, laddie.'

Darren picked up the man's Irish accent for the first time. 'Who are you?'

'Conn Nolan sent us. You and your brother are in the shit. We've come to get you out of it.'

'I don't know what you're talking about.'

'Look down there.' The man indicated out to where a police officer was now kneeling in front of the Astra. 'We're only just in time.'

'So you're not coppers.'

'In one, Darren. But can you think of a better disguise?'

'You're lucky to have good friends in Ireland with their ear to the ground,' said the other man. 'You know Nolan rates you and your brother.'

'He's got a funny way of showing it,' exclaimed Darren Larkin. 'My arm's still aching after grinding all the fertilizer. There was only me and the Tone. No one else offered to help.'

The men laughed. 'That's an apprenticeship everyone goes through. You did fine. Where's your brother now?'

'He went snowboarding in France yesterday for a fortnight. I'll phone him.'

'It's not safe to use mobile phones now. Do you know where he's staying?'

'Yeh. The family's got a timeshare on an apartment in Les Arcs.'

The man pulled out a notebook. 'Write down his address and his mobile phone number. Someone will go and warn him.'

The taller man, watching the real policeman through the window, was growing increasingly agitated.

'Are you sure that white car down there's nothing to do with you?'

Darren flushed. 'Yeh, well . . .'

'We've got to get out of here,' muttered the man.

'I need to pack a bag,' said Darren.

'There's no time. That copper's radioing for back-up. We're going to get caught like rats in a trap.'

They hurried to the door where the shorter man, who seemed to be in charge, halted. 'Let's cuff him,' he said to his colleague. 'That way, if we meet the rozzers, it'll look as though we've already nicked him.'

'Good idea. Darren, put your hands behind your back.'

Before he knew what was happening, Darren felt cold steel closing around his wrists.

The three began going down the stairs. At the last landing, the taller man ran on ahead to fetch their car.

'There's more cops in the next road,' he reported back. 'Something's going down. We've got to leave quickly. Ready?'

The men grasped Darren by his arms and hustled him out. He saw that a car had been backed right up to the bottom of the steps, its boot gaping open.

'What are you doing?' Darren began struggling.

'So no one sees you leave.' Before he could complain, Darren was bundled into the boot. 'Don't make a sound. When we're clear, we'll stop and let you out.'

The boot lid came down, imprisoning him in total darkness.

'That was easy,' said Denny, putting away the police sweaters in readiness for their return to the theatrical costumiers. At the end of the road Rob was forced to stop as two police cars, lights flashing but without sirens, hurtled around the bend, heading towards Darren's home.

'There was something about that white car,' mused Denny. 'Perhaps chummy's really in hot water with the police.'

'Helped us, though.'

A heavy banging came from the car boot.

'Impatient little sod, isn't he?' commented Rob.

'Not the sort of person I could naturally take to,' agreed Denny. 'No wonder the bombers gave him a hard time.'

They drove out of London on the M40 in the late rush-hour traffic before turning north towards Aylesbury. Soon they were travelling along unlit roads, going deeper and deeper into the countryside. The night was pitch black with heavy clouds.

'This just might work, you know,' said Rob.

'It's certainly dark enough. You can't see a hand in front of your face.'

The men chuckled.

'How did you ever find this place?' inquired Rob.

'We shot a *Doctor Who* series there,' replied Denny. 'It was my first TV role. I played a young prince whose people were being threatened by alien slave traders from another galaxy.'

'Didn't you get all the good parts!'

'It paid the bills.'

'You were very convincing as a terrorist back there.'

'Thank you. It's good to know that my time at RADA wasn't totally wasted.' Denny shone a pencil torch on the large-scale map on his lap. 'Next right and then on past the pub. I hope Maddy can find the place.'

'She'll find it,' said Rob. 'She's a pretty determined woman.'

They travelled along a tree-lined lane until their headlights picked out Rob's Peugeot Estate parked alongside a ruined cottage. As they pulled up, Maddy, in jeans and a short coat, climbed out.

'Everything okay?' she whispered.

'Went like a charm,' replied Rob. 'Come and meet Darren Larkin, who helped to make the car bomb.'

'He admitted it, did he?'

'He said that he and his brother ground fertilizer until their arms almost dropped off.'

Rob opened the boot and switched on a torch. Darren's face, bleached by the powerful beam, blinked up at them.

'What do you mean by leaving me in here all that time?' he snapped, struggling to sit up.

'There's someone who wants to see you.'

'Yeh, who?' Darren's arrogance drained away. Something was not right. The man's Irish accent had disappeared. No one was offering to help him out of the boot, nor take the handcuffs off.

'What a worm,' said Maddy.

'You're American,' exclaimed Darren.

'And you're dead,' she drawled.

'Who are you?'

'We lost people we loved when that bomb exploded in Salisbury.'

'But that wasn't down to me. I had nothing to do with that bomb.'

'You helped prepare the big one.'

'But it didn't go off,' he snivelled.

'You *wanted* it to explode and kill innocent people, didn't you?'

'No. No. I never.' Darren began sobbing.

'Take those cuffs off his wrists, they'll leave marks,' ordered Maddy.

Rob unlocked the handcuffs. 'Put your hands out in front of you. And don't try anything or I'll slit your throat here and now.'

Larkin held out his hands. Rob tied them roughly together and pushed Darren back into the boot.

'Let me tell you what is going to happen to you.' The shorter man began speaking in a cold measured way. 'We're going to drive this car to a lonely place and leave you there. In an hour or maybe two, a man will come and open the boot. He will kill you. Maybe he'll stab you. Personally I hope he'll garrotte you. Garrotting is the worst way to die – eyes bulging, tongue lolling, pissing and shitting yourself as you lose control. If the man chooses, he can make your death last a long, long time. And he will.'

'Die badly,' breathed the woman.

She slammed the lid and the three moved away.

'Christ, Denny, where did you get all that stuff from?' whispered Maddy. 'You even scared me.'

'Lines from a film I once appeared in, dear heart,' he replied. 'I thought they were appropriate.'

Darren Larkin braced himself as the car set off again. By the way he was being thrown around, it was clear that they were climbing a steep rough track. The car lurched forward, so that Darren struck his nose against the side of the boot. Eyes watering, he tried to protect his face with his bound hands.

The ropes gave a fraction. He flexed his wrists – and his heart soared. He should be able to work himself loose – if he had enough time. But did he have that time? The car lurched again. This time, the back of his head struck a bag of solid objects. The car slowed down, stopped and began reversing. The engine was turned off. He heard a door slam, then all was silent.

Darren swallowed in fear and worked furiously at the ropes. They gave – but not enough. His murderer was on his way, driving towards him, getting nearer every minute. In a convulsive movement, he drew his knees back into his chest and kicked upwards at the boot with all his strength. Kicked once, twice, three times. Kicked and kicked, accompanying the blows by oaths, threats and pleas for mercy. The boot held solid. Darren sobbed in terror.

Exhausted, with tears streaming down his cheeks, Darren Larkin slumped back and winced again as his head came into contact with the bag. A bag? He scrambled around until his fingers could feel familiar objects through the canvas. Of course, a tool bag. A bloody tool bag.

Darren Larkin managed to undo the zip and touched the cold metal of a spanner. Delving deeper, his fingers brushed the plastic case of a torch. He pulled it out and pressed the switch. A bright beam lit up the inside of the boot. Looking up, he saw that the boot lock was secured to the body of the car by just four Phillips screws.

With difficulty, he positioned the torch to shine on the lock and set to work, holding the screwdriver between his bound hands. The first screw turned easily. So did the second, and the third. The last screw was harder. The weight of the boot lid was pressing on this one screw. It refused to turn more than a millimetre at a time.

'Come on. Come on.' Sweat ran in streams into his eyes and soaked the back of his shirt. 'Got to get out of here.'

How long had he been entombed in this boot? How much longer before his killer arrived? The screw turned a little further. Darren tried again. Now the screw was coming. It was turning freely. With a sigh of relief, he prised out the screw and gently pushed up the lid of the boot. The night was pitch black. He paused for a moment, gulping in mouthfuls of cool air.

The sound of a car engine came on the breeze. Darren struggled to sit up and peer out. He could not see any headlights, only hear the car – but that could mean only one thing. His killer was arriving.

Awkwardly he squirmed around until he managed to get one leg over the rim of the boot. He reached blindly for the ground – in vain.

The car's engine was louder now. Closer.

He *had* to get away. Darren swung his other leg over the boot rim, balanced for a second – and let go.

He felt the cold rush of air on his face. He was falling, falling.

An endless fall through a black void, tumbling through the darkness – as though living a nightmare.

Darren was face down when he struck the rock which drove his ribs into his lungs and heart. The force of the impact pitched him into the air again.

He was still screaming when he struck the water a hundred feet below the edge of the old quarry.

'That worked out well,' observed Rob, approaching the hire car with replacement screws.

Denny shone the strong torch-beam down on the water where ripples were moving outwards in circles from the spot where Darren Larkin had landed.

Of Larkin himself there was no sign.

'Very well indeed,' agreed Maddy.

24

The discovery of the white Astra car prompted a difference of opinion between Tanner, now effectively in control of the day-to-day running of the investigation, and Hayward, still nominally in charge. Hayward wanted to stake out the car to see who returned to it. Tanner believed that the car's location indicated the driver lived locally. He wanted to find him as quickly as possible by going on the knocker.

As a compromise, Tanner agreed to wait until midnight. Then, as no one had approached the car, the street lights were switched off and the area sealed. A bomb-disposal team moved in. Once they declared the car safe, scenes-of-crime officers began working silently.

Just as it seemed that the search was going to be fruitless, a small folded piece of paper, all stuck together, was found under the driver's floor mat.

Twenty minutes of patient work revealed that not only was it a parking permit designed to be stuck to the inside of a car window – but, vitally, that it bore the word *Salisbury*. That was enough. The date was indecipherable but the lab would work on that. This was the car they were looking for.

The first local setting off for work identified the owner of the Astra as the young man who lived in the flat below her. Early twenties, tall, blond hair parted in the middle. She thought his name was Darren. He had a brother with a motorbike.

*

Tanner stood in the middle of the brothers' living room, waiting for Darren Larkin's girlfriend Leila Stebbings – and worrying that their bird might already have flown.

Police had found not only the hi-fi turned on, but also an almost full can of lager on the kitchen table. Both were indications of a hurried departure. On the plus side, Darren's passport was still in a bedside drawer – so he couldn't have left the country.

Women's clothing hung in the wardrobe and a security pass for the current exhibition at the Birmingham NEC in the name of Leila Stebbings lay on the dressing table. Tanner began to believe his luck might be changing – at last.

As West Midlands police worked to track her down, reports came in that two policemen had been seen entering the house early the previous evening. Ealing police and the surrounding boroughs were now contacting every officer who had been on afternoon shift.

Leila was traced to the bedroom of a South African businessman. She had not been happy, said the Birmingham lads when they arrived with her. The businessman even less so.

Leila was a sleek five feet ten with a copper tan and teeth too white to be natural.

'Thank you for coming,' began Tanner.

'I didn't think I had a choice,' sniffed the girl, impatiently tossing her long blonde hair over her shoulder.

'It is important.'

'It'd better be. I've lost two days' work.'

Tanner offered Leila a seat on the sofa and positioned a chair in front of her.

'When did you last see Darren Larkin?'

'When I left here yesterday morning. Why?'

Tanner ignored her question. 'Was he planning to go away?'

'Nah.'

'Does his brother live here as well?'

'The Tone, yeh.' Leila, sullen and defensive, folded her arms.

'The Tone?'

'Darren's little brother Tony. Except he's snowboarding in France.'

'You know where?'

'Nah. Their family's got an apartment in some ski resort, but I've never been invited.'

'How long have you known Darren Larkin?'

'About a year.'

'And you live with him?'

Leila gave a half-shrug. 'Sometimes. I work away a lot.'

'Were the three of you here during the week before Christmas?'

'No. Darren and the Tone were away for a few days together somewhere.'

'Where?'

'Dunno. It was their big secret. I didn't bother to ask?'

'Weren't you curious where your boyfriend was?'

'If I don't ask him, then he doesn't ask me – or he shouldn't. Big spoiled kid.'

'You didn't part on the best of terms?'

'Darren was pissed off because I was going to Birmingham and leaving him alone down here. He doesn't understand that that's what I do for money.'

Tanner did not ask if she was referring to her promotional work or to a more lucrative sideline.

'When the brothers were away before Christmas, do you remember if they both returned on the same day?'

'Shit. Is this really important?'

Tanner leaned forward and locked his eyes into hers. 'Very.'

Leila made a play of trying to remember. 'Yeh. They did. It was the night of a friend's party. We all got wrecked.'

'Was that when Darren brought back the white Astra?'

'Could have been.'

'You drive it, do you?'

'Not often.' There was something behind her eyes now.

'But more often recently?'

'Could be. Look, what's this about anyway?'

'We'd like to find Darren Larkin.'

'Why, what's the creep done?'

'We wish to interview him in connection with the Salisbury bombing.'

'Darren!' The girl gave a contemptuous laugh. 'He hasn't got it in him. He's a prat.'

'Had he ever shown any Irish republican sympathies?'

'He went to college in Dublin but he dropped out.' Leila paused. 'I'll tell you something odd, though. He and the Tone used to live in Irish pubs. Loved the craic, as he used to say. Then suddenly they stopped going.'

'When was this?'

'Towards the end of last year sometime. I don't know. I didn't complain. I never could stand those awful songs.'

'All right. Now think carefully. Do you have any idea where Darren could have gone?'

'Nah. He wouldn't have gone to France. The Tone's the better snowboarder and Darren didn't like that.'

'What about friends?'

'They tend to keep themselves to themselves, in a sort of way. Most of the Tone's mates'll be out snowboarding with him.'

'Write out a list of their mates with addresses and telephone numbers,' ordered Tanner. 'Where do Darren's parents live?'

'The dad's dead. His mother lives in Kensington. She's loaded. She went to the West Indies for New Year. She's still out there.'

'Are the brothers well off?'

'You wouldn't think so, the way they behave,' muttered Leila resentfully. 'Tight-fisted arseholes, especially Darren. But he's coming into his inheritance in a few weeks on his twenty-third birthday. He doesn't know I know that. It's the only reason I put up with the prick.'

*

Maddy stared at the silent boarded-up shops and told herself that she had been right to return.

The streets immediately around the scene of the blast were due to be reopened soon. The shops would be remodelled, the mall rebuilt. The police caravan, centre of the witness appeal in the early days, would leave tomorrow. This was the last chance for Maddy to see where her family had been killed before it changed for ever.

Tanner had promised to escort Maddy here but he and Pottidge had been called to London last night and had not returned. Instead, she was now being accompanied by a young woman detective she did not know.

The shopping mall itself had been shut off as structurally unsafe so she stood at the entrance, where the bomb car had been parked; where she had first met Rob.

It seemed a lifetime ago. In fact it was just four weeks.

Neither Rob nor Denny had wanted to come with her. They had not felt the need, they'd said. But Maddy saw her visit as a pilgrimage made from strength, not from weakness. Since she had embarked on her trail of revenge, she had felt rejuvenated. She now had a purpose – a deadly purpose.

Maddy bent on one knee to place her flowers – early daffodils, Mitch's favourite – against the corner of the toyshop and bowed her head. She found herself remembering the events of last night, and how she and Rob had made love almost as soon as they had walked in through the door.

It was as though killing Darren Larkin had aroused their primeval instincts. They had coupled with a brutal directness. They had been no coquetry, no subtlety. Instead, they had rutted like animals, sweating and grunting until they climaxed.

It had been a long time before either spoke.

'How do you feel?' Rob had asked.

'Good.'

'And about what happened at the quarry?'

'Good,' she replied in exactly the same tone.

'No regrets?' Rob rolled on his side to look at Maddy.

'You keep asking me that. No, I've no regrets at all.'

There was another silence until Rob said, 'It's funny to lie here knowing we're murderers.'

'Speak for yourself, feller. You know what I keep thinking? That's another one of the bastards dead. Does that shock you?'

'Nothing you do shocks me any more.'

'Huh! You wait and see.' Maddy grinned. 'Do you think we're like Bonnie and Clyde?'

'You mean that scene where they're lying on the floor and she slides down out of shot and his eyes pop.'

'No, although . . .' Maddy snaked down his body.

'Aaargh.' Rob grasped her hair and tried to pull her back up. 'Bonnie didn't do that.'

Maddy relaxed her grip to smile up at him. 'How do you know? It was out of shot.'

'Come back up here.'

This time they made love slowly and gently, looking in each other's eyes all the while.

Rob had fallen asleep first. Maddy had pulled his head onto her breast and stroked his hair. Then she had wept softly.

Maddy thanked the woman detective and crossed back through the police tapes into the busy city centre. She was glad she had come here – it had reaffirmed her belief that what she was doing was right, but she'd never go back again.

She turned into the Market Square. Wayne Wallis was standing behind a stall selling leather clothing. She had not seen him since that day he had sworn revenge – and set the others on their path. She hurried over.

'Hi. How are you doing?'

Wayne seemed startled to see her. 'Okay. I'm looking after a mate's stall. That's what life's about, ain't it? Helping mates.'

'We called at your house a couple of times . . .'

'I . . . um . . . had some business in London.'

Maddy fixed Wayne with her eyes. 'We're proud of you,' she whispered.

'Yeh, well.'

'Your secret's safe with us.'

Wayne nodded. 'Um . . .'

'I'm meeting with Rob and Denny later.' Maddy lowered her voice even further. 'We're going to France. Maybe you'd like to come.'

'I don't know I could afford it.'

'We'll work something out if you want. Come to Rob's cottage around seven-thirty this evening? We'll all be there.'

'Yeh, right. I'll see you then.'

Wayne gazed after Maddy as she walked away. *Shit!* She had class. From the way she'd looked at him, Wayne thought he might be in with a chance there.

But what the bleeding hell had she been on about? She knew his secret, and they were proud of him!

Wayne was confused. He'd not been around because he had scarpered to stay with his brother in Wimbledon as soon as that stupid cow Shaynee had threatened to tell her husband about their affair.

Wayne had a golden rule – it was never worth getting beaten up for a shag with a slag. He'd only returned a couple of days ago when he'd heard that she'd picked up with a tyre fitter in the next road. That was fine by Wayne.

For the first time Maddy found fault with her new little home. There wasn't a microwave oven. She made a note to treat the granny annexe to one on her next shopping trip.

Maddy had decided that the easiest way to feed Rob, Denny and Wayne would be to give them a Chinese meal. But the ways of America had not reached Wiltshire. Her assumption that the Chinese restaurant in Salisbury would deliver had been met with polite incredulity, although she was welcome to pick up a takeaway meal herself if she wanted.

Maddy took this as a challenge to her organizational skills and set about ordering a meal over the phone and arranging for a local taxi company to deliver it at eight o'clock. A quick blast in a microwave oven would have perked up the food – except that she did not have one.

She was laying out plates and glasses when she heard a car turn along the narrow lane outside the annexe. It was only ten past seven. The others were not due yet. Maddy peered out into the night. A solitary figure that she did not recognize was sitting in the driver's seat. The sense of foreboding was growing inside Maddy when there was a heavy knock on the door. She cursed England's gun laws. If she'd been home, she'd have had a pistol in her handbag. Her eyes flicked around the room, searching for a weapon. The fireside poker seemed woefully inadequate. The knocking came again. Maddy pulled open a kitchen drawer and snatched up the largest knife she could find.

'Who's there?' she called.

There was no reply.

'Who's there?' she called again, grasping the carving knife behind her back.

'Maddy, it's me. Rose Allen.'

Maddy closed her eyes in relief and opened the door. Rose stepped into the cottage to halt at the sight of the knife in Maddy's hand.

'Are you all right?'

'Sorry. I saw someone sitting in a car outside.'

'I was listening to the end of *The Archers* on the radio. Sorry I scared you.'

'It's nothing.'

'I was just passing and wondered how this morning had gone, in Salisbury.'

'I'm glad I went.' Maddy indicated the drinks on the sideboard. 'Would you like sherry or gin?'

'Not for me, thanks. I'm driving. How was Mr Tanner?'

'He wasn't there. He's been called up to West London on a new development. Do sit down.'

Rose raised her eyebrows. 'Maybe this is the breakthrough he's been waiting for.'

'I do hope so. He's working so hard but he feels the investigation is jinxed.'

'Did he say that?'

'Yes, after that Irishman was knocked down in London. And then there was that man who blew himself up in Ireland at the weekend.'

'Jimmy Burke.'

'Yes. You obviously read the newspapers.'

'Some names just stick in your memory.'

'Well, that's . . . two of the swine dead.' Maddy bit her lip. God, that had been close. She'd almost said *three* – but no one was supposed to know about Darren Larkin. She'd have to watch her tongue. 'My curse is working after all.'

'Do you believe in such things?'

'This is just the start. You'll see. Everyone involved in planting that bomb will end up in jail – or dead. Hopefully dead.'

'You don't really mean that.'

'I do. I'd kill them myself, especially that Teresa Bridges who put the bomb in the litter bin.'

'But the police have no proof against her.'

'Yeh, they do. It just can't be used in court. That's why I—'

There was a knock at her front door. Maddy was relieved that it had prevented her tongue running away with her for the second time. She'd have to be careful what she said, even in front of a friend like Rose Allen.

She opened the door. Rob, Denny and Wayne trooped in.

'There's a strange-looking green thing outside,' exclaimed Rob.

'That's my new hire car,' replied Maddy.

'But it's lime green!'

'Yep. It's a lime-green VW Beetle. Fun car, huh?'

'You certainly don't see many of those around here.'

'Excuse me.' Rose Allen got up to leave. 'I didn't know you were expecting visitors.'

'We meet up once in a while,' said Maddy, feeling unnecessarily guilty. 'You don't have to go.'

'I've things to do.' Rose Allen paused by the door. 'I know what I was going to ask you. Have you heard anything more about the second post-mortem on Mitch?'

'The pathologist that Tanner wants is in the States. He's due back early next week.'

'Take care of yourself. I'm going away for the weekend but I'll call you when I get back.'

Rose Allen was Maddy's second visitor in a few days to leave looking unusually thoughtful.

Wayne Wallis was surprised to learn that he was being credited with killing an Irishman he had never met. And even more surprised to find that this act had led to two further murders. But Wayne was not one to show his emotions. And the more he thought about it, the more he liked the idea of himself as a pathfinder of vengeance. Fact and fiction ran through his life as an indivisible stream. The fact that he was the inspiration for a group of murdering avengers did not worry him at all. He stayed silent, drinking a can of beer, and let the others do the talking. Suddenly he found that Denny was addressing him.

'So you didn't get a note about Mickey Drumm?'

Wayne gathered his wits. 'Nah. Like I said, I know this reporter bloke . . .'

'Whoever it was didn't give us much time with Darren Larkin. It was just as well Denny could get those policemen's uniforms.' Rob Sage laughed. 'You should have seen the way he convinced Larkin that he was a mate of Nolan's.'

Denny chuckled. 'I don't often get the chance to play the villain.'

'Your Belfast accent had me convinced,' said Rob.

'But at least we showed we could react quickly,' said Maddy.

'We managed to busk it,' declared Rob briskly. 'It could easily have ended in disaster. We need to be better organized this time.'

'You're being hard on yourself, Rob. It worked out brilliantly.'

'Er . . . what happened?' asked Wayne. 'How did you top him?'

'We didn't,' replied Denny after a moment's silence. 'He topped himself. That was the genius of Rob's plan.'

'Can we do the same again?'

'I doubt it. Anyway . . .'

The doorbell rang. They all looked at each other.

'It's de fuzz,' exclaimed Denny.

Wayne's eyes widened in fear.

'It's the food,' laughed Maddy, getting up to answer the door. She came back carrying two large carrier bags. 'I hope you all like Chinese.'

Maddy produced newly bought rice bowls and chopsticks, spoons and forks while Rob opened bottles of wine. Wayne copied the others, taking small helpings of one dish at a time. He reckoned he'd eat that posh way the next time he and his mates got a Chinese takeaway, instead of piling everything into their bowls as usual. Then again, if he did, he'd go hungry.

'Why not wait until Tony Larkin comes back to Britain?' demanded Denny, helping himself to a dish of chicken and cashew nuts.

'How do you know that he will?' objected Maddy

'Okay, why don't we simply tell the police about him?'

There was a moment's silence.

'But how would *we* know that Larkin was one of the bombers?' demanded Maddy. 'We'd be compromising ourselves.'

'Tell them anonymously.'

'Aw, Denny, the police aren't going to act on an anonymous tip-off. They'd never take the information seriously.'

'Just a thought, dear heart,' said Denny.

'Anyway, we only have his brother's word that Tony was implicated. And his brother's dead. If Tony Larkin chose to deny everything then the police have no proof. '

'So we're right to act?' asked Denny, that enigmatic smile still on his face.

'Goddam right, we are,' proclaimed Maddy. 'We are the *only* ones who can act.'

'Okay, so talk us through it, Rob,' invited Denny.

'Tony Larkin is snowboarding in the French resort of Les Arcs. It's somewhere I know well because I used to ski there. You can get to Les Arcs in eight hours' hard driving. As long as we don't go in Maddy's green monster, no one should notice us. We'll take my Peugeot.' Rob took a mouthful of wine. 'If we are going to follow Maddy's idea of driving Tony mad before we kill him, then it's going to need at least three of us. Possibly all four. Are you up for it, Wayne?'

'I'm not sure if I can afford the time off, like,' he said with a show of reluctance.

'I'd make sure you didn't miss out financially,' offered Maddy.

Wayne backtracked quickly, thinking that the chance to visit France for free was too good to miss. 'I'd like to come but I don't have any ski gear, or anything like that.'

'You won't need it,' said Maddy. 'Rob and I will keep track of Tony on the slopes.'

'That's all right, then,' said Wayne,

Maddy raised her glass. 'To us.'

'Death and confusion to our enemies,' proclaimed Denny.

'Death to our enemies,' repeated Maddy softly.

'It's a shame about your American passport, Maddy,' mused Rob. 'Usually when you cross the Channel, it's enough just to show a British passport. They wave you through without inspecting it.'

'I've still got Leanne's passport at home,' piped up Wayne. 'But you don't look much alike.'

'Oh, I don't know,' said Denny, looking at Maddy with professional interest. 'I'd need to see Leanne's passport photo – but with a wig and sitting on the far side of the car, I reckon I could get Maddy to pass for Leanne, at least enough to get through immigration.'

'Just don't open your mouth,' said Rob.

'Gee, thanks.'

'We could go the day after tomorrow – Sunday. That'll give me time to get one or two things together,' said Denny.

'We can't be away for too long or our absence will be noticed,' continued Rob. 'And don't forget, we need to think about alibis, just in case.'

'No probs,' said Wayne. 'My brother in Wimbledon'll give me an alibi. He usually does.'

'I'm due to go up to Birmingham to go over the scripts of the next series of the Hospital Horror next week,' said Denny. 'I could go up early to see friends.'

Maddy turned towards Rob. 'That leaves us.'

'A few days camping in the Scottish Highlands, yachting around the South Coast?'

'Not really. Perhaps I'll just be out to callers.'

'Hmmm.' Rob, too, was finding it hard to construct a viable alibi.

'Anyway, does anyone have any suggestions as to how we're going to kill this wretch?'

'He's got his motorbike. Bikes and icy mountain roads don't go well together,' said Rob.

'You'll have to get him on his bike first.'

'I guarantee he'll be on his bike – and crapping himself in terror,' said Denny with relish.

'Any ideas how you're going to get him to do that?'

'Lots,' replied Denny, with an evil smile.

25

'Tony. Hey, Tone.'

Tony Larkin spun around and peered across the crowded bar. An attractive woman with blonde hair under a ski hat was smiling in his direction. She was older than him, but very classy. The anorak she was wearing was top of the range. He couldn't place her, but . . .

Tone glanced at his girlfriend Suzy who was busy getting a bottle of Heineken down her neck. He was about to return the smile when a tall man brushed past him to embrace the woman. Tony gave a mental shrug and promptly forgot about the incident. He decided to finish his beer and get back to his apartment before the rest of his crowd. It was amazing how the apartment had filled up since he'd arrived. It was as though word went out on the grapevine. Tone Larkin's here. Party time. On the one hand, Tone resented being used; on the other, he enjoyed the status and popularity – and a ski bum of a girlfriend willing to exchange sex for a bed.

He pushed his way to Suzy's shoulder. 'I'm going back for a bath before the hordes get in there,' he told her.

'What are we going to do tonight?' she asked.

'Dunno.' Tony unwillingly made room at the bar for a thin-faced man in a cheap anorak. Obviously a Brit, and newly arrived, by his pallor.

'We could go out for a meal.'

Tony knew she meant that he could treat her.

'What about that farmhouse place above Arc 1600 we passed this afternoon? You said they did really good raclettes. We could get there on your bike.'

'The Tannière? It's pricey.'

Suzy looked up at him with knowing eyes. 'Why don't I come back with you and we'll both have a bath? See if I can't persuade you, eh?'

'Sounds cool,' agreed Tone, pleased that she had fallen so easily into his trap. 'But I've got to get a postcard for my brother first.'

'A postcard!'

'It's a tradition, Suzy. On any holiday we send each other the filthiest cards we can find.'

They arrived at the tobacconist shop just as a man moved away from the postcard display to buy a French newspaper. Tony dismissed the various scenes of skiers and mountain views until he found a section of women in bikinis, skiing topless. All very tame.

Suddenly he found he was staring at a photograph of Salisbury cathedral. Salisbury cathedral! Here!

His heart missed a beat. He couldn't help but pick it out of the rack and turn it over.

We know where you are was printed on the back in black ballpoint.

His stomach dropped out.

'Are you okay?' inquired Suzy. 'You've gone as white as a sheet.'

'Yeh, yeh. I'm fine.' Tony replaced the card, thinking that he was going to throw up.

Coincidence? It had to be. How could anyone know he was here? And who was the 'we', anyway? It *had* to be a coincidence – but it was spooky, all the same.

'What about this one?' Suzy was holding up a postcard showing a naked woman draped over the bonnet of a 1950s US sedan watched by two hoodlums in leather jackets. 'This is sexy.'

'Yeh, if you say so. Just get it, and a stamp.' Tone's eyes drifted back to the postcard of Salisbury cathedral.

'I've no money, Tone.'

'What! Not even enough for a fucking postcard?' Anger flashed through him. 'Forget it.'

Tony turned and barged his way through the crowds, taking his fright out on Suzy as she scurried after him back to their apartment tower. At the eighth floor, just he, Suzy and the bloke in a cheap anorak who had been in the bar earlier got out.

'So far, so good,' said Rob as the four of them gathered in the piano bar of the Hotel du Golf. 'We know what he looks like, where he's staying, even where he'll be eating tonight – if that girl does her stuff in the bath.'

'That postcard was a work of genius, Denny,' exclaimed Maddy.

'The opportunity was too good to miss,' admitted Denny, looking pleased with himself.

'I'll tell you one thing,' said Wayne. 'The door of that flat's not locked. Tony and his bird just walked straight in.'

'Perhaps there was someone in there already,' objected Rob.

'Nah. I saw them turn on the light.'

'Well done.' Maddy put her arm around Wayne's shoulders and he glowed with pride. 'We'll try to get in there tomorrow when everyone's out on the slopes.'

'Assuming Tony is going to ride to this restaurant tonight, why not zap him then?' demanded Wayne.

'Because we've nothing against this girl Suzy,' replied Rob shortly.

They agreed that Rob and Maddy should go to the restaurant while the other two stayed behind to watch the apartment in case Tony changed his mind. They'd keep in touch with the pay-as-you-go mobile phones bought especially for the trip.

Rob and Maddy, now without her blonde wig, watched as Tony entered the restaurant with Suzy. The dimly lit room was hot and smoky, with old agricultural implements on the roughly hewn wooden walls and a log fire at one end. The restaurant specialized in raclettes – large half-moons of local hard cheeses which diners toasted at their tables.

It was not a particularly comfortable meal. Maddy had to stop herself staring at Tony Larkin while Rob was too focused on the hours ahead to relax. There was little of the laughter of their previous evenings together. But they did what they had set out to do. And when Tony and his girlfriend finally finished their meal and left, they followed to stand in the shadows and listen.

'Is this your idea of a joke?' Tony held up the tarot card he had found stuck on the speedo of his motorbike.

'What is it?' asked Suzy, waiting to climb on the motorbike.

'It's the Grim Reaper. It means someone's going to die.'

'Don't look at me. I've never seen it before.'

Tone would have dismissed the tarot card if it had not been for the strange postcard earlier. It occurred to him that Suzy had been there, too. But no. She knew better than to piss off the hand that fed and watered her. So who was it? Some sick git among his mates? None of them could have got up here without a long slog – and the freeloaders weren't into expending unnecessary energy.

Tony rode back carefully, a sickly feeling in the pit of his stomach. He was relieved when he finally reached the underground car park.

The apartment was heavy with the stench of feet, dope and beer. There were bodies crashed out everywhere he looked. A couple he didn't recognize were copulating slowly behind the kitchen unit, not bothering to stop even when he turned on the light to get a glass of water. At least there was no one in the bedroom – the only private area in the whole open-plan flat. The dossers knew the rules. The last time Tone had arrived home and found someone in his bed, he had kicked the lot of them out. Thinking about it, he reckoned there were more bodies than ever tonight. Or perhaps he was becoming paranoid. He had no time to count them.

He didn't want Suzy to pretend to have fallen asleep before he made her sing for her supper.

What the fuck! Tony came round out of a deep sleep to find someone's hand over his mouth. He thrashed out. A light came on, blinding him. He balled his hand into a fist and swung. There was a stifled scream.

Tony blinked in confusion. Suzy was clutching the side of her head and sobbing in pain.

Voices called out from the next room. 'Tone, Tone. Are you all right?'

'Yeh, yeh. It's nothing.' He turned to Suzy. 'What happened?'

'You were shouting in your sleep,' she snivelled. 'Then you hit me.'

'Me?'

'You woke me up going on about white lilies or something. You were getting really stroppy, Tone. You started shouting, "Don't you treat me like that." Then you said it wasn't your fault the bloody thing didn't go off.'

'Rubbish.'

'No, it's true. You were getting really heated. I put my hand over your mouth when you started calling out, and you hit me.'

'Never wake sleepwalkers.'

'You weren't sleepwalking. Anyway, who are *they*?'

'No one. It was just a bad dream.'

'If that's a dream, I don't want to be around when you have a nightmare.'

'I didn't realize how much time snowboarders spend sitting around getting in the way,' muttered Rob as he and Maddy watched while Tony Larkin and his crowd sprawled across a narrow piste on the crest above Arc 1800. 'I'm surprised they don't freeze their arses off.'

'You don't like snowboarders, do you?' Maddy smiled.

'Can't stand them,' admitted Rob. 'If you'd ever seen the way they slice off fresh powder, you wouldn't either.'

Maddy breathed deeply, savouring the crisp air. It had been late last night by the time the four had met up and driven down to their hotel in the valley. They were up again early this morning so that Rob and Maddy could hire skis. But there had been no need for them to hurry – Tony and his party did not emerge until half-past eleven when they headed to the very top of the 10,000-feet-high Aiguille Rouge.

The run down the steep black run over the Glacier du Varet towards Villaroger left Rob and Maddy gasping for breath. Snowboarders, they discovered, travelled very fast for short distances, then sat around for long periods, making it easy to keep up with them. They followed the group around the mountain until, just as Rob was beginning to worry that they were not going to take a break, the snowboarders halted outside a soulless self-service cafeteria at the bottom of a long valley.

Rob grimaced. 'When I first came to Les Arcs, this was a magical stone hut serving omelettes in blackened frying pans which used to be washed in the stream. Only locals knew of it, the only way out was up a vertical drag lift and you got high just sitting on the terrace inhaling everyone else's dope. Now look at it. Two crap restaurants, a road going up to Arc 2000 and a car park. Tragic.'

'It's called progress.'

'It's called a travesty.' Rob tensed. 'They're going in. Come on.'

Breda had just finished unpacking when Aoife and Bobby exploded into the kitchen, followed by Teresa.

Aoife threw her arms around Breda's neck. 'I missed you, mam.'

'I was only away two nights, my lovely. Now, have you been a good girl staying with Aunt Teresa?'

'They've both been little treasures,' replied Teresa .

'Are you all right there, darling?' Breda put an arm around her son.

'Ay. Aunt Teresa let us watch a video of *Straw Dogs*.'

'Kept them quiet,' muttered Teresa, stubbing out a cigarette. 'Right, you two. Go and put your things away while I have a chat to your mam.'

'I'm sorry to put you both out . . .' began Breda once the children had left.

'Don't be daft. They're grand, but they gave Dessie a shock. He didn't know how much noise kids make. I told him he'll have to get used to it.' Teresa's eyes strayed to the cupboard where the wine was kept.

'There's a bottle of red open,' said Breda.

'Thanks. I'll help myself.' Teresa poured herself a glass.

'Was Aoife all right at school today? She wasn't bullied, or anything like that, was she?'

'Aoife won't be bothered again. Take my word for it.'

'Sorry!'

'You might as well know. I found her in tears last night. According to Bobby, a gang of girls led by Bridget Morris had picked on Aoife on Friday—'

'I told the headmistress about this a week ago,' interrupted Breda angrily. 'I'll be up that school . . .'

'Don't worry your head. I went straight up to see that Mrs Morris. The cow was full of gob shite so I gave her a good slapping on her own doorstep.' Teresa motioned with her right hand, showing off her heavy rings. 'I warned her that the next time our Aoife comes home in tears, the whole fucking Morris family can call a removal van, for they'll be leaving Dundalk that night.'

'Oh, Teresa.'

Teresa shrugged. 'That Morris woman got the message.'

'You shouldn't have.'

'Why not? I'm not having my niece picked on just because she's bright.'

'Thank you.'

'Listen, what do you think about "Morning Has Broken" for the first hymn?'

'What does Dessie say?'

'What does he always say? You choose. I'm having to do everything. The flowers, the cake, organize the pressie list, the organist, pick the hymns *and* get the order of service printed. I'd no idea there was so much involved in a wedding.'

'It snowballs, doesn't it?'

'Too right – and Dessie's done bugger-all.'

'Are you having a disco in the evening?'

'No. I reckon we'd better get off to Dublin straight after the reception. We've a seven a.m. flight to the Gambia next morning. But is it okay to talk?'

'Ay. Conn had the house electronically swept for bugs before I went away.'

'So how is . . .?'

'Fine. Fine. We talked a lot of things through. The more hardliners we attract, the more difficult it's going to be for the Provos to offer concessions. The fewer concessions, the less likely that the Brits will allow them to share power. The result will be a festering stalemate.'

'If you say so, Breda.'

The British government, Breda knew, would ignore the True Guardians in the hope that they would wither away.

Well, the Brits had a surprise coming.

There was only one way to get their attention – a ruthless new bombing campaign.

Terrifying in its scope, remorseless in its death toll. Unlike anything seen before. Until no one in England felt safe – anywhere.

And the very mention of the Sovereign IRA would make people tremble.

'We've changed our plans, though.'

'Ay?'

'You know we were talking about the Big One, targeting a member of the royal family or a Cabinet Minister. Well, now we both reckon a lot of smaller explosions would do more good, or more harm, depending how you look at it.'

'So where are you going to put these bombs?'

'Anywhere that'll scare the shit out of people. Shopping centres, football matches, tourist attractions, concerts, cinemas, pubs, restaurants – anywhere, and I mean anywhere, that people gather.'

'What about London stations in rush hour?'

'Yeh, sounds good.'

'Or better still. Put bombs in packed railway carriages to explode just after the trains have left the station. If you synchronized, say, three attacks, you'd bring the whole of south-east England to a standstill,' enthused Teresa. 'And what about a bomb on the London Underground? It's everyone's nightmare to be caught in a bombing down there.'

'But we mustn't *just* target London. We'll place devices in places like Newcastle, Exeter, Cardiff, Norwich. The Prime Minister's constituency. Even small towns. So that no one feels safe – wherever they are.'

'Do we have the resources for this campaign?'

'Money's not a problem. Nor is Semtex. And if we run short, Conn can easily get more from Eastern Europe. What we'll be short of is people to plant the bombs. After Salisbury, *we*'re all going to be under close police surveillance.'

'Shit!'

'No, if we play it right, the police themselves will provide us with alibis.'

'So we're going to have to put up with those Larkin brothers again?'

'Afraid so.'

'Tell you what.' Teresa's eyes glinted. 'How about at the end, we give Darren and Tony a couple of duff bombs so they blow themselves to bits?'

'If you say so,' agreed Breda.

Wayne had known that the door to Tone's apartment wouldn't be locked. He'd lived in places like this, with people coming and going all day and only one key which was always getting lost or with the wrong person at the wrong time. People learned very quickly that it was easier not to lock the door at all.

With Denny standing guard at the end of the corridor, Wayne knocked, waited and then slipped inside. Four bunks sat in an alcove immediately inside the door. Wayne turned the corner and found himself in a large single room running the length of the apartment to the balcony. The direct sunlight made the room hot and airless with particles of dust suspended in the still air. Wayne looked round at the untidy piles of sleeping bags and clothing, wondering how he was ever going to know which was Tony's.

Wayne spotted a closed door. He pushed it open to find a bedroom so small that he could not fully open the door because of the double bed. Wayne knew human nature. This was Tone's apartment – so this was Tone's bedroom.

Wayne pulled out a bedside drawer to reveal Tony's passport and, at the back, under pairs of socks, an expensive-looking wristwatch. Wayne picked it up. A Patek Philippe. *Shit!* That was worth a few grand. Wayne slipped it in his pocket. Tony wasn't going to need it. He'd be dead in hours. Wayne placed the calling card on the pillow and left.

Larkin and his crowd were lucky. A table came free just as they entered the cafeteria. Tony claimed a seat and sent Suzy to join the food queue. She returned with two plates of frankfurters and chips and a bottle of red wine.

Tony suggested that they try the floodlit terrain park for 'boarders after their meal. 'I want to hit that rail, man.'

'Bollocks,' mocked a pink-cheeked youngster at the far end of the table. 'You couldn't stay on for five yards.'

'Like a bet.'

'Give you a beer on it, Tone.'

'Make it worthwhile,' taunted Tony, pouring himself and Suzy glasses of wine. 'Say, twenty euros.'

'Nah. A beer.'

'Hey, here's a *Daily Mail*,' announced Suzy, spotting the newspaper as she dumped her meal tray.

'Let's have a look.' Tony stretched out his hand. 'I want to see how Chelsea are doing.'

'Oh, it's ancient,' complained Suzy as she unfolded the paper. 'It's all about that bomb in Salisbury just before Christmas.'

Tony coughed, spewing partly chewed chips over the table.

Someone was trying to wind him up – but it made no sense. The freeloaders didn't know about his part in the bombing. No one knew apart from the Irish – and Darren.

Darren! A suspicion flashed across Tony's brain. Darren could be a sick tosshead at times. He could have been responsible for that postcard and the Grim Reaper card. But if Darren *had* planted the newspaper – he would have jumped out and taken a photo of Tony crapping himself. Tony knew his brother. So, if it wasn't him . . .

Tony pushed away his plate and took a gulp of wine. He almost choked. The food had turned to ashes in his mouth and the wine tasted of sour grapes.

Speeding down through the woods to the terrain park had allowed Tony no time to dwell on his fears but now, as he sat in the snow waiting his turn to try a jump, his brain struggled again to find an explanation for the events of the past twelve hours. Perhaps Darren had bribed one of the crowd to play those tricks on him.

He heard his mobile phone ring deep in his anorak. He felt an absurd sense of relief. This would be Darren now – confessing to the sad japes. Tony took off his gauntlets and fumbled to reach the phone. A text message. And the caller had withheld their number. Frowning, Tony inspected the screen. *Dead Man.*

His heart missed a beat. He looked around to see if anyone from his crowd was on the phone. No. No one missing, either. Who would have his number? It had to be Darren. Trembling, he called his brother's mobile. A voice told him that the number was unavailable. Odd. Darren always kept his mobile switched on. He called their home in Ealing.

A man answered. 'Hello.'

'Hi, Darren.' But as Tony spoke he realized that it was not his brother at the other end. 'Who are you?'

'I'm a police officer. Is that Tony Larkin?'

'What are you doing in my home?'

'We wish to talk to you and your brother. I gather you're skiing in France, sir. Where exactly?'

'Where's Darren? What's going on?'

'We need to talk to you, sir.'

Tony hit the 'end' button. The phone rang immediately. Another text message.

Dead man on a snowboard.

Oh, Jesus. What was going on?

Tony scrambled to his feet and scrolled through the mobile's address book. He hit a button.

'Hello,' said a man in a thick Irish accent.

'Is Conn there?'

'No, he's not.'

'Who am I speaking to?'

'What's that to you?'

'I need to speak to Conn. That's his bar, isn't it?'

'He's not here, I tell you.'

'I was with Conn . . . before Christmas . . . in England.'

'Watch your fucking mouth.'

'But . . .'

The line went dead.

Tony looked again at the last text message. *Dead man on a snowboard.*

How did they know he was on a snowboard? They had to be watching him. Whoever *they* were.

He was getting out of here. He was too exposed on the piste – and it was getting dark. He needed to reach the safety of his apartment.

'I'm off,' he shouted to Suzy. 'You coming?'

'Nah, I'll stay here for a while.'

Ungrateful cow. 'Suit yourself.'

Tony pointed the snowboard into the fall line and headed down to the village as though the demons of hell were after him. It was only when he was outside the door of his apartment that it occurred to him that he was alone. He should have insisted that Suzy accompanied him.

He screwed up his courage to throw open the door. The apartment was deserted. Tony let out a long sigh of relief. He shut and bolted the door behind him before heading into the bedroom. There was something lying on his pillow. He picked it up – and felt the bile rise in his throat. A funeral-service programme.

Anthony James Larkin
28 June 1983–3 February . . .

That was today! Tonys eyes glazed over before he had finished reading. He stumbled back, pressing himself against the wall. His mobile rang.

'We're coming for you,' said a man's voice.

*

'He's on his way,' Rob told Wayne. 'Make sure that rope's secure around the boulder. You'll never be able to take the strain of the impact yourself.'

Rob wrapped a rag around the trunk of the larch and looped the climbing rope around it. On the other side of the winding mountain road – the only way in and out of the resort – Wayne made a half-hearted effort to throw his end over the top of a boulder. After two attempts, Rob became impatient and went to secure it himself. The rope, smeared with mud, now lay across the road. When the slack was taken up, it would sweep Tony off his motorbike.

As Rob waited in the dusk he made out clusters of tiny white lights emerging across the valley, telling of the farming hamlets in the Alpine pastures. Below was the amber glow of the town of Bourg St Maurice.

A faint high-pitched whine of a motorcycle engine in low gear came on the still air. Rob's mobile rang. Denny, hiding two bends up the mountain, confirmed that it was indeed Tony on the approaching motorbike.

'Get ready,' Rob shouted to Wayne. 'Take up the rope.'

Rob could see the headlights above them on the mountain now. The motorcycle's engine screamed as Tony changed down to take a bend.

Just one more hairpin and then . . .

Rob made out the dark shape of the bike through the trees, then Tony swept into the bend. The big motorbike was almost on them. Rob braced himself for the impact.

The rope went slack. Wayne had dropped his end.

Shit!

Rob dashed out just as the bike sped past.

'What was Tony Larkin doing, phoning the bar like that? I didn't know the little fucker had the number.' Conn Nolan crumpled the empty lager can in his ham-like fist and took another from the kitchen fridge. 'Just as well Stozza cut him off when he did.'

'Perhaps Larkin's in trouble,' suggested Breda.

'No, he's just a wanker, like his brother. Did I tell you Tony used to take off his watch before he started grinding the fertilizer because he was scared it might fall in?'

'No.'

'It's some posh thing worth thousands of quid.'

Breda produced a pay-as-you-go mobile phone from a drawer. 'I'm due to call the Pizzaman in five minutes. Will it be all right to drop off his Semtex in the same place as last time?'

'Ay, may as well,' muttered Nolan, still angry about Larkin's call.

'Why don't you send someone around to the brothers' place in Ealing to find out exactly what's going on?' suggested Breda.

Nolan snorted. 'If I find the sods are fucking around, I'll put the fear of God into them.'

'Ease up on the Larkin brothers, Conn. I'm going to need them in our next campaign. That's if they'll play ball again.'

'They'll play ball,' growled Conn.

Out of the corner of his eye, Tony glimpsed a man emerging from the trees. Glancing in his mirror, he saw a second figure appear on the other side of the road. The man was raising his arm, pointing at him. Was he signalling to someone ahead or was he aiming a gun? Tony twisted round to look over his shoulder.

By the time Tony turned back, it was too late.

He was still accelerating as he ran off the road and plummeted down the mountainside.

26

'I don't understand,' grumbled Pat Rodgers. 'Why did Tony Larkin phone Conn Nolan? Why did he phone the Ealing flat?'

'It's a shame that the French police haven't found his mobile phone,' agreed Tanner, taking a sip of his beer.

'Something must have happened to trigger those calls,' insisted Rodgers.

'Graham said . . . Hello, here he is. Hotfoot from France.' Tanner waved to his sergeant from their corner table in the bar of the King's Arms.

'The coordinator said you and Mr Rodgers were down here, sir,' said Pottidge.

'Blame me for that, Graham,' admitted Rodgers. 'This no-smoking rule in your police stations will be the death of every thinking detective. I'm useless without my pipe.'

'And we fancied a drink,' added Tanner. 'You made good time back from the Alps. So, what news?'

'Still no evidence of foul play. Nothing mechanically wrong with the motorbike. The French police are putting the crash down to driver error,' replied Pottidge. 'By the way, the girlfriend Suzanne Worsley claims that Larkin had an expensive Patek Philippe wrist-watch, which is missing. It wasn't found on the body. He used to keep it in his bedside drawer so the French police believe his mates nicked it. They swear blind they're innocent.'

'There's no doubt he was doing a runner?' asked Rodgers.

'He certainly took off in a hurry. He had his passport on him but he left all his clothes behind. A van driver claims he saw two men on the mountain road around the time of the crash. He remembers wondering what they were doing in the middle of nowhere. He didn't learn of the fatality until the next day. The men haven't been traced.'

'Anything else?'

'One sharp-eyed copper found marks around a tree by the side of the road sixty metres before the bend where Larkin lost control.'

'What sort of marks?

'Faint horizontal abrasions a metre or so above the ground, as though a rope had been tied around the trunk. The French got quite excited until they experimented with tying ropes around other trees and found that they left deeper marks. Now they don't know what to make of them.'

'Nothing on the body to suggest why Larkin had taken off so abruptly?'

'No, sir. The girlfriend said Tony had woken up shouting in his sleep the night before – but she doesn't know why.'

Tanner grunted and took a long pull of his beer.

'There are a couple of other things,' continued Pottidge. 'That evening, Tony and Suzy had gone to a restaurant. When they came out, they found a tarot card signifying death placed on his bike. Tony thought it could have been his brother playing a sick joke.'

Tanner and Rodgers looked at each other.

'And, at lunch on his last day, the girlfriend found an old copy of the *Daily Mail* carrying the story of the Salisbury bomb. Tony was really rattled.'

'Sounds as though someone was trying to scare him,' declared Rodgers from behind a cloud of pipe smoke.

'But who?' demanded Tanner.

'Perhaps Nolan's worried that we're getting too close to the Larkin brothers. He might want to rub them out before we can question them.'

'But why scare them first?'

'In a way, you can't help feeling good riddance to bad rubbish,' said Pottidge.

'That's as may be,' said Tanner gruffly. 'But it's not for us as police officers to say.'

Pottidge blushed, embarrassed that he had spoken out of turn – but Rodgers sided with him.

'Graham wouldn't be human if he didn't think that. I know I do.'

'Really?'

'Each time one of those murdering scum blows himself up or gets topped by his own side I say a small thank-you. I know that ninety-nine times out of a hundred, I'll never get a conviction against them, so I look at it as a present from the angels.'

Tanner's mobile phone rang. He listened, then reported. 'An Irish lad has just turned up at the brothers' flat in Ealing. He's blustering on about Darren owing him a tenner. The Met are checking him out as we speak.'

The second post-mortem on Mitch Lipzinger proved as inconclusive as the first. Tanner was disappointed but, to allow Maddy to go ahead with the burial, he agreed for the inquest to be opened and adjourned – despite his gut feeling that something was wrong.

So Maddy returned home with the body of a dead child for the second time. Again, she let Alvin make the arrangements. She was capable of doing it herself but she knew that it made him feel useful after his failure with Sinn Fein. By now Alvin had tempered his earlier blasts against Irish terrorists. His exposure before the TV cameras had reawakened his political ambitions and he knew better than to antagonize the Irish-American vote. He transformed his frustration into attacks on terrorism worldwide and on Islamic extremists. There were few Muslim voters in upper New York State.

Maddy insisted that this trip too would be brief. She still had things to attend to in Britain, she said.

On her first evening home, when her living room was crowded with a sympathetic swell of wellwishers, Maddy produced the parcel that Tom had been carrying – still in its torn original wrapping.

'This is what Tom bought you for your birthday the morning he died,' she told Trixie.

An expectant hush settled over the room.

Trixie, wearing a purple gilet, blinked back tears, brushed her blonde hair back off her face, and reached out to accept her gift. The wrapping came away to reveal the purple cashmere sweater. An audible sigh rippled through the company. The mourners crowded around to marvel at the sweater's exquisite softness – and that was when the tiny purple thong fell out.

There was a collective gasp and then a silence that Maddy could have cut with a blunt knife. A circle of gawping women formed around the thong as it lay on the carpet. Others behind craned their necks for a glimpse.

Maddy picked up the thong. She held it out towards Trixie. 'It's your colour.'

Trixie made a small strangulated sound. 'Tom's little joke,' she muttered before snatching it away to wrap in the folds of the sweater.

Her husband Cy wore a smile which did not reach his eyes.

Trixie was not at the service the next day. She sent apologies, blaming a migraine, although her next-door neighbour said that she'd heard shouting late into the night and had glimpsed Trixie that morning wearing sunglasses which failed to hide a black eye.

Maddy used the visit to see her lawyers. Tom had left her everything so it was a simple matter to transfer his half of the business to her. Maddy and Cy agreed to let things continue as they were, with Maddy as a sleeping partner. Her lawyer would oversee the accounts until she returned.

At the end of their meeting, Cy tried to raise the subject of Tom and Trixie's affair. Maddy declined to discuss the matter other than to make clear that their respective spouses had been cheating on them both for a long time.

She left, cheerfully expecting Trixie to have a second black eye soon.

Alone, Maddy paid one last visit to the cemetery where Mitch now lay next to her brother and their father. She spent a long time in front of their graves, her mouth moving silently as if in prayer.

If it was a prayer, then it was a prayer to the God of Battles.

Maddy was about to step up her personal war.

'If I told you that you were standing within five feet of a bomb, what would you say?'

'I think I'd say, "Holy Mary, Mother of God," or something like that.' Teresa Bridges's eyes darted around her sister's kitchen. 'Are you pulling my leg?'

'No, I'm not.'

Teresa slowly inspected the room. 'I can't see a bomb.'

'You're looking at it now.' Breda, grinning delightedly, lifted up the soft-drinks bottle protruding from the top of the swing bin. 'Here.'

'That's a bomb?' demanded Teresa credulously.

'The first of the Pizzaman's new mini-superbombs. Here. Take it. It's not armed.'

Teresa took the bomb gingerly from her sister, feeling its unexpected weight. Now she looked closely she saw that the inside of the bottle was obscured. The bottom had been sliced off and stuck back again – but you had to look hard to see the join.

'Brilliant,' she whispered. 'No one's going to spot this.'

'It's the Pizzaman's idea to hide the bombs in pieces of rubbish,' explained Breda. 'There's so much crap around nowadays that no one's ever going to look at an empty plastic bottle.'

'Christ, the British government will have to take away every litter bin in England.'

'And won't *that* make the place look untidy.'

'So what's actually in here?' demanded Teresa, trying to peer inside.

'The Pizzaman said something about tiny aluminium offcuts, them being lighter and sharper than nails, around as much Semtex as he could pack in. It's not so much about killing people as making the English so shit-scared that their government will be forced to act.'

'True enough.'

'What we need now are more volunteers to plant them on the mainland. We've only got the singer and her bloke and it takes time to groom a lilywhite.'

'Typical of that prick Tony Larkin to fall off his bike and kill himself just when we needed him again,' sneered Teresa. 'No news about his brother?'

'None, although the police did release the bloke Conn sent round to suss things out.'

Teresa delved in the large shopping bag beside her chair to hold up a small ivory frock. 'Look, I've brought Aoife's bridesmaid's dress for her to try on.'

'She'll look a picture in that,' exclaimed Breda.

'And here's Bobby's white suit with the shirt and tie matching the colour of the frock. Now, you're sure Bobby's all right about this?' asked Teresa, pouring herself a glass of wine.

'He was a bit iffy at first but I found a photo of some English footballers at a wedding, all wearing white suits, so now he reckons that white's cool,' replied Breda.

'You got it right, getting married in a registry office.' Teresa paused to light a cigarette. 'You cannot believe the things I've got to think about. I've found a soprano from the cathedral choir to sing "Ave Maria", Conn's arranging security, just in case, and a mate of Dessie's is doing the photos outside the church and a video at the reception.'

'That's good.'

'And the flights are all sorted?'

'Yes . . . That reminds me, I must change my appointment at the antenatal clinic. I'll be on my honeymoon.'

Maddy Lipzinger turned the glass slowly between her long fingers, holding it towards the candle so the wine assumed a warm rich colour. She smiled softly at Rob and as she did so it seemed to him that all the other sounds in the restaurant muted into silence.

'Do you know the best part of today?' she murmured. 'You meeting me at the airport. It felt like coming home.'

'It's getting to be a tradition.' Rob gazed into Maddy's dark eyes and allowed her to draw him into her. He knew it was a knack she possessed, but she read his thoughts.

'For real,' she whispered.

They were celebrating Maddy's birthday in a restaurant set in an old dower house in the pretty village of Teffont Evias and already she was wishing that they had booked a room for the night. She wore a plain cinnamon silk dress, and her only jewellery was a gold locket around her neck.

'You look like a million dollars,' Rob had gasped when he had first seen her that evening, before adding 'I never knew you had legs.'

'You've seen my legs before.'

'Not when you've been standing on them.'

'Wise guy.' She had kissed him on the tip of his nose, feeling herself blush at his compliment. *God!* When had she last done that?

The journey to bury Mitch had been a closure of sorts for Maddy. She told herself that for ten years her world had revolved around her husband, her children and her home. Now she was alone and a maelstrom of emotions swirled through her. She was so many different people – a grieving mother, her children's implacable avenger, a woman in love.

'No news about your job?' asked Maddy as they began the main course. Maybe because she was aware of her confusion and that she was falling in love their conversation was uneven, with long silences. She hoped the silences came over as comfortable, companionable ones – and she worried that they weren't.

'No. I don't know what to do,' confessed Rob.

'It's Hannah's fault,' replied Maddy tartly. 'Let her stew in her own juice.'

'But I'm not the one who's missing out,' said Rob. 'The only ones paying for Hannah's cock-up are the very people we should be helping. I'm seriously thinking of quitting.'

'What will you do?'

'Don't know. Go and work on a market stall with Wayne.'

'Is he still doing that?'

'No idea. He wasn't there last market day. In fact, I haven't seen him since we got back from Les Arcs. I think he found the whole episode too much.'

'You're still cross because he let go the rope.'

'He flunked it.'

'We had all this out on the way back. He reckons it slipped through his fingers in the cold.'

The first hours of the journey back from the Alps had been taken up by a relentless inquiry from Rob as to what had gone wrong. In place of the quiet, easygoing charity worker, there had appeared a remorseless professional for whom sloppiness and failure were unacceptable. It was a side of Rob that Maddy had not seen before.

A waiter arrived to remove their plates. Maddy inspected the dessert menu while fingering the gold pendant.

'A birthday present?' Rob nodded at the locket.

Maddy was silent for a moment.

'My gift to myself.' She pressed a catch to reveal a tiny braid of hair. Looking closely, Rob could see that it was made up of two different locks plaited together. 'Mitch and TJ's.'

'It's lovely.'

'Yes.' Maddy allowed herself one last glance before shutting the locket. 'Remember, this treat is on me.'

'No way. You can buy me dinner on *my* birthday.'

'I don't even know when that is.'

'End of July.'

'You're a Leo. We're water and fire. Water can douse fire.'

'Fire can also warm up water.'

'Nice thought.'

The coffee arrived accompanied by two vintage cognacs, courtesy of Denny who had gone to Birmingham to begin work on the new TV series.

'Denny did brilliantly to get that funeral-service programme printed in Tony's name,' declared Maddy. 'Wonder how he managed it?'

'I don't know but I'm glad Tony had it on him,' said Rob. 'It'd have been a total give-away if he'd left it behind in the apartment. We mustn't leave things like that to chance in future.'

'You're a machine, really, aren't you?' Maddy sipped her cognac. 'You climbed down that mountain to take that funeral-service programme off Tony's body.'

'*And* get his phone. *And* make sure he was dead.'

'Can I ask you something – if he hadn't been dead . . .?'

'He would have been,' replied Rob shortly, hiding behind his balloon glass.

'I wonder what's next?' mused Maddy. 'Our benefactor has been quiet of late.'

'Perhaps he's annoyed because we went after Tony ourselves. After all, he'd set up the previous bombers for us.'

'You know, I've been thinking about our benefactor again. I wonder if it's Rose Allen.'

'Rose Allen!' echoed Rob.

'Well, she's become a close friend and she feels strongly about what's happened. She may want to help.'

'But how could she know where Darren Larkin lived? Or where Jimmy Burke was going to be at that precise time?'

'She's associated with the police,' argued Maddy. 'Remember that time we were in the incident room, we saw all those details on the boards and in those computers. Maybe she has access to that information.' Maddy saw the doubt creep into Rob's face. 'Okay, maybe she's in cahoots with a police officer who's involved in the investigation. He wants to help so he uses her to pass on information. Whoever it is knows where we and Denny live. Odd that they haven't bothered with Wayne.'

'A good judge of character, I'd say,' muttered Rob.

'Come on. It's easy to make mistakes and he's not had your sort of training in killing people, remember.'

'Charming.'

'My hero.'

The rest of the cognac was sipped in friendly silence before Maddy discovered that Rob had already settled the bill. She insisted on paying for the cab home.

She paused at her front door. 'Would you like to come in for a nightcap? I've got a bottle of champagne in the refrigerator.'

'I don't particularly like champagne,' murmured Rob.

'That's all right. I was lying anyway. Let's just go straight to bed.'

27

'Hello, Detective Superintendent Tanner. It's Rob Sage. I just wanted to let you know that we were the ones who bumped off the Larkin Brothers. Yes, Maddy was involved, too. Hang on, I'll get her. What? Sorry, this is a really bad line. Maddy's saying that Kevin O'Gara's next. The Pizzaman, that's right. Bye.'

Maddy came out of the bedroom where she had been listening on the extension to Denny speaking to a dead phone line.

'Denny, you're a star. If I hadn't known better I'd have sworn that was Rob.'

'Do I really sound like that?' demanded Rob from the sofa.

'To a tee,' said Maddy.

'That's sorted, then,' said Denny. 'When I get the word from you in Ireland, I'll phone Tanner on his mobile so that he can see the call comes from this number. Then I'll pretend to have a three-way conversation with Maddy to establish that you're both here.'

'I still don't know why you're so keen to establish this alibi, Rob,' said Maddy.

'If we continue to take out the bombers, it's inevitable that one day the police will cast their eye over us as potential suspects,' he explained. 'Who better to give us an alibi than the policeman heading the inquiry?'

'We left a trail in Ireland when we got Burke,' remembered Maddy. 'I paid for the flights and hotel on my credit card. I guess I wasn't thinking.'

'All the more reason to get it right from now on,' argued Rob.

'I've booked you a flight to Dublin in Clive's name, Rob. Here's his passport. That photo's so awful you could pass for him, especially now you've had your hair cut.' Denny smiled at the passport photograph. 'Only the airline clerk at check-in will look at it.'

'So why am I going to Belfast?' inquired Maddy.

'Because it's part of Great Britain. Flights there are classified as internal, with fewer security checks. You've got Leanne's passport if they ask. Just don't say anything.'

'Huh! Why don't you just teach me to sound like the English?'

'There's a challenge for you, Denny,' laughed Rob. 'If Professor Higgins could do it for an East End flower girl, you should be able to help a rich New York woman.'

'I suppose I could try to remove some of the adenoidal timbre from Maddy's voice.'

'Gee, thanks!'

'And, of course, the word "gee" from her vocabulary.'

'Perhaps it'd be simpler if I just said nothing.'

'No. No, we'll work at it. As Rob observed, I do like a challenge.'

'We're going to need transport and somewhere to stay,' said Rob as Maddy continued to glower at Denny.

'I can help on both fronts.' Denny smiled. 'I've a friend in Dublin who's currently filming abroad. You are both welcome to stay in his flat in central Dublin and use his car as your own.'

'Brilliant. So we're set,' said Rob. 'Next target, Kevin O'Gara – the Pizzaman.'

'Thanks to Denny, and our mysterious benefactor weighing in again.'

'Any plans on how you are going to deal with O'Gara?' asked Denny.

'Those who live by the bomb should die by the bomb,' replied Maddy briskly.

'You know, we talk blithely about bombs,' said Denny. 'But I haven't a clue how you make one. Rob?'

Rob marshalled his thoughts. 'Take a stable compound explosive like Semtex. You could put a match to it and it would hardly burn. To explode it has to reach a critical temperature. That's the work of a detonator. Basically you make a small bang to set off a much bigger bang.'

'And a time bomb?'

'Okay, the basic time bomb. You wire a clock to a battery. One of the wires is attached to the clock itself, the other to the minute hand. You stick a small piece of metal onto the face of the clock. When the hand comes into contact with the metal, it completes a circuit, sending an electrical impulse to a detonator. That's as simple as it gets, but frequently the simplest ways work best.'

'Do you have the explosive and detonators you need?'

'Donated by Jimmy Burke.' Rob grinned. 'But if we do use a bomb then we have to be careful we don't hurt the Pizzaman's girlfriend.'

'Why not?' Maddy asked angrily. 'She's in it up to her neck. She swore blind that O'Gara was in southern Ireland when he was really in the farmhouse outside Salisbury.'

'It wouldn't be fair on their baby,' argued Rob.

'We'd do the little bastard a favour. With those two dead, he'd be brought up by decent parents.'

Denny poured more wine for the three of them, and changed the subject. 'Do you ever wonder why our benefactor is helping us?'

'Frequently,' replied Maddy. 'But I just say thank you and hope that he'll do it again.'

'I tell you what *is* odd,' observed Rob. 'Neither Burke nor the Larkin brothers figured among the police suspects. They were bang to rights but we were ahead of the police.'

'True,' said Denny thoughtfully.

'There's something else,' said Rob. 'I've been thinking about this note telling us about the Pizzaman. I don't think it's the same as the last two.'

'What are you saying?'

'I don't know.'

The three looked at one another before Denny asked, 'But are you two going to be all right by yourselves?'

Maddy shrugged. 'We have to be. We haven't heard from Wayne since we got back from France. It's Rob's fault for giving him such a hard time.'

'It's better that he's not involved if his heart's not in it,' said Rob.

'I'd *like* him involved, all the same,' said Maddy. 'You know, all for one and one for all.'

'You mean, he can't drop us in the shit if he's already in just as deep,' muttered Rob.

'Anyway, here's to a safe return,' said Denny, raising his glass.

'Yeh, here's to spreading a little grief.' Maddy gave an evil smile.

Shiny paper, sticky tape and a cardboard box. Little Dean O'Gara's favourite things. His mother Lorraine had complained at Christmas how the twelve-month-old got more pleasure out of his presents' wrapping paper than he had from the presents themselves. So this morning, as he crawled around in the hallway of his home, the arrival of a small package through the letter box proved irresistible.

And Dean was bored. His mother had gone back to bed to watch breakfast TV with Kevin, leaving Dean to his own devices. The package fascinated him. There was something inside that rattled when he shook it. Dean scrabbled away at the paper until a brown cardboard box came into view.

Dean lifted up the box in his chubby hands and put it to his ear. It was ticking. Dean began sucking the corner.

During a commercial break, it dawned on Lorraine that Dean was being very quiet. That usually meant he had found something to destroy.

'Go and see what the baby's doing,' she told O'Gara, smoking a cigarette next to her.

'You go,' said O'Gara, refusing to take his eyes off the screen.

'Lazy sod.' Unwillingly, Lorraine got out of bed. 'What are you doing?' She looked down to see Dean shaking a mangled box. 'You little bugger. If you've broken that . . .'

Dean gurgled happily and carried on shaking the box. Lorraine hurried downstairs, opened the security gate and snatched away the package. That was when she heard the ticking.

'Kevin! Kevin! For fuck's sake!' She dropped the parcel and snatched up Dean.

'What?'

'Quick – it's a bomb!'

Kevin O'Gara, naked, white and skeletal, appeared at the top of the stairs.

The ticking stopped.

Lorraine fumbled desperately to open the door into the living room while clinging on to her wriggling baby.

The package began to crackle and hiss.

Lorraine whimpered in fear. She finally managed to open the door and fled to cower behind the sofa.

'Fuck, fuck, fuck!' She curled up, tensing for the blast.

There came a *plop*, followed by the smell of cordite. Lorraine peered over the back of the sofa to see a dark cloud of smoke drift into the room.

'What the fucking hell! Kevin!'

'Stay there.'

O'Gara, now in jeans and a sweat shirt, was carrying a bucket of water downstairs. He picked up the charred package and dropped it into the water. Only when he had disappeared out into the back garden did Lorraine rise from her hiding place.

'What was that about?' she called, ignoring Dean's piercing screams.

O'Gara returned, examining the package.

'Well?' Lorraine was becoming hysterical. 'What is it?'

'Just a hoax,' snapped O'Gara.

'A hoax! There's some sick fuckers out there, if that's a hoax. Dean could have been killed, blinded, anything. Someone's trying to tell you something, aren't they? Admit it.' She began pummelling O'Gara on his chest.

He pushed her away roughly. 'Stop it. I need to think.'

'*You* need to think,' Lorraine mocked. 'What do *you* need to think about? I'm not staying in this house to have some psycho put a real bomb through our letter box.'

'You don't know who's behind this,' he said weakly, knowing that they had got off lightly.

'You said yourself that the Provos wouldn't be happy with you throwing in your lot with Breda Bridges. You were fucking stupid to listen to that woman. I told you from the start she was trouble.'

'Bollocks you did. You were the one who said she paid well. *You* wanted the money, not me.'

'Shit! You want it to buy your stupid pizza parlour,' Lorraine shouted back.

'Better than spending it all on yourself like you do.'

'Anything I have, I spend on the baby.'

'Oh, yeh? Like that cashmere sweater and those new suede boots—'

'Shut up. Shut up. *Shut up!* I gave you that alibi so you could go to Salisbury and look where it's landed us. You make me sick. Either you quit or I'm away from here. Come on, baby, let's get your breakfast.' Lorraine bustled into the kitchen.

O'Gara followed her, watching as she started making herself a cup of tea. Unthinkingly, he switched on the radio. He hated silence. He had to have some sound in the background.

He tried to think. It would be no great loss if Lorraine *did* move out – but that wouldn't solve his immediate problem. Why had this had to happen now of all times? He knew he was going to have to make peace with the Provos – just as he'd agreed to make a stack of bombs for Breda.

When Breda had told him of her idea for the new terror campaign, he'd let her think that the bombs would be difficult to make – so that she'd pay accordingly. In fact, he'd made one last year as a test of his ingenuity – and he was proud of it. It had served as a template for the others – beautifully disguised in such pieces of rubbish as a Coca-Cola bottle, a polystyrene coffee cup, a burger box, a sandwich-shop paper bag, even a can of lager. No one would ever notice them.

Breda had been delighted. At £600 for each bomb so was O'Gara. The first six were already on their way north. He had promised her another eighteen. If he didn't make them, then Breda would get others to copy his work. The bombs wouldn't be as good. He was the Pizzaman. The best bomb-maker the Provos had ever known. And he was paid as such.

'I'll go and have a word with Milo O'Connell,' he told Lorraine finally.

'You do that. You tell him you're out of it, or I'm leaving – and taking the baby with me.'

Three hours later Kevin met Milo O'Connell in a pub near Dublin's Temple Bar. A handful of solitary drinkers sat reading the morning's newspapers in the long room with its frosted windows. Milo's minder Nutter Hains sat on a stool at the bar, keeping an eye on the door. As O'Gara entered he saw O'Connell sitting at a table near the struggling coal fire. The only sound was the ticking of a large wall clock.

'Milo.'

'Kevin. What'll you have?'

'A bottle of stout.'

'Nutter'll bring your drink over.'

'Fine weather,' said O'Gara as he sat down.

'Ay. That it is, for a change.'

'Shame about Mikey Drumm getting himself knocked down like that. A good old soldier, was Mikey.'

'That he was. That he was.'

Hains placed O'Gara's drink on the table and returned to his place near the door.

'Liked a drop, though,' continued O'Gara.

'That he did.'

'And Jimmy Burke.'

'Poor Jimmy.'

'Found his big toe, they say.'

'So they say.' O'Connell took a sip of Guinness and leaned back in his chair, at peace with the world.

A silence grew. Kevin tried to pick the stout emblem off his glass with his thumbnail.

O'Connell asked, 'How's the bairn?'

'Dean. He's fine . . .' O'Gara rubbed the back of his hand over his dark unshaven chin. 'I've got the message, okay? That's me out. Right?'

'Right,' repeated O'Connell evenly. 'That's you out.'

'I'll not be having my bairn and Lorraine troubled, like.'

'No.'

'It's not worth it, is it?'

'No.'

There was another silence before O'Gara asked, 'Do you think you'll be having any work for me? Only . . . you know.'

'Who knows.'

Kevin wished Milo wasn't looking at him with that faint smile that said he knew O'Gara was lying. Of course, he would cut his ties with Breda Bridges – but not yet. He needed time to make the bombs. Not long. A week or so, if he worked through every night. Then he'd have enough money to buy his pizza restaurant.

'Only I'll not work for Bridges or Nolan again, you understand. I want you to know that.'

'Sure.'

'You'll pass that on.'

'Of course.'

'So we won't be having any more . . .'

'Any more?'

'You know.'

'You'll be okay.'

'I have your word?'

'Indeed you do.'

O'Gara emptied his glass in one and stood up. 'Thank you, Milo.'

O'Connell watched the Pizzaman hurry out of the door, then strolled over to join Nutter Hains.

'What was that about?' demanded Hains.

'Fucked if I know,' replied O'Connell.

28

'Three players have died and one has disappeared since the bombing,' said Pat Rodgers. 'But where's the pattern? Where's the link?'

Tanner grunted and looked out at the green countryside speeding by. Rodgers had officially invited the two Wiltshire detectives to come to Ireland to help them understand the background to the case. Unofficially, Rodgers reckoned it was time he gave them an away day on his patch. But first they were all driving north to Dundalk – and, inevitably, mulling over the investigation.

'Anything from Hayward or Kilfoyle?'

'I think those fine birds have bigger fish to fry with the Islamic militants, if you'll excuse the mixed metaphor. But I'm surprised Hayward hasn't taken a closer interest in this case, on a personal level.'

'Why?'

'His older brother Richard was killed by an IRA sniper outside Crossmaglen. Richard was a corporal in the Scots Guards at the time. This was back in 1986 and a certain Conn Nolan was rumoured to be in the frame, although it was impossible to prove.'

'I didn't know that.'

'Hayward doesn't talk about it.'

'It's a shame we didn't find that tape of Mikey Drumm twenty-four hours earlier,' said Tanner. 'I assume his own side took him out when they saw him hitting the bottle again.'

'We assume so, but that's exactly what I don't like about this case

– all these assumptions,' muttered Rodgers. 'We *assume* that Drumm was murdered because he was a security risk; we *assume* Burke was a home goal; we *assume* Darren Larkin has done a runner.'

'In that case, why hasn't Larkin withdrawn any money from his bank account? Why hasn't he used his credit cards or his mobile phone?' objected Tanner. 'And there's still those two coppers who were clocked at his house on the afternoon he disappeared.'

'Just a couple of bobbies being where they shouldn't – and refusing to own up,' said Rodgers.

'That's what everyone says, but I don't know.' Tanner's mobile phone rang. He pulled it out of his pocket to inspect the caller's number. 'Rob Sage,' he announced. 'Tanner . . . No . . . yes, it is a bad line. No, I'm actually in Ireland. Sorry, Maddy's saying what . . . I'm back tomorrow. Sure. Speak then. Bye.'

'Problems, sir?' inquired Pottidge.

'There's a small piece in one of the papers about Breda Bridges and her movement,' explained Tanner. 'I think Rob just wanted a chat.'

They turned off the motorway to pass a row of superstores.

'Welcome to Dundalk,' announced Rodgers.

Dundalk resembled an English county town with its narrow streets and grey stone houses, thought Pottidge looking at the slate roofs glistening in the drizzle. Even the monstrosity of the municipal council office building was depressingly familiar. They drew up in a small car park away from the town centre.

'You see that green steel door down that side street over there?' Rodgers pointed. 'That's Conn Nolan's bar. Fancy popping in?'

'Is that safe?' asked Pottidge without thinking.

Rodgers chuckled. 'Oh, ay. I'm too well known for them to try anything. Besides, we're not alone.' Rodgers let down the window and called across to a blue Volvo parked next to them with three men inside. 'Is Nolan there?'

'Yes, sir. He's at the bar at the moment.'

Pottidge thought it would be naive to ask how they knew.

Rodgers led the way through the green door, Pottidge bringing up the rear. His first impression was of a dark, narrow room with a low dais at one end. A huge green, gold and white flag was spread above the bar. Rough representations of men wearing balaclavas and holding aloft AK47s were painted on the walls.

There were a dozen or so drinkers at the bar, sullen overweight men in their forties or fifties with hard faces. Everyone fell silent as the three policemen walked in. A bull-necked man turned to glower at them.

Rodgers, loving the effect their entrance was having, pointed up to a sign in Gaelic: *Céad Mile Fáilte.*

'Do you know what that means in English? One hundred thousand welcomes.'

'It doesn't include you, Rodgers,' growled the big man. 'You can get out now. We don't serve coppers.'

There was a collective hiss from the drinkers.

Rodgers ignored them. 'Cyril, let me introduce you and Graham to Conn Nolan. Nolan, these two detectives are investigating that awful bombing in Salisbury which killed those small kiddies. Brave deed, that, wasn't it? A real man's work.'

'I've nothing to say to you or your English policemen.'

'I just want them to see you in the flesh. They, like me, are just waiting for the time when we'll met again – in a more formal way.'

Rodgers was taunting the man, saw Pottidge. And Nolan was having to keep his temper. But, by God, he was big. Neither Tanner nor Rodgers could be called lightweights – but Nolan was as broad as he was tall with shoulders like travelling trunks. There was a malevolence around his mouth and a blackness in his eye that were intimidatory. He was a man it would be very easy to be scared of.

'The weasel-faced barman is Nolan's little gofer, Stozza McKenna, who, by the way, was missing the night poor Mikey Drumm met his maker in London,' added Rodgers.

'Bog off.'

'And this is Dessie Fitzgerald.' Rodgers indicated a truculent, swarthy man with curly black hair and heavy eyebrows. 'Dessie doesn't do the dirty work as such; he drives others, as you know.'

Pottidge found himself locking stares with Dessie, who was giving him the hard eye. Rodgers continued, 'Dessie's getting married to his passenger – sorry, partner – Teresa Bridges very soon.'

Nolan placed a massive hand on Dessie's chest as he took an angry pace forward. Rodgers just chuckled.

'Seen enough?' he asked the English detectives. 'Good. Let's get some fresh air.' Rodgers strolled towards the exit, making sure that he was last to leave. At the door he turned. 'By the way, Dessie, you might want to look up how a parent's blood group is passed on to a child. If both parents are blood type O, like you and Teresa are, then the baby cannot be type A.'

Rodgers was out of the door as Dessie exploded in rage.

'Oh, I did enjoy that,' Rodgers chortled, rubbing his hands together in glee.

'What was that about blood groups?' asked Tanner.

Rodgers laughed again. 'Just something Teresa let slip in her hairdresser's salon one afternoon.'

'You bug her premises?'

'Where better to catch women talking?'

'And that's how you know when she's getting married?'

'We don't just know when and where she's getting married, we even know the hymns at the service and the menu at the reception. I'll put everything on the computer so you can see.'

Rodgers murmured to his sergeant to drive off. A few minutes later, he pointed to a hairdressing salon called A Cut Above. 'That's Teresa's place. We won't go in. I've no fears about entering Nolan's bar, but it would be plain madness to go near Teresa while she had a pair of scissors within reach.'

They drove out of town towards the coast, the roads becoming wider and tree-lined until they halted outside Breda Bridges's home. Immediately a curtain twitched.

'We can't stay here too long otherwise Breda'll start hollering about police harassment,' explained Rodgers. 'Seen enough? Good. We'll head back to Dublin and we'll go and say hello to the bomb-maker.'

'The Pizzaman?'

'Poor sod had almost saved enough money to fulfil his dream and buy his own pizza parlour when Lorraine found she was with child. They now have a twelve-month-old son and O'Gara is still delivering pizzas.'

As they set off on the journey back to Dublin, a mental image of Nolan's bar rose before Pottidge's eyes. There had been a head-and-shoulders photograph of a woman behind the counter. Now he realized that it had been Maddy Lipzinger.

'I know,' said Tanner when Pottidge told him. 'I saw her, too.'

Maddy's Dublin guidebook described the district around the Protestant cathedral as having suffered badly at the hands of developers. She would not disagree. It was a nondescript mishmash of an area. The pizzeria sat at the end of a 1970s parade of shops topped by offices, deserted at this time of night. The waiters and waitresses wore the red shirts of Garibaldi while strings of garlic bulbs and red and green capsicums hung on the walls.

Maddy and Rob chose a table at the rear from where Maddy could watch the counter and the door. They ordered American Hot pizzas and a bottle of Chianti, which came in a raffia-sheathed flask.

Maddy cut her pizza into segments to eat by hand.

'That's a very American way of eating,' observed Rob.

'At least I'm eating a pizza, not an emetic.'

'I like spicy food,' said Rob, crumbling dried chillies over his meal.

'So I can see,' observed Maddy. 'It's gone eight o'clock. Where is . . . speak of the devil.'

Rob turned to see a short thin man with a dark stubble, wearing a leather jacket and carrying a crash helmet, walk in through the door. One of the chefs produced a pile of pizza boxes and slapped them down on the counter in front of him. Rob found he was staring and turned back to his food.

'The Pizzaman's being told off,' reported Maddy, striving to overhear. 'I reckon those pizzas have been sitting there for ages. O'Gara's saying he's been looking after his barn.'

'His barn?'

'I think that's what he's saying.'

'Could it be bairn, as in small child?'

'Yeh, right. Now he's stomping out with the pizzas.'

Rob heard a motorcycle engine start up. 'We must have really rattled his cage this morning.'

'See, we're spreading a little grief already,' said Maddy, looking smug.

The previous day, Rob had been relieved to find his secret arms dump easily in the daylight. He had taken away a bag of goodies, including one of the Walther automatics, which Maddy was cross he would not let her carry, and had spent the previous night concocting a firework designed to scare without causing damage. He had rigged the parcel so that a .22 percussion cap ignited a safety fuse which gave off grey acrid smoke as it burned. The fuse fired a British Army detonator, in turn setting off compacted black powder. Rob had deliberately chosen a Coupatan timer with a loud tick to get the message over.

'You like spreading grief, don't you?'

'Poetic justice demands that O'Gara must die by the bomb,' insisted Maddy, picking up her last slice of pizza.

'Ow.' Rob dabbed at his eye.

'What's wrong?'

'I've managed to touch my eye with the hand that I crushed the chillies with.'

'Idiot.'

'Thanks for the sympathy.'

'Don't be a big baby. Go and bathe your eye in cold water, and scrub your hands.'

When Rob returned he found that Maddy had had an idea. 'Could you put a bomb into a pizza box so that it would explode when the lid was lifted?'

Rob glanced at the boxes on the counter. 'Straightforward pull fuse,' he replied. 'But why would O'Gara open a box?'

'Maybe to see if he had the correct order,' suggested Maddy.

'But then we'd have to substitute our box for a real one right under the eyes of the chefs. Not easy.'

'But you *could* make one,' insisted Maddy.

'Yes, but it's not the technology that's the problem, it's the opportunity. And we must be able to isolate O'Gara so that we don't injure innocent people.'

Maddy chewed thoughtfully. 'Okay,' she said finally. 'What about ordering a pizza from the flat? O'Gara'll bring it around. You can slip a bomb in his motorbike pannier while he's at the front door.'

'The restaurant will have a record of O'Gara's orders. You'll implicate Denny's friend. Perhaps if we give a false address and wait for him there.'

Maddy opened her mouth to speak when her eyes bulged in disbelief. 'Oh, my God. Don't turn around.'

'Why? What is it?'

'There's Tanner and Pottidge. They're with that Irish guy Rodgers.'

'You're joking!'

'I wish I was. They've just walked in. They're standing by the door.' Maddy slid down behind the table display of plastic flowers. 'The manager's gone up to them. I think they're asking about O'Gara. There he is. He's just getting off his bike.' Maddy kept up a running commentary. 'He's coming in. Rodgers is saying something to him. O'Gara's gone white.'

Rob began to turn around.

'No, don't,' hissed Maddy. 'O'Gara's absolutely furious. The manager doesn't want to know. Rodgers is laughing. I think they're going. Yes, they are.' She heaved a sigh of relief. 'They've gone. Phew. I wonder what that was about.'

'What are Tanner and Pottidge doing over here?'

'God knows. At least it means that they're not in Salisbury to check up on us.'

They lingered over their meal, having cheese and cassata for dessert while Maddy watched as O'Gara came and went several times. By ten o'clock, the demand for takeaway pizzas had fallen away and he was spending more time hanging around the counter, talking to the chefs.

Rob and Maddy took the opportunity of O'Gara's absence on one of his last calls to pay the bill in cash and leave. They walked across the road to a modern bar from where, sitting at the window counter, they could watch the pizza parlour. They did not have to wait long. Within half an hour the chefs began to pack away the ingredients, the manager let down the Venetian blinds and turned the *Closed* sign on the door. He and O'Gara were the last to leave. The manager walked off in one direction while O'Gara mounted his motorbike and rode off in the other.

'There's nothing else we can do tonight,' announced Rob. 'I'll get hold of one of those pizza boxes tomorrow and see what I can rig up.'

They had just stood up to leave when Maddy grasped Rob's arm.

'Look,' she hissed. 'He's come back.'

O'Gara was turning down the access road that led alongside the pizzeria at the rear of the parade of shops.

'Perhaps he's forgotten something.'

'Then why didn't he park his bike at the front?'

They waited but the Pizzaman did not reappear.

'I'll go and see what's happening,' said Rob.

'I'm coming with you,' insisted Maddy.

Rob knew better than to argue. The two crossed the street and headed down the side of the restaurant. At the far end they peered cautiously around the corner. The service area, running behind the shops, was illuminated only by the faint glow of the street lights from the far side of the buildings. As Rob's eyes became accustomed to the gloom, he spotted the Pizzaman's motorbike parked in a doorway. The man himself had vanished. They were looking around, confused, when they spotted a faint light coming from the nearer of two small frosted windows high in the wall. There was the sound of running water and then the rattle of a roller towel. The light went out.

'He's in there,' whispered Maddy, clouds of vapour forming on her breath.

Rob inspected the rear of the restaurant with its sealed fire door and the two windows. The nearer one, where the Pizzaman had been, Rob reckoned was the gents' lavatory. He knew, from when he'd been in there bathing his eye, that the window catch was broken. The window was wedged shut but not secured.

'What are we going to do?'

'Do you think you could squeeze through that window?'

Maddy studied the space doubtfully. 'I'll try.'

'Stay here.' Rob disappeared, only to return a few minutes later with their car's wheel brace. 'This should do the trick.'

He reached up, inserted the tip of the brace under the bottom lip of the wooden window frame and levered downwards. There was a loud creak. Rob eased down gently, first in one spot and then another until finally the frame was free.

'So far, so good,' he breathed. 'I'll lift you up. From the loo, turn right into the passage until you come to the fire door, push down on the bar and let me in.'

Maddy measured herself against the small gap. 'I'm not going to get through with all these clothes on,' she said. 'Hang on to these.'

She slipped out of her reefer jacket and thick roll-neck sweater to stand shivering in a see-through black bra and black leather gloves. Rob hoisted her up.

The catch in the window frame ripped her bra and left a long gouge down her stomach. A wooden splinter pierced her side. Her hips caught, but she managed to wriggle sideways and then she was through, tilting precipitously into the black void. Maddy made out a white sink directly beneath her. She reached down to grasp it, overbalanced and tumbled painfully to the floor.

'Are you all right?' hissed Rob

'Reckon so.' Maddy rose unsteadily and felt her way to the door. She pulled it open a fraction and listened. For a moment she imagined that she could hear music but told herself that her imagination was working overtime. She could not see a hand in front of her face. She felt her way along the passage until she found the darkness broken by slats of light coming through the Venetian blind. It was enough to allow her to make out the fire door. Maddy eased down on the bar, half-expecting an alarm to sound. She pressed down harder – the bar gave and the door swung outwards. Rob stepped inside.

To Maddy's surprise, he had the Walther automatic in his right hand and a small torch in his left.

'There's no sign of him,' she whispered, pulling her sweater back on.

'No stairs up to the offices above?'

'Not that I've seen.'

Silently, Rob pushed open the doors to the ladies' lavatory and then those of the staff washroom. Both were empty. With Maddy behind him, Rob crept down the corridor to the edge of the restaurant.

'He must have gone somewhere,' breathed Maddy.

A metallic ticking made them freeze until they realized the sound was the ovens cooling down.

Where was O'Gara? He had to be *somewhere*. Then Rob spotted a narrow door tucked away around the side of the counter, partly hidden by a rubber plant. He was about to try the door when he caught the faint sound of pop music. He paused, head on one side.

'What is it?' asked Maddy.

'Can you hear music?'

'I thought I could earlier but . . .' Maddy strained to listen. 'I don't know. It's incredibly faint. Where's it coming from?'

'Maybe someone's in the offices above.'

But Maddy had crouched down, ear close to the floor. 'No. It's coming from beneath us.'

'There's just that one room left.' Gun in hand, Rob turned the handle. The door swung in to reveal a pitch-black windowless room. Rob blinked and peered intently as he made out a faint line of light coming out from the floor in the corner. He turned on the torch. In its beam he made out sacks of flour, catering cans of oil and baskets of peppers and onions. Rob advanced into the storeroom, keeping his eyes fixed on the light. A large refrigerator stood in the middle of the room. Funny place to put a fridge, he thought – then he realized that it had been moved there from the corner. It would normally be hiding something – something like a trapdoor. So the light was coming up from a cellar!

Rob lay flat on his stomach and levered up the trapdoor to see a wooden ladder leading down. By the light from a naked bulb hanging on a flex, Rob glimpsed crumbling brick walls and an arch leading away into another cellar. He could hear the music clearly now.

A shadow moved across the wall through the arch. The Pizzaman. The shadow disappeared out of sight, only to re-emerge a few seconds later.

'Cover me.' Rob handed Maddy the pistol.

Soundlessly, Rob raised the trapdoor and began to climb down the ladder. The cellar was remarkably warm and dry. Near the bottom rung, he held up his arm. Maddy handed him the gun and began her own descent. Once she had reached the cellar floor Rob crept forward. At the archway, he dropped on one knee and peeped around the corner. The Pizzaman was sitting fifteen feet away, bent low over a workbench, facing forty-five degrees away from them.

He was concentrating intently, a watchmaker's glass screwed into his right eye socket, working under the glare of two strong lamps. Music was coming from a radio beside him.

Rob made out a small timer near O'Gara's left hand. Even as he watched, O'Gara was attaching fine wires to a miniature detonator.

'He's making a bomb,' Rob breathed in Maddy's ear.

Now O'Gara was sliding the detonator into a peach-sized lump of plastic explosive. He was taking short cuts that no bomb-maker would normally take. He was either very sure of himself – or in a tearing hurry, thought Rob.

'Can it go off?' Maddy whispered back.

'Yeh. It's a only very small device but he's living dangerously. One slip now . . .'

Maddy was already rising to her feet, a strange smile playing on her lips. Rob made a grab at her but she moved out of reach towards O'Gara. Rob crabbed to one side and dropped into a two-handed firing crouch to cover her.

Maddy glided up to the Pizzaman on his blind side, the music masking her approach.

He was still concentrating, lost in his own world of meticulous precision.

Maddy stopped two paces behind him.

'Boo,' she said.

29

'We were lucky it was a very small device,' said Rob, casting a baleful eye at Maddy. 'What were you thinking of?'

'I couldn't resist it.' Maddy made a grimace of apology.

'It sounds as though you had a narrow escape,' said Denny.

'The explosion was deafening,' said Maddy. 'I still can't hear properly.'

'Serves you right,' said Rob.

'Sorry.' Maddy cupped a hand to her ear.

'Very funny.' Rob poured more of the champagne that Denny had bought to celebrate their safe return home. 'Because we didn't know if the explosion had been heard in the street, we had to get out as quickly as possible. But we couldn't find the ladder for the dust.'

'Our faces were black.' Maddy grinned. 'We really scared a courting couple around the back of the shops . . .'

'They were doing more than courting.'

'I just hope they were too preoccupied with *whatever* they were doing to take much notice of us. Was everything all right at this end?'

'Think so,' replied Denny. 'I spoke to Tanner who's actually in Ireland so that's your alibi sorted out.'

'We know. We saw him.' said Maddy. She recounted briefly how the detectives had come into the pizza restaurant. 'It terrified me.'

'I'm worried that I left my fingerprints on the ladder and the trapdoor,' confessed Rob.

'You haven't got a criminal record so your prints won't be on file,' Denny reassured him. 'You should have nothing to worry about. What about you, Maddy?'

'I wore gloves,' said Maddy. 'I always do in winter. My hands get cold.'

'No problems coming back?'

'No one even looked at our passports.'

'All in all, a very successful operation,' said Denny. 'Even though O'Gara's not dead.'

'Not dead!'

'There was a piece on the news this morning. He's alive but he's blind and he's had one hand amputated.'

'That'll do,' said Maddy.

'Seems like an open-and-shut case,' Rodgers told Tanner and Pottidge as he led the way through the restaurant. 'But I thought you'd like to see the scene before flying back.'

'Thanks.'

'It's amazing that no one knew these old cellars were down here,' said Rodgers. 'That's probably why O'Gara was trying to buy the restaurant. We'd always wondered where he made the bombs.'

Once O'Gara had been taken to hospital, the building had been sealed until explosives and building-safety experts had given the all-clear an hour ago. Now the cellars were swarming with photographers, fingerprint men and scene-of-crime officers.

'O'Gara was lucky he was working on such a small device otherwise he'd have been dead.'

'Another come-on bomb?' asked Tanner.

'Looks like it. We could be about to face a new terror campaign from the Sovereign IRA.'

Tanner nodded towards a green plastic bottle, a can of soft drinks and a brown paper bag blown against the wall by the blast. 'O'Gara was planning to stay down here all night.'

'They're empty. Probably from a previous night's work,' replied Rodgers. 'O'Gara went to see a PIRA godfather called Milo O'Connell yesterday morning. I'd love to know what was said.'

'Not worth asking O'Connell?'

Rodgers gave a barking laugh. 'No. He'd be politeness and charm itself – and tell me bugger-all. I'm off to see O'Gara's girlfriend. Like to come?'

They found Lorraine in a tearful fury, with baby Dean screaming in the arms of a policewoman.

'It's God's punishment,' blurted out Lorraine as Rodgers entered. 'If he'd kept his fucking word, then none of this would have happened.'

'What do you mean, kept his word?'

'I'm not going to spend the rest of my life nursing a cripple.'

'You said he went back on his word.'

'Did I?' Lorraine pulled herself together. 'I don't remember inviting you into my house. Sod off.'

'So O'Gara had promised to stop making bombs, had he?' hazarded Rodgers.

'Did he make bombs?'

'He was an expert bomb-maker . . .'

'If he was so fucking expert, how come he blew himself up?'

A Garda detective beckoned Rodgers from the doorway. Once outside, he held up a soggy, charred package. 'We found this in the dustbin, sir. There's a Coupatan timer inside. It seems to be some sort of crude device.'

'Not the sort of thing you'd expect a virtuoso like O'Gara to make,' remarked Rodgers. 'Let's show it to Lorraine.'

'Never seen it before,' she said instantly.

'Did he make this?'

'Like I said, I've never seen it before.'

'What was the row about yesterday morning?'

'What row?'

'You were screaming at O'Gara.'

'I'm always screaming at O'Gara. He's a lazy fucking sod.'

Tanner, who had been looking around the hallway during the interview, bent to examine a smudge on the wall. Lorraine's eyes followed him.

'Fuck off from there. I didn't have time to clean yesterday, okay?'

'If you'll just go into the living room, Lorraine.'

'It's my fucking house . . .' protested Lorraine as she was led away by two policewomen.

'Soot – and look, here on the carpet, scorching.' Tanner pointed. 'Recent, too. What if PIRA sent this crude device as a warning? That'd explain why the Pizzaman went to see O'Connell.'

Rodgers nodded slowly. 'PIRA was certainly angry when O'Gara went over to Breda Bridges. But why wait until now to act?'

'Letting the dust settle after the Salisbury bomb, maybe?'

'Maybe.'

Tanner was thinking. 'Yesterday we were saying that there wasn't a pattern to what was happening to the Salisbury bombers. But Tony Larkin was frightened into leaving Les Arcs. And now someone's been trying to scare O'Gara.'

'Would PIRA do that?'

'If they wouldn't, who would?'

'The bloody fool. Why now of all times?'

'Hang on. The Pizzaman didn't mean to blow himself up.'

'He might as well have done.'

Conn Nolan opened his mouth but said nothing. This was a side of Breda that very few people ever saw. Nolan sometimes boasted that he was not afraid of any living man but he wouldn't wish to feel the lash of his wife's tongue when she was in a rage. No one believed him. They should have seen Breda now.

'We can use other bomb-makers,' he ventured.

'But they're not as good,' she spat back. 'Fuck it.'

Breda had just returned home from shopping to find Conn waiting with the news. She slammed down a jar of marmalade and banged the cupboard door shut.

'Calm down.' Nolan flinched as Breda's eyes flashed dangerously in his direction. 'We've half a dozen devices. They're a start. You said yourself you weren't going to begin until Teresa was on honeymoon to give her a cast-iron alibi.'

'Everything's going wrong. *You* might not have liked the Larkin brothers but they were useful. Now one's dead and the other's disappeared – just when we need them.'

'You've got the other team, the singer and her bloke. They'll be okay until she's trained up some others.'

'They'll have to be. We need a bomb-maker as well. I suppose we'll have to use Eamon Collins.'

'He's retired.'

'Then he'll have to come out of fucking retirement, won't he? You'll have words with him.'

'Christ, Breda. You can't force someone to make a bomb.'

'You have words with him,' she repeated. 'He'll do it.'

'There's talk that the Pizzaman was seen talking to Milo O'Connell yesterday morning.'

'Was he, now. I wonder why?' Breda paused. 'We must send money to Lorraine. And make sure she spends it wisely. I don't want to be hearing that she's treated herself to a holiday abroad.'

Once Nolan had left, Breda made herself a cup of tea and sat at the kitchen table, looking out at the quiet suburban road and thinking. O'Gara's carelessness could not have come at a worse time. Thinking about possible targets, she had decided on a soccer crowd leaving Manchester United's Old Trafford ground for the first mini-superbomb. The iconic value alone would ensure worldwide coverage.

She'd follow up that attack with Teresa's idea of bombing three packed commuter trains in the evening rush hour. Then the London

Eye, a crowded pub in Newcastle, a shopping centre in Bristol. The list went on.

Breda found that she was looking at Teresa climbing out of her car and waved.

'Yeh, I heard the news,' said Teresa as soon as she entered. 'Silly sod. Should have been more careful.' She took one of Breda's cigarettes from the packet on the table. 'Listen, I need your advice. Dessie's started banging on about the baby's blood group. Some fucker's been winding him up that this kid might not be his after all.'

'Never!' Breda had to suppress a smile at her sister's indignation.

'Right up. But listen, is there any way I can change the kid's blood group if it turns out to be the wrong one?'

'No,' replied Breda.

'Didn't think there would be.'

'Why don't you find out the father's blood group? You're probably getting wound up for nothing.'

'And let him know he's the father of my child? No way!'

Maddy woke on the morning of Valentine's Day to lie rigid with fear, wishing Rob was beside her. With an effort she tried to cleanse the memory of the nightmare from her mind – but the images were too vivid.

In her dream, she had been back in that cellar. The Pizzaman was bending over his workbench. She'd seen herself tiptoe up behind him. Heard herself say, 'Boo.'

Christ, that had been a dumb thing to do! There'd been a flash, a rumble and then clouds of impenetrable dust. They had stumbled, coughing, ears ringing, towards the ladder. Rob had gone up first to open the trapdoor. She was waiting at the foot when she'd heard the liquid, gurgling groan that grew louder and louder. Getting nearer and nearer.

The shape of the Pizzaman emerged through the swirling dust.

His face was a pulped mass of raw flesh, white bone and gristle. Crimson bubbles frothed from the gaping maw that had been his mouth.

Maddy had scrambled upwards, feeling the bile rise in her throat. The blind wretch stumbled into the ladder, pawing at her with a smouldering stump of a hand. Maddy lashed out with her foot. It had connected with the raw pumpkin face and the Pizzaman had screamed again.

Now the shock of the nightmare was passing, she found she did not regret what she had done to the Pizzaman. In fact, she was glad.

But . . . but . . . there'd been an earlier part to the dream, before it had become a nightmare. Maddy fought to cling to the wisp of memory. It had been something to do with Breda Bridges. Maddy had been standing on the doorstep of Bridges's home. Yes, that was it. She'd been telling Bridges that she was taking her children. She was telling Bridges that she owed Maddy her children to make up for Mitch and TJ.

Maddy stared at the ceiling, seething at the memory of how she had been treated by Bridges and her sister.

Yes, this woman did owe her her children. But could Maddy ever hurt a child, even a child of Breda Bridges? Could she? An eye for an eye, a tooth for a tooth, a child for a child.

Could she?

Steve Crowston fished most days now that the wallpaper factory where'd he worked for twenty-four years had folded. Like the rest of his mates from the shop floor he couldn't afford the price of a regular day ticket to recognized fisheries. Instead, they had contrived to stock illegally whatever unattended waters they could find. This flooded quarry had become home to pike, carp, tench and chub. But, above all, to eels. There was something about the dark water's ecosystem that transformed nine-inch eels netted from the local canal into rapacious monsters. So much had they grown that they had begun to prey on other fish. Steve and his fellow fishermen, finding that they had spawned a disaster, now did their best to catch the eels – and kill them.

It was a good day for fishing. The sky was overcast and the waters were protected from the wind by the quarry face. Steve baited a number six hook on a ledger with earthworms and cast towards the middle where he suspected the larger eels lurked. But there was nothing. Not even a nibble. Either the small fish were making themselves scarce, afraid of the larger eels, or they had already been eaten. After an hour, his enthusiasm began to wane. He rolled himself a cigarette and thought about it. He had been doing what every fisherman does – casting far out in the belief that the best fish are always furthest away. He decided to try the deep water immediately ahead of where he stood on a fallen jumble of rocks, close to the quarry face. Seconds after the first cast, the line went tight.

Steve struck. But his elation turned to bewilderment. What he'd hooked was not fighting as an eel normally fought. Instead, the line was being jerked to and fro – but in the same place.

Steve couldn't understand. It was as if something down there was shaking its head to try to free itself but was not attempting to swim away. And whatever it was, it was heavy.

Now he could make out something just beneath the surface. Something pale . . .

A partly clothed body rose through the water. On the end of the line was a struggling eel; its head jammed in the empty eye socket of a long-dead man. As the face broke the surface, another eel, a good four feet long, emerged through the gaping hole where the mouth had been.

Steve screamed.

Neither Hayward nor Kilfoyle could be bothered to hide their resentment at the time they were being forced to spend at Aylesbury police station. The atmosphere was not helped by the local chief inspector. All coppers were jealous of their patch, but Raymond Elmwood had brought surly indifference to an art form. They were on his manor; they would do things his way. He didn't care if they were big noises from the Security Service or the Anti-Terrorist Squad. As for the Wiltshire police . . .

'Dental records confirm the body as that of Darren Larkin,' began Elmwood. 'The body has been in water for at least ten days. The pathologist refuses to be more precise.'

'Was he dead or alive when he entered the water?' demanded Tanner.

'The state of the body precludes a definitive answer.'

Hayward tutted disapprovingly.

'There isn't a lot of it left,' rasped Elmwood. 'Eels have eaten through the chest cavity into the lungs and thorax so it's impossible to tell if Larkin was breathing when he entered the water. Eels have also devoured much of the buttocks, which would otherwise have offered indications of post-mortem lividity, and have consumed any stomach contents that were being digested at the time of death.'

'Anything else?' growled Tanner.

'Severe bruising on the cranium together with the fact that three ribs were driven into Larkin's lungs and heart suggest that he fell from the top of the quarry,' continued Elmwood. 'What's not clear is whether he jumped or was pushed.'

'No evidence of faeces on the clothing? Or that his hands had been bound?'

'No, but rope would disintegrate quickly in that water.'

'So there's no evidence of foul play?' suggested Kilfoyle.

'I wouldn't say that, sir,' replied Elmwood with heavy sarcasm. 'If Larkin had decided to commit suicide, he walked a long way to do it. There's no sign of a vehicle.'

'Is there a way to the top of the quarry?'

'Up a rough track. But any tyre marks would have been washed away by the rain of the past fortnight. I'll show you the scene.'

The visit to the quarry bore out Elmwood's remark that this was not a place you would stumble upon by chance.

'You're right. There are easier ways of topping yourself than slogging up here just to throw yourself off,' declared Tanner. 'When did the quarry close?'

'Some fifteen years ago,' replied Elmwood. 'They shot some episodes of a *Doctor Who* series here soon after. Apart from a few fishermen, no one's been here since.'

'If we accept this *wasn't* suicide, then who killed Larkin?' asked Tanner.

'My money would be on PIRA setting out to teach Breda Bridges a lesson,' said Kilfoyle. 'Maybe those policemen seen at Larkin's home were IRA men. It's the sort of stunt they would pull.'

'So they kidnap and murder Darren Larkin, terrify his brother into running away so he kills himself and then put the frighteners on the Pizzaman.'

'That would also explain why O'Gara went to see O'Connell.'

'But if this *is* down to the Provos, it means that there's a traitor in the Sovereign IRA. The Provos were able to get to Darren Larkin before we could.'

Kilfoyle shrugged. 'They all sleep in the same bed. The traitor'll be someone very close to the centre of power, someone very close to Breda Bridges – mark my words.'

Tanner said nothing but his gut feeling said that something was not quite right here.

Damien Kilfoyle had an unpleasant surprise waiting when he arrived back at his office at Thames House. His secretary was just trying to warn him that his future father-in-law Hector Fakenham was looking for him when the former deputy director-general himself marched in. Fakenham had put the fear of God into several generations of Service officers with his withering sarcasm and unbending ways.

Retirement had not changed him. He fixed Kilfoyle with a steely eye and came straight to the point.

'The DG has tasked me to conduct an audit of agents' payments over the past five years,' he said. 'Now we are about to adopt a higher public profile, we need to ensure that there are no skeletons in the cupboard. Shall we go into your office?'

Fakenham declined Kilfoyle's offer of coffee. He produced a single sheet of paper from a folder, read it from top to bottom and then ordered: 'Tell me about Shamrock.'

'Shamrock!' For a moment Kilfoyle's mind went a complete blank before he realized that Hector was using Jimmy Burke's code name. He didn't know what to say.

'The last payment to Shamrock was made on 20 January,' continued Fakenham. 'And the file was closed on 24 January, marked "Deceased". I gather that Shamrock was Jimmy Burke.'

'Ah, yes.'

'Don't look so surprised. The connection was not hard to make. You weren't paying him a lot.'

'He wasn't that useful . . .'

'Yet you saw him on 24 December, again on the 27th, and then again on 6 January and the 18th. At least, those were the meetings you logged. You may have seen him more often and neglected to report them.'

'No.'

'The point I'm making is that you were seeing him at frequent intervals – and yet you say now that he *wasn't that useful*.'

'He was trying to get close to those who we believe planted the Salisbury bomb.'

Fakenham shot him a shrewd look. 'How do you know he hadn't?'

'He would have told me if he had.'

'Informers seldom tell their handlers everything. He was certainly close to Nolan.'

'How do you mean?'

'He visits him on 31 January. That night Nolan stays sober and the next day he comes to London. Burke must have said something to him. Any idea what?'

'There's a theory that he was warning Nolan about Mikey Drumm's drinking, but that's never been proved.'

'And Burke was blown up on 23 January.'

'The Garda believes it was an own goal. If it had been a PIRA revenge killing, then they'd have taken back their arms.'

'How do you know that they didn't leave behind enough to make a large bang?'

'Um . . .'

'Did Burke have an alibi for the day of the bomb in Salisbury?'

'I think so. His brothers—'

'His brothers! I mean an independent witness.'

'Um, I'll find out.' Kilfoyle swallowed nervously.

'I gather he blew himself up before the Garda got round to questioning him about that duty-free bag from Schiphol found in his bedroom,' continued Fakenham. 'Convenient.'

'I don't . . .'

Fakenham regarded Kilfoyle for a moment, then rose. 'I think that's enough for now.'

He swept out, leaving his future son-in-law feeling as though he had just been through a three-hour interrogation.

Valentine's Day turned out to be cold and crisp. The small puddles in Salisbury's market place were covered in ice and despite the sun's efforts the temperature was not going to climb above freezing all day. Maddy felt foolishly happy. Those memories from that dusty cellar seemed an age away. She wanted to talk about them to Rob, but she was scared that their mention would burst the bubble of her good humour. Maybe over lunch.

'Did you have any post today?'

Rob thought. 'Yes, some bumph about cheap car insurance. Why?'

'I didn't get anything.'

'What were you expecting?'

'Nothing. No flowers either.'

'What! What are you on about?'

'Nothing,' Maddy repeated in a small voice. 'Oh, look, there's Wayne behind that stall.'

'Don't,' hissed Rob as Maddy went to wave.

'Why not?'

'He's pretending he hasn't seen us.'

'You English.' Maddy waved her arm vigorously. 'Hi, Wayne. How are you doing?'

Wayne was trying to put on a welcoming smile – but not trying so hard that he was succeeding. 'I've been away, up in London,' he said quickly. 'Only just got back.'

Maddy was already picking over the stall. She held up a pair of black leather trousers. 'Do you know, I've always wanted something like this,' she said, seemingly oblivious to Wayne's bleak welcome. 'Do you think they'll suit me?'

'You'll look like what's-her-name in *Saturday Night Fever*,' said Rob.

'Don't you mean Olivia Newton-John in *Grease*?' asked Maddy sweetly.

'Yeh, her too.'

Maddy wrinkled her nose up at him. Two young men began inspecting bikers' leather jackets at the far end of the stall and Wayne seized the opportunity to go to talk to them.

'See, I told you he doesn't want to know us,' whispered Rob.

'This pair of chaps looks a bargain,' said Maddy, deliberately ignoring him. 'Like me in these, would you?'

'It'd depend on what else you were wearing.'

'What would you like me to be wearing?'

'Nothing.'

'Huh. In your dreams.'

The two men strolled away. Wayne had no option but to return. Maddy held up the trousers. 'I'll take these, as long as I can bring them back if they don't fit.'

'Sure. No problem.'

'And these chaps.' Maddy caught Rob's eye. 'I can't wait to get home and try them on.'

Wayne began wrapping up the goods, still refusing to look at the other two. Rob became annoyed.

'I take it you saw in the papers about some guy being killed in a motorbike accident in the French Alps,' he muttered to Wayne.

Wayne concentrated on wrapping the package. 'Yeh, I saw something. But I don't want to know. That was a one-off, all right.'

'I haven't a clue what you're talking about.'

'That's all right, then.' Neither Rob nor Maddy spoke. After a moment, Wayne asked, 'Still seeing Denny?'

'He's been trying to get hold of you,' said Maddy. 'He had tickets to get on the set of the hospital series.'

'He was going to introduce you to Sister Sex on Legs,' added Rob spitefully.

'I'll give him a bell. Just to be social, like.'

'You do that.'

Wayne watched as Maddy and Rob walked away, laughing. He suspected they were laughing at him. They were having it off, he could tell. Something had passed between them when she'd bought those chaps. Wayne wasn't stupid. He stamped his feet to keep warm, feeling his resentment grow. He watched them as they went up to Maddy's green VW Beetle. Maddy put her shopping inside and then punched the air with her fist. They disappeared through the door of a nearby hotel, talking animatedly together.

Wayne told himself that he could have made a play for Maddy, but he was too decent – unlike Rob Sage, who pretended to be an officer and a gentleman but all the time had been scheming to get into her knickers. Wayne blew onto his fingers. How come they could afford to swan around, having lunch in one of the town's swankiest places – even if it was stuffy and old-fashioned, not anywhere Wayne would have chosen himself? Still, they were in the warm, and he was stuck out here.

Life wasn't fair.

A woman's voice interrupted his thoughts. 'Mr Wallis, isn't it?'

Wayne swung round to find a woman in a long knitted scarf draped over a topcoat. On her head she wore a Burberry rain hat, pulled down low over a large pair of spectacles.

'I'm Rose Allen. We met at the hospital.' The woman smiled kindly. 'How are you coping with your loss – now that time is passing?'

'Um . . .' Wayne didn't know what to say.

'The passage of time can heal but sometimes it takes longer than others. Everyone said what a treasure your Leanne was. It must be hard.'

'The house is empty without her.'

'How are the others? Maddy and Rob and dear Denny. You see a lot of each other, don't you?'

'Sort of.'

'You've become firm friends, I know.'

'We look out for each other, help each other. That's what life's about, ain't it?'

'Very true, Wayne. Very true. Everyone deals with grief differently. Some bottle it up, others let it out. It's better to let it out, don't you think?'

'Suppose so.'

'It's like the way some people can turn the other cheek, while others thirst for revenge.'

'Nothing wrong with wanting revenge.'

'That's fair enough in *one* way,' said Rose reasonably. 'But there's a difference between revenge and justice.'

'Yeh, but what do you do when some sleezebag politician puts her career before justice? That's when you turn to revenge.'

'Maddy's staying on in this country in the hope of seeing the bombers brought to justice, isn't she?'

'If that's what she says.'

'You don't think so.'

'I think the deaths of her kids and her husband have got to her, if you know what I mean.'

'But what about Rob and Denny?'

'Rob Sage eggs her on and Denny's just a decent bloke who goes along with them.'

'Along with them?'

Wayne opened his mouth to speak and shut it again. What was he saying? This woman could be a copper's nark for all he knew. She certainly had a way of getting people to talk easily.

'Nothing,' he said.

Rob and Maddy left Wayne to walk towards Maddy's rented car.

'He's got the hump with you,' said Maddy when they were out of earshot.

'He shouldn't have bottled it.'

'Bottled it?'

'Cockney rhyming slang. Bottle and glass. Arse. His arse fell out.'

'His ass fell out?'

'In American speak, Wayne found himself to be heroically challenged. We just want to hope that he'll keep his mouth shut. And he's jealous.'

'What of?'

'Me and you.'

'Christ, you don't think I'd fancy Wayne! Not if he was the last man left on Earth.'

'Really the last man on Earth?'

Maddy made a rocking motion with her hand. 'Okay, I've got needs. But I'd have to be pretty desperate. Still, I bet he'd have remembered Valentine's Day.'

'Aaaah.'

They had trouble opening the boot of the unfamiliar Beetle. In the end Maddy gave up and unlocked the car itself. She was about to place her shopping on the back seat when she spotted a plain white envelope next to the handbrake.

'I don't remember that being there. Is it yours?'

'No. Open it.'

Maddy drew out a single sheet of A4 paper. Her mouth fell open as she began reading. After a second, she quickly refolded the paper.

'What is it?'

'The schedule for the wedding of Teresa Sheila Bridges and someone called Desmond Michael Fitzgerald.'

'Teresa Bridges,' repeated Rob softly, looking into Maddy's eyes.

'Didn't Tanner say they thought that Teresa was driven away by the guy she lives with?' She punched the air in elation. 'Thank you, God. Thank you. We're going to turn their wedding into a funeral.'

'Careful. Wayne's still watching us, and you don't know who else. Let's talk about it over lunch, and call Denny this afternoon.'

'Okay.' Maddy thrust the note deep in her shoulder bag and linked arms with Rob.

'Now, wasn't that better than a silly Valentine?'

'This is brilliant,' enthused Maddy as they sat, heads close together, over the sheet of paper. 'The service is for a week today. Look, time of the ceremony, location, where the reception's being held, even what they are going to eat and how many guests.' Maddy looked up, eyes shining.

'Calm down. You definitely want to go ahead with this?'

'God, yes. Remember, it's not enough merely to kill them – we have to drive them mad first.'

'May I join you?'

Tanner, pint of bitter in hand, stood over them. They had been so engrossed in their plans that they had not seen him approach. Maddy's heart missed a beat. She folded away the sheet of paper, hoping that she did not look as guilty as Rob did.

'Of course.' Maddy slid the paper back into her handbag as Tanner, in a rumpled grey suit, lowered his bulk onto a chair.

'Sorry I didn't get back to you,' he said to Rob who looked blankly at him. 'Remember, you phoned me when I was in Ireland and I've been busy ever since with the investigation.'

Rob furrowed his brow. 'Do you know, I can't even remember what I was going to say. Shows how unimportant it was.'

'Doesn't matter.' Tanner took a pull of his pint. 'While I remember, Maddy. Nolan has your photograph up behind his bar.'

'Why's he done that?' she demanded, casting an anxious glance at Rob.

'So that people'll recognize you. I wouldn't go back to Dundalk for a while, if I were you,' cautioned Tanner. 'Now, I don't know whether either of you saw something in the newspapers about a man's body being found in a flooded quarry in Hertfordshire?'

'No,' replied Rob.

'We believe that the man, Darren Larkin, was connected to the Salisbury bombing.'

'What!' chorused Rob and Maddy.

'Darren Larkin and his brother Tony were the gofers for the gang. Tony was killed in a motorcycle accident in France a fortnight ago.' Tanner let his news sink in. 'There seems to be a curse on everyone connected with the bombing. The man who put together the Salisbury device blew himself up in Dublin while I was there.'

'Perhaps my prayers are being answered after all,' said Maddy.

Tanner gave Maddy an old-fashioned look.

Rob realized that he and Maddy were not showing enough curiosity. Tanner was telling them dramatic news. They had to react.

'Wait a minute. We've never heard of these Larkin brothers before.' Rob contrived to sound indignant. 'When did you get this breakthrough?'

'After Tony's death. We matched his fingerprints to a small piece of the farmhouse's door frame which had escaped the fire.'

'And . . . Darren?'

'Darren took the bomb-maker – who has just blown himself up – to Bristol Airport. Darren should have dumped the car. Instead he kept it. We'd just tracked it down when he disappeared. It looks as if he was killed the day he vanished.'

'Who killed him?'

'Could be his own lot, could be the Provos. It could be anyone with motive and opportunity – and the capacity to kill.'

'Not everyone has the capacity to kill, surely?' asked Maddy.

'You'd be surprised,' said Tanner.

30

The Church of the Holy Cross sat squat and alone on its hillside, beneath a glorious stand of elm trees, overlooking its depopulated parish and surrounded by a cemetery of untended graves. It was reached by a narrow track that climbed over the hill past the lych-gate before falling to rejoin a wider lane at a crossroads. Parking would have been a problem if there had been a larger congregation. At the times of its infrequent funerals and even rarer weddings the field across the lane was pressed into service. Teresa had chosen the church for exactly the reasons that it was failing – it was a long way from anywhere, few bothered to read the banns and access to the church was restricted and easy to control.

Conn Nolan had posted a guard on the church from dusk the evening before the ceremony. It was a duty that no one wanted, nor saw the point of. The early man and the overnight man met up at nine o'clock and went off to the nearest pub together. At midnight, the early man drove slowly home and the overnight man fell asleep in his car.

Their vigil was pointless, anyway. An American couple, researching their Irish roots, had called at the church the previous day. By chance, they had found the organist practising for the impending wedding service. She was flattered at their interest in the church and left them nosing around, having promised to return the key to Father Doherty at the parochial house.

All too easy.

From the church, Rob and Maddy had travelled on to Drummore House Hotel where the reception was to be held.

They turned in through the imposing gates to wend their way a third of a mile past stands of trees, clumps of tall bamboo grass and ornamental ponds until they arrived at the hotel's porticoed entrance, flanked either side by the grand stone terrace.

'What an amazing drive,' said Maddy.

'Probably built in the seventeenth century,' replied Rob.

'How do you know that?'

'When you approach a house on horseback, you're facing it – so the drive will be arrow straight. But in a coach, you are looking out of the side windows. Once coaches became fashionable, drives were designed to wind so that you would get different vistas of the house.'

'Full of useless information, aren't you?'

'Yeh, but the drive's largely tarmacked now. It's going to make life harder.'

'In that case, can we get at the bride and groom at the church?'

'Not to get near enough *and* get away again. No.'

'An ambush between the church and the hotel?' suggested Maddy.

Rob shook his head. 'They'll be in a large fast-moving car. We haven't got a sniper's rifle and I can't really plant a bomb on a main road. No, the best chance is here at the reception.'

'There's nothing in the schedule about a taxi,' declared Maddy, thoughtfully. 'So I reckon the going-away car will be brought up here on the wedding morning, ready to drive to Dublin after the reception. Either the groom'll drive or one of their bunch will act as chauffeur.'

'That means we could kill an innocent man.'

'None of that crowd is innocent.'

They climbed the wide steps onto the terrace to stand looking out over the rolling parkland. Away to their right the sun was beginning to sink, sending up crimson rays in a livid sky. They stood silently, very close but not touching, watching the sun creep lower. Dusk always made Maddy feel sad and hollow – the end of another day.

'Do you still think of Mekaela and Alfred as much as you did?' she asked.

'Alfred, especially. I owe that little boy my life and I let him down. In fact, I feel responsible for his death.'

'Only one lot of people are responsible for his death,' exclaimed Maddy angrily. 'Those who planted the bombs.'

'Do you think of your kids, of Tom?'

'My kids, all the time. Their memory drives me. But I think of them even more at moments like this. They're more real, the pain is sharper if you like. You know what I mean.'

'Yes.'

'Any sane person would say, okay, we've had our revenge, let it alone now. But then I hear Mitch and TJ, calling to me, asking me to keep going. I hear their voices, saying, "Come on, Mom. Just do it. Do it for us."' Maddy gave a stifled laugh. 'Sometimes I think I'm going a little crazy.'

Teresa looked a picture, thought Breda fondly. An absolute picture. They had been up since before dawn – but it had been worth it. The heavy ivory silk dress neatly disguised the bulge that was just beginning to show, and her veil and garland softened her short boyish hair.

It had rained overnight but as they drove to the church the sun came out. It seemed a good omen.

'How do you feel?'

'More nervous than ever I did in Salisbury. I tell you that, Breda.'

'You look lovely.' Outside the church, Breda checked that Bobby's shoelaces were securely tied and smoothed down Aoife's bridesmaid's dress one last time before hurrying to her place in the second row. She nodded encouragingly to Dessie, self-conscious in a new suit, fidgeting alongside Conn.

What people went through to get married!

At last. The opening notes of Mendelssohn's Wedding March swelled inside the little church. Heads craned around to catch a glimpse of the bride. Breda wiped away the tear that rolled down her cheek. Teresa – bolshy, stroppy, spunky Teresa – was gliding serenely up the aisle, her hand poised elegantly on the arm of their father's elder brother over from Glasgow for the service. The sight of Uncle Paul reminded Breda that it should have been their father who gave away Teresa, or if not their father, then their elder brother Bobby. But both were dead.

She should have been here to witness this moment – but that, too, was impossible. She had phoned this morning to wish Teresa well. And she'd had a quiet word with Breda, warning her to make sure that the boys were keeping their eyes open. She didn't want anything to happen to Teresa today of all days. Breda had promised to send the video and wedding pictures as soon as possible.

Breda smiled proudly at her younger sister as she glided regally past, brushed away another tear – and caught the first whiff of something foul. Breda wrinkled her nose in disgust. Why couldn't men control themselves? She'd have words to say if she ever found out who was responsible.

God, it was foul! And getting stronger – a gut-wrenching mixture of bad eggs and the worst fart she'd ever smelled. Breda glared around, trying to spot someone looking guilty – but all she saw were people doing exactly the same as she was. One or two of the young ones were smirking. Father Doherty twice opened his mouth to speak and twice closed it, a look of irritation and disgust infusing his already irascible face. There was an eternity of silence before the old priest began coldly addressing the congregation.

It must have been a stink bomb, thought Breda, but not one that you could buy in a joke shop. This was the work of an industrial chemist. She saw Conn scowling in her direction as if blaming her. She shrugged and returned his scowl.

As the congregation rose to their feet for the first hymn, the stench returned worse than ever. The singing faltered. She heard men sniggering. Breda wanted to murder each and every one of them.

'Let us pray.'

Breda leaned forward, clasped her hands together and closed her eyes.

A volley of farts ripped through the church. Breda whipped round to see the congregation in disarray. Some were on their feet, others were still rising, a few still kneeling. The sounds of odd farts were still coming from various parts of the church. Alongside Breda, old Aunt Flora was staring at her hassock in horror. She tried to rise, slipped and sunk down again on the kneeler, which let out a long slow fart.

Teresa and Dessie had turned around to see what was happening, but Father Doherty would not be interrupted. Looking more irate than ever, the old priest motioned for the bridal couple to kneel.

Oh no! Breda wanted to cry out, wanted to stop them. She screwed up her face and tensed, waiting for the inevitable.

As bride and groom knelt, they both apparently let out enormous farts. Giggles broke out afresh, infectious giggles that spread and spread until hysteria swept through the already overwrought congregation. Breda glanced behind her to find whole pews of red-faced guests, their shoulders heaving with laughter. The more she and Conn glared, the more people averted their eyes and choked with helpless laughter. Every so often the temptation to kneel on a hassock became too much for someone.

Teresa's shoulders were shaking. But she was not laughing. She was crying.

Breda burned with shame and humiliation. She wanted to hug her sister – and kill those responsible for this fiasco.

Gradually, the congregation pulled itself together. The older members confiscated the offending hassocks from the younger ones. Father Doherty battled on through the wedding service. He was clearly furious and seemed to blame the debacle on Teresa and

Dessie personally. His address became a brisk, no-nonsense lecture about respecting the sanctity of God's House and the Catholic Church.

And after the hysteria, the collective mood turned flat. The congregation went through the motions, singing hymns without enthusiasm, mumbling the responses. Even the soprano's 'Ave Maria' was subdued and tuneless. When Teresa lifted her veil to be kissed, everyone could see the mascara that had run down her cheeks.

At the end of the ceremony, she looped her arm through Dessie's and marched angrily down the aisle, Aoife and Bobby having to trot behind to keep hold of her train.

'Who the fucking hell . . .?' hissed Breda to Conn as they began to follow.

'I don't know, but when I find out . . .'

'Poor Teresa.'

Outside, the photographer was setting up his equipment in front of the old church porch. Breda went up to Teresa to repair her make-up for the wedding photos.

Above them the bells began pealing.

A shot rang out.

For a moment everyone stood motionless.

Another shot – from very close.

Women screamed. Dessie flung Teresa to the ground and dived down alongside her. A ragged volley sent people dashing back towards the church. Breda peered frantically around for Aoife and Bobby. They were standing in the open, staring open-mouthed at the panicking crowd. Breda ran to her children, dragged them behind a large gravestone and threw her arms around them.

She tried to take stock. Conn was twenty feet away, crouched next to the trunk of an enormous yew, shouting to Stozza and a few of the men who were trying to locate the gunman. Now that Breda listened more intently, the shots seemed strangely muffled. She glimpsed a flash behind the slatted windows of the belfry. As she stared, there was another flash. But no one had been hit. There was no sound of an impact or any ricochet. And by the sound of the shots, they were coming from a twelve-bore.

As the peal of the bells died away, so too did the firing. In the eerie silence that followed, Teresa hobbled out from the church porch where she had finally sought shelter. The heel of her right shoe had snapped off, her chin was covered in mud and the front of her perfect ivory silk dress was plastered with earth and grass stains.

Half a mile away, Maddy passed the powerful binoculars back to Rob.

'Yes. Yes. Oh yessss. You're a star.' Maddy threw her arms around him. 'Teresa Bridges won't forget her wedding day for as long as she lives.'

'That should be less than four hours,' said Rob.

'Who? Who would be sick enough to pull those stunts?' raged Breda, pacing the floor of a bedroom in Drummore House.

Teresa, wearing just her slip, stood by the window, examining her ruined wedding dress. 'I'll get the swine whoever they are,' she hissed.

'*We*'ll get them,' corrected Breda. 'We'll track them down *and* make them pay. By Christ, they'll pay.'

Teresa collapsed on the edge of the bed, her wedding dress in her lap, and began sobbing helplessly. Breda sat down next to her and put her arm around her sister's shoulder.

'I wanted to wear it at the reception.' Teresa flung the heavy gown from her in a fury and took a large gulp of gin and tonic.

There was a perfunctory tap on the door and Conn and Dessie entered.

'Look what we found.' Conn held out thin blue shards. The familiar putrid smell wafted through the room. 'There were glass balls hidden in the organ. The organist said she thought she heard something break when she pulled out a stop to begin the wedding march.'

Conn tossed them into the corridor before holding up two shotgun cartridges. 'These were tied to the bell clappers with tacks to act as firing pins,' he explained.

'And the farting sounds were made by reflatable whoopee cushions hidden in the kneelers,' added Dessie.

'I think we worked that out,' replied Teresa sarcastically.

'What's your wedding dress doing on the floor?' demanded Dessie, scooping it up. 'This was bloody expensive.'

'Because it's fucking ruined. You throwing me on the ground like that.'

'We'll get it professionally cleaned while you're on your honeymoon,' soothed Breda. 'Put your going-away suit on now and we'll get the reception started.'

'Fuck that. The day's already ruined.' Teresa snatched up her broken shoe and hurled it out through the open window. 'Fucking shoes.'

Breda signalled for the men to leave. They scuttled out, only too pleased to do so.

'Come on, Ter, love. You've got to go to your own reception.'

'Why?'

'Because you're my sister and because you mustn't let the fuckers know thev've got to you. Please.'

'If only the devil could cast his net now, he'd have a fine haul,' murmured Pat Rodgers sitting in the snug bar of Drummore House with his sergeant John Mullally.

'A grand gathering of faces,' agreed Mullally. 'There's a few here I wouldn't have expected.'

'It just shows how Breda's influence is growing. I'd have put men like Neilo Close and Brian McIntyre in with the moderates.'

'Maybe they're just being polite.'

'No. This wedding list is as much political as it's social. Any guests here are supporters of Breda's.'

The two detectives were there to keep a quiet eye on things, as Rodgers put it. A separate surveillance team in a bedroom overlooking the entrance was secretly filming the members of the wedding party.

Rodgers chuckled as he picked up the accounts of the disastrous service. Things were not going smoothly here either. The reception should have begun twenty minutes ago but Teresa, blotchy-faced and angry, had only just made an appearance. The wedding guests were currently being hunted out of the bars to file past the receiving line.

Rodgers was puzzled as to who would have gone to such lengths to disrupt the wedding. The Provos were not known for their sense of humour. The Loyalists would have simply blown up the church or, more likely, blown themselves up while trying to destroy the place. But then who? He was puffing peacefully on his pipe – under the *No Smoking* sign – pondering the problem when the duty manager hurried into the bar.

'I'm glad I've found you, Chief Superintendent,' he said breathlessly. 'We've just had a phone call to say that there's a bomb in the banqueting hall. What do I do?'

'Slow down,' said Rodgers. 'What exactly did the caller say?'

'It was a man. He said that a bomb was due to go off in fifteen minutes at the wedding reception.'

Rodgers's mobile phone began ringing. 'Yes?' He listened intently. 'The hotel's received a call, too . . . No, we've no option. Yeh, it is ironic. Cheers.'

'What's happening?' demanded the manager, hopping from foot to foot.

'A man's phoned the local Garda station with the same warning. There's a team on its way to check out the room now. I'd bet a pound to a penny that it's a hoax but we can't take the chance. You'll have to evacuate the building.' Rodgers grinned as the manager scurried off, doing his best not to break into a run. 'You know, John, I'm going to find it devilish hard to keep the smile off my face when I see Teresa.'

'She'll be livid,' agreed Mullally.

'The biter bit. Hey, and where are you going?' Rodgers asked the barman who was making for the door.

'I'm getting out of here.'

'Not until you've poured us a couple of pints first,' ordered Rodgers as alarm bells began ringing.

The two policemen strolled outside to find Teresa and Breda arguing furiously with the manager. 'What the fuck do you mean, a bomb warning? No one would want to plant a bomb in this poxy hotel.'

'Madam, we have to take it seriously. Until the Garda have given the all-clear, we have to evacuate the hotel.' He hurried away before Teresa could reply.

'This is down to the same warped tosser who sabotaged the ceremony.' Breda spotted Rodgers, pint of Guinness in his hand, and headed towards him. 'What the hell are we doing out here?' she demanded. 'You know this is just a lot of baloney.'

'Do I?' asked Rodgers, innocently.

'It's a hoax. Anyone can see that.'

'We have to respect a warning,' replied Rodgers. 'At least they gave one.'

Breda's face darkened in anger. 'And what's that supposed to mean?'

'Whatever you wish it to,' he said evenly.

'What's happening, mam?' asked Bobby, coming up. By now, he had lost the top button on his shirt and muddy patches on both knees of his white suit showed where he had fallen over, playing with his cousins in the gardens.

Breda straightened his tie. 'Wicked people might have put a bomb in the hotel so we'll stay out here until we know it's safe.'

'I'd like to see a bomb go off.'

'That's a horrid thing to say,' complained Aoife. 'Bombs kill people. They're bad, aren't they, mam?'

'Sometimes people are desperate enough to use them,' said Breda.

The wedding guests milled over the lawns, talking together in small clusters. When the Garda bomb team arrived, a handful headed out of sight around the back of the hotel. After what seemed an eternity, the guests were allowed back into the banqueting hall overlooking the parkland. Finally the meal began. The mood lifted as everyone began to drink. Even Teresa began to enjoy herself, helped along by copious amounts of alcohol.

'Today we are witnessing the union of two committed republicans,' began Nolan in his best-man speech. 'A man and a woman who have spent their lives fighting for the just cause of Irish nationalism and freedom. They have a lot in common. They have not sold out as others have and they continue to fight. But they have their differences. Dessie here was unfortunate enough to serve six years. Teresa has never been found guilty of any offence. Now we know who's the lucky one among them.' He paused for the laughter. 'I can tell Dessie that marrying into the Bridges family can be daunting. I should know. But it is an honour and a challenge. And I say to the pair of you, good luck, good health. May your union be blessed. Ireland needs all the sons and daughters she can muster. There may be sacrifices ahead; hard times ahead. I know you will not flinch – and I know we will succeed.'

'Sounds more like a bloody political rally than a best man's speech,' complained Rodgers, listening to Nolan's voice as it was relayed over a hidden microphone to the Garda's room.

'I thank Father Doherty,' continued Nolan. 'The bridesmaid, my own little Aoife. Dessie and Teresa. Bless their union. *Tiocfaidh Ar La.* Our day will come.'

'*Tiocfaidh Ar La*,' replied the guests.

*

Thirty minutes later and Teresa was about to leave to drive to Dublin with her new husband. Breda slipped her arm through her sister's. 'Send us a postcard from the Gambia.'

'Will do.'

'You might want to have a look in the English papers, if they get them out there, especially in the second week.'

'You reckon you'll be ready to . . .'

'I didn't tell you because I knew you had enough on your plate, but we've got enough devices to start the campaign. And we persuaded Eamon to come out of retirement.'

'There they are,' announced Rob, looking intently through the binoculars. 'They're bringing the car around now. They've certainly been to work on it.'

'I'll be missing the fun, then.'

'There'll be other times.' The sisters walked arm in arm out through the wide hotel entrance.

'Oh no!' shrieked Teresa. 'Look what they've done to my car.'

'Just Wed' had been daubed in red lipstick on the doors and bonnet of Teresa's Escort XR3. Green and white balloons and orange lace fluttered from the radio aerial and a line of tin cans trailed from the rear bumper.

'We couldn't just let you get away now, could we?' grinned Stozza.

'Yer evil fuckers,' laughed Teresa. 'You wait until I get back. I'll have you. You'll see.'

But Conn Nolan was looking thoughtful. 'Where's that car been all day?'

'Here,' replied Stozza. 'Around the side in the car park. I brought it up with the suitcases.'

'You mean it's been here since this morning, unguarded.'

'I don't like it, Conn,' muttered Breda. 'I've got that feeling.'

'Come on. Come on. They've got to drive themselves to Dublin.'

'You should have put a guard on the car.'

'How were we to know?'

'Can you get it checked out now?'

'It'll mean someone crawling under it. It should really go up on a ramp.'

'They're looking at the car. Shit. I hope they're not going to change their plans.'

'Teresa's not going anywhere in that car,' decided Breda. 'There's been something funny going on all today and we're not going to risk it.'

'You're right,' agreed Nolan. 'Take my car. Take the Merc. One of the boys can pick it up from the airport in the morning.'

'That's the best idea,' agreed Breda. 'Sorry today wasn't perfect, Ter.'

'What's happening now?'

'They're swapping cars. There's a silver Mercedes on the way from the car park. Wonder if the Escort was a plant?'

Wasn't perfect! You can say that again. Still, who knows, maybe we'll be laughing about this in years to come.'

'That's the spirit . . .'

'But I want someone's arse in a sling when I get back, ye understand.'

'Are you going in daddy's car, Aunt Teresa?'

'Yes, my poppet, as a special treat. Thank you for helping me today. You and Bobby have been really magical.'

'There's a bottle of vintage champagne waiting for you in your room in Dublin.'

'Are they going to stand there nattering for ever?'

Standing well back behind the first-floor window, Pat Rodgers watched as Teresa and Dessie Fitzgerald came down the terrace steps to the applause of the guests waiting to see them off. Teresa threw her bouquet towards Aoife who snatched it out of the air. Breda and Teresa embraced before the bride bent to kiss Aoife and an embarrassed Bobby. Nolan leaned into the car, explaining the controls to Dessie while Teresa wound down her window to continue chatting. Finally, the big saloon moved slowly forward, its wheels scrunching over the gravel. Breda picked up Aoife who waved and waved as the car set off down the winding drive.

'Bye bye, auntie,' called Aoife. 'Have a lovely moneyhoon.'

'Honeymoon, you little thickie.'

'I know that, but moneyhoon sounds funnier.'

The Mercedes disappeared out of sight, only to reappear from behind a stand of laurel bushes. Teresa was leaning out of the open passenger window, waving with both hands.

'Look, mam. Look.'

A radio-controlled model car had appeared on the drive. White, gold and green lace flew from its aerial and it was towing a line of miniature tin cans.

Guests were laughing and pointing at the model car following the Mercedes down the drive.

'That's brilliant.'

'Someone's made an effort. It's really travelling.'

'It's catching the Merc.'

'Who's controlling it?'

Who *was* controlling it? Breda scanned the guests. Then the grounds. Why couldn't she spot who was directing it?

The model car had caught up with the Merc. Teresa had seen it. She was leaning out of the window, pretending to shoot at it.

'Look. It's driven under the Merc.'

Breda went cold.

'Noooo.'

A white flash lit up the dusk. A second later came a dull rumbling crump. In the distance, pieces of the Mercedes were still rising skywards.

It had been fascinating to watch Rob work on the bomb.

'Aren't you scared?' Maddy had asked.

'Only that you'll say "Boo".'

'I promise I won't.' She had smiled.

It was two nights before the wedding. The pair were sitting in the kitchen of the Dublin flat belonging to Denny's friend. The flat had become an anarchist's workshop.

Maddy was taping tacks to the bases of shotgun cartridges to act as firing pins.

In the bathroom, Denny was sandpapering three tinsel balls to make their walls even thinner. The delivery system for his stink bombs.

'All I need is sulphur, sulphate of ammonia and hydrated lime,' he had announced.

'That's all!' exclaimed Maddy.

'You can get sulphur and sulphate of ammonia at any garden centre and hydrated lime from a builders' merchants,' replied Denny.

Having gathered the ingredients, he mixed two ounces of sulphur with four ounces of lime in a saucepan, stirred in a pint of water and allowed the lime to sink to the bottom. Helped by Maddy, Denny poured the yellow liquid into a bucket in the back garden. He added eight ounces of sulphate of ammonia, stirred a couple of times – and then he and Maddy fled, gagging, back into the house.

'Jesus Christ, Denny. That's *the* worst thing I've ever smelled.'

'Isn't it just wonderful?' Denny took a deep breath and rushed back to cover the bucket with a plastic wrap. Later he poured a few drops of the liquid into the balls before replacing their tops and sealing them with wax.

Denny had learned that the wedding organist needed to use the trumpet stop for the opening bars of Mendelssohn's Wedding March. He planned to balance a ball on the stop inside the organ, so when the stop was pulled out, the ball would fall and break. The other two balls would be hidden behind separate stops in the hope that they too would be used during the service.

Denny's second master stroke had been to discover self-reflating whoopee cushions.

And that just left the bomb.

At first, Rob had planned to detonate a device buried in a gravel-filled pothole in the hotel's drive, using a mobile phone to send the electronic signal. But he found that it took an average of seven seconds for the call to get through.

'It's no good,' he'd told Maddy and Denny. 'In those seven seconds, a car doing fifteen m.p.h. will travel 51.3 yards, twenty m.p.h. will cover 68.4 yards and if they're putting their foot down at twenty-five then they'll cover 85.5 yards.'

'What about if someone drove in front of them to regulate their speed?' suggested Denny.

'They could be driving even slower. No, we need a system that will send and receive a signal instantly – like a radio-controlled aircraft.'

'Or a model car,' suggested Maddy, remembering the one she had bought TJ for Christmas. 'We could hide it alongside the drive.'

Denny volunteered to go shopping and returned with a 1/10 scale model of a sporty Dodge Viper.

Rob set the FM radio transmitter to its primary channel and pressed a button. Instantly a light came on in the receiver in the car.

'Shame we can't steer this under the wedding car as it leaves,' murmured Maddy.

Denny cleared his throat. 'I'll have you know that you're in the presence of one of the world's greatest model car racing drivers.'

'What?'

'We were shooting a film in Spain a few years ago which turned into an absolute disaster. We spent days and days sitting around as everything possible went wrong. To pass the time, the crew got into racing radio-controlled cars around the set. I became undisputed champion.'

'You could steer this down the hotel drive?'

'Easily. And it's fast enough. The Viper'll do twenty-eight m.p.h.'

'Right, then.'

Once Rob was satisfied that the transmitting strength of one watt would send a signal to the range of vision, he set to work.

'Are you *sure* that stuff's safe?' asked Maddy as he peeled back greaseproof paper from a block of Semtex.

'Perfectly.' Rob carefully attached two wires from an electric detonator to the radio receiver. 'There you are – a basic initiation set. Keep it away from the explosive until we're ready to assemble the device.'

'So what happens?'

'This servo converts electrical signals into physical movements. Left, right, faster, etc. We don't need reverse gear so we'll connect that servo movement to the detonator. When we want to set off the device, we just hit reverse on the control panel. The inside of Teresa's car will be turned into one whirling mass of shrapnel.'

'And you're sure this'll work?' demanded Maddy.

'Trust me. It'll go like a bomb.'

31

Breda Bridges gazed sightlessly out to where the sullen grey swell of the Irish Sea became lost in the drabness of the late afternoon. A drizzling mist was pearling her black coat in fine beads but she did not notice. Finally, she could help herself no longer and again she looked down at the photograph in her hand. The one of her and Teresa taken not a month ago at their triumphant rally in Castleblayney. Breda was placidly looking at the camera, but Teresa – was Teresa. Her mouth was open as though she was shouting the odds and her right fist was raised in exultation.

Letting out a shuddering wail, Breda keened for her dead sister.

The woman beside her placed her hands on Breda's shoulders and turned her gently so that they were facing one another. Breda gratefully buried her head in the other's bosom, her whole body racked by convulsive sobs.

'I'm sorry,' she managed to gulp. 'I didn't mean to . . .'

'Hush, hush. Cry if you want.'

Breda wiped her eyes and tried to pull herself together. 'I can't believe Teresa's not here. Nothing phased her. She'd head-butt the whole world if necessary. Ter was two months pregnant at our rally. For all we knew we were in for a kicking from the Provos, but Ter was right there alongside me.'

'I know.'

'She was always a right little tomboy. Always getting into fights and brawls and loving every moment of it. She once laid out a copper who was trying to arrest me during a march. She was so brave, so loyal.' Breda's voice rose as she began to wail again. 'Oh my God. What am I going to do without her? I miss her so much. She was my sister.'

'I know,' replied Rose Allen. 'She was my sister, too.'

'At this rate, I'll have no one left to arrest,' joked Tanner.

'It's fine for you,' growled Rodgers down the phone. 'But now I've got to find the bombers who blew up the bombers, so to speak.'

'A case of big fleas having smaller fleas to bite them.'

'A case of what? . . . You're breaking up. Can you hear me?'

'Sorry, we're going under a railway bridge.' Tanner motioned to Pottidge to pull in.

'I was saying that there's not much left of the Merc. Whoever was controlling the model car had to be able to see it but we haven't found his hiding place yet.'

'What about the model itself?'

'A Dublin shop owner remembers the man who bought a powerful radio-controlled car the day before the wedding. Five feet eleven, glasses, bad breath, thick local accent. Said it was a present for his son,' recounted Rodgers. 'We're doing a photofit now. If he was our man, then it's our best lead.'

'What about forensic on the stink bombs and the rest?'

'Nolan destroyed them, or said he did.'

'You're joking!'

'You don't know these people, Cyril. They won't cooperate even to solve the murder of two of their own. Most of them scarpered the moment the bomb went off. You wouldn't believe the trouble we had getting statements from them.'

'Is the man who made the hoax calls the same man who bought the model car?'

'No. I've listened to the tapes. The hoaxer's from West Belfast – which puts him in among the Provos.'

'Are they in the frame?'

'Definitely, but no one can understand the weird happenings in the church. The Provos wouldn't mess around. They'd just take out Teresa and Dessie without any preliminaries.'

'Right.'

'I gather three of the relatives from the Salisbury bombing were in Dublin over the weekend?'

'Yes: Maddy, Rob and Denny. I'm on my way to see them now.'

'Do me a favour, Cyril. Check out their alibis in the nicest possible way.'

'You don't think . . .'

'Look at it this way. They have the motive. Rob Sage has the expertise to make a bomb and, as they were in Ireland, they had the opportunity.'

'I'll have a chat with them and let you know the outcome.'

'Grand. You can't believe the political flak I'm getting over this one. It's as though the President had been slotted, not two murdering toe-rags who deserved to die anyway.'

'I didn't know her as well as you did.'

'You couldn't do. Not the way you . . .'

'That was my decision. Teresa was just a young teenager when we decided that I should go away.' Rose Allen smiled sadly. 'But I could see then what she'd become. I missed being part of her adventures. You must tell me about them. We have all day.'

'Yes.'

Breda felt better now – as she always did on the rare occasions when she met her big sister: the only person in the whole world she would defer to. When Rose was with her, she felt as if the load had been lifted off her shoulders; the responsibility shared. Conn played his part, so too had Teresa, but none of them believed in their cause as much as Rose, as she was now called. No one had sacrificed their whole life – as she had.

'Teresa was so good with kids. Aoife worshipped her. Teresa would have been a good mother. It would have calmed her down; steadied her, like.' Breda wiped at the mist which was falling on her eyelashes like dew. 'They killed her unborn baby. How could they do that?'

'Did you ever ask her how she came to let that American girl see the rings on her fingers?'

'No. And now I never will.' Breda began sobbing again.

'It's all right.'

'And don't forget Dessie.' Breda felt guilty that she had not mentioned him. 'He had his moments. They made a great couple.'

She and her sister stood side by side, lost in thought.

'The struggle must go on, Breda. Now more than ever.'

Breda did not reply.

'I've the singer and her boyfriend jacked up for the next wave,' continued Rose Allen. 'We'll begin with the football crowd at Old Trafford. All you've got to do is get the first six bombs to me . . .'

'On her wedding day. Her fucking wedding day.'

Her sister saw that Breda had not heard a word she'd been saying. 'Tell me about her wedding day,' she coaxed.

'It was a farce. A fucking farce.'

'So who was behind it?'

'Milo O'Connell sent word that it wasn't the Provos.'

'You believe him?'

'Who knows? They'd love to get one over on us but I can't see that they'd fuck around driving us mad first.'

Something stirred at the back of Rose's mind. More than once Maddy Lipzinger had gone on about the idea that those whom the gods destroy, they first drive mad. Rose had thought little of it at the time but now it made her remember Maddy's obsession with revenge, and how she refused to return to the United States until the Salisbury bombers had been accounted for.

What had Wayne Wallis said? '*The deaths of her kids and her husband have got to her.*'

'She certainly had a fucking neck, coming to my house,' exclaimed Breda as her elder sister voiced her suspicions. 'So you think . . .?'

'I don't know. I'll talk to her when I get back to England,' said Rose, before adding thoughtfully. 'There is someone we could lean on, you know. Does Conn still have mates on the mainland he can call on for the heavy stuff?'

'Of course, but he can go himself. There are ways, as you know.'

'That'll be better. Send Conn.'

'And you'll be moving soon.'

'The lease on the furnished cottage runs out at the end of this month. I've put in my notice and I've already begun to move my things to Hemel Hempstead – but slowly, so as not to arouse suspicion.' Rose took Breda's hand. 'But don't worry. I'm going to take a leaf out of Maddy Lipzinger's book. I'm going nowhere until I've found who killed our little sister.'

Tanner and Pottidge pulled up outside Rob's cottage. They climbed out of their car, both glancing up at the slate-grey sky that held the threat of snow.

'Come in out of the cold,' said Rob, throwing open the front door.

Both detectives headed straight for the open fire.

'It's just what you need on a day like this,' said Pottidge, rubbing his hands in front of the burning logs. 'That north wind goes straight through you.'

'Hi. Coffee's on its way,' shouted Maddy from the kitchen.

Tanner wondered again if she and Rob were living together, or if it was enough for them just to live next door to each other.

'You've heard about the couple in Ireland who were blown up on their wedding day?' began Tanner when they were sitting around the fire, sipping coffee.

'Yeh. Teresa Bridges and her bloke. Great result,' exclaimed Maddy.

'Great result?' echoed Tanner.

'You live by the bomb, you die by the bomb,' said Maddy. 'Poetic justice.'

Tanner turned to Rob. 'You feel the same?'

Rob shrugged. 'I'm not whooping and hollering like Maddy, but, yes, I'm pleased they're dead. They had it coming.'

Graham Pottidge was nodding in agreement, but Tanner scowled. 'And you'd rather they were blown up than brought before a court of law?'

'You said yourself that the odds of that happening were growing longer all the time.'

'Yes, but . . .'

Maddy leaned forward, eyes blazing. 'Listen, my daughter said that the woman who planted the bomb wore rings on her fingers. I met with Teresa Bridges. I saw those rings. She killed my family and now *she*'s dead. You expect me to feel sorry? I'll dance on her grave.'

'As long as we know where we stand,' said Tanner, with a sardonic smile. 'Were you aware that Teresa Bridges was pregnant?'

'No. No, how could I be?'

Tanner watched as her eyes flickered towards Rob. 'You said you were going to Dublin this weekend,' continued the detective.

'Yeh, we had a great time. Isn't it a lovely city? And the people are so friendly,' enthused Maddy. 'We stayed in a flat belonging to one of Denny's actor buddies. Say what you like about gay men, but golly, they've got taste.'

'Bit of a coincidence you being in Ireland when Teresa and her groom were killed,' hazarded Tanner.

'Is it? Why?' exclaimed Rob. 'We didn't know they were getting married. How could we? Anyway, the newspaper reports said the wedding was up near the border with Northern Ireland.'

'You didn't leave Dublin?'

'Yes, we hired a car and drove to the Wicklow Mountains. Very beautiful they were too.'

'Hang on,' said Maddy. 'Are we being suspected of killing those scum?'

'No.' Tanner shook his head. 'It's simply that Pat Rodgers has asked me informally to eliminate you from his inquiries. It's just a question of running through your movements while you were in Ireland.'

'That's no problem. We went on Thursday and came back yesterday, Sunday. I've stamps in my passport. I imagine the airline will have records of Rob and Denny.'

'Where is Mr Fox now?'

'He's gone up to Birmingham to record the TV soap. He should be back in a couple of days.'

'And what did you all do in Dublin?'

'We went to Trinity College to see the Book of Kells, visited the Guinness Storehouse – that was fun. Followed in the footsteps of Leopold Bloom. Dublin's a great city to walk around. Everything's so close. Went to the Abbey Theatre to see a very odd play called *The Lieutenant of Innishmore*. I've kept the programme. And we visited that jail . . .'

'Kilmainham Jail,' supplied Rob.

'And lots of bars. Lots and lots of bars. We had a wonderful meal in a hotel near us. It used to be a church. The Davenport, that's right. And, as Rob said, we went off to the Wicklow Mountains.'

'It sounds as if you had a busy time.'

'I kept a diary. I always do on holiday. Do you want to see it?'

'Please.'

'And I *think* I've still got some receipts.'

Maddy was *sure* that she still had receipts. So had Rob and Denny, part of a carefully planned exercise in deception that Rob had insisted upon. Of course, they could provide three ticket stubs for all the places Maddy had mentioned – but then it was very easy for one person to buy three tickets.

Time to go on the offensive.

'Who do the Garda reckon bombed the newly-weds?' asked Rob.

'They've an open mind,' replied Tanner. 'But I can tell you one thing. Breda Bridges and her thugs won't take this lying down.

They'll be out for blood. If they ever get a whiff of who did it, they'll be after them, make no mistake.'

As Tanner spoke, he was watching closely for the effect of his words on Rob and Maddy. They exhibited natural curiosity and interest. There was no sense of fear.

Good.

'This horrific double murder is sending shock waves through the whole peace process. It's a shaky edifice at the best of times, so the last thing we need now is a tremor of this seismic magnitude.'

Petula Anstey leaned back on her office sofa and crossed her legs. She was gratified that both David Hayward and Damien Kilfoyle's eyes dropped to observe the movement. These were men she could do business with. Young, good-looking high achievers – like herself. Certainly not like that old policeman with his flushed drinker's face. What was his name? Tinner, Tanner – something like that.

'The Irish government has asked for our help,' she continued. 'Dublin is furious that they've had such a spectacular killing in the country.'

'Yes, they usually export their murders,' said Hayward drily.

Anstey ignored him. 'I'm told the smart money is on the Provos even though they deny it.'

'Maybe we're *meant* to think it's a political killing,' suggested Kilfoyle. 'After all, Conn Nolan's up to his ears in drugs and racketeering and Dessie Fitzgerald was his associate. It could be part of a drugs war.'

'Whatever. Anyway, Dublin is insisting on a permanent liaison officer from SO 13 to get this investigation moving.'

'We're hard-pressed as it is, Minister. Where are we going to get a senior officer?'

'You still have men working on that Salisbury bomb?'

'Yes.'

'Take someone off that. The peace process comes first. Sinn Fein are already bleating about the bomb being the work of an SAS hit squad. They know it's not true – or rather their leaders do – but it gives them a big stick with which to beat HMG.'

'Even though they might be responsible for the killings themselves?'

'*Especially* because they might be responsible for the killings themselves,' replied Petula Anstey. 'The only way to end this speculation is to find the real culprits.'

'I didn't like the way Tanner went through those bills so thoroughly,' said Maddy once the policemen had left.

'Or the way he went on about Breda Bridges seeking revenge for her sister's death,' added Rob, picking up the coffee cups.

'There's no way she can know it was us,' declared Maddy, following Rob into the kitchen. 'But I'm glad we had those receipts.'

Maddy began washing up the cups and their lunch plates, Rob standing by her side, tea towel in hand. At first, Maddy had complained about the lack of a dishwasher – now she enjoyed the intimacy of washing-up, the opportunity for chatting, the occasional kiss.

'Two to go,' she murmured, breaking the companionable silence.

'Sorry?'

'Just two to go. Nolan and Breda Bridges.'

'What do you propose?'

'Don't know.' Maddy thought back to the squat powerful figure of Nolan she'd viewed through her binoculars. 'I don't think Nolan'll scare easily.'

'Nor Breda.'

'But we know her weak link.' She passed Rob a soup bowl from lunch.

'Do we?'

'Her children.'

'You'd threaten to harm her kids!'

'Might do.' Maddy glanced sideways at Rob and saw that he found the idea distasteful. 'Why not? She dotes on her kids. It's the way to get to her.'

'But you wouldn't actually *harm* the kids?'

'She harmed mine. Christ! She *killed* mine. Why shouldn't I kill hers?'

'Maddy!'

'I don't know,' Maddy said sullenly, aware Rob was regarding her with disbelief.

'I couldn't go along with that.' He took a cup from her, turning it through the cloth in his hands. 'Her children have done nothing wrong.'

'*Mine* had done nothing wrong,' she exclaimed. 'Nor had Alfred.'

'I still wouldn't. We'd become like them.'

Maddy spun to face him, her hands and wrists covered in soapy bubbles. 'Maybe it's different for you. I was a mother. *Was* a mother. Try that for size. How do you think it feels to lose your children?'

'I understand.'

'No, you don't. You can't.' Maddy became aware that she was shouting. 'You adopted a little boy. I gave *birth* to my children and watched them die, thanks to one scheming, bigoted, evil bitch of hell. She *owes* me her children.'

'I'll not help you,' said Rob, so quietly that Maddy was not sure if she had imagined the words.

'Then I'll do it myself.' And again she was not sure if the words were being spoken – or if she had merely thought them.

'It's a terrible business, so it is. A terrible business.' Milo O'Connell gave a sad shake of his white head and watched as a coal dropped in the bar-room fire, sending up a flurry of sparks. 'Who would kill a bride and groom on their wedding day? Not even you've done that, have ye, Nutter?'

'Never had the chance.'

'And her with child, too,' continued O'Connell. 'They'll be missed, I'll be thinking. Breda will miss Teresa. She relied on her sister more than she knew. She'll find out now that there'll be a large hole in her life. But it's Dessie Fitzgerald who interests me more.'

Nutter Hains, used to O'Connell musing aloud, merely grunted.

'Dessie was a prop for Nolan, in a way that neither Mikey Drumm nor Jimmy Burke were. And he was trusted by Nolan, in a way that Stozza McKenna isn't.' O'Connell took a sip of stout, the foam leaving a white moustache on his top lip. 'I'm thinking that Breda's lieutenants are a bit thin on the ground at the moment. She's lost all her top team.'

'Won't she put together a new one?' asked Hains.

'Oh ay, she will,' replied O'Connell. 'But it takes time. There'll be a hiatus – a gap, Nutter – and we must take advantage of it. When's the best time to kick a man?'

'When he's down.'

'Exactly. When he's down. Now is the time to kick Nolan. We'll show others we have long memories and a longer reach.'

'We'll show Nolan too, eh?'

'No, Nutter, he'll be dead. And with Nolan dead, Breda will be isolated. What happens when you cut the head off a body, Nutter?'

'Um . . . um, you kill it. Unless it's a hydrangea.'

'What?'

'It's something I read about. You cut the head off a hydrangea and it grows another one.'

'God save us. That's a *hydra* you're talking about, not a bloody *hydrangea*.' O'Connell sighed. 'Get us another stout.'

But the True Guardians and the Sovereign IRA weren't a hydra. They ran on the will and determination of Breda Bridges and on the broad shoulders of Conn Nolan – but not for much longer.

32

Rose Allen turned the soft-drinks bottle in her hands as if she was holding a precious object. What craftsmanship! To pack that much explosive – that much killing power – inside a one-and-a-half litre plastic bottle and make it look so ordinary and harmless. Genius.

What a shame the Pizzaman would never make another bomb.

She peered up at the kitchen clock. Maddy Lipzinger was due – but she'd be late, she knew. Her few visitors always had problems the first time finding their way to her lonely bungalow tucked away amid a stand of beech trees in a hollow on the very edge of Salisbury Plain.

Rose Allen had grown to like her small home here, its location reflecting her own isolation. But now it was time to reinvent herself again as she had so often in the past. Deep cover, it was called in the trade. Just getting on with an ordinary life and doing whatever job she happened to have – until the call came.

Her work here was done. But before she left, she had to discover if the American woman and her little circle of mourners were behind the deaths of Teresa, Dessie and the others.

She looked around the kitchen, checking that there was nothing to give her away. She had put on her padded corset, tweed skirt, cardigan and large spectacles, slipping into the person Maddy was expecting to see. You could never be too careful. She had drummed that into Breda – who had been a willing pupil. Teresa was a different matter. She was too headstrong, too impulsive . . . *had* been too impulsive.

Rose Allen's nostrils dilated in cold fury. If she found out that that American cow had been responsible for Teresa's death – God help her!

She heard a car and looking out of the kitchen window saw Maddy's distinctive lime-green Beetle turn hesitantly down the track towards her.

'So this is where you live,' exclaimed Maddy as she climbed out. 'You're really out in the wilds, aren't you? There's not another building in sight.'

'Did you have problems finding it?'

Maddy laughed. 'I almost drove onto a firing range but some nice soldiers turned me back.'

'It's wonderful for bird life here. I had a pair of stone curlews nesting last summer and, look, a buzzard.' Rose pointed upwards as Maddy heard a plaintive mewing on the wind.

'Don't you ever get lonely?'

'Not really. Come in. How was Dublin?'

'Wonderful. I tried to phone you Sunday night to have a rave about it but you were out.'

'I went to see friends for the weekend,' replied Rose. 'You enjoyed yourselves?'

'People in Dublin are great. Do you know the place?'

'It's years since I've been there.' Rose crossed the kitchen to where coffee was already percolating. 'I've a Dundee cake, sorry it's from a shop. Normally I'd bake myself but I haven't had time.'

Maddy stopped to admire a montage of a ploughman and his two horses made from strips of different woods. 'That's lovely.'

'I picked it up in Salisbury market.' Rose poured coffee. 'Did you hear about that couple blown up on their wedding day while you were in Ireland?'

'They were the terrorists I've talked about. The bride planted the bomb that killed my family. Thank you.' Maddy took the proffered coffee cup and turned to look out at the view.

'How do you feel about their deaths?' Rose Allen pulled out a large knife from a drawer.

'Tanner asked me that.' Maddy thought she had spotted a movement on the dun-coloured slope opposite. 'I told him I'd happily dance on their graves.'

'Oooh.'

'I'm sure I saw something move on the hill,' said Maddy, staring intently.

Rose Allen moved close behind her, the knife with its eight-inch blade clasped in her right hand. 'Where?'

'Just above that outcrop of rock.'

'Can't see anything. How many of you went to Dublin?'

'Just the three of us – me, Rob and Denny.'

'No Wayne?'

'No, he seems to have dropped off the planet.'

'Ah, there. Roe deer. You can just make out the stag's antlers. You have to know how to look.'

'I can't see them.'

'But, surely, it was a terrible thing to happen to anyone on their wedding day?'

'Sorry?'

'That bombing in Ireland. You've got to feel sorry for someone who's killed on their wedding day?'

'Not that scum. What goes around, comes around. They deserved all they got.'

'Then I expect you wish you'd been there to see it.'

The hairs on Maddy's neck rose. She had a terrible presentiment that she was in mortal danger.

She swung around to face Rose Allen. 'Pardon me?'

'I mean you've talked about revenge so often . . .'

'Just because I talk about it doesn't mean I practise it.'

'But don't you *wish* you'd been there?'

'Rose, I didn't even know they were getting married.' Maddy dismissed her momentary fear as silliness and turned back to look out of the window. 'There's the stag and a doe. I can see them now.'

'Well camouflaged, aren't they?' Rose cut two wedges of cake. 'Come into the living room. It's warmer there.'

'Tanner said that Breda Bridges will be seeking revenge for the death of her sister,' reported Maddy as she sat on one side of the log-burning stove.

'I expect she will,' agreed Rose. 'Who do the police think did it?'

'They've an open mind. Would you believe, Tanner asked us to account for our time in Dublin. Luckily, we had receipts and things.' Maddy delved into her handbag to produce a mobile phone. 'Excuse me. Rob's going to call about going to the theatre. I forgot to switch it on.'

'There's no signal up here. The land line's not much better. It only needs one storm and it goes down,' said Rose. 'Has Rob heard anything about his job yet?'

'Not yet. He's hoping to get another post somewhere in Africa.'

'You'll be lonely without him.'

'To be honest, I don't know if I'd stay in this country once he'd left.'

'If you ever get lonely or fed up, you know where to find me.'

'You're a saint.'

Once Maddy had gone, Rose Allen slowly tidied up the plates, thinking deeply. Her intuition told her something wasn't quite right. She had a feeling that Maddy had been involved in her sister's death – but she wasn't totally sure. She needed to make a phone call that could not be traced. She also needed to get £300 to give to the singer and her bloke – her new lilywhites – to keep them sweet.

Since Teresa's death, she had found the English tweeds she was wearing for Maddy's benefit repugnant. In an act that defied her nature and training, Rose Allen exchanged the pounds-fattening corset, staid skirt and fawn cardigan for a pair of jeans and left her glasses behind.

Rose Allen drove into Salisbury through the early-evening traffic and parked her car in Brown Street. She headed back towards the cashpoints and the Tesco supermarket, forgetting that she was wearing exactly the same clothes, even down to the same black boots, that she had worn when she had called on Mrs Petherton last year to rent Sundial Farm.

That was careless. Andrea Petherton and her husband John were over from Spain to talk to their solicitor about a developer's offer to buy the ruins of their farmhouse. As Tanner had predicted, their insurance company had refused to pay out, leaving them virtually penniless.

It was bad luck that they happened to be in the line of cars crawling out of the city centre just as Rose Allen was hurrying along Blue Boar Row.

Mrs Petherton gulped and grabbed at John's arm, causing him to swerve.

'It's her,' exclaimed Andrea excitedly. 'It's her.'

'Who?'

'The woman who rented the farmhouse.' Andrea twisted in her seat to keep the woman in view.

'It can't be.'

'It is, I tell you. I recognized her straightaway. She's gone into Tesco's.'

'You told that detective you couldn't be sure what she looked like.'

'I can now I've seen her again. We must tell the police.'

'I can't stop here. There's nowhere to park.'

'I told you we should have got a mobile phone.'

'And I told you that we have better things to spend our money on. The little we have.'

'Really, John! Let me out to find a phone or she'll get away.'

Andrea flung open the door and began to scramble out.

The emergency operator was initially confused by the woman who came on demanding the police while burbling breathlessly about a fire. Finally, Andrea managed to calm down enough to explain, 'I've just seen the woman who rented the farmhouse the bombers used. She must be part of the gang.'

'Where?'

'Here in Salisbury, going into Tesco's.'

'And you are?'

'Mrs Andrea Petherton – I've told you.'

The call was relayed to Tanner in the incident room. He had to assume that the woman was armed. Unwilling to risk her taking a hostage when confronted by uniforms, he gave orders to infiltrate Tesco's with plain-clothes men – and positioned an armed-response unit well out of sight around the back. If Tanner could avoid spooking the suspect, he wanted to follow her back to her hideout.

But his planning came to nothing. Rose Allen wasn't in Tesco's by the time the first detective arrived. She had left the supermarket as soon as she'd seen the long queues at the checkouts, deciding to leave her shopping until tomorrow lunchtime when it would be quieter. She actually spotted the armed-response unit arriving – and wondered what was happening. It didn't occur to her that she was the reason for their presence.

'Do you think Mrs Petherton really saw the woman who rented her farmhouse?' asked Pottidge later as he and Tanner settled over a pint in the King's Arms.

'She was pretty positive,' replied Tanner.

'But why has the woman returned to Salisbury?'

'Maybe she never left it in the first place. I'll ask Pat Rodgers in the morning if the new description matches any of Breda's known associates.'

The detectives sipped their beer in silence until Tanner remembered the copy of a newspaper obituary of Teresa Bridges which Rodgers had faxed him.

'According to this republican rag, Teresa wasn't a mass murderer at all. She was a bloody saint who walked on water.' He handed the cutting to Pottidge.

'It says here that she was the youngest of three daughters of noted republican Seamus Bridges and brother of Bobby who both died at the hands of the British imperialists,' read Pottidge. 'I thought Bobby Bridges blew himself up.'

'Shit!' Tanner sat bolt upright. 'He did, but you're missing the point. *Three daughters.* Teresa, Breda. Where's the third?'

Wayne Wallis was in a good mood. He walked home with a lightness of heart that he had not known since Leanne had died. Things were going his way at last. The fake lines in Calvin Klein, Ralph Lauren and other designers were selling well, he was knocking out stolen Berghaus anoraks at the rate of four a week and the leather clothing stall was making money – though it was too cold to stand out for long in this weather. But his best scam was Viagra – not for the old wrinklies but among the builders and young bucks on the estate.

It had started when he'd read that Viagra had become the trendy drug of choice for stars who couldn't perform after a night on cocaine. Wayne had spotted a niche market. Using his brother's credit card, he bought twenty-four tablets for £288 from a site on the Web. He divided them in half and was now knocking them out for £20 each. A clear profit of £572. A nice little earner.

Wayne let himself into the hallway, switched on the light and went through into the kitchen. He reckoned he'd chill out in front of the TV with a few beers before going down the pub to see if there was any business doing.

The house was quiet without Leanne, but he didn't mind that much. You had to get on with life. That was Wayne's motto – get on with life. When that daft tart Shaynee had started to play up, he'd dumped her pronto. That was the sort of bloke he was. A guy who moved on – and didn't put up with anyone's shit.

He picked up a can of lager from the fridge together with two packets of bacon-flavoured crisps and carried them back through the hall, fumbling to open the door to the living room. He stepped into the room – and stopped dead. In the dim light cast by the street lamp outside, he made out the bulk of a man sitting in his chair by the glowing electric fire. The door closed behind him. As Wayne stood rooted to the spot, a second man crossed to the window and drew the curtains.

Damien Kilfoyle and Fliss Fakenham leaned side by side on the balustrade and watched a tug haul barges full of domestic rubbish through the grey waters of the river Thames towards the sea. A small oil tanker was butting its way upstream against the current.

'I always think it's a shame,' said Fliss. 'You have this superhighway running through the heart of London and it's hardly used.'

'Yes,' agreed Kilfoyle, wondering why she had wanted to talk out here and not in the nearby MI5 headquarters where they both worked. He had only just returned to London that morning from yet another conference in Washington on the war on terror. For a people who proclaimed themselves to be the land of the free and the home of the brave, Americans were showing a disturbing degree of national paranoia, he reckoned. He had called Fliss to say good morning as soon as he had reached his office and had been surprised when she'd suggested meeting out here on Millbank.

'I have some good news, darling.'

'Yes?'

'Daddy's given you a clean bill of health for your agent handling.'

'Really! The last time we met he virtually put me through the third degree.'

'I know, that's why I'm telling you now.' Fliss dropped her voice to a conspiratorial whisper. 'Daddy can be the limit sometimes. He's upset a lot of people. Between you and me, the DG called him in and told him to approve everything unless there's a prima facie case of abuse. But Daddy's not going out of his way to put people's minds at rest. And I knew you were worried.'

'I wouldn't say I was worried . . .' Shit-scared would have been a better description – although, of course, he hadn't confessed that to Fliss. 'But it's very sweet of you.' Kilfoyle leaned down and brushed Fliss's cheek with his lips.

'Thank you, darling.'

'Now I'm off to a conference at Scotland Yard on the wedding bombing in Ireland.'

'There's a lot of political pressure coming down on that one,' remarked Fliss. 'Who are you meeting?'

'The usual suspects. David Hayward, Pat Rodgers who's over from Ireland and that Wiltshire detective Tanner, in case there's a link to the Salisbury bombing.'

'Should we invite any of them to our wedding, do you think?'

Kilfoyle considered. 'Hayward definitely. He's going to make DAC, at least. Rodgers, because it does no harm to have friends in Ireland. No point inviting Tanner. He's retiring in a few months.'

'Okay. Now remember we're due at the Johnson-Farrells at eight.'

Kilfoyle groaned. 'I'd forgotten. Can't we cancel? I'm going to be wiped out by then.'

'We promised.'

You promised, thought Kilfoyle, but it was pointless to argue. Fliss was her father's daughter, all right.

'It's significant that the woman who rented the farmhouse has been sighted in Salisbury again,' repeated Tanner, doggedly ignoring the fact that the others wanted to discuss the Irish wedding bombing.

'You're not suggesting that the Sovereign IRA is about to launch another attack there, are you?' sneered Kilfoyle.

'SIRA isn't in a position to attack anyone,' said Hayward. 'They're under attack themselves.'

'Which is why we're here, remember,' rumbled Pat Rodgers.

'I see the newspapers have changed their tunes,' observed Hayward. 'Teresa and Dessie have gone from being martyred lovers to cold-blooded terrorists who had it coming.'

'We had to change public perceptions,' grunted Rodgers. 'If they'd been seen as innocent victims, the hullabaloo would have been even more overwhelming. The pressure from the top is bad enough as it is.'

'How are you getting on with checking the alibis of Maddy and her mates?' inquired Tanner.

'They're standing up – so far,' replied Rodgers.

'You don't seriously believe they're in the frame, do you?' exclaimed Kilfoyle.

'Maddy Lipzinger, Rob Sage and Denny Fox were all in Ireland at the time. Rob Sage has the expertise and all three have the motive,' Rodgers argued staunchly.

'That's preposterous!' Kilfoyle caught Tanner observing him with an amused eye. 'I mean, they're normal people, not blood-crazed murderers. I suppose they blew up Kevin O'Gara and Jimmy Burke as well.'

'You know them well by now, Cyril – what do *you* make of Maddy and co?' asked Rodgers.

'As our colleague says, they're just everyday people. Rob Sage is rather quiet and serious, although, of course, I've only known him since the bomb. I suspect he was rather more . . . carefree before. Maddy, I can see, has a wacky strain in her. But who wouldn't be a bit odd after what she's gone through? Denny is just . . . a normal bloke.'

'Exactly,' agreed Kilfoyle.

'Anyway, if you remember, Pat, Rob Sage phoned me from his home the day the Pizzaman blew himself up,' said Tanner. 'I was with you in Ireland.'

'Ay, I remember. But the word is that PIRA are as puzzled as anyone else about the killings of Teresa and Dessie. That's why this rumour of an SAS hit squad is gaining ground.'

'And that is why our political masters are eager for us to catch the villains behind the wedding bomb,' reminded Hayward.

'What if there was a secret assassination unit operating inside PIRA, known only to a few?' suggested Kilfoyle. 'It would certainly suit their leadership to destroy Breda and her cronies, even if they didn't acknowledge it.'

'It can't be a coincidence that so many of those involved in the Salisbury bombing are dead,' mused Rodgers.

'That's my very point,' argued Kilfoyle. 'PIRA are taking revenge on Bridges's team for daring to plant that bomb.'

'How's the new investigation going, Pat?' asked Tanner.

'Not too well. There's nothing left of the model car so we can't tell if it was the one bought in Dublin. I'd say so, if only because the Dublin model was bought for cash – but it's amazing just how many people in Ireland own radio-controlled cars.' Rodgers shook his head. 'We're not being helped by the way the wedding guests hoofed it after the explosion. I reckon the bomber drove off among them.'

'And nothing from the snouts?'

'Not a dicky bird – which is unusual.'

The men agreed to covertly tap the phones of target republicans in Belfast and the North before Hayward and Kilfoyle began discussing leads to a possible Al Qaeda cell in Nottingham. Tanner turned to Rodgers.

'That obituary of Teresa you sent me mentioned a third Bridges sister. I'd never heard of her before.'

'Mary, ay. She was a right firebrand, getting herself deeper and deeper into the republican movement, and then, one day, around 1982 – just after her father was shot – she just quietly slipped away. It's thought that she went to the States but no one really knows what's happened to her. Breda picked up her mantle and Mary was forgotten about.'

'Strange.'

'Ay, indeed. Now I've a favour to ask. Can you get me the fingerprints of Rob, Maddy, Denny and Wayne?'

'Wayne's easy. He's got a record. I'll get them sent over this afternoon. But why?'

'We've recovered a good set of fingerprints from the ladder down into the Pizzaman's cellar which we can't match. We've also got a blood trace from the window of the gents' loo which may suggest a way of entry.' Rodgers caught the other's look. 'Ay, I know it's far-fetched but Rob Sage still had time to get to Dublin and do the Pizzaman after he spoke to you.'

'But surely the Pizzaman blew himself up.'

'That's what everyone thinks. But as a favour, Cyril, get me those fingerprints – unofficial, like.'

33

Maddy, Rob and Denny sat in the window of the coffee shop, gazing out at the passers-by, muffled up against the bitter cold.

Denny chuckled and picked up a chocolate eclair. 'Didn't we do well?'

'I'm going to buy you a radio-controlled model car for your birthday,' smiled Maddy.

'Don't you think that might be something of a giveaway, dear heart?'

'We want to hope that we won't end up as victims of our own success,' muttered Rob. 'All this fuss might put off our benefactor.'

'I hope not,' said Maddy. 'I just want to get the whole thing over as fast as possible now.'

'Your anger is abating?'

Maddy stared at the table. 'I suppose I'm getting weary. I think we all are.' She raised her eyes. 'But I said I'd see it through – and I will.'

'We're going to have problems dealing with Nolan or Breda Bridges if we're left to ourselves,' said Rob. 'We'll stand out like sore thumbs if we start sniffing around Dundalk – and Bridges knows what we look like.'

'I could go for a recce,' suggested Denny in a thick brogue. 'I do a good local accent.' He smothered a cough.

'Are you all right?' inquired Maddy.

'Just a niggling throat,' replied Denny. He was determined not to tell them about his throat infection, which was stubbornly refusing to respond to antibiotics. Denny had feared something like this would happen – but not quite so soon. He couldn't afford a sore throat – or anything that affected his voice. His voice was his livelihood. Denny had an appointment with Dr Mortenson that afternoon to hear the results of the latest tests. He was not hopeful.

'Oh, look,' exclaimed Maddy. 'There's Wayne.'

'He's still alive, then,' said Rob sourly as Wayne spotted them and waved.

Wayne, in a new anorak, hurried into the coffee shop.

'Glad I saw you.' Wayne smiled around the table. 'I've been trying to phone you at home, Rob.'

'I've been out.'

Wayne pulled out a chair and sat down. 'I take it you were behind that brilliant hit at that wedding?' he whispered, glancing from one to another.

'What hit?' demanded Rob.

'Why should you think that?' asked Maddy at the same time.

Wayne's gaze dropped. 'Yeh, all right. I don't blame you.'

No one said a word.

'Look, I did my bit to start with, okay? But it's just that . . . Remember that reporter from the *Evening Standard*?'

'Not especially,' replied Rob.

Wayne swallowed and pressed on, his nervousness making him speak in rapid bursts. 'We got sort of pally, back in December, and he's doing a follow-up to the bombing. You'll never guess what! Conn Nolan – you know, the bloke who's married to Breda Bridges . . .?'

'Yes, we know.'

'He's going to buy an Irish pub in Bath.'

'Never!' Maddy jerked upright, eyes blazing. 'He can't do that.'

'He can, if he's not wanted for any crime,' said Denny. 'Innocent until proved guilty, and all that.'

'That's outrageous,' shrieked Maddy.

'It does mean that he'll be closer to us,' observed Denny silkily.

Rob scowled at him to be quiet. Wayne intercepted the look. 'No, no. I want to help. I really do. I didn't mean to let go of that rope in France, honest.'

'So what did this reporter say?'

'He got a tip-off about Nolan buying a share in this pub with a mate, or something. Nolan's coming over today to look at the place, he said.'

'You know where this pub is?'

'Yeh, I reckon so. The reporter didn't mention its name but I think I know the one he means. I can find it. If you want, we could suss it out tonight.'

'And you're sure Nolan'll be there?'

'The *Standard* are going to do a story on it.'

'We'd have to act before that was published,' frowned Denny.

'So where's Nolan staying?'

Wayne shrugged. 'I only know that he's due in this pub around half-past seven tonight.'

'I'll enjoy seeing the enemy face to face,' muttered Maddy.

'Hang on. You can't go,' objected Rob. 'Nolan's got your photograph up behind his bar in Dundalk.'

'You can't risk it, Maddy,' agreed Denny.

'I could put on a wig, or something.'

'No.' A ringing sound came from Rob's pocket. He pulled out his phone and inspected the number displayed. 'It's Hannah,' he told Maddy. Rob walked outside, phone pressed to his ear. Maddy followed him with her eyes.

'Important?' asked Denny.

'Might be a new posting.'

Wayne decided to use Rob's absence to explain himself. 'Look, I'm sorry I've not been around but he really had a go at me for dropping that rope. You'd have thought I'd done it on purpose, the way he went on. I didn't need that.'

'That's okay,' said Maddy, who couldn't keep her eyes off Rob. 'Don't worry about it.'

'Yeh, but you've been getting on great guns without me.'

Denny gave him a meaningful look. 'Wayne, mate, the less you know about what we've been doing, the better, okay?'

'Yeh. Right.'

Rob returned, a deep frown etched on his face. Maddy arched her eyebrows in an unspoken question.

'Hannah wants me to go up to London this afternoon,' he announced. 'The big boss is over from Chicago. It's an opportunity to speak to her.'

'You've got to go to put your case,' declared Maddy.

It was clear to Denny that some sort of coded conversation was taking place between Maddy and Rob. He didn't have a clue what it was about, but it was obviously important.

'Why don't *I* go to Bath tonight with Wayne?' he volunteered. 'Then I can report back and we'll take it on from there.'

Rob saw a look of dismay cross Wayne's face. *Odd!* He'd have thought that Wayne would have enjoyed spending time with the actor.

'I'll come to London with you, if you like, Rob,' offered Maddy. 'I can have a mooch around while you're in your meeting. What time do they want you?'

'I haven't said I'd go yet – but they suggested around four.'

Maddy looked at her watch. 'It's just after eleven now. Tell them you'll be there.'

Denny's effort to clear his throat resulted in a minor coughing fit. When he'd recovered, he managed to wheeze. 'Sorry, but I've just thought of a problem. My car is in for a new cylinder-head gasket. I don't know that it'll be ready by tonight.'

'Borrow mine,' offered Maddy instantly.

'What! That lime-green monstrosity?'

'It'll be dark, Denny. No one will see you.'

Daisy M. Gradground, International Coordinator for Waterworks, leaned forward across the boardroom table and fixed Rob with a look of utter contempt. 'Let me get this straight. You allowed Hannah and yourself to get into a confrontational situation with four armed guerrillas. You produced a concealed weapon, shot three of the guerillas dead, then took one of their guns and shot the fourth in cold blood. And you still expect us to give you a job? Get real!'

Rob stared blankly across the table from Daisy to Hannah and back again. The presentation of the facts was so bizarre, so utterly skewed – and yet so basically true – that he was lost for words.

Ms Gradground took his silence for guilt. 'Your request for another post is out of the question.'

Rob tilted his head to one side and regarded Hannah. They had agreed that neither would ever breathe a word of what had happened on that still airless day in the highlands of Tigray. Okay, he had confided in Maddy, but that didn't count.

And if this was how Hannah remembered the incident then he felt sorry for her. She couldn't handle the memory because it had been too traumatic – so she had put her own spin on events. But he was being shafted.

'Is that what Hannah told you?'

'Yeh, sure. You're not going to try to deny it, are you?'

'Hannah?'

Hannah did not say a word.

'I *am* going to resign,' announced Rob. 'But first I'm going to put the record straight. I did *not* deliberately endanger myself or Hannah. I was taking her to see one of our successes, not knowing that the well had been taken over by armed Islamic extremists. These terrorists were charging the villagers extortionate prices for water from their own well. And when they'd have eventually left, they would have poisoned the well. They've done that before.'

Rob could have said that he had told Hannah to stay in the truck and not to inflame the situation. He could have said a number of things.

Daisy snorted disbelievingly. Rob lost his temper.

'The terrorists were about to rape Hannah. Then they'd have murdered us all.'

Daisy's eyes flickered sideways to look at Hannah who was sitting with a dreamlike detachment. A silence settled like a soft fall of snow into the space between them, a silence that grew and grew until it threatened to suffocate them in its weight.

'I'm sure Hannah enjoyed being reminded of that experience,' said Daisy in clipped tones.

'You needed to know the full story.'

'It still doesn't explain why you were carrying a concealed handgun.'

'If I hadn't been, we wouldn't be here now to tell the tale. *You* get real.'

'I've never liked Chicago women,' snarled Maddy. 'There's something . . . repugnant about them.'

Rob motioned to Maddy to keep her voice down as other drinkers in the West End pub glanced curiously at them. He had been saddened rather than angered by Hannah's duplicity – but Maddy was furious, demanding that they go back and make Daisy M. Gradground and her sidekick acknowledge the truth.

Finally she calmed down to announce, 'I've a surprise for you. I'm taking you to see *Chicago* – the musical, that is.' She groaned. 'Oh, no. That's the last place in the world you want to be reminded of right now.'

Rob smiled, in spite of himself. 'It's very kind of you – although I'm going to feel guilty, watching a West End show while Denny and Wayne are risking their lives on this recce.'

'They're not risking anything,' contradicted Maddy. 'They'll have a couple of drinks and look the place over while Wayne drives Denny mad with questions about the TV soap.'

'I hope you're right.'

'I am, you'll see.' She smiled at Rob over the top of her glass. 'So, what does your future hold now you've quit?'

'I don't know,' replied Rob sadly. 'I enjoyed digging wells. I felt I was doing something useful. There's a bloke I know running a Mozambique water project. I'll give him a ring.'

'You could come to the States,' breathed Maddy so softly that Rob thought he might have imagined it. He looked up to find that she was blushing.

'I don't think they have aid projects there.'

'Just a thought.' Maddy slid her hand over his, intertwining their fingers. They sat quietly for a while, enjoying the intimacy. 'Or perhaps I could help you in Africa.'

Rob raised a quizzical eyebrow.

'You know what I'm trying to tell you?'

Rob gave a barely perceptible shake of his head. Maddy locked Rob's gaze with her own and pulled his awareness into her so that, once again, he felt that he filled her whole universe.

'Yes, you do,' she said with a strange half-smile. 'You see, I love you.'

Denny and Wayne set off from Salisbury, heading north-west along the A36 to Bath. Along one stretch the road ran parallel to the river Wylye on their left-hand side. The course of the river was marked by a line of willows and in the gathering dusk the spectral white shapes of a dozen swans could be seen resting in the adjoining fields.

They made good time around the Warminster bypass and pressed on towards Beckington. The sky cleared from the west and a sickle moon appeared along with its consort, the evening star Venus. Soon the dual carriageways ran out and they found themselves on narrower roads, flanked by high hedges. They were keeping up a good speed. Denny liked Maddy's new Beetle – but the colour!

Denny had been bracing himself for a garrulous journey – but instead Wayne was being unusually quiet. The conversation was desultory, each man dwelling in his own thoughts.

Visiting the hospital this afternoon had been as depressing as Denny had expected. No – more so. The latest tests had showed a dramatic fall in his white-cell count – and it was the white cells that helped fight infection, as Dr Mortenson had pointed out. He couldn't understand why the treatment wasn't kicking in as it should have done. Modern anti-retroviral drugs should keep you alive for years, everyone said. But then, Denny had a history of pneumonia. If there was a flu bug going around, he'd catch it. Cut himself and it would turn septic. And that was exactly what the human immunodeficiency virus played on.

Above all, Denny was terrified that his voice would lose its guile and its power. Without his voice, he was nothing.

But while Denny was wondering if he should go to see a specialist in Harley Street, Wayne was fervently hoping that the Micks would not be too disappointed when he turned up at the pub without Maddy and Rob. He was doing his best. He was going to deliver *someone* to O'Gregan's bar, as promised.

He didn't know what would happen after that. Denny would get a good beating, he assumed. It was nothing to do with him. It was Maddy's fault for starting this war of revenge. Go to war and you had to expect casualties – as long as Wayne wasn't one of them.

Wayne wished he'd never seen that bloody Patek Philippe he had nicked off that Larkin wanker in France. He had almost managed to convince those two heavyweights he'd found in his living room that he didn't have a clue what they were going on about. His arse was falling out, but he was starting to believe his own story when the one built like a brick shit house had spotted the watch on his wrist. Things had got nasty then.

In the end they had accepted his story that he was only a bit player who'd been on just the one mission – and then had screwed up. He knew nothing about the wedding bomb and he had never been to Ireland in his life – on his mother's grave. It was all down to that American bird. Off her trolley, she was. Mad with grief, sort of thing. That two-faced git Rob Sage went along because he was trying to get into her knickers. Denny Fox, well, he was all right – but he was a poof, after all.

The traffic became lighter as other drivers peeled off to villages hidden away from the main road. Just past Woolverton with its welcoming Red Lion pub, a sign announced that they were in Somerset. The glow of Bath grew in the distance.

'How's Dr Samson doing?' Wayne broke the silence.

'Rather well, thank you,' replied Denny. 'He's just saved the life of a famous footballer, made a bullying mother confront her beastliness, diagnosed a case of meningitis which everyone else missed, and still found time for a fling with Sister Pidgeon.'

'So you are having it off with Sister Sex on Legs?'

'Yes, but she's hard to work with. She keeps corpsing.'

'What?'

'Evi Townsend who plays Sister Pidgeon is known for giggling during a take.'

They began to descend the long steep winding hill at Limpley Stoke. The road, cut into the side of the precipitous wooded slope, led down to the viaduct across the valley. On their left the occasional house burrowed into the hillside. On their right, there was nothing but a long drop through trees down to the scattered houses of Lower Limpley a few hundred feet below.

'Last week someone put a plastic turd in the bedpan she was carrying. When she saw it, she cracked up and set off the rest of the cast. The director was not best pleased.'

Bang. Denny's head snapped back as the Beetle lurched violently forwards. His first thought, as he wrestled to control the car, was that a tyre had burst. Then, in the dusk, he saw a huge four-wheel-drive vehicle sitting right on his tail. The black 4×4 with tinted windows crashed into them again, sending the smaller car careering across the road. The monster accelerated to draw level with them.

Denny wrenched the wheel over but despite his efforts, they were being pushed sideways across the road. The larger vehicle slammed into them again. Denny tried to brake but the sheer power of the 4×4 was forcing them inexorably towards the edge. The Beetle cannoned into the crash barrier and bounced back to be shunted again, even harder.

Now Wayne knew why the Irishmen had asked what car Maddy would be driving. The lime-green Beetle, of course, he'd replied. Her pride and joy.

Then Denny, Wayne and the Beetle plunged over the drop.

34

'We should have heard from Denny by now,' said Maddy. 'I can't understand why's he not answering his cellphone.'

'Maybe the battery's flat. You know he's always forgetting to charge it.'

'But there's no reply at his home either.'

'Perhaps they had a drink too many and stayed over in Bath,' suggested Rob, buttering the last of the breakfast toast. 'Denny has friends there – although I don't know whether he'd have wanted to introduce Wayne to them.'

'You've really got a down on Wayne, haven't you? Once you take against someone, God help them.'

'I thought he looked shifty yesterday.'

'He always looks shifty. Anyway, I'm worried about my car.'

'Maybe Denny's pranged it and he's trying to get it repaired.'

'Very funny. *And* I've not heard from Rose. We were supposed to be going shopping together this morning. Now you're going to have to take me into Salisbury.'

'Me?'

'Well, I don't have a car, do I? We'll call in at the coffee shop to see if they've heard anything there.'

Rob sighed. 'If you want.'

'My hero. Now I must get dressed.'

Maddy was trying to pretend that yesterday she had never told Rob she loved him. Rob had lifted her hand to his lips and kissed her fingers. He had kissed her lips. In fact he had been as sweet as he could be – without responding.

Maddy had berated herself for being too forward. Clearly, Rob wasn't ready to commit himself. What did it matter that they had just made love four times in the night? Maybe Rob was just in it for the sex. Maddy couldn't bear to think that. No, Rob was just a typical reserved Brit. She'd have to give him time.

They parked by the cathedral and made their way to Denny's coffee shop. They were greeted by Betty. No, she hadn't heard from Mr Fox that morning, but that wasn't unusual. Would they like a coffee and a selection of pastries? she asked, showing them to the window table.

'Seriously, I'm worried about Denny,' continued Maddy. 'What if Nolan recognized them? Do you think we should tell someone?'

'Tell them what?'

'I don't know, but they should have been in touch by now.' Maddy looked up to catch sight of Rose Allen passing the window. Maddy banged on the glass. Rose started and looked around. Her jaw dropped before a welcoming smile lifted her face. Maddy waved for her to join them.

'Are you all right?' she inquired as Rose approached their table. 'You looked as if you'd seen a ghost.'

'I'd just remembered that I was supposed to have phoned you. It completely slipped my mind. I'm so sorry. What can you think of me?'

'No problem. Sit down, sit down.'

'Thank you. I've had such a frantic last couple of days.' Rose put her large shopping bag on the floor at her feet, took off her rain hat and began unbuttoning her topcoat to reveal the same shapeless fawn jumper. 'Do you remember that poor old man who was robbed of his coin collection? Well, he's been burgled again. Now he refuses to leave home. I'm trying to arrange for him to place a supermarket order over the phone. Of course, he doesn't buy much so it's proving difficult.'

Betty brought another pot of coffee for Rose.

'Have a pastry,' urged Maddy.

'I was going to phone you last night but then something happened and I forgot,' confessed Rose, beginning to break up an eclair with her fork.

'You wouldn't have been able to reach me, anyway. I was in London with Rob,' replied Maddy. 'He's resigned from his job.'

'Good heavens.' Rose turned an inquisitive eye towards Rob as he carried on quietly tucking into a pastry.

'He's already arranged to see a friend who runs another aid project tomorrow morning,' said Maddy with a note of pride in her voice. 'Oh, look, there's Mr Tanner.'

Tanner rolled in through the door, his bulk out of all proportion to the delicate tables and chairs and the little old dears who populated them.

'Coffee would be grand, but I've got to stay off the cakes,' he replied to Maddy's invitation to join them.

'You know Rose Allen, don't you?' asked Maddy by way of introduction.

'Of course.' Tanner smiled a greeting before turning his attention to Maddy. 'I've some news for you. The woman who hired the farmhouse for the bombers was seen in Salisbury two days ago. We're just about to issue a photofit to the press and TV.' The detective held up his hand to stay Maddy's questions. 'And there's more news, although we don't know whether it's relevant or not. Breda and Teresa Bridges have a third sister – Mary, who disappeared twenty years ago.'

'Someone must know where she's gone,' Maddy said after Tanner had explained. 'No one can just disappear like that.'

'Don't you believe it,' said Tanner.

'You don't know that this Mary had anything to do with the bomb, though, do you?' said Rob.

'True. We don't even know if she's still alive. But the Garda are checking to see if anyone matching her description attended Teresa's wedding.'

Mentioning the Garda reminded Tanner that Pat Rodgers had asked him to collect Rob and Maddy's fingerprints. Now was the perfect opportunity.

'So the bombing inquiry's not dead?' murmured Rose Allen, speaking for the first time.

'Far from it,' Tanner reassured her. 'There's still forensic evidence to come out of the burned remains of the farmhouse itself, to say nothing of the unexploded bomb car. People don't understand how incredibly painstaking these forensic scientists are. They only need one fibre from that car, or even in the fertilizer of the bomb itself and we'll have the unshakeable basis of a case. They can't afford to miss anything or to contaminate the evidence.'

'Like the mills of God, grinding slowly but thoroughly,' said Maddy.

'Indeed,' replied Tanner. 'That reminds me. The Garda have found some interesting fibres of blue cashmere in O'Gara's bomb cellar.'

Instinctively Maddy's eyes dropped to the sleeve of her reefer jacket resting on the table. She felt her face flame.

Tanner pressed on. 'It now seems that O'Gara was working on a new type of minibomb disguised as everyday bits of litter.'

'Had he finished any?'

'About half a dozen – judging by sums of money he'd paid into his bank account. If the Garda can't find them very soon, then security throughout the mainland will have to be stepped up.' Tanner's mobile phone rang. He left to take the call outside the cafe.

'Can you believe it!' exclaimed Rob. 'Another bombing campaign.'

Maddy did not reply. She was deep in thought, deciding that she'd have to destroy her favourite jacket. She'd seen a similar one in lambswool in a shop window. Tanner would never notice the difference. But then if the police ever demanded a sample fibre she'd be in the clear.

Tanner returned, his face set and grim. He looked from Maddy to Rob and back again.

'I'm afraid I have bad news. Maddy's car has been found at the bottom of a steep embankment near Bath. It contains the bodies of Denny Fox and Wayne Wallis.'

Tanner sat alone at the coffee table, thinking how an almost tangible fear had passed between Rob and Maddy when he'd broken the news. Rob had taken the news almost as a physical blow, while Maddy had sat, pale as the winter sun, and sobbed helplessly. The only one who had not reacted had been Rose Allen – but then, Tanner assumed, she was used to dealing with crises. The waitresses were all crying softly.

'Why were Denny and Wayne driving your car?' Tanner had asked Maddy gently.

'Denny's car was in the workshop,' she'd explained. 'He and Wayne wanted to go to Bath so I told them to use mine.'

'What were they going to do in Bath?'

Again he saw a look pass between Rob and Maddy.

'Something about the theatre. I don't know exactly what.'

'Wayne had ideas of becoming an actor,' added Rob. 'Denny was being good to him.'

'But what happened?' demanded Maddy, twisting a lock of her hair through her fingers.

'It seems that Denny lost control on the steep hill at Limpley Stoke. It's a notorious accident black spot. There are crash barriers but the wooden posts supporting them were rotten. Ironically, they were due be replaced next week.'

'Was it definitely an accident?' As soon as Rob spoke, he realized that he had made a mistake.

'As far as we know. Why? Is there any reason it shouldn't be?'

'No.'

'The car left the road to plunge a couple of hundred feet down into the valley below. It wasn't found until this morning. Accident investigators are at the scene now,' replied Tanner. 'Do you know what time Denny and Wayne were travelling?'

'Early evening, I think,' replied Rob. 'Maddy and I were in London so we don't know for sure.'

'And you're positive you can't remember why they were going to Bath?'

'I'm sorry.'

When the others had left, Tanner had stayed behind, pretending to make some notes. He gathered up each individual's pastry fork, put each one in separate plastic bags and labelled them. The waitresses did not notice.

This afternoon Pat Rodgers would have the fingerprints he wanted.

Maddy stared blankly at the empty grate and cradled the glass of wine in both hands.

'Poor, poor Denny. He was such a lovely guy.' She stifled a sob. 'What do you think happened?'

'It could have been an accident, like Tanner said.'

'He said that first indications *suggested* it was an accident.'

'You're right. It's too much of a coincidence,' decided Rob. 'It's a bad road but Denny used to drive that route to Bath every day when he was in panto there.'

'But if it wasn't an accident, then they must have been murdered,' said Maddy. 'Maybe Nolan recognized them in the pub, killed them and *then* put their bodies in the car and pushed it over the edge.' She shuddered. 'I wish we had the name of that Irish pub.'

'Why?'

'We could go and ask if Denny and Wayne ever got there.'

'Maddy, don't you think it might be foolish putting your head in the lion's mouth?' Rob could not stand looking at the empty grate any longer. He began raking out last night's ashes. 'Anyway, it wouldn't be easy to drive a car through the crash barriers and then get away unhurt.'

'But if Denny and Wayne weren't killed in the pub, then it means that Nolan forced them off the road on the way to Bath.'

'If they *were* ambushed, Nolan must have known what car they were driving. Maybe he thought you were in it.' Rob swiftly placed fresh kindling in the grate.

'Me!' exclaimed Maddy in horror.

'Your car *was* pretty distinctive.' Rob put a match to the kindling and watched as the flames spread. 'But more than that, Nolan knew where to be at the right time.'

'He couldn't have.'

'Clearly he did. Maybe Wayne betrayed us.'

'Come on, Rob. You've just got a down on the guy . . .'

'Hang on a minute. Remember how he didn't want to know after France, then suddenly he pops back up, all eager to do his bit. I thought it odd at the time.' Rob placed some lumps of coal on top of the burning sticks. 'Maybe Bridges is trying to get her own back for her sister's death. She's turned into a revenge freak.'

'Like me, you mean?' demanded Maddy coldly.

'No. Not at all.'

'But that's what you're thinking, isn't it? You were about to compare me to Breda Bridges.'

'Maddy, I swear I wasn't.' Rob busied himself with the fire to avoid meeting her stare.

'I don't want to feel responsible for Denny's death,' she said in a small voice.

'You're not.' Rob looked up to see that Maddy was weeping again. He held her clumsily, trying not to touch her with his blackened hands. 'You didn't kill Denny. He was doing what he wanted to do. He volunteered, remember.'

'But what if Nolan knows he made a mistake?'

'Then Bridges will try again.'

'Welcome home. You killed the wrong ones.'

Conn Nolan froze in the act of hanging up his coat. He had not been home for ten seconds and already Breda was picking holes in him. Since Teresa's death she had become unbearable. Nolan grunted in reply and kicked his overnight bag to one side.

He found his wife exactly where he had left her when he'd set off for England – sitting at the kitchen table with a full ashtray and a bottle of wine, dark circles under her eyes. He thought she must still be wearing the same clothes. She certainly hadn't washed her hair.

'You killed the wrong people,' she repeated. 'Can't you get any fucking thing right?'

'They were all involved,' muttered Nolan, switching on the kettle to make himself a cup of tea. He was tired, grubby and not in the mood to listen to Breda harp on. It was late in the afternoon, and he still had to go to a drugs meet that Stozza had set up.

'Those two were nothing. It's that American cow and her fancy boyfriend you should have gone for.'

'We did. Wayne insisted that those two would go to Bath themselves. How was I to know that Fox and that little toe-rag would take their place? Anyway, Fox was in Dublin with the other two so he must have been involved in Teresa's murder.'

Breda snorted impatiently and lit another cigarette. Nolan ploughed on in the hope that Breda's mood would improve.

'You know that Wayne almost had me and Leary convinced he wasn't involved. If I hadn't spotted that posh watch of Larkin's I'd have fallen for his bullshit.'

'Where's the watch now?'

Nolan held up his own thick wrist. 'Here.'

'Very nice,' said Breda in a bored voice. 'But Lipzinger and Sage are still alive – and – I – want – them – dead.' She punctuated her words by pounding the table with her fist, making the wine bottle jump.

'I can't go back again,' muttered Nolan.

Breda behaved as if she had not heard him. 'Bobby's wet the bed every night this week and Aoife woke up screaming twice last night with nightmares. That fucking bomb not only killed my sister and her unborn baby, it's threatening to ruin the lives of my kids. I'm taking them to see a psychiatrist or they'll end up scarred for life.'

Nolan showed what he thought of psychiatrists by curling his lip in contempt. Breda flew at him.

'If you had done a proper job on security like I told you to, then none of this would have happened. I warned you that American cow was bad, mad and dangerous.'

Her daughter was not the only one to have nightmares – except, since Breda had hardly slept, hers were waking ones. In her mind, time and time again, Breda saw the Mercedes lift off the ground as though in slow motion, saw the white and gold flash, heard the dull explosion and felt the blast's shock wave in her face.

By the time she had reached the car, it had been engulfed in flames. She had been held back, forced to stand helplessly at her sister's funeral pyre.

Breda roused herself. 'Anyway, while you've been taking your time getting back, I've heard from Mary.'

'Yes?'

'The Garda know that O'Gara completed six devices but they can't locate them. The police on the mainland are about to go on a higher state of alert so we're moving quickly. Mary's going to get the singer and her bloke to plant the first one at Manchester United's ground on Sunday afternoon and then hit the three commuter trains on Monday evening at rush hour. That operation's going to involve her personally because the bombs will be planted simultaneously. Then, towards the end of the week, just as the publicity's dying down, the lilywhites will bomb the London Eye. I'll make the bastards pay.'

'But that won't help kill Lipzinger or Sage.'

'You can't count, can you?' sneered Breda. 'One in Manchester, three on the trains, one for the London Eye. How many does she have?'

'Six.'

'Right, then. And one for the bastards who killed Teresa.'

Even though he felt tired, Nolan was glad to get out of the house with its atmosphere of poisonous menace. It was impossible to talk to Breda. He hadn't wanted this drugs meeting now, but Stozza had phoned to say there was a middleman from Birmingham with South American connections who was looking for a business partner in Ireland. He didn't want to set up in Belfast because a deal with the Provos meant that you made enemies with the Loyalists, and vice versa. Dundalk – just over the border – was a perfect base, especially as Nolan already had a distribution network.

But Nolan was concerned about the way Breda was taking her sister's death. She was going to have to get a grip on herself, or she'd end up going round the twist.

Still, the ambush had worked a treat. Shame the American bitch and her bloke hadn't been in that car. He just hoped Leary would take the big 4×4 to a garage he could trust to get its damaged bodywork repaired.

Nolan headed out of Dundalk in the Nissan car belonging to his bar and turned inland, over the rolling hills towards Monaghan. Stozza had arranged to meet the middleman at Dead Mare's cross-roads up on the moors. Stozza and a couple of the boys should be there already.

Nolan was less than a mile from the crossroads, travelling along a narrow sunken lane, when he rounded a bend to find his path blocked by a white builder's van with a tube-holder on the roof.

Nolan slowed down and sounded the horn. He rolled right up to the van and leaned on the horn again. There was no one in sight.

Nolan felt a prickle of apprehension. What was a builder's van doing out here in the middle of nowhere? And parked in such a way that it blocked the road so that no one could get past it.

Some instinct screamed danger.

Nolan had just slammed the car into reverse when he heard a muffled bang.

Something flew out of the tube on the roof of the van. Something that was coming straight towards him – growing larger and larger.

The rocket-propelled grenade smashed through the windscreen into his car to explode in a fireball.

35

Rose Allen put the cake in the oven, pleased that she had managed to finish off the last of her flour, currants, peel and eggs. How efficient. On the stove she was making marmalade from the last of the Seville oranges.

The fruit cake and the marmalade would be perfect gifts for her new neighbours across the country in Hemel Hempstead. And perfectly in keeping with her reinvented character. The neighbours were already warming to Janice Gray, the kindly widow who was moving there to make a clean break after the death of her beloved husband. A photograph of the couple already stood in a silver frame on the sideboard in the new flat.

It was not hard to conjure up the documentation, the paper trail that allowed her to set up a bank account, acquire credit cards and a forged driving licence – especially if you had done it as often as she had.

Most of her possessions and clothes were already at her next home. Today she was taking the penultimate load, leaving her just enough clothes to get through the next week.

She had arranged to meet her lilywhites at the Membury services on the M4 motorway to hand over the first device and explain how to set the timer so that it would explode as the soccer crowd streamed out after the game.

The thought brought a grim smile to her lips.

Now, on with the tasks in hand. She couldn't risk heading off north across the Plain until she had topped up the car with petrol. She'd have to go to the nearest garage in Shrewton, even though the journey meant that she'd be going back on herself. She was annoyed that she'd allowed the petrol to run that low in the first place. It wasn't like her.

Rose hauled a large suitcase out to the car, looking up at the sky as she did so. Patches of washed-out blue were at last appearing in the west. The ground was littered with twigs and small branches, evidence of last night's ferocious storm.

She liked this part of England – but she would not miss it. Home was wherever she was – whoever she was. By this time next week, Rose Allen would have faded away as though she had never existed. Gone to live with a non-existent brother in Spain. She wouldn't be saying goodbye to many people – especially not to Maddy Lipzinger and Rob Sage. They would already be dead. She was keeping back the last bomb – just for them.

Maddy was having a slow start to her Saturday. Rob had left early to go off to Swindon to see his contact. It seemed that engineers were in short supply. Maddy was in two minds about Rob's application. He had still not responded to her slip of the tongue. Maybe he never would – in which case his departure for Africa would mean the end of their relationship. Maddy tried not to think about it.

She was scruffing around in jogging bottoms and a sweatshirt – building up to taking a shower – when the phone rang. She picked up the receiver to hear Tanner's rumbling voice.

'Hi. And to what do I owe this pleasure?' she asked.

'I don't want to alarm you, but you should know that Breda Bridges left her home in Dundalk suddenly last night and she's now on the mainland.'

'What!'

'Her husband was blown up in an IRA ambush yesterday afternoon.'

'Yeh, we saw that on the news last night.'

'Bridges walked out on a houseful of mourners, collected her two children from friends and vanished. She arrived at Fishguard this morning.'

'But couldn't the police hold her?'

'You'd have thought so,' replied Tanner heavily. 'Somehow she was allowed through.'

'You don't think she'd come here, do you?'

'I've no idea but I'm told she was already taking the death of her sister very badly. Yesterday's events could have sent her over the edge.'

'Shame,' muttered Maddy ironically.

'Grief does strange things to people,' continued Tanner. 'It might be just as well to keep your eyes open. Bridges is driving a blue Citroen Espace people carrier with Irish Republic registration plates. Tell Rob to be on his guard, too.'

'Rob's not here. He's gone to Swindon,' said Maddy before asking, 'If Breda Bridges *was* coming this way, how long would it take her to drive from Fishguard?'

'Three or four hours. The ferry docked late because of the storm but she could be near you by ten o'clock.'

'I'll be all right.'

'If Bridges is acting irrationally, there's no knowing what she will do.'

'No, really, I'll be fine.'

She heard Tanner sigh as though reaching a decision. 'Maddy, it's beginning to look as if your car was deliberately forced off the road.'

'What!'

'I'm at the scene now. There's black paint marks on the Beetle's rear wing which appear to have come from another vehicle.'

'Shit!' Maddy shivered as the full impact of Tanner's news sank in.

'I think I'd better get a bobby to come up to keep an eye on your place.'

Maddy frowned. If Breda Bridges was really on her way to kill her, a British bobby with a truncheon was not much protection. 'It's okay. I'll go and see a friend until Rob gets back. I'll stay out of harm's way.'

'All right,' Tanner agreed reluctantly. 'All units are looking out for Bridges so we should get a fix on her soon. I'll call you on your mobile if there are any developments.'

'Thanks.'

Maddy had decided to go and see Rose Allen in that remote little bungalow of hers. No one would ever find her there. She dialled Rose's home. An operator's recorded voice told her that the number was temporarily unavailable. Maddy remembered that Rose had complained that her line went down every time there was a storm.

Maddy looked at her watch. Twenty past nine. Rob was to due to have his interview in ten minutes. On the spur of the moment, she called to wish him luck and mentioned that she was going to spend the morning with Rose Allen.

She did not want to worry him before his interview so she did not tell him that Breda was in England.

Maddy looked out of the window. The sky was clearing after the night's storm. She picked up the phone again and called a taxi. Then she went off for a shower, making sure that the doors were locked and bolted.

Breda Bridges was keeping going on a rocket-fuel mixture of adrenalin, grief and searing anger. She had not slept since God knew when. The news of Conn's death had been brought by a policewoman and a Garda detective who would have shown more compassion if a dog had been run over. As word had spread and people began to arrive, Breda had sent Aoife and Bobby off to stay with friends. Stozza and the boys from the bar turned up, followed by their wives, neighbours, Conn's mates, party members and business associates until the house was full and Breda began to feel trapped.

There was only one person she wanted to see – her sister Mary. Breda had allies, comrades in the struggle, even disciples – but no one she was close to.

Word was that Conn had fallen in a PIRA ambush and there was talk of war as everyone pointed the finger at Milo O'Connell for taking advantage of SIRA's weakness to exact revenge on Conn.

But why had SIRA been weak? Breda asked herself. Because so many of them had been killed or injured in the wake of the Salisbury bomb. And who was to blame for that? Maddy Lipzinger. Snivelling bloody cow – just because her whelps had been killed. They'd died for a cause; died in a war. What did Americans believe in? Nothing. Nothing but the dollar and Mc-fucking-Donalds. Shit-scared of terrorism – but they were the biggest terrorists on the planet in the way they supported the Zionist oppression of the Palestinians. *Bloody Americans.*

Breda needed to see her sister. She needed Mary. Only then could she cry.

She tried to think clearly. If she went directly to Mary's bungalow she could spend a couple of days there and no one would ever know. The kids had to come as well.

Mary had those bombs.

The American lived close by.

Breda's thoughts were dark and tangled – but it was possible. She'd kill the American and that Rob Sage.

And now she had crossed the Severn Bridge into England. The kids were squabbling in the back of the people carrier, fractious and tired from the rough crossing that had made it difficult to sleep.

Maybe the storm was why Mary's phone was not working. Breda had tried to call her sister on her mobile but there had been no reply to that either. Breda had stayed at her sister's place for one night back in October while they'd planned the Salisbury bombing. She had only a vague idea how to find the bungalow again. She knew that it lay on a lonely road, right on the edge of the British Army firing range, past a pub named after an unusual bird. What was the name of the pub? The Buzzard? The Bittern? No. She forced her tired brain to work. The Bustard. That was it. She'd find it. There was a service area coming up. She'd stop there and buy a map.

The kids were squabbling again, but she was not even hearing them. She was concentrating on reaching Mary's. A mantra entered her head, repeating itself over and over again like a cracked record stuck in a groove. *Mary – the bombs – and Lip – zin – ger. Mary – the bombs – and Lip – zin – ger.*

Rose Allen was carefully placing the black plastic sack in the boot of her car when she heard a vehicle in the distance. Apart from British Army Land Rovers and lorries, traffic was rare up here. She watched from behind a beech tree as a taxi appeared. It slowed down and indicated to turn down her track. With an exclamation, she scuttled back into the bungalow, slipped hurriedly into her padded corset and skirt and put on her glasses.

She arrived back in the kitchen just in time to see Maddy Lipzinger climb out of the taxi. Rose Allen wondered what she wanted, turning up here out of the blue. There was only one way to find out. Rose opened the door, a welcoming smile on her face.

'Oh, Rose, I'm sorry to descend on you like this,' called Maddy. 'I did try to phone.'

'What's wrong?'

Maddy thought she'd appear foolish if she told Rose that she'd fled because Breda Bridges was on the mainland.

'Mr Tanner phoned to say the police think the deaths of Denny and Wayne weren't an accident. They were forced off the road by someone who was trying to kill me.'

'Never!'

'I was by myself in the cottage when Tanner called. His news just freaked me out. I had to see someone. And I thought of you,' she ended lamely.

'You're always welcome, you know that.'

'If I could stay with you until Rob gets back from Swindon.'

'Of course. Come in. I'll put the kettle on.'

Maddy paid off the waiting taxi, then followed Rose into the kitchen.

'What lovely smells,' exclaimed Maddy as she entered. 'What's in the pan?'

'Marmalade, and I've a cake in the oven. Now sit down and I'll make tea.'

Rose Allen bustled around, putting on the kettle and stirring the marmalade. All the time she was thinking. *Never look a gift horse in the mouth.* Yes, it would mean a change of plan – but what was a slight inconvenience for such a major prize? That was the advantage of living in rented accommodation. It cost you nothing if you destroyed it.

Payback time had come early.

Rose made the tea, poured milk into their cups and then, behind Maddy's back, tipped the rest away down the sink.

'Please don't let me stop you doing whatever you were doing,' Maddy was saying.

'No. I often bake on Saturday mornings.' Rose made a show of looking in the refrigerator. 'Oh dear, I thought I had more milk. I'll have to pop out and get some. And I need caster sugar.' She tutted in exasperation. 'I spent so much time yesterday trying to help that poor old man that I didn't get round to shopping for myself.'

'I'm sorry to be a burden.'

'Don't be silly. In fact, you can help me. Will you stir this saucepan regularly while I drive to Shrewton? I won't be that long but you have to watch marmalade like a hawk or it'll burn.'

'Of course.'

'I'll set the oven timer to ping at eleven o'clock when the cake'll be ready. I should be back by then – but just in case.'

Maddy began stirring as Rose tidied up around her. She did not see Rose place a large plastic drinks bottle in the rubbish bin in the corner of the kitchen.

Rose Allen seemed in a hurry to get away. 'I'll be back as soon as I can. Remember to take the cake out at eleven and watch the marmalade.'

'I won't forget.' Maddy smiled, thinking she had never seen Rose fuss so much.

Rose picked up her handbag. 'Lock the door if you feel safer.'

Once her friend had driven away, Maddy continued to stir the thick saucepan, savouring the warm baking smells and comfortable in the silence. But then, looking around, she began to think that the kitchen looked somehow different from the way it had been on her previous visit. She couldn't work out why, until she saw that the wooden montage she had previously admired was missing. And surely there'd been an earthenware vase of teasels near the window and a bread bin in the corner. In fact, the more Maddy looked, the more she noticed that the kitchen was bare. *Odd.*

Maddy gave the marmalade one last stir and decided to poke her head into the living room. Her eyes popped wide open. The bookcase was empty. The Russian dolls on the mantelpiece were missing. Pictures had gone from the walls. In fact, the place had been stripped of all Rose's personal belongings.

Maddy stood stock-still, puzzling over her discovery. The silence ceased to be comforting. Instead, she began to feel afraid. Maybe she should lock the door. After all, she was all by herself, marooned up here miles from anywhere.

As she tried to find a logical explanation for the missing articles she caught the sound of a car engine on the breeze. Perhaps Rose had forgotten something.

But instead of Rose's small silver car, a blue people carrier was coming slowly down the road as though looking for something – or somewhere.

Denny Fox and Wayne Wallis had not stood a chance, Tanner saw. Their car had smashed through the barrier just below the Rose and

Crown pub – at the steepest part of the hill. It had plummeted thirty feet over the retaining wall and then crashed down the hillside, cutting a swathe through immature ash and whitebeam trees until it came to rest almost down in the valley itself.

Tanner watched the sling under the Chinook helicopter grow taut and the car slowly lift off the ground. Accident investigators had concluded that the Beetle had been forced off the road – and that made it a murder inquiry. Christ knew what the salvage operation was costing – but at least it was coming off the Avon and Somerset force's budget.

Tanner's mobile phone rang. He half-expected the call to report progress in tracking down Breda Bridges – but he was surprised to find it was Pat Rodgers.

'Christ, Cyril, you certainly know how to throw a man,' began the Irishman. 'Those two sets of fingerprints you sent us . . .'

'Yes.' Tanner found that he was holding his breath.

'It's a puzzle and no mistake,' continued Rodgers. 'Neither matches the ones we found in the Pizzaman's cellar . . .'

Tanner sighed in relief.

'But – do you know who one set of prints belongs to?'

'No.

'Mary Bridges.'

'Sorry?'

'Breda's elder sister Mary. The one who's been missing these past twenty years.'

'What . . . but . . .' Tanner was lost for words. 'Are you sure you haven't mixed them up at your end?'

'Are you sure *you* haven't?'

Tanner's head swam. It didn't make any sense. He had sent Rodgers Maddy's fingerprints – banking on her having worn gloves, as she did invariably. But he had substituted Rose Allen's prints for Rob's. Maddy obviously wasn't Breda's sister – therefore . . . Jesus Christ!

Tanner made himself stay calm. 'You're sure, Pat? No room for any mistake?'

'It's a perfect match.'

Tanner remembered Mitch's death. He had always thought that had been suspicious. And Rose Allen had been at the hospital early that morning. Had she killed Mitch?

Rose Allen must have been the woman who had booked the farmhouse and set up the bombing. No wonder she'd been spotted in Salisbury a few days ago. She'd never left it – merely changed her appearance.

And how much had Maddy inadvertently been passing on what he'd told her about the investigation?

Tanner explained quickly how he had come by the fingerprints. Apart from Maddy and Rob, there had been another woman at the table. A victim-liaison woman known to them as Rose Allen. He must have sent her fingerprints by mistake, which meant that she was . . .'

'Hell's bells,' breathed Rodgers.

Tanner ended the conversation to call Maddy and warn her. She was not at home and her mobile phone was on voicemail. He called the incident room to alert the on-call Divisional Superintendent. They needed to trace Rose Allen's home address and car registration number while summoning the tactical firearms adviser.

Tanner was speeding back towards Salisbury, driven by a grim-faced Pottidge, when he thought to phone Rob.

'It's Tanner. Where are you?'

'On my way back from Swindon, coming over the Plain. Why?' replied Rob, startled by the urgency in the policeman's tone.

'I've got some dramatic news for you. Rose Allen is Breda Bridges's missing sister.'

'Rose Allen! But Maddy's just gone to see her.'

'Hell! Do you know where Rose Allen lives?'

'Yeh, I helped Maddy with directions when she went to visit her a few days ago. She's got a bungalow off the back road past The Bustard, near Orcheston. Can't you contact Maddy?'

'There's no mobile signal up on the Plain.'

'Why did she have go to Rose Allen's *this* morning?'

'I warned her that Breda Bridges had arrived unexpectedly in England. For all we know, she could be on her way to see her sister.'

'Listen, I'm not too far away from Orcheston. I'll go and get Maddy.'

Tanner thought about Rob's offer. It made sense. Not only was he closer than any police unit but he could also bring out Maddy without raising Rose's suspicions.

'Be careful. We have to assume that Rose Allen's armed.'

'Okay.'

'And don't let her suspect that we know who she really is. We don't want her to take you and Maddy hostage,' said Tanner. 'As soon as you're both safe, we'll move in. Best of luck.'

Tanner called the incident room to pass on the location of Rose Allen's home. Back-up armed-response units were already on their way from the north of the county. One advantage of such an isolated spot was that the police could seal off the few roads over the Plain within minutes.

'No sirens. Silent approach only,' warned Tanner. 'You can hear a siren two miles away up there.'

When he finished the call, he slid down in the passenger seat, wincing as Pottidge sped around a blind bend, and recalled that night in January.

Tanner had thought at the time that it had been an extraordinary chance spotting Kilfoyle.

Sometimes Tanner drove home past Rob's cottage just to keep an eye on him and Maddy. The supergrass story had just appeared in the newspaper and he'd been worried about its impact on Rob, considering his previous memory lapse. And, being a copper, he was curious about the relationship between the two now that they lived cheek by jowl. They were decent people and he wished them well.

He wished them justice, too, but he was coming to doubt if he'd be able to deliver it.

Tanner's inquiry into the Salisbury bombers was being hampered, endangered even, by the police's eagerness to collect evidence. They'd been so eager that they had broken the rules. Rules that had not been in force when he'd been a young bobby. Rules that Tanner, like most coppers, believed had swung too much in favour of the villain. Sometimes, he thought, English justice not only had to be seen to be done; it had to be seen to be believed.

The politicians' decision not to use Mikey Drumm as a supergrass defied belief. A political decision, not a judicial one. Hayward had cut his protests short.

'They are looking at a bigger picture, Cyril,' Hayward had said, managing to be simultaneously smug, condescending and patronizing.

Tanner disagreed. The politicians were not looking at a bigger picture, they were looking to cover their own arses. The government had invested a vast amount of political credibility in keeping the Northern Ireland peace process alive. Now they were willing to let mass murderers walk free for the sake of their own careers.

Tanner's thoughts were running along those well-worn grooves when he'd driven home through Rob's village that Friday night and spotted Kilfoyle's sporty little Audi parked up the lane from the cottage. He'd slowed down.

Tanner had not known that the MI5 man was on his patch. Was he dealing with Rob and Maddy directly, cutting out the local police? That was the sort of thing he'd expect from MI5 – but what could they tell Kilfoyle? And it was late. Almost midnight. There was no light on in Rob's cottage, nor, as far as he could see, in Maddy's annexe. Just then, he made out Kilfoyle emerging from the shadows near Maddy's front door. Stranger and stranger.

It had been the start of an eventful weekend – Mikey Drumm had been released and killed and on the Sunday a massive explosion had killed Jimmy Burke who, it turned out later, had been the passenger in the bomb car.

The next day, in Maddy's cottage, Tanner had spotted the overnight bag with the airline cabin-luggage label. And the Irish newspapers that Rob had gone to great lengths to hide. Tanner had said nothing – because it was just too implausible. But the more he thought about it, the more it hung together. Rob knew about explosives. And he'd served with special forces, although he was too shy to talk about it. So they had the capability. They certainly had the motive. But did they know who to target, and where? That was where Kilfoyle had come in. But why would Kilfoyle target Burke, of all people?

It had not taken Tanner long to come up with a theory.

His argument went like this: Burke hadn't even been a name in the frame when he'd been killed. But those who *were* in the frame had been put there by Kilfoyle. So why would Kilfoyle finger Burke? Because he was a threat. What if Burke had been Kilfoyle's snout – and, say, he'd gone on the bombing raid? If anyone found out, Kilfoyle would be in ten feet of shit.

The disappearance of Darren Larkin – just before the cops had arrived to arrest him – and the death of his brother Tony strengthened Tanner's theory. The brothers were the weak link who might have told the police about Burke and thus implicated Kilfoyle. The discovery of the duty-free bag in Burke's bedroom confirmed that Burke had been one of the bombers. But by then Kilfoyle had nothing to fear. He could get on with his new job, pursuing Al Qaeda terrorists. Now there was no one to help Maddy and Rob. No one to give them the vital information of how and where to find the rest of the killers. So Tanner had stepped in.

Maddy watched from behind the kitchen curtains as the blue people-carrier with an odd-looking number plate turned down towards the bungalow. There was a woman behind the wheel. The Espace drew to a halt and after a moment the driver climbed out.

Breda Bridges.

Maddy staggered back against the wall, feeling the vomit rise in her throat. This didn't make sense. Was she dreaming? Having a nightmare – in the middle of the day? A boy and a girl were getting out of the people carrier. The children she had spoken to outside Bridges's home. So this wasn't a dream. The kids looked tired and fed up and they were squabbling. Their mother too appeared exhausted and dishevelled. God, they were heading towards her.

Maddy prepared to flee. But where? She couldn't get out of the bungalow without being seen. She was trapped. She retreated back into the living room, turning off the hob as she did so. To leave on the gas burner would be a tell-tale sign that someone was in.

The clock on the cooker said 10.47.

There was nowhere to hide in the living room. Maddy ran into the bedroom, where she scrambled under the bed, wrinkling her nose at the musty dampness. She heard the door open and then the sound of voices.

'She can't be far away – this saucepan is still hot and there's something in the oven,' Breda Bridges told her children. 'We must have missed her by minutes.'

'I want to go to the lavvy,' complained the little girl.

'It's through there on the left.' Breda began exploring the kitchen. 'Maybe she's gone shopping. The fridge is almost empty. Not even a bottle of milk. Shame, I could do with a cup of tea.'

'No orange juice?'

'Afraid not, Bobby.' There was a sound of cupboards being opened and shut. 'There's nothing here at all. I'm going to have to go and get some food.'

'I don't want to go back in the car,' wailed Bobby.

'All right. Why don't you two stay here and watch TV while I go and see if I can get a signal for the mobile phone? Right?'

'Yeh, if you say so.'

'I won't be long. Now don't touch anything.'

'I don't want to watch stupid football,' wailed Aoife as the TV came on, showing a soccer preview.

'Sort it out between you and no fighting,' snapped Breda. 'I'll be as quick as I can.'

Maddy faintly heard the Espace start up and pull away. The sound of the football pundits was replaced by an American cartoon. 'I was watching that,' shouted Bobby.

'Football's boring.'

'It's not boring.'

'Play with your stupid Game Boy,' ordered Aoife.

'It's not stupid. You are.'

Maddy lay in the dust, remembering the conversation she and Rob had had last night, after learning that Nolan had been killed. Rob had suggested giving up their war of revenge.

'Breda Bridges has lost her sister and her husband. Isn't that enough?'

'No. She's still got her children.'

'We do not wage war on children. If we did, we'd be as bad as Bridges.'

'Okay. I'll be as bad as Bridges. I can handle that.'

'Maddy!'

'She owes me her children. She took mine, now she owes me hers.'

'I think something's happened to daddy,' said Aoife.

Maddy smiled at being reminded how quickly children could switch focus. One minute the little girl had been fighting for the TV control, the next she was discussing the family in a grown-up way.

Bobby grunted. 'What do you mean?'

'All those people came to our home; then mam sent us to play at our friends' and *then* she turned up and drove us here. I haven't even got my pyjamas or my toothbrush. That's not like mam.'

'She's gone crazy,' said Bobby.

'It's scary,' agreed Aoife.

'Hi,' said Maddy, appearing in the doorway.

*

Rob put his foot down, feeling the power in the old diesel engine as he surged past a Land Rover and horsebox. Rose Allen, the third sister. It was unbelievable.

When Tanner had phoned, Rob had been thinking about the future and the choices before him. The interview for the job in Mozambique had been a formality. He had begun to wonder if he'd dare to ask Maddy to accompany him to Africa. He thought not. Instead, he'd suggest that they stayed in touch and maybe one day he'd go to visit her in Tonawanda. Maybe.

And then had come the bolt out of the blue. Suddenly Rob realized just how much Maddy meant to him. When she had laid her pride on the line to say that she loved him, he should have had the courage to tell her, 'I love you, too.'

What had stopped him. Cowardice? Reserve? Fear of being hurt?

Not any more. His future was her future. Her future his. Their future together.

He said a silent prayer to protect Maddy and vowed that if Rose Allen so much as harmed a hair on Maddy's head he'd kill her with his bare hands. With a snarl, Rob pressed his foot to the floor.

'Hi,' said Maddy, smiling at the children.

They looked up from the old sofa, curious but not alarmed. The girl had straight brown hair and an earnest expression and despite the boy's snub nose and freckles, which gave him a pugnacious air, it was clear that the girl was in charge.

'Are you our aunt?' asked the boy.

'Er . . . no. Are you guys expecting to meet her here?'

'Suppose so.'

'Does your aunt know you're coming?'

'Mam didn't tell her,' replied the girl. 'She tried to phone but she couldn't get through.'

'Mam's gone weird,' muttered the boy, bending his head over his Game Boy.

'Really.' Maddy went into the kitchen to look out at the road. It was clear for a mile in either direction. A soft-drinks bottle was protruding from the top of the swing bin. Instinctively, she pushed it down out of sight and gave the cooling marmalade a stir.

'So, what are your names?' Maddy called out gaily as she opened a drawer and found the same long-bladed knife that Rose Allen had held when Maddy had been here before.

The girl came to the doorway. 'That's Bobby. I'm Aoife.'

'That's a pretty name. Is it Irish?'

'Yes. It's spelled AOIFE.'

'So what are you doing here, Aoife?'

'Don't know. Mam didn't say. We think something's happened to daddy.'

'He's dead,' Bobby shouted from the living room.

'Why do you say that?'

'Our Auntie Teresa was blown up on her wedding day. We saw it happen.'

'Really!'

'Mam wants to kill the person who did it.'

'Does she know who it was?'

'It was an American woman.'

'How does she know that?'

'Don't know.' Aoife shrugged. 'Why do you talk funny?'

Rose Allen pulled onto the forecourt of the petrol station in Shrewton deep in thought. Her hasty departure would pose problems – but the prize was worth it.

Shame her new neighbours would have to do without their gifts but the cake and marmalade were pinning Maddy Lipzinger to the kitchen. The bomb was set to explode at eleven o'clock – just as Maddy should be taking the cake out of the oven. If it went off early, she would be stirring the marmalade, just feet away from where the bomb was hidden in the rubbish bin. Either way she was dead.

To be doubly sure, as she had left, Rose had loosened the tops of the four liquid-gas cylinders sitting in their cage just outside the kitchen. The blast from the Pizzaman's bomb would set them off – and once they went up, there'd be nothing left of the bungalow but a pile of matchsticks.

Since she had to go back on herself to head north, she should only be a mile or so from her cottage when the bomb went off. She should be able to hear the explosion. She'd certainly see the plume of smoke that would mark the end of Maddy Lipzinger.

And that left Rob Sage. That wasn't a problem to Rose Allen – or Janice Gray, as she had already begun thinking of herself. It was enough for her to know that one day in the future – next month, next year, maybe even longer – she would hunt down Rob Sage and kill him.

The petrol pump switched off automatically. The tank was full. Rose paid in cash and climbed back into her small silver car. She had just buckled on her seat belt when her mobile phone rang. She pulled it out of her handbag and inspected the caller's number. Her mouth dropped open.

'Everyone talks like this where I come from.'

'Where's that?'

'A long way away.' Maddy was trying to make sense of the situation. 'Have you ever met your aunt?'

'No.'

'What's she called?'

'Dunno. Mum never mentions her name.'

The terrible realization pierced Maddy like an icicle to the heart. Breda Bridges had come here to see her sister. The missing sister. Mary – now known as Rose Allen.

Panic surged inside Maddy. She was stranded in a lonely house miles from anywhere. Any minute her two deadliest enemies would return – and then what?

Her stomach began heaving with terror.

'Are you all right?' The little girl was looking at her with concern.

'Yeh, sure.' *Wait a minute.* Rose Allen. The woman who had sat by Mitch's hospital bed for all those hours. And Mitch had died – just after she'd begun to describe the woman who had planted the bomb. Rose Allen's other sister.

Maddy knew then that Rose Allen had killed Mitch.

And she must have been behind Denny and Wayne's deaths. She hadn't turned up to go shopping yesterday morning because she'd believed Maddy had been killed when her car had been forced off the road.

Maddy made herself think. Clearly Rose Allen had not been expecting her sister – and Breda Bridges had gone to phone to try to make contact. Once they met up, they'd exchange notes and they'd come back together – to kill her.

Let them come. Maddy was not frightened any more. Dark, bloody thoughts raced through her mind. She had the long-bladed knife and she had the kids.

Let the evil sisters come.

Breda Bridges longed to close her eyes. Setting off to try to find her sister was proving a journey too far. The adrenalin that had kept her going had finally burned out, leaving her sweating with a prickly tiredness. She dug her fingernails into the back of the hand gripping the steering wheel to keep herself awake and lit yet another cigarette, her mouth tasting stale and foul. The mobile phone was still not showing a signal.

She came to crossroads and junctions and turned this way and that at random. The storms had washed the air wonderfully clear so she could see for miles over the gently rolling countryside. Once she yielded to temptation and closed her eyes for just a second, only to wake with a start, fearing that she was falling asleep over the wheel.

Part of her wanted to go and see where Maddy Lipzinger lived. It didn't look far on the map – but it was too far at the moment. She'd go this evening to take a look round – after she'd taken a nap.

At last! The phoned showed that she had a signal.

'Hello.'

'It's me.'

'What are you doing, phoning me now?'

'I'm here. I've got to see you. They've killed Conn.'

Rose Allen caught the desperation in her sister's voice. 'Who's killed Conn?'

'Provo swine. There's only you now.'

Conn's death was news to Rose Allen. 'Slow down and start again. Where exactly are you?'

'I don't know. On Salisbury Plain somewhere. I'm coming up to what looks like a military camp both sides of the road. There's field guns at the gates. I'll stop.'

'Breda, it sounds as though you're at the Royal Artillery base at Larkhill,' said her sister urgently. 'It's crawling with security cameras around there. Keep driving.'

'I'm so tired. I can't think straight any more. I went to your house but you weren't in.'

'You went to my house!'

'I left Aoife and Bobby there. Shit! Fucking madman!'

'What's wrong?'

'Some lunatic doing a ton in an estate car almost crashed into me.'

'Breda, listen, this is important. When you were at my place, did you see Maddy Lipzinger?'

'Maddy Lipzinger! Are you crazy? I didn't see anyone.' Breda gasped. 'You mean she's there? My kids! She'll kill them – I must get back.'

'Breda, it's worse than that. I've set up Lipzinger. The biggest device from the last batch the Pizzaman made is in the rubbish bin in the kitchen. It's due to go off at eleven o'clock.'

'That's in seven minutes.'

'I remember you,' said Aoife. 'You gave us £10 each. Mam said we must never ever talk to you again. You're not the American woman, are you?'

'Is she very bad?'

'She's a witch.'

'We saw Auntie Teresa blown up on her wedding day,' announced Bobby. Maddy looked at him keenly. He had said almost exactly the same words not five minutes ago. She wondered if he was suffering from some kind of post-traumatic shock.

'Do you think about that often?' she asked him softly.

'All the time,' said Bobby. 'Booommm.'

'I dream about it,' volunteered Aoife. 'Mam says she's going to take us to see a paediatric psychiatrist.'

'Those are big words,' said Maddy, smiling. God, this little girl was so like Mitch. Sharp as a button. She found herself wondering if they would have got on if they'd known each other. Or would they have been too much alike?

'I've got a reading age of twelve, even though I'm only nine,' said Aoife proudly.

'That's very good.'

'I'm hungry,' whined Bobby. 'Why can't we eat the cake in the oven?'

'Ye-es,' encouraged Aoife. 'It smells so good.'

'You'll end up with indigestion if you eat cake when it's hot,' warned Maddy.

'Don't care. Just a slice.'

'When did you two last have something to eat?'

'Dunno. Please, just a slice. No one will mind.'

'Come on, then.'

'Yippee.' Bobby ran into the kitchen where he and Aoife began tussling to see who could stand closer to Maddy.

She looked at the clock on the stove. Rose Allen had said the cake would be ready at eleven o'clock. Just five minutes to go. It shouldn't do any harm to take it out now.

A blast of hot air greeted Maddy as she bent to open the oven door. She wrapped a tea towel around her hands and brought out the currant cake. She inserted the tip of the knife and was rewarded by a delicious cloud of steam. Aoife and Bobby crowded round her.

'Now be careful,' warned Maddy as she put a slice onto a plate.

Bobby began juggling with a piece. 'It's fearsome hot.'

'I did tell you,' smiled Maddy.

Aoife was more circumspect. She tore off a tiny piece and pushed it around the plate to cool.

'Our mam never bakes cake,' she said. 'She doesn't have time. I hope she's going to be all right.'

'Why shouldn't she be?'

'I told you, she's gone weird. Something terrible's happened, I know it.'

'Get out of the fucking way.' Pottidge gave an aggressive blare on the horn. 'Moron.'

Tanner glanced at his sergeant. He would have been amused – Pottidge seldom swore – if he hadn't been so worried that they were about to crash. Pottidge was driving like a madman, doing 120 m.p.h. around the Warminster bypass, headlights on full and warning lights flashing. The police radio was silent in case anyone was earwigging but Tanner kept receiving constant updates by phone. The outer perimeter of roadblocks was in place. Now it was a question of tightening the circle.

Breda Bridges's people carrier had been spotted at Larkhill. She was thought to be alone and heading east. Three minutes later came a report that she had backtracked and was now heading west at high speed. Rose Allen had been sighted at the petrol station in Shrewton. She'd been seen talking on a mobile phone and then she too had taken off like a bat out of hell, heading towards her home. Something was going on. But what?

'Faster,' Tanner told Pottidge.

Rob Sage had made good time along the straight stretch across Knighton Down, although he'd almost come to grief with a people carrier that had swerved into the middle of the road at Larkhill. He turned left and headed up past The Bustard inn where squaddies at the vedette on the edge of the firing range eyed him suspiciously as he sped past the sign saying 'Slow'.

Soon Rob could make out the stand of beech trees that Rose Allen had mentioned in her directions. The wooden-clad bungalow came into view. Where was Rose Allen's car? If she'd killed Maddy and done a runner . . .

Rob took his foot off the accelerator, coasting to a stop at the top of the track leading down to the bungalow eighty yards away. Maddy emerged from the kitchen door. He heaved a huge sigh of relief and jumped out of the car. He and Maddy ran towards each other to meet halfway.

'Are you all right?' he demanded, holding her in his arms.

'Yes. I'm so glad to see you.'

'Where's Rose Allen?'

'She's gone to Shrewton.'

'You haven't heard the news. She's Breda's sister.'

'I know. Bridges has been here. She's gone off to find a phone signal. I was scared the sisters would come back together.' Maddy slid her right hand into the left sleeve of her jacket and pulled out the long-bladed knife. 'Bridges left her kids here.'

Rob stared at her.

'They're all right,' Maddy said in answer to his unspoken question.

'I've been feeding them cake.' She gave a stifled cry. 'They're just like my kids.'

'Look.' Rob pointed to where a small silver car could be seen racing down the road towards them.

'That's Rose Allen,' hissed Maddy.

'She's not hanging around,' commented Rob. 'Back to the car, quick. She could be armed.'

But near the road they spotted a blue Espace people carrier speeding towards them from the other direction.

'Bridges,' gasped Maddy. 'We're trapped.'

Rose Allen braked violently to a halt beside them and leaped out.

'Where're the kids?' she screamed.

'I like this cake,' said Bobby, taking advantage of Maddy's absence to help himself to another slice. 'I'm going to ask mam to make one like this.'

'You'll get indigestion if you carry on,' said Aoife, repeating Maddy's warning as she looked out of the window. She didn't understand what was happening. First, a man had come haring up in a blue car. He and Maddy had run to meet each other. Then they had run back to the road as a silver car arrived. A woman had got out of the new car. She was looking towards them and waving her hands.

'I'm thirsty,' complained Bobby. He began opening kitchen cupboards, looking for something to drink. He spotted the soft-drinks bottle poking out of the top of the dustbin. 'Look what I found.'

'It's rubbish. Put it back.'

'There's something in the bottle.'

'They're in there,' replied Maddy, nodding to the bungalow. 'They're safe.'

Rose Allen began running down the track. 'Aoife. Bobby. Get out of there. Get out! Now!'

Two small faces appeared at the kitchen window.

'Come out. Now. For the love of Jesus.'

The force of the blast blew out the glass windows and made the wooden walls bulge.

Rose Allen stumbled, recovered and ran on desperately towards her home.

Rob went to follow her, but Maddy grasped his arm. 'It's too late.'

Rose Allen had reached the kitchen door. She pushed it open. A sheet of yellow and red flame erupted in her face. She flung up an arm and stepped into the inferno.

Rob shook free of Maddy's grip. 'I'm going to help.'

He had taken just two paces when the gas cylinders exploded. The second blast blew the wooden building apart and sent Maddy and Rob reeling back, their ears ringing. Pieces of wood and other debris rained down on their heads.

The blue people-carrier slewed to a halt and a dishevelled, gaunt-faced woman staggered up to them, her mouth contorted in a silent scream.

Breda Bridges and Maddy Lipzinger looked at each other. Over the roar and crackle of the blaze came the sound of sirens.

Epilogue

To: ADG (Ops) G.
From: Dep Director (ICT) G.
SECRET

As requested, please find executive summary of the investigation into the deaths of those responsible for the bombing in Salisbury, Wiltshire on 23 December last year.
The full report is attached.
Taking the deaths in chronological order:

1 Michael (Mikey) Drumm was knocked down and killed by fellow members of SIRA. Not only did his heavy drinking render him a security hazard but SIRA had become aware through the actions of politicians (see Addendum A) that he was considering turning Queen's evidence. The Garda believe that Steven (Stozza) McKenna and his cousin Malcolm Leary were responsible for Drumm's death. The investigation is ongoing.

2 James (Jimmy) Burke died either in an accidental explosion or he was the victim of a cross-border smuggling war. The Garda favour the former theory, on the grounds that had Burke been killed the rival gang would have stolen the hidden arsenal to sell the arms back to PIRA.

3 Darren and Anthony Larkin were killed by Conn Nolan with the

aid of person or persons unknown. Anthony's Patek Philippe watch, which went missing at the time that Anthony was killed, was found on Nolan at the time of his death. In light of the discovery, French police have reopened the investigation into the death – so far without further success.

4 The injuries to Kevin O'Gara, aka the Pizzaman, were self-inflicted in his hurry to fulfil a bomb-making contract for Breda Bridges before PIRA discovered that he was double-crossing them. That haste, causing him to take dangerous short cuts, was generated by a hoax bomb sent by PIRA on the morning of the accident.

5 The deaths of Teresa Bridges and Desmond Fitzgerald on their wedding day are believed to have been the work of a secret PIRA assassination squad. This squad was set up specifically to destroy SIRA and its political wing The True Guardians whose dissident republicanism was perceived as a threat by the Provisional leadership. The murder of their rivals in such a spectacular way was intended to serve as a public warning to others to toe the party line.

6 The deaths of Denny Fox and Wayne Wallis can undoubtedly be ascribed to Conn Nolan, probably acting with the help of Malcolm Leary. A Mitsubishi off-road vehicle, discovered in a garage in Kilburn, has dents in the offside wing and traces of lime-green paint which match the paint on Mrs Madeleine Lipzinger's car.

7 Conn Nolan himself was killed by the same PIRA assassination squad that killed Teresa Bridges and Fitzgerald. Again, the method of execution – a rocket-propelled grenade fired from a tube mounted on a builder's van – was guaranteed to grab the headlines and serve as a warning.

8 Aoife and Robert Bridges were the innocent victims of a plot by their aunt Mary Bridges to blow up Mrs Lipzinger.

9.1 Mary Bridges perished in the fire, trying to save the children.

9.2 A further five litter-bin bombs were recovered from the boot of her car.

10 The children's mother Breda Bridges is now in a secure psychiatric unit in Dublin, where she exists in a catatonic state. (See Addendum B.)

In view of the above findings, Garda speculation that Madeleine Lipzinger and Robert Sage were responsible for some or all of the above-mentioned deaths in a war of revenge is as far-fetched as it is groundless.

Damien Kilfoyle